Acclaim for JL Crosswhite

"This is a very suspenseful story and I'm looking forward to the next book in this series."—Ginny, Amazon reviewer

"I was impressed with the suspense in this book as well as the romance. Great storyline. Morality issues were great. An overall great read."—Kindle customer

"Absolutely loved it. Fast paced and kept me guessing concerning the outcome. I highly recommend it to all who like a good mystery or suspense."—Linda Reville

"Very well written, with interwoven stories and well developed characters"—Mary L. Sarrault

Other books by JL Crosswhite

Hometown Heroes series
Promise Me, prequel novella
Protective Custody, book 1
Flash Point, book 2
Special Assignment, book 3

The Route Home series, writing as Jennifer Crosswhite
Be Mine, prequel novella
Coming Home, book 1
The Road Home, book 2

Contemporary romance, writing as Jennifer Crosswhite
The Inn at Cherry Blossom Lane

Nonfiction, writing as Jennifer Crosswhite
Worthy to Write: Blank pages tying your stomach in knows? 30 prayers to tackle that fear!
Posts from the Pencildancers: Short Bites to Improve Your Writing Today

FLASH POINT

HOMETOWN HEROES
BOOK 2

Blessings!
(old cover!)
Jennifer

JL CROSSWHITE

Tandem Services Press
SOUTHERN CALIFORNIA

Copyright

To all the first responders who keep us safe.
Thank you for your service.

For the Spirit God gave us does not make us timid, but gives us power, love and self-discipline—2 Timothy 1:7

PROLOGUE

Orange County, California, 2000

DUST DRIFTED ACROSS THE ROAD ahead as Joe Romero sped down nearly deserted Irvine Boulevard, bypassing the infamously jammed El Toro Y, the conflux of Interstates 5 and 405. Were the Santa Ana winds kicking up? But the eucalyptuses lining the road tucked between the foothills and the recently deserted El Toro Marine Corps Air Station weren't swaying. Their leaves remained perfectly still. Eerily so.

So where was the dust—

It wasn't dust. It was smoke.

A car sprawled sideways in the intersection, shards of metal and glass scattered across the pavement. Skid marks across the intersection led to a second car impaled on a light pole, front end crumpled nearly to the windshield.

Orange sparked around the edge of the smashed hood.

A cell phone would be handy about now. As a broke community college student, he couldn't afford one. No pay phones were nearby. He pulled over and hopped out. A man eased out of the car in the intersection.

"You okay?"

The man nodded.

Joe jogged past him. The flames were creeping around the hood of the impaled car.

The driver was a woman with the steering wheel embedded in her chest. Blood ran down her face from a gash in her forehead that corresponded to the spider web of broken glass in the windshield. The woman didn't turn her head. "Please, can you get my baby out?"

He looked in the back seat, the crying just now registering with him. A red-faced toddler screaming his—or her—lungs out. Joe glanced at the approaching flames.

"Please, hurry!"

The mom was in more danger from the flames, but given how she was wedged in there, he didn't think he'd be able to free her. He looked around. A car slowed as it approached Sand Canyon, driving around the debris in the intersection. He tried to make eye contact with the driver but couldn't. He hoped they'd call for help.

Someone came around him to the front of the car. The man from the other car. He carried a fire extinguisher and was reading the instructions. Good, maybe he could get that fire out while Joe worked on the baby. It was the only thing he could do for the mom.

The doors were crunched shut, and the windows had popped out. Lifting the edge of his shirt, he wrapped it around his hand and cleared out the rest of the broken glass. He leaned through the window. "Hey there." He turned to the mom. "What's your baby's name?"

"Brandon."

The other driver must have figured out the fire extinguisher because with a hiss, white powder covered the hood of the car, repelling the flames.

Joe studied the car seat buckles for a minute. "Hey, Brandon. I'll get you right out of here. Okay? How do you work these things anyway, huh? I bet you can figure it out before me." He finally found and pushed the release button, undid the chest strap, and slipped Brandon out of the harness. Making sure the baby didn't graze any of the broken glass, Joe pulled him out of the window.

"See, Mom? We're safe." Though he wasn't too sure about her. The flames were growing again.

The baby nearly threw himself out of Joe's arms, trying to get to his mom. "Whoa, buddy. Hang on there. We'll get your mom in a second." What was he going to do with the baby? He needed to set him down somewhere to get to the woman. His car? It'd have to do. He grabbed a couple of the toys next to the car seat. "I'll be right back." Brandon snatched the red furry one from Joe. With its googly eyes and big orange nose, it had to be some monster from Sesame Street.

The mom didn't say anything. Her face was ashen, and her eyes were closed. They didn't have much time.

He put the baby in his car, giving him the toys. "Stay here, Brandon. I'll be right back."

Brandon stuck a toy in his mouth and grabbed the steering wheel.

This wasn't a great solution, but what choice did he have? He eased the door shut and ran back to the car.

The other guy was yanking on the door with no success.

Joe went to the other side and leaned in the window. The dashboard was pushed back over the woman's legs, pinning her to the seat. No way were they going to get her out. He eased out of the car. "Where's the fire extinguisher?"

"It's empty."

He scanned the area. No sirens yet. Had anyone even called? The smoke traced across the sky, leaving a clear signal some busybody should notice. "We need to stop this fire. We aren't going to be able to get her out of here ourselves. Got a shovel?"

The man shook his head.

Joe strode around the car. Debris and trash littered the dirt on the side of the road. Maybe there was something here they could use. He grabbed a couple of discarded scraps of wood.

"Here. Use this." He handed one to the guy and then used his to start flinging dirt on the car. The grit pelting the hood of the car sounded like rain. He couldn't tell if it was helping or not. Dust stung his eyes and filtered into his mouth.

He heard something. Was the baby crying? He looked up. No, Brandon was chewing on the steering wheel.

Sirens.

Relief poured over him. He'd never been so glad to hear that. He tossed another load of dirt on the fire, then ran around to the driver's window. He put his hand on the woman's shoulder. "Did you hear that? The fire department's on its way. You'll be out of here before you know it. And don't worry about Brandon. He's having a good time. I think you've got a future race car driver on your hands, the way he's going after my steering wheel."

That got a faint smile out of her.

The noise was nearly deafening as an Orange County Sheriff's unit drove up followed by the fire engine. Firefighters swarmed the car. Joe stayed next to her, explaining what was happening as they put out the fire and pried the front end of the car off of her.

One of the firefighters leaned over his shoulder. "This part is going to hurt her a bit. Think you can keep her distracted?"

"I can try." Joe could see Brandon, so he gave the mom a running commentary of Brandon's fascination with the lights and activity.

When they were ready to extract her, Joe got out of the way and sprung Brandon from his car. The sheriff's deputy came over to get Joe's statement about the accident. Satisfaction, and something else, mixed in Joe's bloodstream as the cop lifted Brandon from his arms to head to the hospital. The firefighter from earlier came over. "Good job there. Have any experience with this kind of thing?"

He gave a short laugh. "I'm just a college student." But there had been a time when this was all he'd wanted to do. He had even put out a fire with his friends as a kid. But that dream was gone, smashed in the wreckage of bad choices.

"Well, if you're interested, we're hiring. There's an information meeting Wednesday at seven at the high school. You should check it out."

"I might do that."

The firefighter nodded and walked off.

Joe climbed in his car and sat there a moment before starting it. His steering wheel glistened, and it took him a minute to realize what it was. Baby slobber. He grabbed a napkin and wiped it off.

A firefighter. Huh. He'd thought that dream had died. But maybe … He'd be graduating in a couple of weeks with a business degree but no firm job prospects. Maybe he'd check it out. After all, it was just an info meeting. Likely nothing would come of it.

He turned the key in the ignition. Something red on the floor caught his eye. He reached down and picked it up.

The furry Sesame Street monster.

Chapter One

Orange County, California, Present day

THEY WERE CALLED THE DEVIL winds. Fire Captain Joe Romero thought it an apt description of the dry winds that blew down from the desert, funneled through mountains that acted as a chimney, and pushed back the normal Southern California ocean breeze. More often than not, the Santa Anas brought out the arsonists.

A trickle of sweat ran down his neck, adding to the wetness already gluing his shirt to his back under his turnout gear. He rolled his aching shoulders as best he could while holding the hose. The smoke and embers blowing in his face didn't help. He pulled his shroud higher over his nose to block the smell of a campfire gone wrong.

Focus. Fatigue was as big of an enemy as the fire. Scanning the area, he forced himself to be aware of his surroundings and his team. Probationary Firefighter Zach Akino manned the hose with him. "See this expensively landscaped yard we're yanking our hose through?"

The rookie nodded, his eyes widening.

"It won't mean anything if we don't save this house. I know it's our third day on the fire, and we're not going home any time soon. But keep focused and be aware. You can't let your guard down." Joe adjusted the hose on his shoulder. The wind swirled, lifting dust, ash, and smoke in a vortex. The fire made its own weather, the heat sucking the flames skyward into a wall of red-and-black heat.

Joe blinked his eyes to ease the grittiness caused by the smoke, heat, and lack of sleep. Wouldn't be able to put in any study time on his classes that would enable him to move up the fire department ranks. The testing dates moved for no man or woman. Looked like he would miss this round of promotions. A hard ball formed in his stomach at the thought, but he shoved it from his head. No point in dwelling on what he couldn't control.

A crashing noise ended in a metallic clang. A boulder banged into the wrought-iron fence. He swiveled around, looking for more. He closed the nozzle and dropped the hose. Grabbing Akino's shoulder, Joe yanked him back as a chunk of granite shattered where his boot had been. Fragments pelted their turnout gear. A chill raced over his sweat-slicked skin.

Akino gave him a wobbly grin. "Thanks."

Joe snatched up the line again. "With all the noise from the fire, wind, and support aircraft, you won't hear a rock coming until it's usually too late to get out of the way. And there are a lot of big rocks in these foothills that can easily work themselves loose as the fire burns away their support." They needed every man to hold this line. They couldn't do that if any of their thinly-stretched crew got injured.

The Global SuperTanker roared overhead, slightly louder than the fire and the wind. Nineteen thousand gallons of red slurry dropped from the tanker's belly, temporarily pushing back the wall of flames.

Joe nodded at Akino, then braced himself and opened the nozzle. The stream of water knocked down the flames flaring up between the house and the line made by the tanker-dropped fire retardant. Firefighters Jeff McCoy and Andrew Hardin covered the other edge of the house.

More snapping brush. Joe scanned for another rock, but a small deer broke through the chaparral and slammed into the fence. It tried to scramble over. Snakes, rabbits, and mice had been running across the lawn all day. Poor thing. It could see safety, but it just kept pawing at the metal bars, panicked.

"Air Fire 3, coming in for a second pass closer to the line. All personnel be advised." The call came over Joe's radio. He closed the nozzle. "Akino, this one'll be closer. Move back from the drop zone." Jeff and Andy already loped across the lawn, closer to the house, taking cover under the wide patio.

Joe glanced back at the deer. Wait, it wasn't a deer. It was a dog with dirty, singed fur. If he could get it to follow the fence line around the corner, the dog could escape down the greenbelt.

He ran toward the dog, waving his arms. "Go on. Shoo!"

The dog sat and whined, tail thumping.

"Joe! The drop!" Jeff's voice rose above the crackle of the flames and the roar of the approaching plane.

He waved off Jeff and sneaked a quick glance at the sky. He had time. Hopefully.

The dog pawed harder at the fence, eyes wide, ears flat.

He didn't want to spook the animal into hurting itself. "It's okay, boy. Come on." He patted his leg and moved down the fence, hoping the dog would follow. "You can get out of here."

"Joe!"

He ignored Jeff's voice. The guys were always teasing him for having a soft heart. He liked saving people. And animals. So sue him.

They say smell is the sense most closely related to memory, but Joe always thought it was the adrenaline rush, the split-second decision making, that so often brought back the memory of a steering wheel buried in a young mother's chest and a red-faced toddler screaming in the back seat. Images of his first rescue flashed across his brain at every scene.

He planted his boot on the fence and levered himself halfway over, reaching down. "Come here, boy. Up!"

Someone grabbed his legs. Jeff. "I got you. Get the dumb dog, and let's get out of here."

He grabbed the scruff of the dog's neck and heaved himself back, taking the dog with him over the fence. And toppling over on top of Jeff.

Scrambling to his feet, someone grabbed his collar, yanking him up. Akino.

The roar of the SuperTanker announced its arrival. They ran, ducking under the covering of the house's wide patio as the heavy, red rain fell.

He leaned against the wall, catching his breath. "Thanks, rookie. But obey orders next time." He grinned and looked over at Jeff. Blood ran down his face. "What happened to you?"

"Your boot. You kicked me in the face when you grabbed that stupid dog." Jeff dabbed at his nose with his shroud.

"Aw man, I'm sorry. Do you want—?"

"Nope."

Joe studied Jeff a moment. Deciding there wasn't anything to be done—the bleeding had stopped—he unscrewed the lid on his water bottle, taking a long drink of water nearly as hot as coffee, washing the taste of cinders from his mouth. "Where's the dog?"

Akino gestured to the patio table. "Under there."

"Probably a good move. That drop could have killed him." Joe squatted down and let the shepherd-collie mix sniff his hand. The dog licked it, and Joe scratched its neck, the fur thick with ash and crispy where it was singed. No collar. Why did people let their dogs out if they didn't have a collar? At a time like this, they'd be lucky to see the mutt again. He was somebody's pet, most likely. He hoped some little kid wasn't going to be heartbroken.

Battalion Commander Dan O'Grady strode around the corner. "Everything under control? Jeff, what happened to your face?"

Jeff tilted his head in Joe's direction. "Oh, you know. Joe was helping. Again."

O'Grady raised his eyebrows and focused on Joe a moment. "Okay. That last drop bought us some time. Gather around." He waited until Andrew Hardin pushed off the wall and joined them. "The heavy winter rains have made these foothills bloom and thickened the growth of the chaparral brush. The winds are sucking the moisture out of every living thing. It's all tinder dry and ready to burn. Wind-driven embers are bursting into spot fires the minute they land. We're making our stand here. If this house goes, the whole neighborhood goes. With tile roofs and a wide greenbelt, these are defensible. Everything north of here is on fire, and the winds aren't forecasted to abate anytime soon. You are the center of our containment line."

He studied each man's face then his gaze drifted beyond. He frowned. "Hey, you know whose house this is?"

Jeff shook his head. Hardin and Akino shrugged.

Joe glanced around. Should he? "The negative edge pool, the outdoor kitchen complete with top-of-the-line stainless steel Weber grill and a fireplace is standard for this neighborhood. So, nope."

"Tony DiMarco, that big land developer." O'Grady tapped the granite countertop he leaned against.

"Really? How do you know?" Joe pulled off his helmet and ran his hand through his sweat-soaked hair.

"My wife dragged me to that charity home tour last Christmas. This was one of them. It'd be ironic if it burned."

What was Joe missing? No one else seemed to get it either. "Oh?"

"Don't you remember? His company was investigated for arson and insurance fraud last year on that empty business park." O'Grady slapped Joe's back then pointed at Hardin and McCoy. "Keep those hot spots down and hold here. Romero, don't give Jeff any more injuries helping. Rookie, listen to your elders. I'll be back with an update." Lifting his radio, he moved off.

"Half the county's burning, and you guys are kicking back. About what I expected." Detective Kyle Taylor appeared around the corner of the house. He wore jeans, boots, and had a bandana around his neck. His Laguna Vista PD badge was clipped to his waistband and his gun visibly holstered.

"Hey, Kyle. Figures you'd bring a gun to a fire. You didn't happen to bring us anything along with your attitude, did you?" Joe stepped forward and fist-bumped his best friend.

"Never go anywhere without it." Kyle handed each of them a cold bottle of water out of the backpack he wore.

Joe drained his without coming up for air. Nothing tasted so good. He capped the empty and tossed it to Kyle. "What brings you up here? Other than your gift of water."

"Checking the neighborhood to make sure everyone's out and nobody's trying to sneak back in. And I don't have to tell you about the pressure from the city council to keep looters out of this neighborhood in particular." Kyle leaned against the wall. His radio squawked, and he turned it down slightly. "So, talked to Sarah?"

"Sarah?" Heat flashed through Joe. No, he hadn't talked to her. Only thought of her nearly every waking moment.

"Sarah?" Kyle echoed. "You know. Sarah, the one you spent all your spare time with last month, the one you can't stop talking about, the one—"

"Been a little busy. Hate when work interferes with my love life." Joe glared, gesturing to the glowing hills in front of them.

"Wait." Jeff turned. "You have a love life? Since when?"

Hardin snickered. Akino, for once, didn't look terrified.

The tanker overhead, the traffic on the radio, and smelling smoke made for a weird background while discussing his life. They were talking like it was a normal day, like they were shooting hoops or something, instead of protecting people's homes.

Jeff stepped forward. "I've been trying to set you up with my sister. She's a former cheerleader. Perky and happy all the time. She might even appreciate your 'helping.'" He made air quotes.

This wasn't awkward at all. He needed to change the subject quick. "Hey, we need to get after a couple of those hot spots. Akino, grab the hose. Thanks for the water, Kyle."

"No problem. Want me to tell Sarah you said hi?" Kyle grinned, enjoying this too much.

Joe shoved his shoulder. Something exploded off in the distance. The smoke obscured all but a slight brightening to the west.

Hardin peered off in the distance. "Sounds like the fire just hit that grove of eucs off Via de los Arboles."

Joe reached for his radio. "Who's over there?"

"Station 42."

Akino looked from Hardin to Joe. "Eucs?"

"Eucalyptus trees. The volatile oils in their leaves and other desert-adapted plants make them particularly vulnerable to fire. They're basically time bombs, dangerous to anyone or anything around them. Hardin, you and McCoy go check it out. The rookie and I will hold down the fort here."

Joe started to follow Jeff off the patio. Something brushed his leg, and he looked down. The dog stared up at him, whining. Great. Now he had a shadow. Maybe Kyle could take him. No, Kyle had left. Ah well. Joe gave the dog a final pat then joined Akino at the hose. They searched for hot spots and flare ups. Every time he looked back, the dog was still there, watching him.

"Looks like he knows you saved his life," Akino shouted over the roar of water and fire. "You've got a dog for life."

He didn't want a dog. All he really wanted was a hot meal, a shower, and a long nap. And to call Sarah and see if she would have dinner with him. Yeah, that's what he wanted. But he wasn't going to get it until this fire was contained.

Sarah Brockman dumped her saddle-leather tote purse on her office chair. Coffee. She needed coffee. She slipped her computer out of its sleeve, snapped it into the dock, and booted it up. Twisting open her blinds, she gazed out over her second-story view of tree tops, but she'd take that over a parking lot. Today, billowing smoke filled the skyline as the foothills in the distance burned. Joe must be out there. *Lord, keep him and the other fire-fighters safe.* Maybe Heather would have an update from Kyle, who was also probably working the fire.

The Pandora app opened, and her playlist of soothing music started, which made her office feel more like a spa on a tropical island than an architectural firm. It pulled her mind away from the fires and onto work. While AutoCAD booted, she mentally went down the project list. Final drawings would be due—

Mark Rankin, her boss and mentor, knocked on the door-jamb of her office. "Come see me?"

"Sure. Just let me get some coffee, and I'll be over."

Mark disappeared. He was a great guy, not old enough to be her father, more like a quite-a-bit-older brother. But he was a good boss, and his profit-sharing plan allowed her to make her own hours and do quite well the last couple of years.

She grabbed her mug and headed for the break room and kitchen area. Popping in her favorite hazelnut pod, she waited for the machine to fill her cup. What did Mark want? It wasn't unusual for him to ask to see her, but never first thing. Which could mean what? Her mind whirled at the possibilities. An unhappy client? Or coworker? A new project? The possibilities were endless.

The machine sputtered out the last of the coffee. She popped the top, pulled out the pod and tossed it, then heavily dosed her coffee with cream. Fortified, she headed to Mark's office.

He gestured to the chair.

She sank into the buttery leather and took a sip. "What's up?"

Mark toyed with a pen. Not a good sign. "Before you say anything, hear me out."

Oookayy.

"You know I've been talking about retiring—"

"But not for a few more years. Your five-year plan, right?"

He tilted his head side to side. "There's been a change. I'm pushing it up." He held up his hand as she opened her mouth. "Just let me finish. Then you can ask questions."

She nodded, gripped her mug tighter.

"Martha's been diagnosed with dementia. It's still early stages, but there are some things we want to do—travel, see the grandkids, things like that—before it gets worse and we can't."

A small gasp escaped Sarah's lips. "Mark, I'm so sorry." She reached for his hand and squeezed it. Tears pooled in her eyes. "What do you need me to do? I'll do anything I can to help." She could pick up more of the workload, handle clients, mentor some of the younger architects—

"Become managing partner."

Her heart stopped. Pressure filled her chest. She sat back in her chair, pulling her hands into her lap. She hadn't expected that. But she hadn't expected Martha to be diagnosed with dementia. If her heart was heavy, Mark must be devastated.

"Sarah, I know how you feel about this. But trust me. I've watched you over the years. I know what you're capable of. Do you think I'd offer you the job if I didn't think you could handle it?"

He didn't need to be worrying about the firm. That was something she could give him. "Of course, I'll take it. If that's what you really want. Are you sure there's no one else you'd rather have?"

"I know you can do this." He leaned back. "But if you decide not to, I'll ask Eric. But you're still my first choice."

She nodded. "Thanks for thinking that I could do it. That means a lot, your confidence in me." She leaned forward. "Please don't worry about the office. We'll make it work here. I'll be praying for you and Martha, so please let me know if there's anything I can do. Or anything the team can do."

Mark cleared his throat and swallowed. "Thanks."

Recognizing his emotion and not wanting to cause him embarrassment, Sarah stood. "Need anything else?"

He shook his head. "Close the door behind you."

She gave him a soft smile and left, giving him his privacy to grieve. Back in her office, she eased into her chair and opened up her task list for the day. But she couldn't focus on the words.

What had she gotten herself into? Managing partner. Sure, Mark had been hinting for a while, but she thought he'd be around to show her the ropes, answer her questions, ease her into the job, and help her recover from her mistakes. But now, she had to take that load off of him. He didn't need to worry about the firm when he needed to be focused on Martha.

But she could go to Eric and talk to him about it. Maybe there would be a way for the two of them to divvy up the responsibilities. One that kept him away from dealing with the office staff.

Eric Garrity. Why on earth would Mark consider him? Yes, he could handle the financial aspect of the job, but he had no people skills. She could think of two people who would quit the moment they learned Eric was in charge. And they wouldn't be the last once Eric bullied his way through the staff like they were the opposing football team. So maybe that wasn't the best option.

What did *she* want? She didn't really know. She was happy doing just what she was doing. But that wasn't an option. And did it really matter what she wanted? She had to help Mark.

Her peaceful music wasn't helping. Between worrying about Joe and Kyle, and now Mark and Martha, her brain wouldn't settle into work mode. Normally, some fresh air and sunshine would help, but there was none to be found under the smoke-saturated skies. She opened the Bible app on her phone and began to pray through the Psalms.

But her mind wandered. She couldn't wrap her brain around Mark's news. Mark was her mentor. He *knew* her and had guided her career, giving her advice and opportunity. He was more than her boss. Her heart broke at what he and Martha were facing. She didn't want to add to his problems. But she'd never seen herself as managing partner.

However, if she didn't take the job, Eric Garrity would. Creating another set of problems. There was no good solution.

CHAPTER TWO

SARAH GLANCED AT THE MAPS app on her phone clipped to the dash of her Acura. A few days ago, the fire had burned within a couple of blocks of one of her job sites. Laguna Vista PD had just opened the roads to traffic that morning. The lot was around here somewhere, but where? Unfortunately, her landmark for this area, a grove of eucalyptus trees, had burned down.

She looked at the phone again. Turned it around. Which way was she going, anyhow? No signal. No GPS either. Sigh. Nothing around here ran in a straight line. Instead, streets followed the curves of the coastal foothills. Which also blocked cell reception. And this was an undeveloped area that wasn't on any map yet. Sigh.

The fire-charred hills brought a certain firefighter to mind. Built like a football player, with wavy dark hair and dark eyes that focused on her when they were talking, like what she was saying was the most important thing to him in that moment. Had Joe worked this part of the fire? She kind of thought she would have heard from him by now. Or maybe she was just hoping. He was kind, picking her up to visit their mutual friends, Kyle and Heather. It helped that they lived in the same condo complex. Part of her hoped that he would ask her on a date, just the two of them.

But maybe it was for the best. He was a firefighter, and she couldn't imagine giving her heart to someone who had such a dangerous job. She was terrified of fire. She didn't even like bonfires. And don't even try to tell her roasting marshmallows was fun.

Her head snapped up as her car hit the curb. Oh crud! Hoping she hadn't blown her tire with that brilliant move, she pulled parallel to the curb. She wished she were better with directions. It was disgraceful the architect couldn't find the job site.

She clicked the phone's screen off and gave up. She had no idea where she was. Clearly, her phone didn't either. Easing away from the curb, she wiggled the steering wheel. The car seemed okay. She'd just drive around until she figured something out. It was probably the most illogical idea she'd ever had. Why would Mark ever think she should be the managing partner if she couldn't be smarter than this?

The answer to her prayers appeared in the form of two men standing outside their cars on a vacant piece of land. Probably developers. They should know where they were.

She pulled up next to them and rolled down her window. The air still smelled like a campfire. Flashing what she hoped was an I'm-a-stupid-woman-come-help-me smile, she picked up the phone.

Both men turned and looked at her. The tall one—a contractor, she figured by his build—smiled back. He was blond and muscular.

The shorter one was almost his exact opposite. He was probably the financial guy based on his impeccably-tailored suit. His dark hair was slicked back, and he frowned at her, tapping one of his expensive shoes. Not practical for a job site. She always kept a pair of boots in the trunk of her car. Along with flares, jumper cables, a gallon of water, antifreeze, a thermal blanket, a flashlight, a small toolkit, and power bars.

"Hi. I think I'm lost. Can you help me?"

The tall blond took two long-legged strides and bent down to look in her window. "Where are you headed?"

"Via de los Arboles."

"That's the problem. We're not on the maps yet. And no cell reception either. Hang on a sec." He walked to his truck and leaned in, then returned with a piece of paper.

"Hey, Greg!" The dark-haired guy pointed to his watch, his brow cut with deep grooves.

The tall guy—Greg apparently—handed the paper to her. It was a site map.

"Just go down here—" he pointed back the direction she came—"and it looks like it's just two streets down on your right."

She pulled the map closer. How could she have missed it? Heat crept up her face. What a stellar morning. Still, she gave him another smile. "Thanks so much. I really appreciate it."

"Sure. No problem." He straightened but didn't back away from her window. She thought he was going to say something else, but he didn't. He wasn't looking at her either. She followed his gaze to the dark guy, who glared at her, hands stuffed in his pockets, rocking back on his heels. Seemed like she'd interrupted an important meeting.

"Well, thanks again."

He glanced at her distractedly. "Sure. Um, would you—" He stared over the roof of her car.

She looked up, eyebrows raised. Would she what? He'd better not be asking her out. She had enough drama today.

"Uh, nothing. Okay. Have a good day." He stepped back from the car.

She waved and drove off. Glancing back in the mirror, she saw the two talking again. Impatient Guy must really have been ticked at her interrupting their meeting. Greg kept gesturing for him to calm down.

Sorry. Didn't mean to crash their little rendezvous.

Rubbing his eyes, Joe sat up. The early evening news had come on. He was sure one of the stories would be on the mop-up of the brush fire. The faint scent of smoke clung to him. Man, he hated how sleeping during the day made him groggy. As he got older, it seemed to get worse. Maybe he could go shoot some hoops with Kyle. He had to do something to shake off this fog and still get tired enough to sleep tonight.

His squad had finally gotten off the line at four this morning. He was proud of the rookie. Zach Akino had stayed close, paid attention, and not done anything stupid. With a little guidance, he'd be a good firefighter.

A wet nose nudged his hand. A slobbery ball dropped next to the couch. One of his old baseballs. Where had the dog dug that up? A memory flashed through his mind of tossing this ball around in the front yard with Pops. That moment in time where they really were a happy family, not just pretending to be one. Someday, maybe, he could do better with his own family.

The dog nudged the ball toward him, looking up expectantly. A condo was no place to throw a ball around. Poor dog. He'd probably lived with a family in a big, fenced in yard. Maybe with a couple of kids. His heart twisted. That sounded like a pretty good life. And not just for a dog.

Joe'd tried to turn him in to the animal shelter rep at the staging center, but they were full. And seeing how attached the dog was to him, the worker had suggested Joe take him home. She took his number and said she'd call if anyone reported a missing dog matching his description. So far, no calls.

He'd followed Joe everywhere, as if he were eternally grateful to Joe for saving his life. He had to admit the company was nice to have. Guess the dog would need a name. And a bath. He'd have to get him to a groomer's soon, get some of the singed fur trimmed off. And a trip to the grocery store for food for the both of them.

He should call Kyle and see if he was up for some basketball tonight. He picked up the phone, letting it dangle between his knees for a moment. If he went to the grocery store now ...

Or, he could go running. If he went running, he could stop by Sarah's, see if she was home. Show her the dog. Ask her out to dinner finally. That beat shooting hoops with Kyle. And the dog would get some exercise.

"Wanna go for a run?" He rubbed the dog's head.

He pulled his shirt out and sniffed. Smoky. It didn't make the most sense to take a shower before running, but if he was swinging by Sarah's first, he didn't want her to be repelled.

Tossing the phone on the bed, he headed for the shower.

At the knock at Sarah's front door, she put down her pencil. She had been playing around with elevations on her dream house. She needed the escape dreaming and doodling provided her. It was all on AutoCAD but something about holding a pencil and drawing brought out her creativity. Probably all in her head.

She left her home office and opened the door of her condo to Ryan's smiling face. "Oh, hi, Ryan. What brings you by?" She had been expecting Heather, not the good-looking worship pastor from church. She ran a hand over her head, hoping her hair wasn't sticking out in a million directions. She should have glanced in the mirror before opening the door.

"Sorry to just drop in on you, but I need your help." He flashed her his movie-star grin that made her knees a little weak.

"Um, sure. Come on in. I have some passion-fruit iced tea, and we can sit on the back patio. Heather's supposed to stop by in a bit. We're going out to dinner."

"Terrific! This won't take long."

She headed into the kitchen and grabbed a pitcher out of the refrigerator. Ryan slid open the wood-and-glass door while Sarah carried a tray with the pitcher and glasses to the back patio. She set the tray down then sank into a teak chair padded with an ice-blue cushion. She loved her patio. It didn't have a view, but the Asian-inspired garden she was trying to create within its stucco walls was the perfect escape. Almost as good as the beach and a lot closer.

Ryan took the chair next to her. "Thanks for letting me barge in on you like this. But I didn't know who else to ask. You're so good with people. You always seem to know the right thing to say."

Sarah poured two glasses and handed one to Ryan, hoping her hand wasn't shaking. He'd noticed more about her than her singing? A bit of warmth ran through her. She took a sip of the sweetly tart drink to cover her nervousness. "I'll be happy to help however I can."

Ryan took a drink. "Hey, this is good." He leaned back. "So you know Linda, right? Every Monday I get a report from her on how the weekend service went. It's always so negative." He mimicked her voice. "It was too loud. The tenors were off. The altos came in late." He grinned.

She couldn't help but grin back. With Ryan, everything was entertaining. It made choir practice fun.

"I've tried joking with her, blowing her off, but nothing seems to work. How do I get her to stop?"

"Have you tried asking her to stop?"

He shook his head. "No. I don't want any conflict." He sat up. "But maybe you could talk to her for me."

"I don't know about that—"

"The music budget is pretty small, so I don't have an assistant, which I really need. Someone to deal with things like this. But you'd be doing me a favor if you could help me out." His gaze was steady on hers.

Her stomach quivered. People probably didn't turn Ryan

down. She turned her glass in circles on the table. "I'm sure Linda just wants the music program to be at its best. So many people connect with God through music. I'm sure she thinks she's helping. Maybe just acknowledge that you value her insight, and you'll take it into consideration."

Ryan grabbed her hand, shooting tingles up her arm. "Sarah, you're brilliant! You sure you don't want to be my assistant? We could make beautiful music together." He laughed at his own corniness. Typical Ryan.

He continued holding her hand, rubbing his thumb over it. "Actually, I've been wanting to ask you something."

Joe hadn't even worked up a sweat before Sarah's unit came in sight. She lived just on the other side of the complex. If she wasn't home, he could check again on his way back. Of course, he'd smell a lot worse then. He hoped she was home now.

The dog trotted happily by his side, tongue lolling. Joe had to admit he liked the company.

No car, but that didn't mean anything. He bet she could fit hers in the one-car garage. His truck was too big, so he always parked out front. Of course, even if he had something smaller, he had too many toys in his garage to get a car in there.

The blinds were open, and the light in the kitchen was on. Her place was a mirror image of his own, with the kitchen at the back of the combo living-dining area. Except hers looked a lot nicer. She had redone the whole interior before moving in, something he'd noticed before when he'd picked her up to hang out with Kyle and Heather.

Maybe she was out on the patio. No way to tell from here. He jogged around the back of the building. Laughter drifted around the corner. Hmm, someone was with Sarah? Or was it a neighbor he heard? Working his way through the landscaped greenbelt, he didn't try to be quiet. The dog's collar jangled, and they sounded like they were hacking their way through the jungle. It was just as well. He didn't want her to think he was sneaking up on her. The ground here was lower than the wall. Unless he pulled himself up, he couldn't see over it.

A male voice drifted over the wall. Who was that? He couldn't keep standing here eavesdropping. He moved over to the gate to knock on it. The leash jerked in his hand as the dog lunged after a cat. "Hey, stop that." He tightened his hold on the leash and took a few steps.

The gate swung open.

"Joe?"

He turned. "Hi, Sarah. I—"

"You have a dog? When did you get him?" She knelt down, and the dog came over to lick her hand.

Ryan appeared behind Sarah. What was he doing here? Heaviness filled his stomach. This was a bad idea.

"Ryan Bradley." Ryan stuck out his hand.

Joe shook it. He knew who Ryan was from church. "Joe Romero."

Sarah petted the dog. "What's his name?"

"He doesn't have one. I rescued him during the fire, and he won't leave me alone. We were just going out for a run, and I'd thought I'd stop by. I heard voices and came back here. Didn't mean to interrupt."

"You're not interrupting. We were just having iced tea and talking about choir business." Sarah straightened from petting the dog. "Come join us. You and your shadow." She smiled up at him, and his heart melted a little. "Hey, that's a good name for him." She met his gaze with her pretty dark-green eyes.

He suddenly didn't know what to do with himself. "That is a good name. Thanks. What do you think, buddy? Want to be called Shadow?"

The dog licked his hand.

He grinned. "Shadow it is." Then he caught Ryan staring at him over Sarah's shoulder. Were they really just talking about choir business? Or did Ryan have another reason for being here? He hated the idea of leaving her here alone with Ryan. Yet, what could he do? Ask her out in front of him? A bold but stupid plan. Time to punt. "Thanks for the offer, but we'd better get a run in before it gets too late. Maybe another time."

"Yes, that would be great." Sarah stepped back into the patio. "Thanks for letting me meet Shadow. Have a good run."

He nodded and turned to move off.

"Joe?"

Sarah's voice stopped him. He turned back.

"Glad you made it back safe from the fires. You were in my prayers." Her gaze on him was soft. The sun lit up the edges of her reddish-brown hair, making it glow.

"Thanks, Sarah." This time he turned and started jogging. Once around the corner of the building, he broke into a run. Shadow kept pace with him. Dang it! He should have said something sooner. But when? He'd gone straight from helping Kyle protect Heather from the gang that wanted her dead to fighting that brush fire. Probably should have said something to Sarah while they were with Kyle and Heather one of those nights. At least let her know he was interested.

He ran out of the complex and up the hill. As his feet hit the pavement in cadence, some of his anger drained away. Even if Ryan was interested in Sarah, she wasn't off-limits yet. He always liked a good challenge.

The beginnings of a plan drifted together in his mind as he crested the hill.

Sarah stared after Joe until he disappeared around the building. Ryan might have movie-star good looks, but Joe's broad shoulders and dark eyes would give Ryan a run for his money any day. Of all the times, why did Joe have to show up with Ryan here? Suppressing a sigh, she started to close the gate when she heard, "Hey, wait up!"

Heather McAlistair's smiling face appeared around the

corner. "Guess you didn't hear me knock. Then I heard voices over here. Was that Joe just leaving? Did—"

Sarah held up her hand and widened her eyes. "Ryan also stopped by." She stepped back so Heather could enter the patio.

Heather's eyebrows lifted, but she came inside. "Hey, Ryan."

"I'll grab another glass."

"I'm going to run. I know you guys have plans." Ryan squeezed Sarah's shoulder and leaned close, his breath fanning across her ear. "I'll call you." He winked and let himself out the gate.

Sarah locked it securely behind him then collapsed in a chair, head in her hands. "Can this day just be over?"

Heather scanned the area. Then she stood. "Let's go eat. You can tell me about your boy drama over chips and salsa."

Over fajitas, chips, and smoky, fire-roasted salsa at their favorite Mexican restaurant, Sarah told Heather all about the bomb Mark had dropped.

"You'll be great at it." Heather popped a salsa-laden chip in her mouth. "The staff loves you, the clients love you. Anything you need to know, Mark can teach you. He wouldn't have offered you the job if he didn't think you could do it. He doesn't want his firm run into the ground."

Sarah nodded slowly. "I guess you're right. I just never planned on doing anything like that. But, Mark has done so much for me, it feels like I should do this for him in return."

"A year from now you'll look back and wonder what on earth you were worried about." Heather grinned.

Sarah rolled her eyes. "I don't know about that."

"Tell me what I walked in on back there. Joe leaving, Ryan on your patio. I didn't see any blood."

"Please." Sarah gave Heather a quick recap while piling grilled meat and veggies on a tortilla.

"Obviously, Ryan's going to ask you out."

"You don't know that." Sarah took a bite.

"I doubt he was going to ask if you wanted to sing a solo this Sunday. He knows the answer to that, and he never asks. He just assigns." Heather picked up her iced tea. "Ryan is pretty cute. You'll definitely be the envy of more than a few women."

"Not my goal in life." Sarah leaned back in her chair. With Ryan's Chris Evans good looks, who wouldn't be flattered to be showered with his attention? "I just want to design buildings that make people feel safe and happy. I don't need to run the firm. And while I admire Ryan's passion and wouldn't mind spending time getting to know him better—not to mention he's easy on the eyes—I don't want to be in the spotlight. And he loves it." She paused. "And then there's Joe."

"Yeah. You guys really seemed to hit it off when you were so gracious to keep me company during my 'confinement.'" Which was a nice way of saying the protective custody Kyle had put her under after she'd witnessed a gang-initiation robbery gone wrong. "I thought for sure he'd ask you out."

"The fires did get in the way. He's dedicated to his job. I think today was his first day off." Sarah stopped, chip halfway to her mouth. "Was that why he came by? I thought it was to show me his dog. But …"

Heather wiggled her eyebrows. "I'd bet money on it."

"And then he saw Ryan." Sarah let out a groan.

"What are you going to do?"

"Build a time machine and go back to yesterday?"

Heather laughed. "Wrong direction. You'd just have to live today over."

"Oh yeah." She leaned her arms on the table and propped her head up with her hand. "I'm taking suggestions."

"Speaking from experience, sometimes it's not a bad thing when God shakes up your world. Not pleasant, but not bad." And Heather knew what she was talking about. Her life had been turned upside down recently.

Sarah's phone buzzed in her purse. She picked it up. Ryan. Plus two other missed calls from ... Ryan.

"You can't keep putting it off. He'll call all night. You might as well answer while I'm here and can listen in." Heather grinned.

Sarah made a face. She wished she'd had time to come to some understanding of her own feelings. She punched the phone on. "Hi, Ryan."

"I just realized ... You were out to dinner with Heather, weren't you? I'm so sorry. I forgot. I wondered why you weren't answering."

"It's okay. I didn't hear my phone."

"I won't keep you then. I, uh, I wondered if you'd go to dinner with me Thursday night."

Sarah's heart pounded. She glanced over at Heather, who had covered her mouth with her hand, but it was easy to see she was laughing. Sarah made a face at her.

"Sure. That sounds nice." What else could she say?

"Great! I have an idea, but I think it'll be a surprise. I'll pick you up around six, okay?" His enthusiasm leaked through the phone. It was hard not to be excited around him.

She smiled. "Sounds great." Surprises were not something she enjoyed. Plans, advance notice, those were things she could get behind. Still, there was no reason to disappoint him. And a nice dinner out would be fun. Wouldn't it?

Even if it wasn't with Joe.

"I've gotta run. I'm playing basketball with Sean and Nick, and I took a chance on calling you during a water break. I'll see you at rehearsal on Wednesday."

"I'll see you then." She punched the phone off and stuck it in her purse.

Heather studied her. "So, a date Thursday? I wonder what he has planned. Knowing Ryan, it'll be memorable."

Sarah sighed. "Yeah. I just would rather get to know him in a more low-key way."

"Like you did with Joe."

"Yeah." Why couldn't Joe have been a little bit earlier?

"Hey, it's not like you agreed to marry the guy. It's just a date. Go, have fun." Heather motioned to their server for a refill on her iced tea.

"I honestly don't even know what he sees in me. I've never tried to catch his eye. He seems more the supermodel type."

Heather stared at her. "Are you kidding? With that gorgeous wavy auburn hair? And your beautiful voice? The fact that you haven't thrown yourself at him, unlike every other single woman in church, probably makes you that much more intriguing."

"Maybe." But what she really wanted to know was what Joe thought of her.

Chapter Three

J OE BLINKED AS THE SCREEN blurred. It had been slow at the station, a good thing since he still hadn't recovered from the brushfire stint. Today he definitely felt older than thirty-three. They'd spent the day cleaning and checking gear and equipment, but Sarah had been on his mind. That'd been the downside of a slow shift. Nothing to distract him. Still, he'd take it. None of the guys was mentioning the lack of calls, but their gaze would drift to the clock or their phones. No one wanted to comment on it and jinx it.

While the guys were running drills and putting Akino through his paces, Joe studied for the next exam until the words swam in front of his eyes.

"Hey, Captain?"

Joe looked up at Jesse Lin's voice. Behind him stood a man with slicked-back dark hair in a tailored suit and expensive shoes. A local businessman? Joe got to his feet.

The man extended his hand. "Tony DiMarco. I hear you guys saved my house, and I wanted to come by and give my thanks in person."

Joe shook his hand. So this was the guy. Too bad the chief wasn't around. He'd be able to tell his wife that he'd actually met the guy with the gorgeous house. "Joe Romero. We're just happy it all worked out."

"Regardless, I'd like to at least buy you guys dinner. Barbecue, okay? I'll have my secretary make arrangements."

"Not necessary, but much appreciated." This guy was smooth and clearly wasn't going to take no for an answer.

DiMarco reached into his pocket and handed Joe a card. "Here's my number. You or any of your guys ever need anything, let me know. I have a cabin in Big Bear that I'd like to make available to you. You guys need a break or a team-building retreat, it's the perfect place. Just call my secretary. Her number's on here." He shook Joe's hand again and slapped him on the shoulder. "I gotta run, but expect dinner soon." He pulled out his phone as he turned, striding away.

Well then. Joe glanced at the card then tucked it in his pocket. Not that they could use the cabin or any of his "help." Who knew how many regulations that would break. Guys like DiMarco thought if they threw enough money around they could get whatever they wanted. Must be a nice illusion to have. But, the guy hadn't yelled at them for messing up his yard. And at least they were getting dinner out of it.

Which reminded him. He grabbed his phone, moved to a quiet spot, and called Kyle.

"Hey, I have a favor to ask. Can you run by my place and let the dog out? I've got to come up with a better long-term plan."

"Sure. No problem. Dog have a name yet?"

"Shadow. Sarah named him." Joe leaned against the wall and closed his eyes.

"Sarah? So, you two have plans?"

"Nope." Joe let out a breath. "I went over there yesterday, but Ryan was there."

"That doesn't necessarily mean anything. Heather said Ryan's been interested in Sarah for a while, but Sarah's not too sure about him. You need to make sure Sarah stays unsure about him."

"He doesn't seem her type. Too showy. He's a great singer and good looking … and he knows it." The image of Ryan leading worship, blond hair catching the lights, emotion pouring through his voice flashed through Joe's mind.

"My thoughts exactly. What are you going to do?" A police radio squawked in the background through Kyle's phone.

"Not sure yet."

"Hey, why don't you ask Sarah to watch Shadow on your shifts?"

Joe paused. "That is a great idea."

Kyle said something, but raised voices coming from the apparatus floor cut through the air.

"I gotta go." Joe pocketed his phone and headed out front. More shouting. He rounded the corner to see Andrew Hardin facing off with Jesse Lin. A couple of the guys arrayed themselves on either side.

"It was an accident, dude. I said I was sorry. Chill." Lin's hands were up and out to the side.

Joe pushed between them. "Is there a problem here?" He bore his gaze into Andrew, then Jesse.

Jesse shrugged. "Not with me."

Joe turned to Andrew and raised his eyebrows.

Andrew scowled and stalked off.

Joe watched him go. The other guys moved off. What had gotten into Andrew lately? He'd been edgy and grumpy. Problems at home? He'd have to look into it. Distracted firefighters were a danger to everyone.

Alarm tones sounded. Joe ran for his pants and boots. So much for the quiet shift. But maybe when they got back, they'd have a still-warm dinner.

"I want a bigger cut. I'm taking all the risk."

Tony shook his head. Greg was harping again. He thought they were done with the conversation when that chick drove up. "You gotta be kidding. You're not the one fronting the money, convincing certain people that their interests are our interests."

Greg shrugged his big shoulders, towering over Tony, but he refused to take a step back. "I can always go to the press. Since the Bedroom Burglar was caught, the *South County Times* could use a good investigative piece."

Tony gave a harsh laugh. "You do that and you'd never work in this state again. Or any other for that matter."

A vein throbbed in Greg's forehead as his face reddened. That was okay. Tony could ride out the explosion. He was used to it. Greg's unpredictable temper and lumberjack appearance intimidated subcontractors, which generally made them jump to do Greg's—and by default Tony's—bidding. It had served him well in the past.

Greg was obviously stuck on this subject, so Tony would have to throw him a bone to pacify him. Maybe—

His jaw exploded in pain as his neck snapped to the side. What the—

He caught his breath and touched his jaw gently. "What are you, stupid?"

Greg's face was fast approaching the color of a bad sunburn. "There's more where that came from. You believe me now?" His fists remained balled at his side.

No way was Tony putting up with that. But in Greg's condition there was no reasoning with him. Tony needed a way to get him to calm down. The pain in his face was making it hard to think. "How much you want?" The words were hard to get out.

"Half."

"What are you smoking? No way are you gonna get half. Not even close." He started to shake his head, but it hurt too much.

Greg stepped closer, crowding Tony's space. This time he did take a step back.

He'd had it. "Don't push me. Or the DEA might get a tip about someone using building sites as drug drops."

Greg's eyes narrowed.

Ha! He hit a nerve. "Remember who you're dealing with."

Greg took another step.

Smelled like Greg had had beer with dinner, probably quite a few. "You're not getting the message." Tony shoved him away.

Greg stumbled a step then caught his heel on the curb and gutter. He fell straight back, windmilling his arms. Hard to catch your balance when you've had too many beers. Like a cut tree, he landed hard on his back, bouncing slightly, then was still.

Tony watched, keeping his distance, rubbing his jaw.

Greg didn't get up.

He must have fallen harder than Tony thought. Got the wind knocked out of him.

Tony took a step toward him, kicked at the booted foot. Nothing.

Another step. And in the fading light of the day, he saw the glint of dark liquid underneath Greg's head.

Chapter Four

JOE WASN'T BEING STALKERISH. NOT at all. It was just a coincidence that, as he stepped outside to let Shadow water the plants, he happened to see movement in the direction of Sarah's unit. Sarah. Walking in the opposite direction. With her earbuds in and tennis shoes on, it looked like she was going for a walk. Okay, this could work.

He hustled Shadow inside. "Wanna go for a walk, boy?" He put on his running shoes. He checked the mirror, running his hands through his hair. It looked okay.

Back outside, he couldn't see her. He started off at a run—Shadow trotting by his side, tongue hanging out—in the direction he'd seen her headed until he reached the end of the complex at the street. He looked both ways. The street curved around, so he couldn't tell if she went uphill or down. But knowing Sarah . . . They headed up the hill. Nope, he wasn't being stalkerish at all. Stalkers didn't have dogs.

Sure enough, as he rounded the bend in the road, he saw her. He didn't want to scare her by running up on her. "Sarah!"

Her step faltered before she slowly turned her head. She stopped and waved.

They caught up with her, slowing. "Hey, do you walk every morning?"

"Hey, Shadow." She ruffled the dog's fur, and they started up again. "Nearly. Well, I kind of got out of the habit the first month I was here. Too exhausted from remodeling then moving. But pretty much every day the last month."

"Surprised I haven't seen you before now."

"Do you usually run this way?"

Joe hesitated. "We do PT at the station. On my days off, I run, but not at any set time."

Sarah glanced at him then Shadow. "Guess you'll be getting outside more now that you have him."

This could be an opportunity to outflank Ryan. "I saw you when I stepped outside this morning. I figured the company would be good. Not that Shadow isn't company, but ..." There was no good way to finish that sentence without making it sound like he was comparing Sarah to a dog. This was off to a stellar start.

A half smile from her. Good. "But you're not running."

"That's okay. Same benefits, just takes longer to cover the miles. I might run later. I don't know what kind of endurance Shadow has yet. How far do you go?"

"I usually loop around to Rue de Valore and back home."

"About a mile and a half, hills included." Nothing like Joe's typical workout, but he wasn't here to get in shape. He was vying for a chance to connect with Sarah.

"I used to do two miles at my old place, but it was flatter. The hills here are killer. My legs still aren't used to it yet."

It was cool in the mornings, the typical June gloom marine layer that didn't burn off until afternoon, so it made sense that Sarah wore yoga pants instead of shorts. From what he could see of her legs, their shape looked good to him. "You and Heather have any plans this week for a girls' night out? I owe

Kyle a rematch at basketball, and I wouldn't want to crowd their couple time." It sounded like a halfway decent excuse. He didn't expect her to flat out tell him she had a date with Ryan, but who knew what he might learn.

"I don't know. We have choir practice tonight, so we may set something up. Her sisters are coming down this weekend. She hasn't seen them since before all that craziness happened with the gang. Glad that's over."

"Me too. Kyle's couch is comfortable, but it's not the same as my bed." Not that he was a cop or anything, but it had helped ease Kyle's mind to have another able body in his house to protect Heather. Though Joe knew he was really acting more as a chaperone. A role whose importance he understood far too well. He would have done anything to keep his friend from making the same mistakes he had. Wanting to change the subject, he asked, "Is the choir singing this weekend?"

"Yes. Not sure what yet. Guess we'll find out tonight?"

Joe raised his eyebrows. "Isn't that a little late?"

Sarah laughed. "I hope not. It happens occasionally. I think it'll be a song I already know."

Joe racked his brain while they walked, trying to think of a way to get her to say something about her plans with Ryan. The only way he could definitively find out, short of flat-out asking her, was to ask her out himself. But the thought of her turning him down made his legs go weak. There had to be a better way. He just couldn't think of it yet.

As the complex came into view again, Joe was reluctant to let her go. But she had to get to work. He walked her to her porch and made sure she got her door open. "I don't work tomorrow. Want to do this again?"

"Sure." She smiled. "The company keeps my mind off the pain in my legs." She petted Shadow. "Bye, boy. Be good."

"Okay. I'll pick you up at seven." It was almost like a date.

"Sounds good. Have a good day." She waved as she stepped inside.

"I will." It'd already started out pretty good. Sarah seemed to really like Shadow. Maybe she wouldn't mind watching him while Joe was at work. His stomach rumbled. He needed to eat breakfast. And think about his next move.

Sarah walked from her car to the choir practice room, forcing down the nervousness. How was she going to act around Ryan? The whole thing was weird. Just act normal. Whatever that was.

She pushed open the door and walked in. Ryan was in the back talking to someone. He looked up when she walked in, giving her a big smile and a wink, cranking up her nervousness and reassuring her at the same time.

A floaty feeling enveloped her, and somehow she made it to her seat, knowing Ryan's eyes were on her. She tried to keep her movements casual but couldn't help but feel like she was on stage.

Heather leaned over her shoulder, and Sarah nearly jumped. "So?" Heather wasn't doing a good job of concealing her smile. And the way she kept glancing back at Ryan.

"Is he looking this way?"

"Yep."

"Thanks for the subtlety, Heather."

Heather smacked her music against Sarah's shoulder. "Oh. Almost forgot. If you don't have other plans"—she raised her eyebrows—"Aimee and Kellie are coming down for sure Saturday, and we are planning a shopping marathon. South Coast Plaza and Fashion Island in one day. Come with us if you dare."

Sarah rolled her eyes. Heather's sisters were fun, creating a dynamic Sarah—as an only child—didn't have. A shadow passed over her heart. She hadn't always been an only child. "We'll see how it goes. I'm still trying to wrap my mind around Mark's proposal."

"Have you given Mark an answer about the managing partner position?"

Sarah shrugged. "Not exactly. But I don't have much of a choice, do I? I can't add one more worry to his pile." She sighed. "Maybe a day of shopping is what I need to take my mind off things. Are Kyle and Joe playing basketball Saturday then?"

Heather raised her eyebrows. "I don't know. What makes you say that?"

"Oh, I ran into Joe and Shadow when I was walking this morning, and he mentioned it."

Ryan stepped to the front. "Okay, let's get started." He gave Sarah a long look.

"Talk to you after," Heather stage whispered and headed back to her seat with the sopranos.

Sarah tried to concentrate on rehearsal. Was it her imagination or did Ryan look at her way more often than usual? Did anyone else notice? Every time she glanced over at Heather, she was looking at Sarah with a knowing smile. She stopped looking over there.

Ryan called her up to work on her solo while the choir provided backup. While he was complimentary, he didn't seem any more attentive or affectionate than usual. Relief with a tinge of confusion spread through her. She didn't want him to act differently, did she? That would be embarrassing.

As rehearsal was winding down, she was a little unsure of what to do. Should she stay and talk to Ryan? They had set a date for tomorrow night. If she just knew what the rules were, she could live with that. *Yes, Sarah, go ahead and go home, and I'll call you so we can talk in private. Or, Why didn't you stay to talk to me after practice when we were both right there?* Ugh. She couldn't win.

Ryan was talking to a couple of guys. She wasn't going to walk up to him and hadn't caught his eye. Luckily, Heather came over to her, and Sarah pretended like she was paying attention. Heather knew she wasn't, and played along, bringing up random subjects that didn't require much input from Sarah but still allowed her to keep an eye on Ryan. Sarah was grateful that Heather knew her so well.

This was ridiculous. She was leaving. If Ryan wanted to talk to her, he could come find her. "I'm going to go. I'll call you tomorrow."

"Okay, don't forget about Saturday."

"I'll try to go."

Without giving Ryan another look, Sarah headed out the door into the dark.

Someone grabbed her arm.

Heart pounding, she spun.

Ryan. "Hey, you weren't trying to leave without saying goodbye, were you?" He pulled her against him in a side hug. "So, about tomorrow—"

Choir members streamed out of the door. "Night, Ryan. Night, uh, Sarah." A few confused looks, a few half smiles, but no one said anything.

Her face heated. She gave a small wave. If her potential relationship with Ryan was a secret before, it sure wasn't now.

Ryan draped his arm over her shoulder. "Wear something nice, dressy. You're going to love it." He kissed the top of her head just as the choir's biggest gossips, Chris and Sharon Roberts, left the room.

Tony searched through the stack of papers again, this time reading each one carefully. It had to be here. He'd pulled every scrap of paper connecting Greg and his "nonpublic" dealings out of Greg's truck. Then Nick had driven it to a trailhead pullout on the Ortega Highway. The twisty road made it easy to get in and out of there without being seen.

It wasn't here. He had to find it. Not only could it connect Greg and him in a very damaging way if it fell into the wrong hands, it had the information he needed to keep working on the site. They'd spent a lot of money to create their plan. Too much to re-create it. He had to avoid doing that, if at all possible.

He had to find it.

Why wouldn't it be in Greg's truck? Had he planned on using it as leverage against Tony? He picked up his phone and hit a button.

"Nick, I need you to head over to Greg's house and find something for me. If it's not there, check his office. Tonight."

If Greg had planned to pressure Tony, he could have hidden that map anywhere.

And Tony was going to find it.

Chapter Five

SARAH PACED ACROSS HER LIVING room, heeled sandals clicking on her red oak floors. She had fifteen minutes but didn't want to sit. Picking up the remote, she flipped on the TV. It would provide background noise and maybe a distraction to make time go faster. Ryan had a tendency to run late.

Unlike Joe, who'd been right on time this morning for their walk. They hadn't talked about anything important, but she had been uneasy the whole time about her date with Ryan looming over her head. She didn't want Joe to hear about it from someone else, but there was no good way to bring it up. So she didn't. Besides, it was one date. There probably wouldn't be another once Ryan realized she wasn't his type.

The blonde newscaster prattled on about the happenings in LA. Orange County didn't merit its own TV station, and coverage consisted of whatever bones the networks wanted to throw it. Then again, not much happened here. Outside of brushfires followed by rain-induced landslides or winter storms pushing waves against multi-million-dollar beachfront homes, the OC didn't get much coverage. Most of the damage here was done by nature, shoving man back from where he'd encroached.

Of course, it was her job to help that encroachment. While her firm concentrated mainly on business parks now, she'd done her share of housing developments. Now that OC was nearly built out, she pretty much only saw a home design for a remodel. Or to replace something that had burned in a brushfire. Which was why she enjoyed working on her own dream-home plans so much.

She checked the mirror one more time as the clock clicked over to six.

"Our top news story tonight comes from Orange County."

Really? Sarah turned toward the TV. What house fell into the ocean?

"The owner of a large construction company has been reported missing."

A picture of a blond-haired, ruddy-faced man flashed on the screen. He looked familiar. She knew a lot of the contractors in the area.

"Greg Connor was last seen Tuesday in the Foothill Corridor development area of Laguna Vista. His secretary reported him missing when he didn't show up for work for two days, and she couldn't locate him. If you have any information on Greg Connor's whereabouts, call the Laguna Vista Police Department." The number crawled across the bottom of the screen.

Sarah blinked. Foothill Corridor. That's where her job site was. She thought back. Tuesday. She'd been up there. It was a fairly large area, but still. She mentally walked through her visit to the site, but nothing seemed unusual.

Wait. Before she got to the site, when she'd gotten lost—

The doorbell rang. Ryan.

What should she do? *Answer the door, dummy.* She shook her head at herself. She should call Heather and get Kyle's number. Would Ryan be upset if she put a wrinkle in their plans? Talking to the police about a man's disappearance certainly didn't fit in to her definition of a good date. She pondered her options while she pulled open the door.

Wow. Ryan was wearing a dark-blue button-down shirt and dress pants. She rarely saw him out of jeans or shorts.

"Hi, Sarah." Ryan stepped inside and kissed her on the cheek. "You look fabulous. These are for you." He handed her a wrapped bouquet of flowers.

"Thank you. I'll go put these in water." She moved to the kitchen, searching for a vase. "I can't remember the last time I saw you dressed up."

"We have a reservation at Five Crowns."

She nearly dropped the vase she had just grabbed. That was an awfully expensive place for a first date. "Wow." She filled the vase with water and dropped the flowers in. She moved the vase to the table. The news had moved on to another story, and she picked up the remote and flipped the TV off.

But what to do? Ryan had gone to a lot of trouble. And with traffic, they might end up pressed for time to make their reservation. But would Kyle want her to come in and talk to him? How did that work?

"Sarah? Ready to go?" Ryan looked a little confused. She must be making a weird face.

"Oh, gosh. Sorry. Yes, I'm ready. Just let me grab my jacket." Great, now she was babbling. Couldn't she just forget she saw the report? It was just chance that she had the TV on. She glanced at her watch. What did she really know about the missing guy, anyway? Other than he had given her directions. Still, someone's life could be at stake. Who knew what little bit of information she might have that could crack the case open?

Ryan reached out and rubbed her arm. "Are you okay? Is this not a good night?"

She turned to find Ryan right behind her. Really close. She realized she was still standing in the middle of the living room with the remote in her hand. Mmm, he smelled good. Soap, shaving cream, aftershave.

"No, we can go. I just heard on the news that a contractor is missing, and I think it's a guy I saw the other day near one of my current job sites. I'm sure it's nothing, but I probably should let Kyle know."

"Call from the car." He squeezed her shoulder.

Relief washed over her. Good, he wasn't upset. Grabbing her purse and jacket, she followed Ryan out the door. Her purse was a large, soft leather tote that she kept all of her necessary things in. It was fine for every day, but it was a little large to take on a date. Too bad she hadn't thought to switch to a smaller one. Too late now. She locked the door behind her—double checking to make sure it was locked—as Ryan waited by his Mustang. She climbed in, buckling her seatbelt as he backed out, then tugged her phone out of her purse which she had wedged on the floor next to her leg.

He glanced over at her, giving her one of his movie-star grins that made women everywhere swoon. "You look great, by the way."

"Thanks." She should be flattered that he'd turned his sights on her. She smoothed the front of her dress. A plum, fitted sheath, it rode up a bit in the car, exposing several inches of skin above her knees. She called Heather, who was probably at Kyle's, which would simplify things.

By the time Sarah finished explaining to Heather, then Kyle, what she knew, Ryan had exited the freeway and was heading down MacArthur Boulevard toward PCH. The sun wasn't setting yet but hovered low on the horizon, Catalina Island a dark smudge off the coast.

Kyle asked her a few questions, most of which she couldn't answer. She didn't think she'd given him any earth-shaking information. She set her phone to silent then tucked it in her purse. Taking a deep breath and letting it out, she pushed the phone call and the missing contractor out of her mind and concentrated on what she was supposed to be doing: being on a date.

"All done?" Ryan beat out a rhythm on the steering wheel.

"I hope so. I'll give a statement tomorrow. He's going to check into a few things and then get back to me if he has any more questions."

"So are he and Heather together now after all that gang stuff she witnessed?"

"Yeah. They seem pretty happy."

Ryan nodded but didn't say anything.

When they arrived, the valet opened Sarah's door, and she slid out. Ryan rested his hand lightly on her back as they walked up to the restaurant that looked like a Tudor-style country inn, complete with vines crawling up the front and an English garden. At Christmas they would have Victorian carolers strolling through the restaurant.

She took in the surroundings and forced herself to relax. She was going to enjoy this evening. And since she'd known Ryan awhile, this first date wasn't nearly so awkward. While it was like Ryan to make a big show of things, she was still surprised that he'd chosen a place as elegant and expensive as Five Crowns.

The hostess seated them near an enormous brick fireplace. Sarah glanced at the menu full of lamb, roast duck, salmon, swordfish, shrimp and scallops, but it was only for show. She was ordering their prime rib. With five different cuts, it was what they were renowned for.

They discussed music, where Ryan saw the church's music ministry headed, things he wanted to accomplish personally and professionally. It was nice. She liked listening to him, and it kept her mind off herself. Ryan had this way of talking, holding her gaze, making her feel like she was the only person in the world. When the waiter discreetly arrived, the spell was broken.

He set a steaming chocolate soufflé between them, cutting it open to pour chocolate sauce and raspberry purée over it. Sarah thought she was full, but she could nearly taste the hot, fluffy chocolate. The perfect way to end a wonderful meal.

After dinner, they drove down a couple blocks to where the street ran along the cliffs above the ocean. Sarah loved this neighborhood and wished she could afford it. Small bungalow homes, some fifty years old with quaint gardens, lined ordinary streets until suddenly the Pacific Ocean opened up at the end. Of course, in the summer the streets were jam packed with tourists who wanted to avoid the parking fee for Corona del Mar State Beach. Sixteen bucks was worth it to her not to lug everything up and down the steep path to the beach below.

They parked along the cliffs. She tucked her purse on the floor of the back seat, out of sight. She hated to leave it, but it was too bulky to carry while walking along the beach.

She shrugged into her russet moto jacket to stave off the cool ocean breeze. Ryan grabbed her hand while they walked down the sidewalk to the middle of a grassy area. It overlooked the cove that formed the beach. A few fire pits twinkled below, a warm contrast to the inky blackness of the cold ocean.

He put his hands on her shoulders, sliding them up and down, rubbing her neck, heat trailing his fingers. She let out a breath, forcing herself to relax and be in the moment. He was a physically affectionate person, demonstrative, often hugging people, squeezing shoulders during practice and services. But how did he feel about affection in a dating relationship? She'd only known him to date one woman since he'd been at their church. Not that others hadn't nearly thrown themselves at him. But the woman he dated wasn't a singer or musician, so she rarely saw them together.

He stepped in front of her so she was facing him, taking her hands in his, rubbing his thumbs over the back of her hands.

Her eyes darted over his shoulder to the dark Pacific beyond. Was he going to kiss her? This was a bit faster than she was comfortable with. "Thank you for dinner. It was wonderful." She finally looked at him.

His gaze roamed her face, a smile on his face that she couldn't interpret. "My pleasure. Thanks for going. I'd like to do it again sometime. Want to catch a movie tomorrow?"

A bubble of panic rose in her chest. She needed a bit more time. "I have a proposal due Monday I need to get finished. I may be working late. I'm trying to get some things off my boss's plate."

"I'm a night owl. We could hit the late show."

Yeah, she knew that. She didn't know how he made it to Sunday morning sound check. Usually, he rolled in late with a venti Starbucks, his eyes barely open. He was so not a morning person. "Let's see how it goes. I already told Heather I'd try to meet her Saturday for a day of shopping with her sisters. If I stay out too late, I won't want to get up in the morning."

"Aw, come on. The movies with me or shopping with Heather? Is there any contest?"

She smiled. "I don't know. Fashion Island has quite a hold on me."

"Hmm." His eyes dropped to her mouth for a second then back up. "Nice to know my competition." His voice had lowered, the joking tone nearly gone, replaced with a more intimate one.

He was going to kiss her. If she backed away, he'd feel rejected. For all his bravado, she'd seen hurt in his eyes a few times that he couldn't quite cover. She didn't want that. She didn't know what she wanted. This was why she hated dating.

"Sarah!"

She jerked her head. Someone was calling her name. Why? Who? She stepped away from Ryan and looked around.

A red Chevy Silverado truck idled at the curb, the passenger window rolled down. The driver leaned over. "Sarah!"

Joe! What was he doing here? Her face heated. And what had he seen? She hurried over.

"Hop in. Kyle needs to see you at the station about that missing contractor. He tried calling you."

Her phone was in her purse. In Ryan's car.

Ryan was right behind her. "I'll take her then."

Joe shook his head. "Kyle sent me. He'd have my neck."

"Um …" She turned back to Ryan. "I have to go. I need to get my purse." She hurried over to the Mustang, not waiting to see if Ryan followed. When she heard the chirp of the alarm and the doors unlock, she tugged open the door and grabbed her purse. Striding back, she pulled her phone out of her purse. Sure enough, a couple of missed calls and texts. This was why she should have brought a smaller purse, so she could have kept her phone with her.

She pulled open the truck door.

A hardness had replaced the warmth in Ryan's eyes. "Sure. Civic duty and all. I'll call you tomorrow." He kissed the top of her head.

She slid in the truck, glancing back.

Ryan stood with his hands in his pockets, watching them drive away.

Nick had turned up nothing.

Tony drove aimlessly, headed generally in the direction of the site. Driving helped clear his mind, and he knew if he could just think for a moment, he'd figure out what Greg had done with that map. Passing the site, he parked on the street, right where that girl in the black Acura had parked the other day.

Could that have been more than it seemed?

Greg had been pretty friendly with that girl. Could it have been a set-up? The way Greg had turned on him, he could have been planning something. Something about the Acura tugged at his mind.

He replayed the scene in his head. Greg went back to his truck and handed the girl a piece of paper.

Tony would bet his profit on this project that that girl had his map. And he was going to get it back.

Question was, who was she? And what did she know?

She'd asked about Via de los Arboles. Was that just a cover or the truth? Only one way to find out. Tony put the car in gear and started back down the street. Greg had been pointing this direction. If anyone found out what was really on this site, a lot of time and money would be down the drain. This was the project that would set him for life. He'd do better than his dad—and live longer too. If this girl didn't mess it up.

He passed two streets of vacant lots before he came to it. He turned onto Via de los Arboles. Just more vacant lots. Except …

Up ahead was a sign, the kind they always put up on a new project listing the developer, the engineering firm, and the architect. This was the only thing around here. The girl must be associated with one of the firms. Maybe a secretary or an assistant. He remembered what her car looked like. A black Acura.

A piece clicked into place. On a pad of notes he'd found in Greg's car was a line about a black Acura and a license plate number. Greg must have been planning to track the girl down himself.

Good. Tony had two ways to pursue this. He'd get one of his sources to figure out who the plate number belonged to. Meanwhile, he'd work on it the old-fashioned way. All he had to do was drive by each of these businesses until he found the one with her car.

Then Nick could take over.

Joe tapped his fingers on the steering wheel as he pointed his truck toward the Laguna Vista police station. The questions he wanted to ask, but couldn't, hung heavy in the air between him and Sarah. Seeing her tangled up with Ryan plummeted his heart down somewhere near his toes. Maybe he should just give up. Though when they'd gone on their walk this morning, she seemed glad to see him. Not that she had mentioned her date with Ryan for tonight.

What was Kyle thinking in sending him? Kyle could have come himself; his excuse about being too busy and putting Sarah at ease with someone she knew instead of a patrolman was as flimsy as a newspaper. Kyle had thought he was doing Joe a favor. Some favor.

He glanced at Sarah who stared straight ahead, arms wrapped around her middle.

"You cold?" He flipped on the heat and adjusted the vents. The marine layer at the beach could make summer nights chilly.

"I'm fine." She gave him a small smile. "Just tired."

"Kyle didn't give me a lot of details, just said you had some information critical to a case." It was a safer topic than what he really wanted to ask her about: her date with Ryan. On second thought, maybe he didn't want to know.

She sighed, and her shoulders sagged. "I don't know how much help I can be, but I'm willing to try." She turned in her seat toward him. "Did you hear about the missing contractor?"

"Yeah. It wasn't too far from us."

"Apparently, I was the last one who saw him. Well, he was with someone else, but no one seems to know who that was. I've been wracking my brain for what I might have missed."

Without thinking, Joe reached over and covered her hand with his. "It's going to be okay. Kyle knows what he's doing, and he'll walk you through everything."

She gave him a soft smile. "Thanks, Joe."

That lifted his heart out of his toes. He was the one helping Sarah through this stressful time, not Ryan. Maybe Kyle did know what he was doing.

Police stations were cold. That was Sarah's first thought as her and Joe's footsteps echoed across the industrial tile floor to-

ward the front desk at the Laguna Vista police station. But
Joe's hand—resting lightly on her lower back—was warm, even
through her dress.

"Hey, Sarah. Hi, Joe." Kyle appeared on the other side of
the bullet-proof glass partition. "Thanks for coming down." He
disappeared from view for a moment then a door clicked open.
Kyle held it and motioned to her. "Come on back. You too, Joe.
Thanks for picking her up."

"As much as I help you out, I should get paid by the LVPD
as well as the LVFD."

"Yeah, it's a real hardship on you." Kyle smacked his
shoulder.

This was why Sarah loved hanging around these guys. The
had such a solid friendship. They were always there for each
other. Any guy that was loyal to his friends wouldn't abandon
his girl. She faltered, and Joe reached for her arm, steadying her.

"You okay?"

She nodded. Where had that thought come from? Especially since less than an hour ago she had been on a date with
Ryan. She pushed the thoughts away. At this moment, she had
a job to do.

They walked down a hallway a bit until Kyle stopped
and opened the door to a conference room. He held the door.
"Have a seat. Can I get you something? Coffee? Diet Coke?"
He smiled on the last one. He obviously well knew her and
Heather's affection for—possibly even addiction to—the stuff.

"No thanks. I'm fine." She twisted her fingers together, just
wanting to do her civic duty and get this over with.

"Joe?"

"I'm good."

She reached for a chair, but Joe beat her to it, pulling it
out for her. He slid into the one next to her.

Kyle sat and opened his laptop then started asking her

questions about her visit to the site, what was said. She wished she'd paid better attention. She'd been so focused on figuring out where she was and how to get to the job site that she hadn't really noticed much about the contractor or his friend. She described them both as best she could, but it felt inadequate. Maybe if she had Heather's artistic skills, she could draw them. But all she could draw were buildings, not people.

"This guy he was with, what else can you tell me about him? Even just impressions."

She leaned back in her chair and closed her eyes then opened them. "I just assumed he was a developer. I thought both of them were. He seemed more like the money behind the project. I don't know why I thought that." She was silent for a moment, trying to grab a fragment of a memory. It came to her. Shoes. "He was wearing dress shoes. Most guys wear work boots on the site."

Kyle nodded and took notes. "What else?"

"I got the feeling I was interrupting something, like a meeting. He seemed annoyed at me. Or annoyed that Greg was stopping what they were doing to give me directions. In contrast, Greg was very nice to me."

"Back to his giving you directions. He seemed familiar with the area?"

"Yeah. He said we weren't on the map, which was why I couldn't find the site. Then he brought me a map of his own—a site map he'd drawn up probably for a project he was working on—and showed me where I needed to go." Sarah saw him handing her the paper. But she hadn't handed it back. "I don't think I gave it back to him. I bet it's still in my car."

Kyle closed his laptop. "It's late. I'll swing by in the morning and get it on my way to work."

She turned to Joe. "Sounds like that might interfere with our morning routine." She grinned, relief at having this part over, lightening her mood.

Kyle's eyebrows raised. "You kids got something going on

I don't know about?"

Joe slid his arm around Sarah's shoulders and squeezed. "Yeah, we have this deep commitment ... to walking in the morning."

For a moment, Sarah wanted to melt into his shoulder, pretend it was real.

Kyle laughed as he stood. "Get this woman home. Both of you get some rest. Joe, we can't have the city unsafe because you're too tired."

Sarah stood, and Joe's arm slid away. She immediately missed the warmth.

What a weird night. Though ending a date night at a police station with a different guy than she started out with was not anything she ever imagined doing, being with these two was far more comfortable than she had been all night with Ryan. And it allowed her to dodge a bullet as far as Ryan kissing her went. For now.

Unfortunately, her civic duty wasn't done just yet.

Chapter Six

J OE WAITED AS LONG AS he dared. He didn't know how early
Sarah got up, but he wanted to check on her before he left
for work. She had to be worn out after last night. Maybe
Saturday she'd want to do something to get her mind off things.
He had to ask her before Ryan did. He reached down and ruf-
fled Shadow's fur. Plus, he had an excuse to see her.

Grabbing his spare key out of the drawer and then clipping the leash onto Shadow's collar, he headed out the front
door. A slight breeze carried the spicy tang of eucalyptus trees.

Shadow made his round of sniffing and peeing as they
worked their way over to Sarah's condo. The blinds were closed,
but light spilled out around the edges. Maybe she was up. Or
maybe she left a light on. No way to know. He knocked.

A moment later the door opened. When Sarah saw them,
she smiled. Her pretty reddish-brown hair was pulled back into
a ponytail, and she would look like a teenager if it weren't for
those dark circles under her eyes. "Hey, Joe. Hey, Shadow." She
put her hand down for Shadow to sniff and then scratched his
ears. "Want some coffee?"

He was pleased all out of proportion. It was only coffee, and Sarah was the type of woman who was always polite. She probably read Miss Manners. Or whatever the current equivalent was. "Wish I could. I just have a second before I have to get to work. Can you believe it? They actually expect me to pull people out of wrecked cars and fight fires instead of drinking coffee and walking around the block."

She laughed, like he hoped she would. He liked making her laugh, even if her smile didn't quite reach her eyes.

He might regret this, but he couldn't help himself. "You look tired. Have trouble sleeping?" He watched her face for a reaction.

She ran her hand over her face. "A little. It feels like that paper in my car is burning a hole. I couldn't stop thinking about it."

"Want me to go check? I'm good with fires."

She laughed again. Two for two.

He had to go, or he'd be late. And he still hadn't asked her about Saturday. But he couldn't bring himself to pull away. Realizing he was staring at her, and she probably thought he was losing it, he scrambled to think of something to say. For once he was at a loss.

Shadow licked his hand. Oh yeah. "Hey, I wondered if you could do me a favor today?" He pulled out his spare key. "Could you let Shadow out after you get home from work? I haven't adjusted to having a dog yet and keep forgetting that he can't go the whole twenty-four hours of my shift in the condo."

She reached for the key, and he could have sworn there was a spark when their fingers touched, as clichéd as that sounded.

"I'd be happy to. We'll even go for a walk, won't we, Shadow?" She scratched his ears again. "Actually, it'll be kind of nice to have company. This whole thing has me rattled."

"Text me any time. I mean that. If I can't answer right

away, I'll get back to you as soon as I can. Okay?" He was going to be late, but it was worth it.

"Okay. Thanks. I appreciate that, Joe." She smiled again, and his heart did a funny thing. "Anyhow"—she shook her head—"you've got to get to work. I'll let you go do your heroic duty. Shadow and I will do the walk-around-the-block thing tonight since someone has to." Her phone buzzed, and she pulled it from her pocket.

He couldn't read the text message, but he saw who it was from. Ryan.

She shoved it back in her pocket.

A car pulled in the parking slot in front of her condo. A Crown Vic. Kyle. Great timing.

Joe was not going to ask her out as Kyle was coming up the walkway. Maybe a text later when he had time at the station? No, that was a lame way to ask a woman out. But she was watching his dog, and they did live in the same complex. He'd figure something out.

Sarah stared after Joe as he and Shadow left on a light jog back to his condo. Her phone buzzed again in her pocket as Kyle came up the steps. She ignored it.

"Morning, Kyle. Want some coffee?"

"I'm good." He tilted his head toward Joe's retreating form. "Early morning visitors?"

"We've been walking in the mornings. Today, he wants me to let Shadow out while he's on shift." She stepped back inside, and Kyle followed her. She put Joe's key on the counter and then moved to the door leading to the garage. Leaning in the passenger door, she searched until she spotted it. The paper had floated to the floor, which was why she'd forgotten about it. Normally, she didn't leave anything in her car. She picked it up and straightened, glancing over it before heading back into the house. Holding it between her and Kyle, she pointed on the map where she and Greg Connor had been and where she had been trying to go.

Her eyes roamed over the page as Kyle studied it. She frowned. "This is odd."

Kyle's eyes met hers. "What?"

She leaned against her table, careful not to knock over the vase of flowers from Ryan that stood in the middle. "Well, this looks like part of a grading plan. But I don't know why these areas are marked and circled here. These are cut-and-fill amounts listed here, the amount of dirt they need to remove or add to a site, generally to level it for building pads. The thing is, the site is on a gradual slope, not in the side of a mountain like these amounts would indicate. I'm not a soils engineer, but these amounts don't look right to me." She turned the paper over. "There's no soils or civil engineer's name on this."

She handed it to Kyle. "It's probably nothing. Just seems a little odd. Maybe it's just an idea for a project."

"I'll call the city building department and check it out. Maybe something will turn up."

"You can find out if they've issued any grading permits for the site or if any plans have been submitted."

Kyle nodded and looked at his watch. "What does your day look like? Do you have time for lunch? I'm supposed to meet Heather. She'd love the company. I know it's what she misses most about freelancing from home now."

"Sounds great."

"Baja Fresh okay?"

"Sure. I'll meet you there."

Kyle headed out to his unmarked unit, and Sarah finished up a few things before leaving for the office. But those cut-and-fill amounts nagged at her. Something was off about this whole thing. She pushed it out of her mind. Kyle would track it down.

It was in his hands now, and she had done all she could. Hadn't she?

Settled in at the office, Sarah was engrossed in a proposal when her cell phone buzzed on her desk, pulling her out of deep work mode. She glanced at it. Ryan. Again. She'd forgotten to call him back. She couldn't dodge him forever, even if she hadn't decided to go with him tonight. When she was with him or talking with him, she liked being with him. He paid attention to her, there was chemistry. But when she was away from him, she found herself doubting. It was like he was sucking her in, and she had to make sure she wasn't just going out with him to avoid the conflict of saying no to him. She hated conflict, but it wasn't fair to date someone just to avoid it either.

Sighing, she turned away from AutoCAD and answered the phone.

"How are the proposals coming?" Ryan did have a great voice.

"Good. I think I'll be done today. If nothing goes wrong."

"Great. I'll pick you up at seven. We can get something to eat at the food court and head over to the movies." Ryan never had a problem being direct about what he wanted. A trait she envied.

All she had to do was say *okay* or *no*. *Okay* would be the easiest. *No* would bring on an argument that Ryan would win. He always won. Either with charm or persuasion. Off the top of her head, she couldn't remember anyone saying no to him.

"Sarah?"

"Um, sure. Seven's fine." That would give her time to give Shadow a quick walk. A night at the movies sounded good. Didn't it? And she'd still get home early enough to go shopping with Heather and her sisters on Saturday.

She glanced at the time on her computer. "Oh, wow. I didn't realize it was almost lunch time."

"Lunch plans?"

"Not really. Well, just Heather and Kyle." She put her computer to sleep and grabbed her purse.

"Sounds like fun. Where at?"

"Baja Fresh."

"Hey, how about I meet you guys there? It'll be like a double date."

"Um, sure." It wasn't like she could say no. It was a public place. He could show up if he wanted to. But she could picture the look on Kyle and Heather's faces.

"See you in a few."

She disconnected the phone and stared at it. She wasn't as hungry as she had been a minute ago.

Joe pulled a bottle of water out of the refrigerator at the station. They'd been running all day from one accident to another. Did anybody know how to drive anymore? He shut the refrigerator door and leaned against the counter. He was mostly annoyed that he hadn't had a chance to talk to Kyle about Sarah and the contractor thing. He'd managed to get one call into Kyle and got his voice mail. After taking a long drink of water, he headed for his cell phone.

Voice mail again. He tossed the phone on his bunk just as the tones sounded. Minutes later they were rolling through the door of the truck bay and down the street. The traffic stopped for them, and they made the turn onto Portola Parkway. In front of them, cars pulled to the side of the road at the lights and siren, but a few with their windows up and their music cranked too loud didn't see the truck until it was nearly on them.

Jeff McCoy blew the air horn and stopped at every intersection, and there were three of them to go through in the scant mile to the wreck. Lights from police cruisers flashed and illuminated the underside of the toll road overpass. The engine lights added to theirs. The wreck was just on the other side. McCoy pulled the engine next to the wreck. A small car—now pointing the wrong direction—had collided with a big truck, the small car the obvious loser.

Joe jumped out, opened the engine's compartments and grabbed two of the medical cases. He was the paramedic on the shift, so he headed for the injured. Andrew Hardin and McCoy would deal with the wreck. "Akino, with me."

Joe hurried over. The passenger door was open, a cop peering inside, talking to the driver. Joe saw it in the cop's eyes as he straightened: It didn't look good. Joe popped open one of the cases. "Hi. Can you talk to me?"

"Uh huh." Blood covered the person's face. He could barely tell it was a woman, mostly by the long, straight blonde hair. She had her head against the headrest, eyes closed. The airbag had deployed, probably saved her life, and broke her nose in the process.

Joe assessed her as he pulled on nitrile gloves. "What's your name?"

"Cait Bellamy."

"I'm Joe. I'd ask you how you're doing, but I suspect you've had better days. Where's it hurt?" He pulled out gauze and crawled partway in the car, swabbing away the blood so he could see where it was coming from. Nose for sure. A cut on the head. Those always bled terribly.

"My side. Hurts to breathe."

"Okay. Just take easy breaths. Not too deep. Just nice and easy." Looked like the shifter—and possibly the airbag—had gotten her in the side. She was a small woman and airbags could be almost as dangerous as helpful to them.

He looked past her, out what was left of her window, to where Hardin was pulling equipment out of compartments. McCoy was powering up the compressor for the tools. "Akino, get in here." He touched Cait's shoulder. "Hang on a sec. I'll be right back."

She closed her eyes.

Joe moved out of the vehicle and said to Akino, "Keep her company. I don't care what you talk about, but don't freak out over the blood. She's got lacerations to the face, probably a broken nose, and possible internal injuries. She's in there pretty good. We're going to have to take the car apart around her."

Akino gave a quick nod and crouched down where Joe had been a minute before. "Hey, my name's Zack."

Joe nodded. Good start. He moved over to Hardin and McCoy. "Let's get her out of there."

Hardin turned and headed back to the truck without a word. What was with that guy? Joe had to talk to him, when they could get a spare moment. Something was definitely up. He jogged to the truck, grabbed a blanket, a half backboard, and a c-collar.

Traffic was slowing down, backing up. The cops were doing their best to direct it away and keep people moving. They had flares marking off this side of the street and traffic was moving in the center turn lane. People always wanted to look. Couldn't seem to help it.

He strode back to the car, setting the stuff down outside next to the boxes. He tapped Akino on the shoulder. Akino jerked out of the vehicle, nearly whacking his head on the roof.

Crawling in the car again, Joe noticed a bulletin from his church on the floor. He thought she looked vaguely familiar. It was a huge church, but he knew her face. "Hey, Cait. You sing in the choir, don't you?"

"Um hmm."

"I thought you looked familiar." He reached for the c-collar. "I'm going to put this around your neck to protect it." He continued to talk while he worked. "So you must know Sarah Brockman and Heather McAlistair. Sarah lives in my complex, and Heather's boyfriend, Kyle, and I have been best friends since fourth grade. Small world, huh?"

She attempted a smile. "I'm friends with both of them. Don't think I'll be singing this weekend, though."

"Probably not. I suspect you'll have two nice black eyes by tomorrow and an interesting story to tell of your ride in the ambulance." Working on people you knew was the hardest thing. It was a big enough city that it didn't happen too often. Still, when it did, those were the calls he remembered.

He took her BP, checked her pulse, listened to her breathing. She was stable. He spread the blanket over her, covering her completely. He checked to make sure Akino was watching and listening. And he was. The kid was on it. "I'm putting this over you to protect you from any pieces of flying metal. They're going to take the car apart so we can get you out with as little pain as possible. The car's already wrecked, so it won't hurt it to wreck it some more. You, however, we need to keep as comfortable as possible."

"Hey, watch it!" McCoy's raised voice caused Joe to turn his head. McCoy had Hardin by the back of his turnout coat and was pulling him back from near the traffic lanes. The cop directing traffic scowled at both of them. Joe took a quick glance at McCoy's tight face. "Everything okay?"

McCoy gave him a short nod and then a sidelong glance at Hardin. Joe let out a breath, and then remembered Akino. His wide-eyed gaze darted from McCoy to Hardin to Joe to Cait. So, they were going to have a teaching moment back at the station. For now, they still had a job to do.

Joe put the BP cuff and stethoscope back in the boxes and closed them, then reached for his helmet, pulling down the face shield. He signaled for Hardin and McCoy to begin.

A few loud minutes later, enough of the car had been peeled away to get Cait out. Joe slid the half backboard behind her while the EMTs from the ambulance pulled up a gurney.

Carefully, all of them working together, they slid her out of the remains of the car and onto the gurney. The EMTs strapped her down.

"Joe?" Cait's voice didn't have much strength behind it. He moved closer so she didn't have to strain. "Tell Sarah to call Grayson."

"Your boyfriend?"

"Yeah."

"I will. You guys have a choir prayer chain or something, right?"

"Uh huh."

"She'll take care of it."

They loaded her into the ambulance. She was stable enough that Joe didn't need to ride along. An EMT climbed into the back with her, and they sped off.

A cop was guiding a tow truck through the traffic. Now for the cleanup.

Joe took his helmet off and wiped his forehead with the back of his hand. He directed Akino to pack up. He'd call Sarah once they were back at the station. He couldn't imagine being Grayson and getting that call.

Chapter Seven

SARAH HAD JUST SAT AT a patio table with Kyle and Heather when Ryan bounded up. He kissed her cheek before pulling out the chair next to her, the metal legs squealing across the stamped-concrete patio.

Luckily, she'd had a chance to warn them Ryan was coming. Heather had greeted the news with raised eyebrows, but Kyle had said nothing.

Kyle reached across the table to shake Ryan's hand. "How's it going?"

"Good, good." Ryan slipped his arm around Sarah's shoulders and squeezed then took his seat.

A server delivered Ryan's food, and they all dug in. Conversation flowed around church and choir activities. Sarah was thankful Kyle didn't talk about the case. She needed a break from thinking about it.

Her phone buzzed in her purse. Someone from the office? She pulled it out. Joe was calling. She punched the phone on. "Hey, what's up?"

"I've got some news for you. Cait Bellamy was in a car

accident today. I'm sure she's going to be okay, but they took her to Saddleback Memorial. She asked me to call you so you could let Grayson know and put her on the prayer chain."

"Of course." She slid out her chair and moved away from the table. Kyle and Heather both watched her. Ryan was busy finishing his burrito. "So you must have responded to the accident. What happened?"

"Yeah. The car was pretty well wrecked. Looks like a truck ran a red light under the toll road overpass."

"Wow." She paused, trying to absorb all the information. Her lunch turned to stone in her stomach. "I'll give Grayson a call right now and then get it put on the prayer list." Cait's boyfriend, Grayson, was a real estate developer, and Sarah had worked with him in the past. He also sang in the choir. He and Cait had been together about five months now and by all accounts, things were serious. He would definitely want to be by her side. "This afternoon I'll call the hospital to see how she's doing and if she needs anything. Thanks for letting me know. I'm sure Cait was glad to have you there." If Sarah was in trouble, she could think of nobody better than Joe to have by her side.

"It can be hard working on people you know, but in this case, it turned out all right. Quick change of subject. Any more information on that missing contractor?"

She sighed. "No. I gave Kyle the paper Greg Connor had given me. There were some weird things that didn't add up, but nothing conclusive. Kyle was going to run down a few more leads. I'm actually having lunch with him and Heather." She hesitated but had to tell the whole truth. "And Ryan. Um, but Kyle hasn't said if anything else has panned out."

There was a longer pause on the other end. Sarah inwardly cringed. "Well, if there's any information to be found, Kyle will find it. He's the best at his job."

"I know. I just feel like I'm missing something, like I should be able to do more."

"I think if you help Cait out, you'll have done a lot for the day."

"I'll do that right now. Thanks again for letting me know."

"No problem. And, hey, when you find out her condition, could you let me know? Just leave a message on my cell if I don't answer."

"I will." She ended the call and dialed Grayson. Luckily, he picked up and she was able to tell him what she knew. He'd keep her posted once he was at the hospital and found out more.

She moved back to the table. Kyle and Heather looked at her steadily. Ryan concentrated on his food. She sat.

"What about Cait?" Heather asked. "Was she in an accident?"

"Yeah. Sounds like a bad one. I let Grayson know."

"Why'd Joe call you?" Ryan's tone held a note of something in it. Displeasure?

"Cait asked him to."

Heather wadded up her wrappers and tossed her napkin on her plate. "Cait and Grayson have been together for a while. It's pretty serious. Grayson has got to be worried. I'll get her on the choir prayer list. Maybe we can see if she needs meals or something."

Ryan looked up. "I'll get her on the church prayer list too."

"Thanks. I'm sure she'll appreciate that. Grayson's on his way to the hospital. He'll let me know when he knows more." Sarah took a sip of her iced tea, but it didn't really ease the knot in her stomach.

Cait would be okay, and Sarah was glad she could help. But Joe must see this kind of thing multiple times a day. How did he deal with it? She couldn't imagine. He was always calm and upbeat. Did it ever get to him? And how would it be to be part of a firefighter's life? The constant worry about their being in danger must be overwhelming. But there were women who did it. She swallowed and refused to let her thoughts go any further.

"This is terrible timing, but Grayson might know

something about that project area. He was putting together a real estate deal at the beginning of the year up there. It fell through, but he knew all of the players. Though I'm sure he has his mind on other things right now."

Kyle nodded. "I'll check in with him later. You never know what might turn up. That was a good idea, Sarah."

She gave a small nod, glad she could help a little, but it was a small consolation. "I'd better get back to the office." She slid out her chair.

Ryan was staring at her, but she couldn't read his expression.

She turned to Heather and gave her a hug. "See you tomorrow bright and early."

Ryan slung his arm around her shoulders and kissed the top of her head. "See you at seven." He loped off.

"Yeah." She looked back to find Kyle's eyes on her, his expression unreadable.

Joe hung up and rubbed his hand over his face, leaning back in his desk chair. Talking to Sarah on the phone wasn't as satisfying as he thought it would be. He put his phone back. He had reports to write, and he needed to get to the bottom of what was going on with Hardin.

McCoy stuck his head in the office, knocking on the doorframe.

"Come on in. Have a seat." Time to start figuring out what was going on.

McCoy looked around then stepped inside.

Joe folded his arms across his chest. "What was going on out at the scene?"

McCoy let out a breath. "It was like he was sleepwalking. Every movement was slow. Twice I had to take over for him because he just wasn't moving fast enough. And then he almost wandered into traffic. He wasn't looking where he was going.

That's when you saw me yank him back. He say anything to you about being sick or tired?"

"No. And I was focused on the victim at the scene and training Akino." He raised his eyebrows. "Maybe he just needs a good night's sleep."

McCoy shrugged.

Joe tapped his fingers on his desk. He wasn't buying it either. Hardin *had* been off lately. Irritable, getting into it with Lin. Personality conflicts were one thing, but not performing on a scene raised his concern to a new level.

"Thanks, Jeff. Send Hardin in, would you?"

McCoy nodded and left the office. Joe settled into his chair and waited several long minutes. He was about ready to go grab Hardin when he made his appearance, flopping into the extra chair.

Hardin stared at Joe, not saying a word.

Joe let the silence hang between them. Partly so he didn't respond in anger at the blatant disrespect Hardin was showing. He mentally flipped through all the management training he'd been through about handling troublesome subordinates.

He leaned forward, elbows on knees. "Andy, what's up? You haven't been yourself lately."

Hardin said nothing, but his knee jiggled up and down. After a long minute, "Nothing. I'm just tired."

Neither Joe nor McCoy really believed that. Still, giving Hardin some space to work things out himself might be the best solution. *If* he could do it.

"Get some rest before next shift. That's an order. And if things don't change, we'll have to look at other options. If you're too tired to do your job right or get along with your teammates, there's a problem."

Hardin briefly met Joe's gaze before standing. "That it?"

Joe stared at him. "Dismissed."

Tony studied the building in front of him, idling his Lexus just beyond the view of the windows. Just one office in a complex where each low-slung building looked like the next. This was the last place on his list. Rankin and Associates, an architectural firm.

He would never admit it to Nick, but he was beginning to question whether this path would pan out. Maybe he should just let Nick handle this with his contacts and stay out of it. Tony's dad had been a control freak, having to be in charge of every detail. That's what kept him from growing his business and put him in an early grave. *Come on, Tony, isn't that your mantra? Do the opposite of whatever Dad would do.*

Well, if this didn't work out, he would. He scanned the parking area, the landscaping making it difficult to take in the whole area at once. He pulled around the corner and—there it was. A black Acura. Slowly driving past, he checked the plate. That was it. So the girl worked here.

He seated his Bluetooth wireless headset more firmly in his ear before dialing.

"Rankin and Associates, this is Malia."

The voice was too young. "Hi, I was talking to one of the gals in the office ... I'm terrible with names, I can't remember who it was. Can you help me out?"

"Was it Sarah Brockman, one of the architects? She's the one that usually works with clients. Besides me." She gave a small laugh. "I can transfer you."

An architect? Not an office girl? He wouldn't have guessed that. Then again, it made a lot more sense for an architect to be out at the job site. "Okay, thanks. I appreciate it." As soon as he heard the phone click over, he hung up.

This complicated things. She might actually understand what was on that map. Which made it even more imperative that he get it back.

He speed-dialed another number. "Nick, I found her."

Sarah took her Diet Coke and Junior Mints from Ryan. "Which theater?"

"Fourteen." He picked up the popcorn and his drink and nodded for her to lead the way.

Threading her way through the Friday-night crowd, Sarah found the entrance to the theater. She paused, letting her eyes adjust to the dim lights, a contrast to the neon profusion of the lobby.

Ryan stood just behind her shoulder. "Where do you want to sit?"

She glanced over the seats, counting up twelve rows. Good, no one was there. "Up here okay?"

"Sure."

She headed up the stairs to the ideal row. At least in her mind. She didn't think she should share with Ryan the fact that she always sat in the twelfth row if she could. He might think it was weird, though what was weird about finding the ideal spot in the movie theater?

Ryan stopped at row nine. "This is good."

Sarah hesitated. She really wanted to sit in the twelfth row, especially since it was empty. "Um, can we go up a few more?"

"Okay."

She hurried up the steps to row twelve before Ryan could stop again, scooting across the seats to the middle and plopping down.

"Are you sure this isn't too far back?" Ryan eased into the seat next to her, fitting his drink into the holder on his right.

"No. It's great." She needed to change the subject quick but couldn't think of anything. "So, you think we're ready for Sunday?"

He tossed a handful of popcorn in his mouth and talked around it. "Yep. You sound great." He flipped up the armrest between them, slid his arm around her shoulders, and gave her a quick squeeze, leaving his arm there.

She scooted in her seat a little closer to him. This was nice. And kind of weird. Ryan, who was always up on stage, who everyone loved, was sitting here with his arm around her.

"Hey, Ryan."

"Hi, Sarah."

Sarah looked over to the aisle. Chris and Sharon Roberts. Lovely. She pasted on a smile. Great. She had hoped Chris and Sharon might think the quick kiss to her head Ryan had given her after choir practice was more friendly than romantic. But being at the movies with his arm around her definitely blew that idea out of the water. By Sunday, there would be plenty of speculation about her and Ryan. She cringed.

"Hi, guys." Ryan didn't move his arm from her shoulders. She didn't know if he was making a statement, but at least he wasn't ashamed to be seen with her.

"So, what are you guys doing here?" Sharon gave a high-pitched laugh. "As if it's not obvious."

"Yes, dear," Chris said, "I think we can see they're on a date. Ryan doesn't usually take his soloists to the movies." He gave what Sarah thought was supposed to be a conspiratorial laugh, like they had discovered some big secret.

"Not when Lou sings, that's for sure," Ryan said.

He was so much better with the quick comebacks than Sarah was. She was just going to keep her mouth shut and let him do the talking.

"We should find our seats and let you get back to what you were doing." Sharon laughed again.

Sarah's smile had frozen in place. The fakeness of it had to be obvious, though maybe the dim lights helped to hide it.

"I don't know." Chris drew out the words like he was talking to a child. "Maybe we should sit behind them and be their chaperones."

No, Lord. Please no. If they did that, she and Ryan might as well walk out of here now for as much as she'd enjoy the movie. Every word and each movement would be analyzed, dissected, and passed around the choir until the end result was something like what happened when you played Telephone at a slumber party. No thanks.

Chris stepped into their row to let someone pass him on the stairs. Sharon elbowed her husband, nearly knocking his popcorn out of his hands. "No, dear. Let's let them be alone. Don't you remember what it was like?"

"It was so long ago. We're not as young as they are."

Sarah wanted to roll her eyes. Chris and Sharon were only about ten years older than Ryan, but they always treated him like an inexperienced child, giving him advice on how to handle the choir and what the church music program needed.

The lights faded to black, and the music started.

"You guys have a good night," Ryan said. "It was nice running into you, and we'll see you Sunday." He lifted his hand in a half wave.

Chris didn't get the hint until Sharon tugged on his arm. This time a few popcorn kernels trickled off the top of the bucket. "Sharon, will you wait? You're making me spill."

"We need to get some seats. It's starting."

Neither of them had lowered their voices which echoed loudly during a lull in the sounds, causing some rumblings from other movie goers.

Ryan held the popcorn bucket out to her, effectively dismissing Chris and Sharon. She took a handful, salt and butter colliding in her mouth, while Sharon argued that she wanted to sit closer because her eyes weren't working so well anymore. Good grief, you'd think she was eighty instead of mid-forties.

Sarah wanted to talk to Ryan about what they were going to tell people. Did he want it known they were dating? She supposed it didn't matter anyway since Chris and Sharon would make sure it got spread around. It'd be hard to play the "we're just friends" angle when he had his arm around her. But the previews had started, the loud sound negating any chance for conversation. Maybe after the movie they'd talk, though she had no idea how she was going to bring it up. *So, Ryan, kinda weird running into Chris and Sharon like that. Do you know they'll go straight home and use the prayer chain to ask people to pray for our new relationship?* Ugh. Sometimes she hated the lack of privacy in churches.

Ryan pulled her closer to him. "Comfortable?"

"Um-hm." She snuggled up next to his shoulder. A preview for the latest terrorist action movie flickered on. The voice-over guy told them in a suspenseful tone that police and firefighters surrounded a building, ready to deal with the aftermath if the hero didn't get there in time and the bomb went off. But the hero always got there in time.

Joe's face flashed in her mind. Must have been triggered by the firefighters in the preview. What was he doing tonight?

Sarah couldn't stop the series of yawns that overtook her as Ryan drove her home from the movie. It had been an exhausting week, and she just wanted to get into bed.

Ryan pulled up in front of her condo, and she hopped out, walking quickly toward the door.

"Hey, what's the hurry?" Ryan was on her heels.

"Sorry, I'm just tired. Ready to crash." She pulled out her keys and turned toward him. "I had a nice night. Thanks."

He put his hands on her shoulders and gazed at her face, his glance dipping to her lips.

He was going to kiss her. Mixed emotions swirled through her stomach. She wanted him to, didn't she? Why was she feeling anxiety instead of anticipation? She turned toward the front door, fumbling with her keys. "I just remembered. I have to go check on Shadow." She had walked him earlier, but he should still be let out before settling down for the night.

"Who's Shadow?" Ryan furrowed his brow.

"Joe's dog. Joe's on shift, and I said I'd look out for his dog."

An unreadable look crossed Ryan's face.

She opened the door. "I did have a nice time tonight. Thanks. I'll see you Sunday bright and early for sound check." She forced lightness into her voice as she slipped in the door.

He gave her a slow nod. "See you then. Night." He spun and headed back to his car.

She closed the door and headed to the kitchen where she'd stashed Joe's spare key. As her hands closed over the key, she paused. She'd like some company tonight. And she bet Shadow would like to spend the night here with her instead of in an empty house.

It'd been a long time since she'd had a dog. She swallowed. A very long time. An image of the small brown mutt that had been her dog as a little girl flashed through her mind. She'd loved that dog.

She picked up her phone to text Joe that she was taking Shadow, forcing away the bad memories of Gaucho that always came fast on the heels of the good ones.

Chapter Eight

J OE PULLED INTO THE CONDO complex, the sun just beginning to warm the day. Should he go to Sarah's place first or home? Her late-night text had sent his heart racing until he read that she was just letting him know she decided to keep Shadow overnight at her place for company.

During a week day, this wouldn't be too early. But considering when her text had come through, she was probably sleeping in. Had she been on a date with Ryan? Or hanging out with Heather or one of her other girlfriends? It wasn't really his business, but he couldn't keep his mind from going there.

He pulled in front of his condo. He'd take a shower first and then text Sarah. They'd had a busy night last night, and if he laid down, he'd fall asleep. He needed to pick up Shadow before that.

And maybe Sarah would have some information on Cait. He'd seen worse, way worse, but this one hit close to home. Luckily, Cait had Grayson to help her through a difficult time.

Hopping out of the truck, he headed inside, straight for the shower. Sarah wasn't having an easy time of it herself. That missing contractor was really bothering her. Yet here she was helping him with Shadow and helping Cait and Grayson. But who was helping Sarah? Probably not Ryan. He didn't seem the type. Though maybe Joe wasn't giving him enough credit. Maybe taking Sarah out helped keep her mind off things.

He dried off and threw on shorts and a T-shirt. Cait's accident could have been so much worse. He saw it every day. One thing his job taught him was that life is short. He needed to go after Sarah now. Especially given his line of work. Though he got a lot of security from the fact that God already knew the number of his days, they weren't granted an unlimited number. He wanted to be with her for whatever time they could have together. He needed to go for it. Who cared what Ryan was doing?

He grabbed his phone and sent a text to Sarah. She responded immediately. Guess she was up. Shoving his keys and phone in his pocket, he headed over to her place at a brisk walk.

Her door was open with Shadow looking out the screen door. "Hey, buddy. Did you have fun last night?"

Sarah opened the door, hair pulled back in a ponytail, wearing yoga pants and a T-shirt, eyes still shadowed by sleep. She looked like something he wanted to see every morning.

To distract himself, Joe ruffled Shadow's ears, getting a lick on the hand in return.

"Want some coffee?"

"Sure." He stepped inside. He was so tired, he doubted it would keep him up. Besides, it'd be worth it to spend some time with her. "How was the boy last night? Give you any trouble?"

Sarah's gaze darted up then relaxed. "Shadow? He was fine." She poured two cups. "Black, right?"

"You remembered." He smiled.

She brought the cups to the living room, her coffee significantly lighter in color than his, and set them on the coffee table. She settled on one end of the couch. Joe grabbed the other. Shadow plopped on the floor between them.

"He must have been someone's dog. He's really well behaved. I can't believe no one has claimed him." She reached down to pet him.

"I know. I keep thinking I'll get a call about him, but it's been long enough now, that I doubt it'll happen." Joe reached down too, grazing Sarah's hand.

"He seems pretty happy with you. Did you have dogs growing up?"

A shadow passed over his heart, and he tamped it down. Someday, maybe he'd tell her, but not now. Only Kyle and Scott knew what his childhood had been like. "Um, no. My parents didn't like dogs." He cleared his throat. "What about you?"

She stared into her coffee cup and nodded. "Yeah, we had a dog. Gaucho." She looked up with a sad smile. "Cute little brown mutt. Didn't obey worth a darn. He was an escape artist. We should have called him Houdini. He was always trying to get out." She looked at her phone and groaned. "Heather and her sisters are going to be here in an hour. I'm not sure I'm up to a marathon shopping session today."

"Sounds more fun than my day of laundry and grocery shopping. Though I might sneak in a basketball game with Kyle. Any more word from him on the missing contractor?"

"Nope. You'd think in this day and age it'd be hard for someone to just disappear. Grayson did text me, though. Cait's coming home today. She ended up with a broken nose, a couple of broken ribs, and they kept her overnight for observation on her concussion. She'll be sore and bruised for a while with some lovely black eyes. I may head by there tomorrow after church. Plus, Grayson may be able to help with the missing contractor. He worked on a land deal in that area earlier this year. Maybe he'll have some insight. Kyle said he'd look into it, but if I'm over there, I might as well ask."

"That's good news. Glad to hear Cait's going to be okay."

Joe drained his coffee. It was now or never. "Hey, if you're not too tired tonight after your McAlistair girls' marathon, we could grab something to eat."

Her wide smile warmed his heart. "I'd love to. That sounds great. I'll text you when we get back."

He stood, mentally giving himself a fist pump. For once, he'd outflanked Ryan. "Sounds good. Thanks for the coffee. I'll see you tonight. Come on, Shadow." He patted his leg and clipped on Shadow's leash. He waved at Sarah as they left the condo and jogged onto the street. He was feeling so good, they might as well take a run around the neighborhood.

Sarah flopped on Heather's couch. Her feet and her back hurt. She needed to be in better shape to go shopping with these girls.

Heather handed her a Diet Coke before landing next to her. "Whew! I can't believe my sisters wanted to drive home after all that. Well, I can see Aimee wanting to get back to Darryl, so I guess Kellie didn't have a choice. I suppose that means next time we have to head up their direction."

Sarah took a sip. "I wonder how Cait's doing. She should be home by now."

"Wanda and Sharon are coordinating meals. I'd wait to call her until tomorrow. That first day back from the hospital is always exhausting. Besides, Grayson is going to be busy taking care of her."

Sarah nodded, deferring to Heather's more recent knowledge of hospital visits. "I'll sign up to take them a meal next week." She glanced up at Heather and gave a dramatic sigh. "If I live that long."

Heather tossed a pillow at her, almost spilling Sarah's Diet Coke.

"Hey!" Sarah sat up holding the can out to the side.

"You're fine. Don't be such a baby."

"Just because you run and lift weights doesn't mean some of us don't prefer quieter forms of exercise like yoga and walking."

"Walking with a certain firefighter I know?"

Sarah could feel the telling heat in her cheeks. "He's nice. We're becoming friends, I think. Besides, I'm dating Ryan. I guess. Though I'm having dinner with Joe tonight." She rubbed her face with her hands. "Why does this have to be so difficult?"

"Uh huh. You've been on two dates with Ryan. Not really dating him. You still have options. Which you must know, otherwise you wouldn't be going out with Joe tonight." Heather met Sarah's gaze. "You want my thoughts? Long term, Joe seems more your type. Ryan's great at what he does, but he's all about the spotlight. You're not. You've spent some time with Joe as friends hanging out. You know what kind of guy he is."

Images of Joe's melted-chocolate eyes and warm smile flashed through her mind. "Yeah, I do." Her voice was soft. "If he'd just asked me out before Ryan, I wouldn't be in this mess."

"Hey, it's not Joe's fault you don't like conflict. You can tell Ryan no, you know." Heather squeezed Sarah's shoulder. "You'll survive, and he'll survive, even though I don't think anyone has ever told Ryan no."

"That's what I'm afraid of." She let out a long sigh. "Hey, at this rate, I'm seeing more of Kyle than anyone. I hope they find that Greg Connor. Did Kyle tell you about it?"

"A little. He doesn't talk about work too much, but since you were involved …"

"I just wish I could be more helpful. He was talking to the other guy, who apparently hasn't come forward. Either he doesn't know Greg is missing, or he doesn't realize he was one of the last people to see him, or he doesn't care or want to get involved. Obviously that guy knew Greg. He must have information that would be helpful to the police."

Heather stood and headed upstairs. "Hang on. I've got an idea."

Sarah could only imagine what Heather's idea was.

She clattered back downstairs with a sketchpad and pencil. "Have you tried drawing him?"

"No. I can't do that kind of drawing. I'm an architect, not an artist."

Heather gave her a look. They'd had this argument before. Sarah considered Heather the real artist.

"All right. After I took a stab at drawing Alex, the guy who shot at me, I did a little research into forensic art. At the station they have a computer program, but we'll work with what we've got."

Sarah was skeptical that it would work, but at this point she was willing to try anything. With Heather guiding her, she took some deep breaths, relaxed, and walked through the day, just like she had with Kyle, but feeling free to add more emotion and impressions to the facts.

She and Heather worked on the sketch for over an hour. It still wasn't right, but Sarah couldn't figure out why. She ran her hands through her hair. "This is just frustrating me. We're not going to get it. And even if we do, so what?"

Heather looked a little deflated. "I know. I felt the same way. I never did get Alex's face right, but when I saw him in the lineup, I knew it was him. Maybe it'll help stir up your subconscious."

"It might."

"Let me make a copy of this and you can play around with it later if you want." Heather disappeared upstairs again. She was seeing his face in her dreams. Why couldn't she see it when she was awake?

The sound of a Dodgers game filtered into Joe's consciousness. He had fallen asleep on the couch watching the game. He grabbed his phone off the coffee table. A text from Kyle about shooting hoops had just come through. That must have been what had awakened him. He looked at the time. He couldn't believe he'd fallen asleep and almost missed their game. He texted back.

Leveraging himself off the couch, he grabbed a bottle of water, a towel, his keys, and his basketball shoes. The park where they played wasn't far from his condo complex, so he clipped a leash on Shadow, and they headed out at a jog.

In the parking lot, Kyle was leaning against his truck. "Thought you might stand me up."

"Fell asleep on the couch watching the Dodgers lose. Even Shadow was bored."

Kyle petted Shadow. "No one's claimed him, huh? You could have a worse roommate."

"Yeah, like Scott." Joe wandered over to a bench, clipping Shadow's leash around the leg. Kyle and Scott Blake had roomed together in college. Kyle kept things neat and clean. Scott … did not. Now that he was in the navy, they'd probably trained the sloppiness out of him. "Heard from him lately?"

Kyle sat next to him as they changed their shoes. "Yeah. He's gonna be up here in a couple of weeks for the Fourth. I thought we'd have a barbecue at my place." Kyle nudged Joe. "Bring Sarah."

"Maybe I will. We're going out to dinner tonight."

Kyle nodded, grabbing the basketball. "Nice." He ran onto the court and tossed Joe the ball.

Joe dribbled, eying Kyle. They'd been playing basketball together for so long, they knew each other's moves. "She's still worried about that Connor guy."

Kyle raised his eyebrows, and Joe moved to the hoop for a layup and missed. "I saw her this morning. She kept Shadow overnight."

Kyle took the ball down court and touched the halfway mark. "Convenient, that dog." He brushed past Joe's screen and sunk a three-pointer. "What's with your game?"

Joe grabbed the ball. "Not much sleep. Last night was

rough. Lots of calls. Personnel conflicts. Maybe I'm just getting old." He grinned. Kyle was older by three months.

They played to twenty-one, but Joe only got sixteen points. They sank on the bench and cracked open water bottles.

Joe pulled out his phone. No text from Sarah. Maybe they weren't done shopping yet.

Kyle's phone dinged. He looked at it. "Hey, the girls are at Heather's place. They're inviting themselves over to my house and want us to bring pizza and a movie." He smacked Joe on the shoulder. "Just like old times."

"Without a gang going after Heather." When Heather had been in protective custody for witnessing a gang initiation gone bad, Joe and Sarah had brought over food and movies to keep them from going stir crazy. It was how he'd first gotten to know Sarah.

"Better than old times." Kyle shoved the basketball and shoes in his bag. "Go grab a shower. I'll get the movie and ice cream. You can get the pizza. See you at my house."

Joe nodded as Kyle jogged to his truck. He unclipped Shadow's leash and headed for home. He looked at his phone again. Still no text from Sarah. What should he make of that? Did she not want to be alone with him tonight? Was this her way of getting out of their date? But she'd seemed so happy when he'd asked earlier. Maybe she was just being nice.

He unlocked his front door and headed in. Regardless, he was getting to spend time with her tonight. He'd take what he could get.

Pacing in Kyle's den as he and Heather were busy in the kitchen, Sarah hoped Joe wasn't upset with her. Her phone had died, so she hadn't been able to text him. Then Heather suggested they all just meet at Kyle's for pizza and a movie. Would Joe think she was trying to get out of their date? He was so easy and comfortable to be around that it wouldn't have been hard to be alone with him. But until she sorted out things with Ryan—okay ended them—it felt weird to be going out with Joe. Heather, perceptive as always, had cut through Sarah's dithering with a plan to hang out at Kyle's.

The front door opened, and Joe stepped through balancing pizza boxes. "Hey!" He spotted her and broke into a wide grin.

She smiled back. "My phone died. That's why I couldn't text you." She tilted her head toward the kitchen. "This was Heather's plan. I hope it's okay?"

The hand not juggling pizzas squeezed her arm. "It's fine. Unless Kyle picked the movie. Then it might be torture."

She shook her head and laughed. "You two could be brothers."

"Growing up as the youngest and only boy in a house full of girls, I was desperate for a friend by fourth grade. That's how I got stuck with that guy." He nodded toward the kitchen. "I'm going to put these down and see what the movie option is. Want a Diet Coke?"

"You know me too well."

His smile softened, but his eyes smoldered. He winked at her. "Be right back."

She plopped on the couch, not knowing what else to do. Then she realized it had been quiet in the kitchen. Heather and Kyle were now greeting Joe, but they had been mysteriously silent when she and Joe had been talking. Eavesdroppers. But she couldn't help but grin.

Joe returned bearing two plates and two sodas. "Sausage and mushroom for you, pepperoni and olive for me. A Diet Coke and a Dr. Pepper. The makings of a great dinner." He slid the plates and drinks on the table in front of her. "And Heather had input on the movie, so we should be okay."

He sat on the couch next to her, close enough that she bumped his arm when she reached for her plate. But he didn't move away. And neither did she.

When would she ever get used to the fact that Joe always remembered what she liked? He paid attention. Her heart melted a little. She'd spent most of her life not being noticed by the people around her, and that was fine. She'd gotten used to it and now preferred it. But she also liked this, how her preferences mattered to someone. To Joe.

Kyle and Heather joined them and started the movie. Sarah ate her pizza and trained her eyes on the screen. But she couldn't have said what the movie was about. She was acutely aware of the heat coming from the man next to her. If she tilted her head, she could rest it on his shoulder. What would it be like to snuggle up with him on the couch?

One thing was clear. She needed to screw up her courage and end things with Ryan. Tomorrow after church.

Chapter Nine

JOE WALKED THROUGH THE SIDE door of the church. He was early. The choir was still doing sound check. Sarah stood in front of the choir, holding a mic, and listening to something Ryan was saying. He watched for a moment, waiting to see if she'd turn his way so he could wave.

Last night had been great. She'd sat next to him on the couch, close enough that he had no idea what movie they'd watched. He spent the whole night wondering if he could put his arm around her. The smell of her mango shampoo haunted him. He could still smell it now.

He spotted Heather up in the risers. She was biting her bottom lip. Was sound check not going well? He took a step closer. Ryan was speaking, but because he wasn't mic'd, Joe couldn't make out the words.

Ryan held out his arm toward Sarah. She ducked her head and moved closer to him until he had his arm around her. He pulled her up next to him while he said something to the choir then kissed her on the cheek. The choir broke out in cheers, claps, and whistles. Sarah's face glowed bright red, but Ryan's attention was on the choir.

Joe's stomach clenched like he'd fallen through a roof. He glanced up to see Heather's reaction. Her eyebrows drew down, and she frowned. He risked a look at Sarah again. Her chin was down, and she shifted her weight from foot to foot. Ryan didn't have a clue.

He needed to get out of here before Sarah saw him. He turned and got two steps toward the glass door before he saw Kyle coming from the other side. He stopped and let Kyle come to him.

"Hey. Get us seats yet?"

"Uh, no." Joe looked around the worship center which was now beginning to fill up.

Kyle's brow furrowed. "You okay?"

"Sure." He shoved his hands in his pockets. "Let's get a seat."

Kyle didn't move but looked toward the stage. He waved.

Joe turned around. Heather was waving back. He lifted his hand, trying not to look at Sarah and Ryan, but he couldn't help it, like the rubberneckers drawn to a car wreck. Ryan's arm was still draped over her shoulders while he chatted. Sarah saw the direction Heather was looking and spotted him and Kyle. She gave them an embarrassed smile and half wave before turning her attention back to the choir.

He scanned the worship center, trying to find them seats. Kyle's hand landed on his shoulder. "I bet you'd wipe the court with him in basketball."

Joe gave a short nod but didn't say anything. He appreciated Kyle's effort. "Let's get a seat."

Sarah trudged into the green room, sighing, the weight of this morning still heavy on her shoulders. Then she caught herself. She glanced around, hoping no one had noticed. She had to act as if everything was fine. It wasn't, but she didn't need any more emotion displayed this morning.

The faint scent of pear preceded a hand on her shoulder, and she relaxed into it. Heather.

"You okay?" she whispered into Sarah's ear.

Sarah nodded, but tears started to clog her throat. Crud. She hated when that happened. It would be easier if Heather weren't so nice to her. People milled around the green room, getting their things and leaving. Sarah focused on remembering where she left her purse.

"We're going out to lunch with our small group. Want to come and relax?"

Sarah just wanted to go home and be alone to recover from being the attention of so many people all morning. And having her plans blown out of the water. How could she end it with Ryan when he'd just made a huge show of their "relationship"? And why hadn't he even talked to her about it beforehand? She wanted to scream. There was her purse, sitting on a chair. She headed toward it. Grabbing it, she slid the straps over her shoulder and turned to face Heather. "I don't know. Maybe I should just go home."

Heather raised her eyebrows. "And what? Brood?"

Sarah gave her a look. "No, I just—"

"Come to lunch with us. You don't have any good excuse, and I'm not taking no. Besides, I drove, remember? You don't have a ride home."

"You need a ride home, Sarah?"

Ryan. Sarah closed her eyes for a moment before turning around. "Oh, no. I don't think so. Heather's just twisting my arm to get me to go to lunch with her and Kyle."

"Where at? I can meet you guys there."

She put her back to Ryan and looked at Heather, eyes wide with pleading.

Heather swallowed. "I think Kyle said Chili's, but I'm not sure."

"I've got to finish up a few things here, but I'll meet you there in a few. Call me if plans change." He squeezed Sarah's shoulder and moved off.

"Sorry. I didn't know what to say. I can't think on my feet. But this could be a good thing. Maybe he can take you home, and you can have that talk you need to with him then."

Sarah sighed. "It's okay. Let's go find Kyle. I'm hungry."

They stepped out of the green room and nearly ran into Kyle and Joe coming in.

"There you are." Kyle slid his arm around Heather's waist and kissed her cheek. "I was starting to wonder what was keeping you."

Joe smiled at Sarah. "Hi. You sounded great."

"Thanks." She'd seen him walk in with Kyle this morning but didn't know how much of Ryan's spectacle he had seen. Her cheeks warmed, and she darted her gaze away. Joe was such a great guy, and they'd had fun last night. And then Ryan, without warning her, told everyone they were a couple during sound check. Now what was she going to do?

Why hadn't Joe asked her out before Ryan had? Then she wouldn't be in the mess she was in now. But as Heather said, it wasn't Joe's fault Sarah didn't like to deal with conflict. She let out another long sigh. Why was life so complicated?

They headed out to the parking lot. The ocean breeze had picked up. The day was going to be a gorgeous one. Kyle touched her arm. "Oh, Sarah. I thought you should know. The missing contractor, Greg Connor? The sheriff's department found his truck pulled off on Ortega Highway. No sign of him, though."

"What does that mean?"

Kyle shrugged. "Any number of things. He could have gone for a hike and gotten lost or injured. Someone could have parked his car there to make it look like that's what happened. We don't know. It was pulled off into a more remote area that's not heavily traveled, so I doubt we'll end up with anyone who saw him."

A chill passed over her leaving a shiver in its wake. The whole thing felt odd. She looked up.

Joe was watching her. "Cold?"

"Just tired, I think. And this Greg Connor thing. It's—I don't even know how to explain it."

They'd arrived at Kyle's truck and Joe's red Chevy Silverado that had played a big role in Kyle and Heather's lives the last few months. Considering all her friend had been through in the past two months, Sarah thought it was remarkable Heather wasn't a basket case. On the other hand, she had Kyle who took really good care of her. She didn't think it'd be too long before they'd announce their engagement. It was obvious they thought the world of each other, but how did Heather know Kyle was the one? Did it take someone sticking with you through a life-threatening situation to know? Hopefully not.

"You want to ride with me?" Joe was talking to her.

"Sorry. I'm fading. Sure." Heather could ride with Kyle, and they could have time together, short as the ride was.

Joe held the door open for her and made sure she got settled before closing it.

She leaned her head back against the seat and smiled. A trace of smokiness mixed with the clean-car smell.

Joe climbed in and shut the door then started the truck. "What?"

She shook her head. "Your truck. Sparkling clean, and it already smells a little like smoke."

"Really? I'm sorry. Occupational hazard, I guess."

"No, it's okay. Smells a little like a campfire. That actually brings back good memories. A family in my church growing up often took me with them camping. They had a lot of kids, something I wasn't used to. But every night the dad would play his guitar around the campfire." She didn't love campfires at first. Fire terrified her. But something about the dad's gentleness and how he explained all the ways he was keeping the fire safely contained and all the precautions he was taking eased her fear. Seeing the other kids having fun made it feel not quite so dangerous. "We would sip hot chocolate and sing." Someone would always roast Sarah's marshmallow for her. She never got that close to the fire. But for a few minutes, Sarah could imagine she belonged.

"Hmm. Me too. Never thought about it before, but I wonder if that was one of the reasons that attracted me to firefighting. I've always thought it was because I liked helping people, but Kyle's dad used to take us and our friend, Scott, hunting and fishing and camping. Those were definitely good memories." He glanced over at her before turning onto the street. "I wonder how many of our decisions as an adult are influenced subconsciously by trying to recreate good things or avoid bad things from our childhood."

Sarah sat forward. "I don't know." But she knew she did. She'd ordered her whole life around avoiding bad things from her childhood.

Joe hopped out of the truck and opened Sarah's door, taking her hand to help her down, wishing he didn't have to let it go. Kyle and Heather were waiting on the sidewalk.

They had just reached the restaurant door when a blue Mustang rumbled into the parking lot, top down. Ryan.

Joe watched Heather and Sarah exchange a look. Heather looked up at Kyle. "Oh, I forgot to tell you. Ryan said he was coming."

Kyle raised his eyebrows but said nothing. He didn't have to. Joe clenched his jaw.

Ryan came jogging up. "Looks like I got here just in time." He slid his hand under Sarah's hair and squeezed her neck. Joe could have sworn she stiffened. But if the attraction was only one-sided, why was she going out with him? Nobody was forcing her to. Lunch suddenly seemed like a bad idea. He had no appetite but no way to gracefully leave. Pressing his lips in a firm line, he stepped away from Sarah and toward the door.

"Let's go inside." Kyle motioned them in. "I'm sure the others are already here."

Ryan draped his arm across Sarah's shoulders as they went in and found the others. They scooted chairs around and made room for Ryan. Who was too busy chatting with everyone to get Sarah's chair, Joe noticed. He pulled it out for her before seating himself next to her. She smiled her thanks.

The waiter brought drinks and took their orders. Ryan was dominating the conversation. Which was fine with Joe. He didn't feel much like talking. He took a drink of Dr. Pepper—the sugar-caffeine combo waking him up—then leaned over to Sarah. "You look like you'd rather be home taking a nap. We didn't keep you up too late last night, did we?"

She gave him a small smile. "No. Last night was fun. It was nice to hang out, watch movies, and eat pizza and ice cream without worrying about someone trying to kill Heather. But this thing with Greg Connor runs through my mind whenever I'm not thinking about something else. So I'm not sleeping all that great. I would have thought after yesterday's shopping expedition, I'd sleep like a baby. Those McAlistair girls know how to shop. It's like an Olympic sport with them or something."

Heather looked up from farther down the table. "Hey, I resemble that remark." She turned to Melissa Ellis sitting on the other side; she was part of Heather and Kyle's small group. "You should come with us next time."

Melissa laughed. "I'm more in Sarah's camp, I think. But, yeah, I'd go. It'd be a nice break from work, which is all I seem to do lately."

Joe leaned closer to Sarah. "So you're not into extreme shopping?"

She sighed and rested her elbows on the table. "I don't mind shopping, but generally I have something specific in mind to add to my wardrobe. I got a couple cute summer things, picked up a few books I'd been wanting to read. But Heather and her sisters are really fun. I enjoy hanging out with them more than anything. The shopping is just an excuse to get together."

Joe glanced up. Ryan gave him a steady look. Okay. He sat back.

Ryan's gaze dropped to Sarah, and he slid his arm around the back of her chair. "So did everyone hear the big announcement at sound check this morning?"

Melissa glanced around the table. For a few beats no one answered. "No. What happened?" Her gaze darted to Sarah before coming back to Ryan.

As Ryan proceeded to regale the table with his story, Sarah seemed to shrink. Joe shook his head. Couldn't Ryan see Sarah hated the spotlight as much as he loved it? Probably not. Poor Sarah. He wanted to catch her eye, but she took a sip of her Diet Coke, and then kept her focus steadily on her plate.

Even Melissa seemed to regret asking, though she kept her attention politely on Ryan between bites.

Heather leaned over to whisper to Kyle, and Joe caught her eye when she did, seeing the sympathy there. Though, after he thought about it, he wasn't sure if that was for Sarah or him. He wished he could think of a way to get the attention off Sarah. His mind scrambled.

"Hey, Ryan. How's your workout been going? Ever get all the way through P90X?" That should keep him talking for a while.

Sarah glanced at him out of the corner of her eye.

Ryan hesitated and looked at him for a moment before launching into his latest workout regimen, something way better than P90X.

Finally, the waiter brought the check. Joe was astonished to see that Ryan let Sarah pay her own way. Joe almost paid for her himself, just for spite. What did she see in that guy anyway? Surely she wasn't so shallow as to go on looks alone? No, Sarah wasn't like that. What was it then? He didn't know. Who knew how women's minds worked anyway? He sure didn't.

Outside, he sensed Sarah's indecision as they headed for their cars. "I can give you a ride."

"You didn't drive?" Ryan asked her.

"No, I came with Heather this morning."

"I'll take you home then."

Joe was feeling particularly contrary. "It makes more sense for me to since we live in the same complex."

Ryan looked at him, and Joe didn't look away. Ryan glanced at his watch. "I'm supposed to meet with Pastor Tom in a few minutes anyway." Leaning forward, he gave Sarah a quick kiss. "I'll call you tonight."

She nodded and headed for Joe's truck without looking back. Joe waved at the group still standing on the sidewalk, talking, before opening her door and helping her in, but he noticed the tension drop from her shoulders the minute Ryan's car left the parking lot.

After a short but silent drive, Joe pulled up in front of Sarah's condo. He turned to look at her. "Are you okay?"

She ran a hand over her face. "Yeah, just really tired. Think I'll take a bubble bath then go to bed early."

He turned off the truck. "I'll walk you to the door."

"You don't have to."

"I know." But for some reason, he wanted Sarah to notice the difference between Ryan and him.

She unlocked the door and opened it, taking one step in before faltering back into Joe.

He put his hand on her arm to steady her and looked around. Her place was a mess. That wasn't like Sarah; she really must be tired. Then he saw it. The ripped cushions on the couch and the overturned chairs definitely weren't Sarah. He grabbed her around the waist and pulled her back with him. "Get in the truck."

Chapter Ten

SARAH TURNED TO LOOK AS another car pulled up in front of her house. Kyle. Two cop cars were already here, and the neighbors had been peeking out their windows. A woman across the greenbelt was even standing on her balcony watching. Sarah wanted to hide.

Kyle got out of his truck; Joe had called him first. Joe had been great. He hadn't left her side, keeping his hand either on her shoulder or her back while Officer Patino and the others checked out her condo and then asked her questions.

"You okay?" Kyle asked.

She nodded, arms wrapped around her waist.

"We didn't go inside." Joe rubbed her shoulder. "As soon as I saw what happened, I pulled her out of there and called you."

"Can you take her over to your place? I don't want her to go too far as we'll still have some questions for her. But we're going to be awhile, and she doesn't need to be standing around here."

"No problem."

Sarah wanted to object to the two of them making decisions for her, but frankly, it sounded like a good idea, and she was too rattled to think straight anyway.

"Is that okay with you, Sarah?" Joe studied her face.

Had he read her mind? "Yes. Thanks."

Since Joe's truck was now blocked in by police cars, they walked through the complex to Joe's unit. The sound of voices and the crackling of radios faded as they got closer to Joe's. She tilted her head to each side and tried to let some of the tension drain out. It didn't help much.

Joe unlocked the door and let her in. Shadow whined and sniffed her hand. She scratched his ears.

"I'm going to let him out real quick." He grabbed a leash off the hook by the front door. "I'll be right back."

It was strange being in his apartment even though she'd been here before to pick up Shadow. It looked just like hers had before she remodeled it. Except his couch was under the window instead of facing the gas fireplace. A huge TV and recliner dominated the small living area. Obviously, his priorities weren't interior design. She sank down on the couch and set her purse on the floor.

Joe and Shadow came back in through the front door.

"Quick trip," she remarked as Shadow bolted for her. She rubbed his fluffy neck as he settled on her feet.

"I don't think he wanted to leave you alone. Can I get you something? I don't have Diet Coke, though."

"I'm fine. Thanks."

Joe sat in the recliner and leaned forward. "It'll be okay."

She rubbed her arms and sighed. "I know that. In my head. It's just ... The idea of someone being in my home, going through my things, messing stuff up. Overwhelming, I guess. I hope my computer and plans are okay. I've got backups of the computer at work on the server, but the drawings on paper would be a lot of work to redo." That was an understatement. Her dream house plans represented a lifetime of ideas and solace. If they were destroyed, she didn't have the energy to redo them. They couldn't be recaptured. A deep emptiness threatened to engulf her.

Joe picked up his phone and pushed buttons. "Hey, Kyle.

Have you seen Sarah's office yet? What's it look like?" He met Sarah's eyes.

She held her breath, watching Joe's face for any type of reaction.

"Okay, why don't you talk to her?" He held out the phone.

When she reached for it, her hands were shaking. "Hi, Kyle."

"Sarah, your office looks about like the rest of the house. Things are pulled out of drawers, paper and files everywhere. And I'm sure they were on your computer. But nothing's ripped or destroyed. I can't say if anything was taken; you'll have to let us know about that."

Swallowing, she hoped her voice would be steady. She could barely get the words out. "There were some house plans, drawings, on my drafting table. Are they still there?"

Rustling in the background. "Yeah, they're still here. They've been moved around, but it doesn't look like they're damaged. The only things that were actually damaged were your couch and mattress. Both of those were knifed. I'll make sure you get all the info you need to file a claim with your insurance company."

She closed her eyes. Guess she wasn't going home tonight. Who would do this? Did it have to do with Connor's disappearance? That was the only unusual thing in her life. But she didn't know anything. She hoped Kyle would find some answers soon. "Thanks, Kyle. I appreciate it."

"No problem. You can always call and ask me anything. Heather will want you to stay with her tonight, I'm sure."

Sarah said goodbye, hung up the phone, and handed it to Joe.

"Are your plans okay?"

"They're the only things." She shook her head. Too many questions. She couldn't even voice them.

He flipped on the TV. "Put your feet up. Close your eyes. Take a nap and try to forget about all of this until you can actually do something about it."

She couldn't sleep, not in front of someone. But lying down sounded good. She tugged her feet out from under Shadow, slipped off her shoes, and stretched out on the couch. The cool leather helped relieve the sick-to-her-stomach feeling. Joe was changing channels. That was one big TV. It took up the whole wall of the living area.

The day's events clicked through her mind like a vacation slideshow, though she didn't particularly want to relive them. She and Ryan, except when they were singing, had been moving out of sync all day. Proof that she needed to break things off with him. They just weren't right for each other. But after his big announcement, there was no way to do that without making everything a huge deal. She just wanted it to all go away.

Still, she should probably call him and let him know what happened. But she didn't particularly want to talk to him. She glanced over at Joe, whose gaze collided with hers. Warmth flooded her along with a sense of safety. She definitely didn't want to talk to Ryan with Joe around. In fact, she didn't want to think about Ryan. Joe would keep her safe.

Maybe she would just close her eyes for a minute.

Joe watched Sarah sleep, the baseball game on TV forgotten. He'd never thought he could get so much pleasure watching someone sleep. The tension in her face had eased, leaving a peacefulness in its wake. What would Ryan think if he could see her now?

He eased out of his chair, not wanting to wake her. The thought of Ryan made him restless. He headed for his room. The game couldn't hold his interest, but maybe the book next to his bed could. He picked it up then set it back down. His room could use a little straightening. The doorway was at the end of the hall, so it was visible from the living room. He picked up dirty clothes and tossed them in the hamper. It was overflowing. He'd have to do laundry soon.

The phone rang, and he yanked it out of his pocket, hoping to get it before it woke up Sarah. Kyle's name flashed on the screen.

"We've finished at Sarah's. I've got a couple of questions for her, and then do you mind taking her to Heather's? They got to her car too."

He closed his eyes. Sarah didn't deserve this. "I'll bring her over."

"Thanks."

Joe put the phone next to the bed and ran his hand through his hair. It was not going to be easy on Sarah going back there. Maybe he should call Ryan. Would she want him there? The thought turned his stomach. He'd let her decide, but she hadn't called Ryan yet. Maybe she didn't want to. She had Kyle and him, and she was going to Heather's.

He headed out to the living room. Sarah was sitting up, smoothing her hair.

"You're up. How'd you sleep?"

"Okay, I guess. I didn't even realize I had fallen asleep." She glanced at her watch, and her eyes widened. "Two hours!"

"I think you needed it. That was Kyle on the phone. They've finished up, but he has a couple of questions for you. You can get some of your stuff; then I'll take you to Heather's."

She nodded, picked up her purse, and stood.

Joe guided her out the front door, telling Shadow to stay, and then locked the door behind them. He rested his hand lightly on her back until he was sure she was okay. When they got to her place, only one unit and Kyle's truck remained.

Sarah's face paled as she walked into her house. There wasn't one thing that had been left untouched. Every cupboard was opened, every drawer emptied. Flour, spices, and other pantry items had been opened and scattered across the kitchen. It smelled like his mom's cooking, a comforting scent that seemed strangely out of place in the destroyed kitchen.

Her eyes took in the room, but she didn't say anything as she moved down the hall. She looked into the first room, which served as her office, stilled for a moment, and then moved down the hall. When she got to her bedroom she put her hands over her face. "I don't even know where to begin."

Joe touched her shoulder. "You don't have to deal with any of this tonight. Just get what you need for Heather's, and then you can come back tomorrow, take pictures, and talk to your insurance company."

She didn't move for a long moment. Finally, though, she nodded and went into her closet. Everything was lying in a heap on the ground, but she rooted around until she found an overnight bag and a few things.

Joe felt helpless. She knew what she needed; he didn't.

He looked in the master bath. Every bottle had been upended and every bit of makeup smashed and dumped out.

He tamped down his anger as he headed back down the hall to where Kyle was in the kitchen. "What happened? This isn't a burglary or someone trying to find something. This is a personal attack against her."

"I know." Kyle sighed and glanced toward the hallway, lowering his voice. "Look, she's going to need to lean on you. Ryan—I don't know what's going on there, but despite what he may think or say—Sarah's not into him. And I have that on good authority from Heather. You need to forget about him and be what Sarah needs. That's what you want, right?"

Joe nodded. He and Kyle didn't mess in each other's business. Unless they needed to. He'd had a few hard words for Kyle regarding Heather last month, so now it was his turn.

"You need to see this." Kyle took a few steps and opened the door that connected the garage to the house, flipping on the light. Sarah's Acura was parked in the garage, a relatively neat space compared to the rest of the place. He could see through the windshield that her seats had been ripped open and the contents of the glove box strewn around. But the windshield itself was the most shocking thing.

Red letters—looked like lipstick, probably Sarah's—were printed on the glass.

I WANT WHAT'S MINE. I'LL BE BACK.

Chapter Eleven

SARAH LEANED BACK IN HER chair and stretched. It was only ten, and she was already having trouble staying awake. Usually drowsiness didn't hit her until mid-afternoon. It probably had something to do with the fact that she didn't sleep well on the couch at Heather's. Though after what had happened Sunday, she wouldn't have slept well anywhere.

The insurance adjuster was supposed to meet her at her place in a while. As much as she'd wanted to start cleaning, both Joe and Kyle had stopped her. She'd had to leave everything as it was until the adjuster inspected it and made a report.

She stood and headed to the break room. Maybe she should just take the day off. She had to go shopping sometime today to replace, well, everything. Luckily, her large purse had her extra makeup, face wipes, and moisturizer. Knowing what she had to face at home was more than enough to send her over the edge.

Opening the small fridge, she grabbed a Diet Coke.

Mark walked in and refilled his mug from the coffeepot.

"How are you holding up? You look tired." She had showed him pictures of the house yesterday and brought him up to speed.

He'd been on a call most of the morning, so she hadn't wanted to disturb him with her plans for the day. "I'll feel better once the insurance company does their thing, and I can start putting things back together. I'm heading over there soon and will probably be gone the rest of the day."

"Do you need anything?"

She sighed. "A shovel." She gave a short laugh.

"Take all the time you need and hire a cleaning crew. You don't need to be here. Eric can handle things."

"Some stuff I have to do myself, but the cleaning crew's a good idea." Inwardly, she groaned. Did Mark not see how people bristled when Eric came in the room? He was a great architect, maybe even brilliant, but his people skills were terrible. "I'll be back tomorrow. Work helps keep my mind off things I can't control anyway. How are things with Martha?"

He grimaced. "I know this is bad timing. You have a lot on your plate. But after Friday, I won't be coming into the office on a regular basis. You and I can set up regular meetings and calls, but you'll be running the show." His shoulders slumped, and he seemed to age before her eyes. "Martha wandered off yesterday while I was sleeping."

"Oh, Mark! You must have been terrified. Is she okay?"

He nodded and swallowed. "Yeah, just a little dehydrated. But I can't leave her alone. I've been making arrangements all morning. It's time."

She touched his arm. "I'm so sorry. Is there anything I can do?"

He squeezed her hand. "You're doing it. I'm not worried about the business. I know you'll do a great job." His phone buzzed. He glanced at the screen. "I have to get this." He touched the screen and moved off.

She returned to her office and rubbed her hands over her face. Why did life have to be so difficult? For her, for Mark, for

Heather. She felt so out of control. There had to be something she could do.

Kyle had showed her the message the intruder left on her car. She had no idea what it meant. Who was this person, and what did they think she had? She popped open her can and took a sip, the carbonated bubbles waking her up. Kyle was reassuring, and she trusted him. But the whole situation was frustrating. And scary. How could she give them what they wanted if she didn't even know what it was? Maybe they were mistaken, confusing her with someone else. The only thing this could possibly be related to was Greg Connor's disappearance. He'd given her that site map ...

Maybe she could do something. She clicked on a couple of files until she had several open on her screen. They'd done multiple projects in the Foothill Corridor area. She didn't know what she was looking for, but maybe she would when she saw it. What did she hope to accomplish? Probably nothing, but if there was one thing she hated, it was not fully understanding a situation.

Sarah studied the aerial topographic surveys of the area she'd opened. Yep, they overlapped Greg's site as she'd hoped. She moved the aerial photographs around until they were side by side. One was from about six months ago, the other a couple of weeks ago. They covered different areas, so she zoomed and resized the windows until the areas were approximately the same size. Even the most recent photo still showed the eucalyptus grove still standing that had burned last week. She glanced between the two pictures, focusing on the grove and the surrounding area.

Something was different. This was the area, right? Yes, she matched up the streets. But the topography was different. The land contours had changed between the two pictures. What was going on? There'd been no recent mudslides.

She shifted in her chair, trying to stretch her back. That couch definitely wasn't comfortable.

The site map. It had cut and fill amounts on it. She con-centrated on remembering what it said. She hadn't really looked at it until she handed it to Kyle.

If they were grading the site, that would explain the contour changes. So what? Why would they care if she had their cut/fill sheet? Maybe they were grading without a permit. Not legal, but not that unusual.

It was probably nothing. Grading was not that big of a deal, certainly not worth trashing someone's house over. And did she really want to get any more involved in this thing? She should just leave the investigation to the pros and not give someone another excuse to come after her.

She closed her eyes. She couldn't do that. She'd come up with something, no matter how small, and she should call Kyle and let him know. Kyle was nice; he wouldn't make her feel stupid if what she'd found was nothing. Which it probably was. She picked up the phone.

***

Joe threw another load in the washing machine and closed the lid. The sound of water filling the tub echoed through the small closet off the kitchen that served as his laundry area. He picked up the clean clothes and carried them to the couch. He sort of folded things the way his mom had showed him. He hated doing laundry and put it off until his hamper was overflowing.

He could take it over to his mom's. She'd do it for him, but as much as he hated doing laundry, that felt like too much of an imposition on her. However, when he'd been fighting brush fires for days on end and was completely wiped out, she'd come over and done his laundry, stocked his fridge, frozen some meals for him. She took good care of him. His sisters complained that he was spoiled, that Mom never did those things for them. Which was true. There were a few perks to being the only male in a family of girls.

The thought squeezed his chest. He'd been the only male since his dad had died when he was in high school. That was a mixed bag of emotions. Things had been good between them when he'd died, but a life of alcoholism had taken him all too soon, something Joe had a hard time forgiving his father for. Among other things.

His stomach growled. He carried his clothes to the bedroom, put them away, and started thinking about lunch. What was Sarah doing? She'd been on his mind all day yesterday while he'd been on shift. She and Heather had come over to let Shadow out and feed him last night, still thoughtful after all she'd been through. Though he and Shadow got through their morning workout faster by running, he'd missed her company. Shadow did too, it seemed. He kept looking at Joe like, "Where is she?" He'd give her a call. Most likely she'd be coming to her condo today, and he didn't think she should be there alone.

He shoved the last drawer shut and pulled out his phone. She picked up on the first ring. "Hey, just checking to see how you were doing, and if you were heading over to your condo today."

"I have an appointment with the adjuster in, oh"—he heard the phone shift—"half an hour. I've got to get a rental car so Heather can have her car back. Then, depending on how much I get done, I might be back over there later. But I'm staying with Heather again tonight."

"I'm off today, so let me know when you get over here. I don't think you should be in your condo alone. And I'll go with you to pick up the rental car."

"You don't have to do that. I feel like I've imposed on you a lot lately." Her voice was soft in his ear.

"It's not an imposition. I want to help."

A moment of silence, then a sniff. "I appreciate that."

"I'll see you in a few." He slid the phone back into his pocket but stood there for a moment. She hadn't mentioned Ryan. And obviously Ryan wasn't helping her with the adjuster or her rental car. So maybe things weren't so solid in that area. He shook his head. He couldn't figure out why Ryan wasn't doing those things for her. Those were the kinds of things you did for … people you cared for.

Sarah sat in the parking lot at work in Heather's Miata, driver-side door propped open to let the heat escape while the air conditioning started working. One of Heather's CDs shuffled on.

The weight of everything that had happened pressed against her chest. Tears spilled out her eyes, and she dashed them away. All of her things could be replaced. So why was she so upset? She hoped Joe couldn't tell over the phone. She was glad he was going to be there. The thought of entering her condo again alone was something she hadn't let herself think about.

She put the phone away then checked her hair and makeup in the rearview mirror. Her hair was past her shoulders now—probably needed a trim—and felt a little wilder than usual since she had to use styling products meant for Heather's straight hair and not Sarah's wavy mane. Of course, that could pretty much sum up the last twenty-four hours. Even the car smelled like Heather's pear lotion. She shook her head. Time to go.

Cool air now blew out of the vents, and Sarah headed toward her condo. She switched off the CD, needing the quiet to soothe her. Until she could get her condo back in shape, she'd have precious few moments of alone time staying with Heather. She would need what she could get if she expected to stay sane through this nightmare.

She pulled in front of her condo, and a chill washed over her. It was weird parking out here and not in her garage. How was she going to feel when she got inside? At work, she'd been able to focus on Mark's problems and take care of what needed to be done for the office. But here it all came crashing back.

As unpredictable as her emotions had been, she had

mixed feelings about Joe meeting her here. She didn't want to be emotional in front of him. And yet, his very presence made her feel safe.

She got out of Heather's car. Joe was walking across the parking lot. She smiled and waved. He covered the ground between them and rubbed her shoulder.

"Where's your shadow?"

"I left him at home, under great protest. It's like he knew I was coming here. I think he likes you better than me."

"That's because he knows I have doggie treats." She stepped up to the front door. Her hands were shaking, causing the keys to clack together. She jiggled them unnecessarily so Joe wouldn't see. Sliding the key in the lock, she turned it until the deadbolt *thumped* back into its housing. A lot of good it did. The guy who broke into her place had pried open one of the windows enough to slip the lock.

She dropped her hand to the doorknob, coated with black powder, and held it for a moment. Then she turned it and pushed the door open. It was no better or worse than she'd remembered. All she could see was a huge mess to clean up. It would take forever. Especially since she had absolutely no energy to deal with any of it. "Maybe I should just let a cleaning crew come in and get rid of it all and start over."

"A lot of things here are salvageable. We can help." Joe was close behind her, so close she could feel the warmth coming off him.

She was glad he'd come. Doing this by herself would have been overwhelming. She headed straight to her office. Plans were strewn all over the floor, files dumped out, books pulled off the shelves.

Joe's hand landed on her shoulder. "The adjuster is going to want to see everything. Why don't we wait outside? The sun feels good, and you won't be itching to put things to right."

"You're right." He already knew her pretty well. How did he know that her fingers fairly tingled to get things back in order?

They went outside and leaned against Heather's Miata, his shoulder touching hers, warming it. Taking comfort from his presence, she said, "I talked to Kyle before I came over. I couldn't sleep last night trying to figure out what that message on my car meant. The only thing I could think of was it was related to that map Greg Connor had given me. So I pulled up some aerial topos from our projects in the area. It doesn't fully cover the lot I saw Greg and that other guy on, but part of it definitely showed some unusual grading.

"Anyhow, I told Kyle what I found, and he was going to the building department to look into it. Maybe he'll find something and all of this will be over. He was going to call Grayson today too. None of it makes any sense."

A sedan pulled up next to them. The adjuster. Sarah showed him inside and briefly explained what happened. She gave him Kyle's card with the police report number on it. He moved through the house, making notes, taking pictures.

When the adjuster was done in Sarah's office, she headed in there, clearing a path so she could get to her desk, putting books back on her built-in shelves as she went. Gathering up papers off the floor, she pulled out her ergonomically-correct chair—thank goodness it hadn't been knifed—and sat and turned on her computer.

Joe knelt on the floor, gathering papers and stacking them, returning books to the shelves. "Maybe if you have one area under control, the rest will feel more manageable."

As soon as the desktop came up, she knew someone had been on it. It was a mess. Files in the trash, names changed. Her heart pounded as she clicked open her dream home plans. They were buried a couple of files deep. No one should have even known they were there.

The file opened. The screen loaded. Someone who knew AutoCad had been in here. Her drawings had been messed with. She zoomed out to see the whole drawing. It was salvageable, especially if the backup files hadn't been destroyed. But someone had drawn geometric designs over her plans and filled them with patterns until her original drawings were completely obscured.

Closing her eyes, she willed back the tears. But they leaked out anyway. And then the dam burst. Tears flowed, and she wiped them away with her sleeve. Where was her tissue box? Who knew?

Joe nudged her shoulder, a wad of toilet paper in his hand.

She gave him a watery smile and wiped her nose. Lovely, not how she wanted him to see her.

He put both hands on her shoulders and leaned in behind her, speaking into her ear. "It's okay. Better to let it out than stuff it down. This is a pretty big deal."

His breath sent tingles down her neck. She hoped they weren't visible. She nodded. He was right, but she didn't want to cry in front of him. Maybe tonight on Heather's couch she could let her guard down.

"Did you look at your computer and your plans? Was everything okay?"

Sarah put her hand over her face and shook her head. "They were in there. I think it's fixable, but it'll be a lot of work."

Joe pointed to her house plans on the screen. "What was that supposed to be?"

She sighed. "Just a personal project." She paused. He'd already seen her cry. He wouldn't make fun of her dreams. "It's my dream house. I've been working on it forever." She dug around the desk until she came up with the paper copy and handed it to him. "Luckily"—she moved to her drafting desk—"these were okay. This is what it's supposed to look like."

Spreading out the slightly wrinkled plans, she was amazed—and thankful—that was the only damage. "I have a couple of different elevations, but the floor plan's basically the same."

Joe leaned over her shoulder. He wasn't as tall as Ryan. But he was solid bulk. She wasn't used to sharing these plans with anyone. She wrapped her arms over her middle. It was nice of Joe to be interested, though.

Joe studied it. "Wow, this is really cool. I love the office area with the bay window and a fireplace." He put the plans on her desk and tapped them. "That would be a fabulous place to live. Where would you build it?"

She ducked her chin. No one had ever asked, not that she had shared them with many people. "I have some land up in the foothills I'm making payments on. Can't afford those payments and to build the house both. But some day."

"That is so great. You have a tangible dream. Something to work toward."

She tilted her head. "Someday. Maybe." His encouragement did funny things to her heart, but she couldn't deal with any more emotions today, even good ones. She had one more thing she needed to do.

She opened Quicken. It was okay. She shook her head and closed the program.

"What?"

"This is weird. If someone wanted to mess with me, it seems like they would start with my financial files. But they're fine. They messed with my house plans instead. This has to be connected to Connor's disappearance. That's the only thing that remotely makes sense. I have no idea what the connection is, but someone obviously thinks I do."

The adjuster rapped on the office door frame. "I'm finished here. Just need you to sign a few things."

She stood and moved to the living room where she signed the forms, said goodbye to the adjuster, and closed the door behind him. "Now I'm free to clean up." She stretched her shoulders. They felt like they'd been carrying two-by-fours all day.

"Let's go get your rental car. Then, let's see who all we can get over here, maybe order a pizza and get through as much of this as we can so the cleaning crew can come in tomorrow.

What do you think?" He studied Sarah.

She nodded. Joe had come up with a manageable plan when she couldn't, and she was supposed to be the planner. Her brain must really be on overload. "With everyone here, it might not seem so bad." She met his gaze and saw the intensity there.

She clasped her hands in front of her. "Let me call Heather and let her know what's going on. Then we can go. Kyle had my car towed to the police yard so they could investigate further. When they're done with it, they'll tow it to the shop. The rental place isn't too far from here." She was babbling; it happened when she was nervous. But why should she be nervous around Joe?

He grinned. "Yeah, I know. Remember when I couldn't drive my own truck because of Kyle?" His gaze was steady on her.

She rummaged through her purse to find her phone, using it as cover to hide her heating cheeks. Could Joe be attracted to her? Unless she was so emotional that she was misreading things, Joe was making his interest in her obvious. This was beyond the easy friendship they had developed. And if she was honest with herself, her attraction to him had moved them past friendship in her mind.

Her hands stilled at the thought. She grabbed the phone and speed-dialed Heather, pretending to be staring aimlessly, but sneaking a peek at Joe to see if he suspected anything. He was strolling around the room, probably regretting how much work he'd gotten himself into. She watched how he moved, athletic, but comfortable in his own skin, not like he was trying to make a statement. Not like Ryan.

"Hey, girl." Heather answered the phone, saving Sarah from her disconcerting thoughts.

Sarah explained Joe's plan.

"Great. I'll have Kyle drive us over when he gets off. We'll bring sodas. So there'll be five of us?"

"No, uh, no." She hadn't even thought about asking Ryan. It felt odd to think of him here with Kyle, Joe, and Heather. It was always just the four of them. Should she ask him? She bit her lip and snuck a glance at Joe. The look he gave her made her stomach turn flips. She pushed thoughts of Ryan aside, something to deal with later.

Heather didn't seem to notice her hesitation or lack of a mention of Ryan. "Oh. Okay. That's fine then. I have Diet Coke for us, and Dr. Pepper for the guys. I'll raid the stash I keep here for Kyle."

"Thanks. I'll order the pizza when you guys know what time you'll be here."

Shoving the phone back in her purse and picking up the address from the adjuster, she took a deep breath and let it out. "Want to follow me?"

"Sure." But his soft eyes and gentle smile said more. What were they really talking about?

Chapter Twelve

SARAH SAT IN THE WARM sand, digging her toes deeper to find the coolness. In another couple of weeks, the sand would still be sizzling at this time of day, too hot to walk on barefoot. She still wore a blouse and pants from work. Visiting the beach had been a spontaneous thing. Not like her at all. But after Joe had helped her get a rental car and then offered to return Heather's car to her, Sarah just couldn't imagine heading back to the office. So she'd come here seeking the peace and solace the ocean usually provided.

She rolled her shoulders and her neck. She'd been ready to leave fifteen minutes ago, but her car wasn't. It had a flat. Now she had to wait on the rental company to send out road-side assistance. So she was stuck for at least another hour. There were worse places to be stuck. Maybe God was telling her something. Giving her a forced time out. She took a deep breath of the salty air. And listened. Leaving her phone in the car had been a good choice, giving her a chance to decompress and pray. Or try to.

The afternoon rays played across the ocean, turning the film of water left by a receding wave the color of champagne.

It was beautiful, relaxing, perfect … yet she felt none of those things. Too many issues tumbled through her mind, and she struggled to make sense of them all. Greg Conner, her trashed house, the site grading, Ryan …Joe.

She needed to have a conversation with Ryan. Being with Joe today confirmed to her that she had to talk to Ryan sooner rather than later. No matter how embarrassing choir would now be, it needed to happen. Like ripping a bandage off. The faster the better. But as long as her phone was in her car, she could ignore all of it.

Being stranded was an oddly familiar feeling, but not a comfortable one. She needed one of the Little House books she read as a girl. They used to keep her company while she waited and waited and waited.

The sand under her today was a lot softer than the con-crete bench she had sat on after school so many days. Her eyes drifted to the parking lot, ostensibly looking for the road-side assistance, but she found herself counting cars. She never had lost that habit. Probably part of her desire to control things.

A few more minutes, a couple of deep breaths of the salt-crusted air, and hopefully they would be here. She shook her head. That was weird. She just had a mental flash, picturing the driver as Mr. Simpson.

Guess it made sense. Mr. Simpson had given her a ride home from school that day. Odd, she hadn't thought about him in years. Her mother had had a fit when she found out. Later she would learn of Mr. Simpson's reputation for being overly-affectionate with female students. She sat through a lecture on the dangers of riding with people she hadn't explicitly been given permission to be with while she wondered the whole time why her mom wasn't more concerned about her being left alone at an empty school.

"Sarah!"

Her head snapped up. Was she hearing things?

Apparently not, because there was Ryan. Striding down

the bike path and headed her way. Had she conjured him up by her thoughts? Was this God's way of answering her prayer? And how'd he find her?

He grinned, like he expected her to be thrilled at his presence. She couldn't help but smile back. But she didn't know how convincing it was. He stepped onto the sand, crossing over to her, his boldly appreciative gaze a little unnerving. "You're not answering your phone." He eased down into the sand next to her, draping his arms over his knees. Even on the wide-open sand, Ryan seemed to take up more than his share of space. He looked back at the parking lot. "And where's your car?"

"At the police station. My house was vandalized last night, probably related to the missing contractor. They also trashed my car, so Kyle had it towed in for their techs to go over before it can be fixed. Now I have a rental. But it's got a flat. I'm waiting on their road-side assistance."

"Let me look at it." He pushed to his feet and held out his hand to her.

She hesitated and then took it. He didn't let go until she had to dig in her pockets for her keys.

He bent down and looked at the deflated tire sagging over the rim. "Pop the trunk."

When she did, he lifted the floor mat and pulled up the spare and the jack. He scowled at the tire and shoved everything back in.

"What's wrong?"

"The spare's flat too."

"Well, we can wait for the road-side assistance to come." She reached in the car and grabbed her phone out of the console. No calls from them but a bunch from Ryan. A few texts too. She slipped her phone in her pocket and leaned against the car, watching the parking lot entrance.

Ryan moved in front of her, his feet touching hers.

"How did you know where to find me?"

He leaned against the car, bracketing her inside his arms.

"When you didn't answer the phone, I called your office. Malia said you weren't coming back to the office. So I texted Heather and asked where you were. She told me about the break in and your trashed house and that you liked to come here when you needed to think." He shook his head. "Why didn't you tell me?"

She didn't meet his gaze. Heather had sent Ryan here so they could have a private conversation. She just needed to open her mouth and speak. She swallowed and cleared her throat.

He grimaced. "That's so bad for your vocal cords."

"I know. Sorry." She shook her head. Ryan gave them a lot of lectures about that. "There's just been a lot going on. I've had to deal with the police, the insurance adjuster, the car rental. Plus stuff at work." She didn't mention the clean-up party tonight, and, interestingly enough, he didn't ask her how she was going to handle all of it or if he could help.

The fact that Joe had been there for her through all of that instead of Ryan spoke volumes. She needed some space from him. She put her hands on his chest, but he leaned in and kissed her.

A flood of thoughts and emotions poured through her, and she couldn't sort any of them out.

Ryan slid his arms around her and pulled her close, kissing her more deeply.

Finally, one overarching thought came to the front: She didn't want this. She pushed back and turned her head.

He grinned at her, his eyes dark and heated.

She gave him a small smile. "Uh, don't really want to do that here where people can see." Or at all. She searched the nearly empty parking lot and wiggled out of Ryan's grasp.

"We didn't get a chance to talk much at lunch after church, but I think our big announcement went over pretty well." He toyed with her hair. "Sorry I didn't have a chance to talk to you about it beforehand. I meant to, but I was running late. After we ran into Chris and Sharon at the movies, I figured the best way to deal with the gossip and rumors was to hit them head on and tell everyone what was going on."

A shadow crossed his eyes, and he eased back. "You're such a strong Christian woman, Pastor Tom was happy to hear the news. He's already planning the wedding, I think." He moved next to her to lean against the car.

"Yeah. About that …" She scanned the highway, hoping she'd find some miraculous words there. Someone in a Chevy Avalanche was cruising the aisles of the parking lot. He looked a little rough around the edges with two-day stubble and longish hair. She met the man's gaze. Fear spiraled out of her stomach. Wait. He was looking at Ryan. Of course. Silly. Probably someone who recognized him from church and was just curious as to who she was. Was she ever going to get used to that? She preferred being in the background, but people were always stopping to talk to Ryan.

Ryan saw her staring and followed the direction of her gaze. "Hey!" He pulled on her hand, tugging her in the direction of the Avalanche. "Nick, what are you doing here?"

The guy stopped the truck and leaned his elbow out the window, revealing an arm covered in a full-sleeve tattoo. "I had a job nearby, and I thought I'd take a break and enjoy the ocean. Didn't expect to see you here."

"Same with us. Nick, this is Sarah."

"Hi, nice to meet you." Good. Someone Ryan knew, not some weird stalker. Her imagination was really going wild. She needed to get some good sleep.

"Hi, Sarah." He switched his gaze back to Ryan. "Still on for basketball tonight?"

"Yep. Never miss it."

Someone he knew well enough to play basketball with. Ryan had a ministry of sorts playing basketball with whoever he could get to bring their friends, hoping they would see Christians were normal people and not weirdos. It was one of the things she liked about him. Looking past Nick's truck, she saw a tow truck coming. She watched, hoped, as it got closer. It turned in to the parking lot. She'd never been so happy to see a tow truck. But she knew the reprieve was only temporary. Relief and annoyance battled for prominence as once more, her conversation with Ryan got put off.

Joe flipped open the lid on the pizza box and snagged the last piece. He was finished with the kitchen. Everything salvageable was back on the shelves and the rest left for the cleaning crew.

Heather and Kyle and done a good job in the living room and now were tackling the back bedroom. Had anyone else but him noticed how often Kyle checked out the front window? He'd brought over a motion-detector light for the front porch and installed it first thing. The homeowners' association was going to love that. But Joe was pretty happy with the video-enabled doorbell that would let Sarah see on her phone anyone who came near her door.

They were all doing their best to help Sarah get things back to normal. The question nobody seemed to bring up was, where was Ryan? Yeah, it was work, but hadn't he made a public spectacle about their relationship? On the other hand, Joe was glad Ryan wasn't here. Less awkward that way.

He walked through the rooms, categorizing what needed to be done. Out of habit, he checked for smoke detectors. In the kitchen, a fire extinguisher sat on the counter next to the stove. Good. And yep, a smoke detector was mounted on the wall. Wait. Two? Maybe one was broken. Hmm. He turned and looked at the living area. It had two smoke detectors too and a carbon monoxide detector. Heading down the hall, he poked his head in every room. All of them had two smoke detectors. As did the garage, which also had another fire extinguisher. He wished more homes were this well prepared.

He grabbed a Diet Coke. Sarah was in the office since she was the only one who knew how to put her files back in order. She sat on the floor, cross-legged, surrounded by piles of paper, jazz streaming from her computer's speakers. With her hair pulled back in a ponytail, she had that same young look as when she went walking.

"Need some help?" He popped the soda open and handed it to her.

She took it from him with a smile. "Thanks. Yeah, find a space."

He pointed above the doorway. "What's the story with two smoke detectors in each room? Is one broken?" He reached up to hit the test button and a piercing noise emitted. "Not that one." He hit the button on the other detector with the same result. "They're both fine."

Faint pink suffused Sarah's cheeks. "It's just a precaution. In case one fails."

He pulled one of the detectors off the wall. "These have ten-year batteries, and they're only a year old."

She shuffled papers around. "But if there was a defect in them, I wouldn't know until it was too late."

"That's what the test button is for. And why you have one in every room. If one misses it, the others will get it."

She just shrugged and continued sorting. Something else was going on here, but with all that had happened recently, she probably didn't need anyone poking at a sore spot. But he hoped someday she felt comfortable enough to tell him what it was about. He pushed a mess of papers to the side and joined her on the floor.

"The piles are labeled. Just try and put all that loose paper into one of them. If you don't know where something goes, just ask."

"Sounds like a plan."

They worked in silence. Joe sorted through insurance papers, warranties, and receipts. Pretty straightforward. He was making a dent, clearing enough space that he could see more of the hardwood floor. Leaning over he tugged another pile closer. Photographs, cards, and notes. He picked up a few pictures. Based on the way the prints had faded to an orange tint and the hair and clothes styles, these were pictures from when Sarah was a little girl. He looked on the back. *Sarah Brockman, 5th grade, 1998.*

"Where'd you go to school?"

She looked up, eyebrows raised, and he turned the picture toward her.

"Oh, that. I went to a private school."

"So you were one of *those* kids." Joe smiled, teasing her.

She rolled her eyes. "Believe me, I would have rather gone to school with the neighborhood kids instead of a bunch of stuck-up rich kids. It wasn't the great academic institution my parents thought it would be. I asked all the time to be allowed to go to the local school, but they wouldn't hear of it. I guess sending me to an expensive private school made them feel like they were doing their parental duty." She sorted through papers, not looking at him or the pictures. "It worked out okay, I suppose, because I did get a good college scholarship."

Now she looked at him and smiled. "Just toss all the pictures in that pile over there. You grew up around here, right? You and Kyle?"

"Yeah. Kyle and our friend Scott grew up on the same street. I moved here when I was in fourth grade, and we pretty much became the Three Musketeers."

"It's pretty rare these days to know someone who still lives in their hometown." She put down the papers in her hands. Staring at nothing for a few beats, she then moved her gaze to him for a long second. "Can I get your opinion on something?"

"Sure. What?"

"Hang on a second." She stood and left the room, coming back a moment later to insert a small jump drive into the side of her computer. Sitting in the chair, she clicked open a couple of folders until an aerial photograph came on the screen.

"Sorry I don't have another chair in here. We could pull one in from the kitchen."

"I'm fine. What's this?"

"That aerial topo of the Foothill Corridor I was telling you about this morning. I've got a couple of projects there." She moved the windows around. "Here's where I saw Greg Connor before he went missing. Do you know anything about this area?"

Joe nodded. "Recently, it almost burned in that fire we had. In fact, I saw that grove of eucs—eucalyptus—explode."

"Yeah. That's how I got lost. I used that as a reference when I was driving around up there."

Lost? Sarah incapable of something was an odd picture. But kind of cute. "We used to go up there sometimes as kids. It was a pretty decent bike ride from home, about seven miles. So don't tell my mom. I don't think she ever knew we went that far. But there was always a bunch of junk up there. Farming equipment, old smudge pots they used to use to keep the oranges from freezing the few times we'd get a cold snap. Someone started a rumor of an old Indian burial ground up there. I don't think there was any truth to it. Probably just a product of a boy's overactive imagination supported by finding a couple of artifacts. And a burial ground is so much spookier than a garbage dump, which is really more what it looked like."

"But there were artifacts found?" She turned in her chair to look at him.

"Oh sure. I actually found an arrowhead. Other guys found pottery shards, pieces of baskets, stuff like that."

"Have there been any official studies or designations of that area?"

Joe shook his head. "Not that I know of. I think it would have made the news."

"That's what I'm thinking." She looked back at the map.

"I wonder how long the current owner has had the property." She opened the internet and went to the county records site. "Hmm. DiMarco family trust, 1990. Newport Beach address. This only gives me the current owner, but I bet if I ordered a title search we'd find it belonged to a DiMarco before it went to the trust. I think we can safely say he's got to know about the Indian artifacts. Which would explain why they'd be grading without a permit. Kyle needs to see this."

Joe got to his feet. "I'll get him. I need to unkink my legs anyway."

He nearly ran into Kyle in the hall. "Sarah has something she thinks you should see."

"Okay." Kyle followed him back into the office. "What's up, Sarah?"

She turned in her chair to face them. "I was asking Joe about the site where I last saw Greg Connor. Kinda near those topos I showed you. He was telling me you guys used to go up there when you were kids and that some Indian artifacts had been found there."

"Yeah. I still have a couple of those arrowheads." His words were casual, but his intent look meant Kyle had shifted into cop mode.

"I pulled up this title search on the property. It's owned by the DiMarcos and has been for some time. I bet they know about the artifacts, and that's why they're grading without a permit. If Indian artifacts are found on a land under development, everything is brought to a screeching halt until experts can be brought in to evaluate the site and determine if it has significance to the local tribes. If it does, Mr. DiMarco can kiss his development goodbye. Considering this is one of the routes under consideration for the new toll road, that's a significant amount of money. Even if he got fined for grading without a permit, it's a drop in the bucket compared to what he stands to make if they choose his land for the route."

Kyle nodded slowly. "If Greg Connor knew any of this,

DiMarco has motive for wanting him to disappear. Sarah, write that info down for me, and I'll look into it. Might have to pay a visit to Mr. DiMarco."

Joe looked at Kyle while Sarah copied the information from the screen. "Is this Tony DiMarco? He paid us a visit at the fire station to thank us for saving his home in the fire."

"Could be. Or maybe it's a family business. Either way, it's something to go on." Sarah handed Kyle a piece of paper. "Did you talk to Grayson yet? He could tell you."

"He had meetings all day today, but we've got an appointment for tomorrow."

Joe crossed his arms. "Maybe I'm missing something here, but none of that tells us why he's after Sarah."

Kyle gave him a steady gaze tinged with steel. "I know."

Tony's cell rang, and he picked it up. "DiMarco."

"Good call on having me bug her house." Nick's voice came over the line. "It's paying off. Our friend thinks she's figured something out. And it sounded like she was pretty chummy with the cops. That detective was already at her house. And your name came up."

Tony slammed his fist on the desk and swore, causing his crystal bowl of Jelly Belly jelly beans to jump. His contact at the city had just called to tell him someone had been asking around about his land. And now this. He'd hoped they could still get the map from her. Now it was too late. And if someone was poking around … He had to hope that the innocuous looking paper would stay that way, that no one would figure out what it really meant. This was going to cost him. But it was still cheaper than the alternative.

He tossed a handful of jelly beans in his mouth. They'd helped him break his two-pack a day habit but hadn't helped his waistline. Though he could blame that on his love of good food.

"Tony? What do you want me to do?" Nick still needed an answer.

Tony munched on the candy, not sure he had one. He started to run a hand through his hair then stopped. He didn't want to mess it up. He clenched and released his fist then let out a breath. "Keep an eye on both of them. Then move to the next step tonight. She has to be convinced to stay out of this."

He hung up and rooted around in his candy dish. The cappuccino ones were his favorite.

Chapter Thirteen

SARAH TAPPED HER PEN AGAINST the pad of paper, ignoring her computer. After finding herself staring blankly at the screen for the third time that morning, she switched gears. Kyle had just left. She'd printed out the topos for him. He had brought the cut/fill sheet, and that seemed to explain the contour change, though it still looked like they were moving a lot of dirt. Elevated pads, basements? Not typical. Kyle said the building department hadn't issued any permits for the site. He'd also talked to Grayson, who had had some dealings with DiMarco, who confirmed that the guy would do anything to get his way, even though nothing was out-and-out illegal.

They had a lot of hunches and guesses, but nothing solid. And still no idea why they were after her.

She had to do some shopping, and Heather would probably enjoy that. She really didn't want to be alone, which proved just how much this whole thing had shaken her up.

She was going in circles here. Standing, she stretched her back. She couldn't wait to get off Heather's couch. The goal was to be back in her own, new bed tonight. And there was a lot to do to make that happen.

The cleaning crew was due at her place in thirty minutes. She shut down her computer, slipped it into its sleeve and then her bag. Heather had offered to meet her there.

Fifteen minutes later, Sarah drove up to her condo to find Heather sitting with the top down on her Miata, seat tilted back, face to the sun, CD playing in the background. Sarah would feel worse about interrupting Heather's day if she didn't seem to be enjoying it so much. Heather turned her head to look as Sarah pulled into the adjacent spot with her rental car.

Heather waved, and the seat moved back into the upright position.

Sarah got out of the car. "Thanks for coming."

"Any excuse to get out of work. Actually, I'm ahead of schedule, so it's fine."

Sarah glanced at her watch. They still had ten minutes before the cleaning crew was supposed to be here. She really didn't want to wait inside. She unlocked the door and opened it, the dark coolness spilling out into the warming day. She flipped on the light by the door then headed toward the French doors that opened to the back patio. "If we leave the front door open with just the screen latched, we'll hear them if we sit on the patio."

"Let's do that then."

She loved this patio. A sense of peace enveloped her every time she stepped outside and the scent of warmed lavender and rosemary greeted her. Aromatherapy at its best. She was incredibly grateful the intruder hadn't bothered anything out here.

The calmness washing over her gave her the burst of energy she needed. She started a list. "I'm sure the cleaning crew will be here at least two hours. We can replace the bare necessities during that time."

Heather reached out and touched her hand. "You know, when I was under police protection, I had to keep reminding myself that God hasn't given me a spirit of fear, but of power and of love and a strong mind. You in particular have a strong mind."

Sarah's eyes got hot as she blinked back tears.

Someone knocked on the screen. She jumped, her heart pounding. Shoving back her chair, she saw the cleaning crew. She took a deep breath. Everything was fine.

As she crossed through the house to let the crew in, her shakiness subsided. The crew came in, and she explained what needed to be done. The normalcy of assigning tasks and going down a list calmed her heart. But as she and Heather were driving off, she couldn't help but wonder. When dark fell and everything got quiet and there was nothing left to do, would she be able to spend the night here?

Heather rubbed Sarah's arm. "There's no rush to leave my place."

"I know. You're a great friend." Sarah gave Heather a tight smile. "But I have to do this." *I can do this.*

She hoped. Maybe she and Heather would come up with a solution to her other pressing problem: Ryan. They had choir practice tonight. And she had to talk to him. She only hoped that didn't blow up in her face as well.

"Mr. DiMarco, Detective Kyle Taylor and Detective Steve Collins are here to see you." His secretary's voice came over the intercom. Tony popped a cappuccino Jelly Belly in his mouth and thought for a moment. Pressing the intercom button, he said, "Send them back, please."

The door opened to his office a minute later, and two men, obviously cops by their upright, confident bearing, strode in.

"Mr. DiMarco? I'm Detective Kyle Taylor; this is my partner, Detective Steve Collins." He flashed his ID. "We'd like to ask you a few questions."

Tony motioned to the chairs in front of his desk. "Please,

have a seat. Can my secretary bring you anything?"

"No, thank you." The taller one, Taylor, waited until Tony was situated behind his desk.

"How can I help you?" Tony folded his hands on top of his desk. He knew how he appeared to these men. The well-appointed office with dark woods, rich upholstery and carpet, the view out his window all gave the message that Tony DiMarco was a successful, well-respected businessman. And that was what they needed to believe.

"Do you know Greg Connor?"

"Yes. We worked together on a few projects. I was absolutely stunned to hear about his disappearance. If you think a reward would help generate information, I'd be happy to put one up."

"When was the last time you saw him?"

Tony thought for a moment. "Let me check." He pulled out his phone and hit the screen a few times. Only his public dealings with Greg were on his phone. "We had lunch on the fifteenth. But I talked to him on the phone, oh, what day was it? It was during the fires. I was staying at a hotel since we'd been evacuated, and he called to see how my house was."

"How well did you know him? Did he have any enemies, anyone who might want to harm him?"

"We've done several projects together, like I said. We're friends, we'd do lunch, dinner, stuff like that. If I had my choice, I'd pick Greg to GC all my projects. But so would a lot of guys. Greg keeps busy. I can't imagine him having a problem with a developer. He's good at what he does. Maybe a sub might have a problem with him, because Greg could push pretty hard." Tony smiled. "That's why developers like him. I'm sure his secretary would have a list of the guys he's worked with."

"What's GC and a sub?" Collins asked.

"Oh. GC is general contractor, the guy on-site in charge of the project. He hires all the subs or subcontractors, the different trades needed to do a job."

Detective Taylor made notes. "Tell me about your project in the Foothill Corridor."

He'd expected this. "Not much to tell. We're in the process of putting together proposals for some parties interested in the area if it gets selected as the route of the future toll road."

"Are you grading without a permit?"

This would take a bit of finesse. He chuckled. "You caught me. I don't know how familiar you are with the building process. The city can take a really long time approving grading plans. And in my business, time is money. If an investor can't get a project done within a certain time frame, he's going to move on to something else. I can't have the city costing me money because their workers take every other Friday off. So we get a little grading in ahead of time. No big deal. If the city fines us, we pay it. They're happy, my investor's happy, and I'm happy."

The other one, Collins, leaned forward. "So you're comfortable operating outside the law."

"I don't think of it that way. I don't know any developer who does. It's simply how a businessman has to deal with the bureaucracy of government. I'm sure you guys have your share of paperwork and politics that you don't like. Besides, the city seems to forget that it's my land, and I have a constitutional right to use it."

Taylor stood. "Thank you for your time." He handed Tony his card. "Call us if you can think of anything related to Greg Connor's disappearance."

Tony stood as well and walked them to the office door. "I will. Let me know if there's anything I can do to help."

At the door, Taylor turned. "I used to ride my bike up in the area of your project when I was a kid. Have you owned the land long?"

"Been in the family for years."

"I remember finding some arrowheads and stuff like that up there. Does that kind of thing turn up anymore?"

Cold seeped into Tony's bones. This guy was just fishing.

"No, just a lot of garbage. We had to clean a ton of it out of there. Everybody and their brother used to dump their old couches and stuff out there. What a mess. I wish we'd found something as interesting as arrowheads."

The detective nodded and left. Tony closed the door behind them. There was something behind that detective's question. Sounded like Miss Sarah Brockman had been talking to the cops. Well, she was about to get another message tonight. Maybe it would teach her to keep her nose out of other people's business.

"When are you going to talk to him?" Heather whispered to Sarah at the back of the choir practice room, waiting for Ryan to arrive and start rehearsal.

Sarah leaned her head against the wall. "I don't know. But soon." She had to end this torture in at least one area of her life.

Ryan strode into the choir practice room, Christian recording artist Ethan Tate next to him. Ethan was touring in the area, doing a gig at the Honda Center arena, and had stopped in to sing with them this weekend as part of the patriotic concert they did each year the weekend before the Fourth. Everyone was looking forward to it.

"Running late as usual," Heather whispered to Sarah as they hurried to their sections.

As everyone turned around and noticed who walked in, the room started buzzing. Ryan and Ethan headed to the front of the room. Ryan motioned for everyone to quiet down. "Hey, everyone. Guess you know who this is."

A round of applause and hollering began. Ethan waved and smiled then stuck his hands in his pockets and looked to Ryan.

"We're doing two of his songs, and we've got a lot of work to do with all the extra songs we're doing this weekend, so let's get to it. Sarah, Heather, come on up." He turned to Ethan. "These two and I will sing backup for you."

"Great." He shook hands with them. "Hi, Heather. Hi, Sarah. Thanks for singing with me."

"It's going to be fun." Heather unclipped her mic from the stand.

"Our pleasure." Sarah smiled and grabbed her mic. Ethan seemed like a nice guy. She willed the nerves away. She did not want to mess this up.

After everyone had mics, Ryan signaled to the sound guy to start the track. They would rehearse with the band later tonight after they'd all done it separately.

The first time through the song went pretty well. Sarah shot Heather a nervous smile. At least they hadn't screwed up.

Ryan pulled Lou out of the choir to direct them so Ryan wouldn't have to juggle that with singing his own part. Then someone raised a hand with a question.

Ethan moved next to Sarah. "Great job. I hope I can keep up. I see you've got the home-court advantage here."

She laughed. She always admired people who knew how to put others at ease. "We've been looking forward to singing with you ever since Ryan announced it."

Ryan turned back to them. "Next song."

Maybe Ethan's kind words jinxed it because the whole thing fell apart. The choir's timing was off, and the altos didn't know their part even though last week they'd nailed it.

Ryan ran his hand through his hair and gave Ethan a small smile. "Let's try it again."

It wasn't much better. But Ethan didn't seem too concerned. "What's good to eat around here? Any favorite hole-in-the-wall places?"

She opened her mouth to respond when Ryan shot her a look with narrowed eyes and a furrowed brow.

"I'll get back to you. Ryan, why don't I go help the altos?"

"Thanks." He glanced at his watch. She knew what he was thinking. They needed to be up in the worship center soon to rehearse with the band. And they weren't ready.

She moved in front of the alto section and started them on their part a cappella. They got it.

Ryan cued the music, and they started again. It was still rough, but the altos came in stronger this time. Still not good enough for the weekend. He stepped back toward Ethan. "Sorry about this, man. They had it last week."

"I'm not worried. Sarah's doing a great job with them. They follow her lead real well."

Her cheeks heated.

Ryan nodded and moved back to the front.

They ran through the song one last time. It was better, but she knew it still was not where Ryan wanted it.

"Okay, everyone. Head up to the worship center." He started to join Sarah, but Lou grabbed his arm. Still, he kept his gaze on her.

She looked away. Tonight would not be a good night to end things with him. Already things were not going his way. He was being embarrassed in front of someone he wanted to impress.

Ethan stepped up next to her and grabbed the door. "Lead the way. Especially since I have no idea where we're going."

She laughed. It was almost as if Ethan knew she'd had a bad day and he was trying to make her feel better. He didn't, of course, but it was still helping.

Forty-five minutes later in the worship center, rehearsal was over. It had finally come together at the end. Sarah walked over to where Heather sat on the risers and joined her. Choir and band members were talking in small groups, some were filing out. Ethan and Ryan were talking. Both men glanced their way.

"I think they're talking about us." Heather nudged Sarah. "Ryan doesn't look happy."

"We sang great. Ethan said so."

"Yeah, I think that's the part Ryan doesn't like. Ethan. Talking to you."

Sarah rolled her eyes. "Whatever. He was just being nice."

"All right, well I'm in the mood for something sweet." Heather hoisted her purse on her shoulder. "Let's grab some coffee and dessert."

Ethan clapped Ryan on the shoulder and hopped off the stage. A couple of people stopped, wanting to talk to Ethan.

Ryan headed over to Sarah and Heather as they stood.

"Ryan can walk us out." Maybe that would mollify him. She smiled at him.

"Maybe Ethan can." Ryan shoved his hands in his pockets.

Sarah took a step, closing the space between them. "What's that supposed to mean?" She kept her tone even, but his remark was uncalled for.

"Just that your phone calls were pretty short today with me, but you're all smiles with Ethan tonight. You two seemed to hit it off well."

"Today was rough. I had to replace everything in my house from the vandalism. It was a little stressful."

Ryan frowned. "But you got through it okay, right? And now you have a fresh start."

"Yes." She suppressed a sigh; he didn't get it.

Heather moved over to the edge of the stage and started talking to someone else, obviously not wanting to be part of this—what? It wasn't a fight, but it confirmed Sarah's feeling that she needed to end this. Any other night and she'd use the frustration she was feeling to bolster her courage and say so. Instead, she shook her head. "As for Ethan, I was being nice. He's a nice guy, and I like his music. Big deal."

"Well, he certainly seems to like you. Asked about you, in fact. Until I told him you were my girlfriend. Or did I get that wrong?"

And there was the perfect opening. She glanced around.

No one was watching them. But people were around, and this needed to be in private. Her courage fell flat like a punctured tire. "Ryan, I'm sure he didn't mean anything by it. He's probably like this at every church he visits. He wants to be charming so they'll ask him back."

He stared at her, hard, for a long minute. "Ready to go?"

Heather had already moved off the stage. Sarah returned his gaze for a moment, refusing to feel like a scolded child. She picked up her purse and followed after Heather.

Ethan looked up from where he stood talking and waved at her and Heather. She smiled and waved. Glancing over her shoulder, she saw Ryan giving her an unreadable look before taking long strides to catch up with her and Heather.

Sarah swirled her coffee in the cup. It wasn't doing anything to loosen the tension in her shoulders. She glanced at Heather sipping a latte across from her. "I think we need some chocolate to go with this." Chocolate cured everything, didn't it? Too bad they weren't at Jitter Bug. They had the best desserts, including a chocolate raspberry cheesecake that was to die for. But considering Heather's last visit there nearly got her killed, it was scratched off the list.

Heather left her seat. "Mmm. I agree. I'll go see what they have."

She hadn't gotten two steps before Sarah's cell phone vibrated. Ryan. She debated answering it. What was she going to say? Ryan was blunt and up front with people. She generally respected it as long as he didn't cross the line and hurt someone's feelings. She'd never seen him do it intentionally, but he had hurt people with his forthrightness. Tonight though, it seemed like he was edging toward being mean on purpose.

It wouldn't hurt to hear what he had to say while she was waiting for Heather to get back with her chocolate fix. "Hello?"

"Hey, it's me. I'm sorry about tonight. I guess I was just tired and frustrated."

Yeah, she could see that. "Apology accepted." Heavy silence filled the air. She knew he wasn't happy with her response, but what did he expect?

"Thanks. Look, things have gotten a little sideways between us. You've had all that stuff going on with your condo. I'm trying to juggle the whole patriotic concert weekend. So I was thinking tomorrow we should head to the beach after work, grab a fire ring, roast hotdogs, make s'mores, and just hang out. How does that sound? The beach closes at ten, so we'll make it an early night."

She closed her eyes. Tension built in her chest. She forced herself to concentrate on the feel of her lungs inflating and deflating as the air moved in and out. She forced out of her mind the image of flames leaping around her. Nobody knew about her fear of fire. Or why. Her face still felt hot when she could find her voice. "Uh, it's just that I was planning on staying late the rest of the week to make up all the work I've missed dealing with the whole condo thing. With Mark leaving the office on Friday, I have a lot to do." There, her voice sounded nearly normal.

"The sun doesn't set until around eight, so we could leave by seven and still make it in plenty of time." He was using his persuasive voice. She should have known. "That would let you work a little later." He paused. "The whole staff is going to the Ethan Tate concert Friday, and then we've got this busy weekend. I really don't want to wait until next week to see you."

She could wait. But putting this off wasn't going to make it any better. Still, neither ending it with him over the phone or on a beach date was a good idea. It would be a stressful weekend, and she didn't want to add to it with awkwardness between them. Feeling like a complete coward, she said, "I'm sorry. I just can't. I'll see you this weekend. I've got to go." She punched the phone off before he could say another word. She dropped the phone on the table and put her head in her hands.

Heather slid into her seat with a big piece of something chocolate. She pushed the plate between them and set down two forks.

Sarah forked up a bite. Yum. Chocolate fudge cake. She concentrated on the texture and the flavors exploding in her mouth. Anything but the images Ryan's offer had conjured up.

"Ryan?" Heather asked around a mouthful of cake.

Sarah nodded.

"Did he apologize?"

"Was it that obvious he needed to?" Sarah took a sip of coffee. Nothing was better than the combination of gooey chocolate and hot coffee. She savored it, living in the moment. Not the past.

"Not to anyone else. Just me. He didn't seem too happy with how much Ethan was talking to you."

"He wasn't. But I think he was just stressed out. Still, he couldn't understand why I was so upset about my condo being vandalized."

Heather reached across the table and touched her hand. "You'll figure it out. Change of subject? Kyle and I are having a barbecue at his place on the Fourth of July. I'm going to invite our Bible study and a few people from choir. You can see several different fireworks shows from his patio. His friend, Scott, the navy pilot, will be there. And of course, Joe, if he's not working. You want to come?" Heather wiggled her eyebrows.

"Sure. What do you want me to bring?"

Heather grinned. "I haven't thought that far ahead yet." She reached down and pulled her phone out of her purse. "I was kind of hoping you'd help me plan it."

Chapter Fourteen

J OE HEARD THE CAR. HE peered out the window, waiting until the headlights weren't blinding him so he could identify it. Yep, it was Sarah's rental. It felt a little creepy waiting for her like that. But until they knew who had trashed her condo and why, he was keeping an eye on her. At least that's how he was justifying it to himself. Not that he really needed a reason to want to spend time with her.

He glanced at his phone. Should he call her? He grabbed the phone and dialed before he changed his mind. He did have something to offer he thought would help.

She sounded a little breathless when she picked up. "Hi, Joe. I just walked in the door."

"Choir practice, right?"

"Yeah, then coffee with Heather. And a little chocolate." Her smile came through the phone.

"I wanted to see if you'd like Shadow to spend the night."

The silence stretched out, and he was about to say something about it being a dumb idea when she spoke, her voice full of emotion. "That's really sweet of you. I think I'd like that."

"We're on our way." He hung up.

He grabbed Shadow's leash, the dog instantly alert. "Let's go see Sarah, boy."

Shadow pranced as Joe clipped on the leash, and they headed out the door.

Sarah was waiting and opened the screen door when she saw them. Shadow walked right in and laid down next to Sarah's feet.

She laughed. "Guess he feels at home here."

Joe unclipped Shadow's leash. "How are you doing with everything?"

"Okay. It's finally sinking in, I guess. We'll see how everything goes tonight, but I think I'll be fine. Especially with this guy here." Shadow licked her hand.

"I work tomorrow, so you can leave him at my place or keep him here if that makes you feel better."

"Are you off on the Fourth?"

Interesting change of subject. "Scheduled to be unless I get called in."

"Good. Heather and I just planned a barbecue at Kyle's place for the Fourth."

"I'll be there." He turned toward the door. "I'd better go and let you get to bed. "Let me know if you need anything. Even if you hear a weird noise or just can't sleep. I'm used to being woken up in the middle of the night. It won't bother me to come over. Otherwise, I'll see you in the morning for our walk."

"Thanks, Joe. I really appreciate it. You're a good friend." She stepped closer and wrapped her arms around him.

Stunned, it took him half a second to respond. But once his arms were around her, it felt right. For this moment at least, he was keeping her safe, protecting her. Too soon, she pulled back, and the sense of loss was immediate.

She tucked her hair behind her ear and dropped her gaze before meeting his again. "Thanks for everything."

"My pleasure, Sarah."

They said good night, and he headed back to his place. He was glad she trusted him, but he wanted to be more than her friend. Was there any chance of that? Tonight seemed like a step in the right direction. He was definitely looking forward to the Fourth. And not just for the fireworks display.

The lights of the fire engine flashed into the dark as they pulled up to a fully engulfed structure under construction. Joe glanced at Hardin whose head was leaned back and eyes were closed. The tones hadn't roused Hardin, and Joe had had a hard time getting him out of bed. Joe gave Hardin's shoulder a shove as he hopped off and assessed the situation.

"Akino, get a line on that hydrant. Hardin, mask up. We'll begin a primary search." Hopefully there wasn't a transient in the building, but they were often the cause of vacant building fires. This one didn't even have electrical to it yet. It didn't look like they'd be able to save it. No other structures were in the vicinity, but there was lumber and other building supplies. Plus, being a construction site and dark, there were any number of hazards.

What was taking Hardin so long? McCoy, their engineer, was already at the control panel. Akino was hooked up to the hydrant. Hardin was struggling with his SCBA. Joe hefted the tank the rest of the way onto Hardin's back. He clipped them both to lines, and they entered the building. They moved through the search pattern. Most of the area was wide open, the lights on their helmets barely piercing the smoke. They came to the end of a hallway. "You go left, I'll go right." Joe pointed.

Hardin nodded and moved off.

Joe searched the area, poking his light in the corners, yelling "Fire Department! Call out!" Nothing but black and smoke.

Battalion Chief Dan O'Grady's voice came through his mic. "You got about a minute. Fire's reached the roof."

Joe spun his light through the area one more time.

A high-pitched squeal sounded. A PASS alarm. Hardin was down somewhere.

O'Grady's voice came over the radio. "We need a RIC. Romero, report!"

Joe retraced his steps, running his gloved hand down his line, feeling the knots every twenty feet. Hardin's line couldn't be too far. "Hardin's last known location was the C/D corner. He can't be far from me. Heading there now."

Hardin's line appeared in the patch of light. Joe grabbed it and moved hand over hand as fast as he could. The firefighters on the rapid intervention crew would be right behind him. His light hit Hardin's helmet first, lying on the ground. Then Hardin on the ground behind it, blood oozing from a gash on his forehead.

Joe keyed his mic. "Hardin located! Unconscious, head injury, and no mask. Placing him on air and need assistance for packaging and extrication." He deactivated Hardin's PASS alarm and grabbed Hardin's mask. It didn't appear to be damaged. He put it back on Hardin and checked the seal. His SCBA system looked good. The RIC arrived and looped cords around Hardin's SCBA straps and legs, dragging him back the way they came.

As soon as they all were out the door, McCoy and Akino got water on the fire.

Hardin opened his eyes as the team got him over to the engine, where they set Hardin down.

Joe began his assessment. "Let me take a look at that gash on your head. What happened?"

Hardin shook his head, then stopped, wincing. "Don't know."

Joe requested transport over the radio then grabbed his medic cases and cleaned the wound.

"Just butterfly it." Hardin brushed his hand away. "I'll be fine. I don't need stitches."

"You're going to Saddleback Memorial. That's an order."

Hardin gave him a long stare, then slumped.

Joe watched him for a moment then moved over to O'Grady. Akino and McCoy had the fire pretty well knocked down. They'd have this out soon, barring any unforeseen complications. Overhaul wouldn't take too long. But arson would be here after the sun came up, he was sure.

"What's your read on Hardin?" O'Grady turned to him.

"Sluggish, slow to respond. And that was before he hit his head somehow. Which he doesn't remember. He's going to get checked out."

The lights from the engines flashed on a wooden sign announcing the project that was coming soon. Not so soon anymore. One of the names caught his eye: Rankin and Associates. Wasn't that who Sarah worked for?

The ambulance rolled up and loaded Hardin in while Joe gave the EMTs the rundown.

Thirty minutes later, the sky was lightening on the eastern horizon, and they were poking through the remains of the future office building searching for hotspots.

Joe let his mind wander. Cleaning up Sarah's place the other night had actually been fun. The four of them got along well, almost seemed like they belonged together. Except for the small problem of Ryan. He turned over a loose two-by-four and checked it. Ryan was an okay guy; he just didn't treat Sarah as well as Joe thought she should be treated. Sarah's life had been turned upside down, and Ryan didn't seem to think it was a big deal.

He tossed the wood back. It was Sarah's problem.

But Andrew Hardin was his problem. And he had a feeling he wasn't going to like the report from the docs.

Sarah trudged into her kitchen and grabbed a mug. She really wanted to go back to bed. It had taken awhile, but she'd finally drifted off to sleep last night out of exhaustion. But she'd spent two nights in her house, so that was something. Joe was on shift yesterday which meant he probably wouldn't be home before she left. If she missed her morning walk, who would know?

"You would mind, wouldn't you, Shadow?" He'd slept next to her bed, the new one that had been delivered. It had been a blessing to have him. She trusted his keen hearing to let her know of any danger. He truly was a shadow, following her as she put stuff away and replaced items over the last two days. Her cabinets now held only the essentials. It was one way to declutter, though a rather traumatic one.

She poured coffee and had just returned the cream to the fridge when her phone rang. Her heart skipped a beat. No good news came this early in the morning. She leaned across the counter and picked up the phone. Joe. She frowned. "Hello?"

"Sarah. I didn't wake you, did I? I wanted to catch you before you left for your walk."

His voice warmed her in a way that coffee didn't. "No, I'm up getting coffee. Debating with Shadow about our walk. What's up?"

"Your office is doing a project over on Via de los Flores, right?"

"Yes. One there, and we just started one on los Arboles. Why?"

"It burned down tonight, and it looks like arson."

Joe's words registered, but Sarah couldn't get anything to come out of her mouth. She shook her head before realizing he couldn't hear that. "Wow. I don't know what to say. Any idea who or why?" The image of flames consuming the building overwhelmed her, and she almost didn't hear what Joe said next.

"No. Arson will be investigating. They may come by and ask you some questions. Are you okay? I know it's kind of a shock."

"Yeah, it's just … I don't know." Greg Connor. Martha Rankin. Her house ransacked. And now this. One thing after another. It was too much to process.

"Call me if you need me. I'll be heading home shortly."

"Okay. Thanks, Joe, for letting me know."

"I figured you'd rather hear it from me. I'll call you if I learn anything more."

Sarah hung up the phone and stared at it, her hand shaking. The thought of one of her "babies" lying in a pile of ashes sent a chill up her spine. She always wondered how the architects and builders felt when they saw one of their buildings being demolished. This was the first time it'd happened to her. And by fire, no less. A cold and empty pit filled her stomach. All that hard work down the drain. It was just a building, but still …

She leaned against the counter and sipped her coffee. She'd made it through the night okay, thanks to Shadow. So that was one good thing. The cleaning crew had left everything spotless, and the only sign that anything had happened was the empty spot where her sofa used to be, some empty cupboards, and the rental car she was driving.

Still, she couldn't shake Joe's call. Why? The project could be rebuilt. There would be a delay, but it could be done. But it was the fire that disturbed her. Her old fear coming back to haunt her.

Taking a deep breath, she stared at her coffee cup. It wasn't at all appealing anymore. "Come on, boy. Let's go for our walk." She grabbed his leash before she could change her mind. A walk would help her burn off the anxiety flowing through her veins.

Shadow pranced excitedly. At least someone was happy this morning.

Joe was dozing on his couch, the TV providing mindless background noise, when his cell rang. He picked it up and saw O'Grady's name on the display. He punched it on.

"Just wanted to let you know that Hardin was released from Saddleback Memorial."

"How's he doing?" Joe sat up and his feet nearly landed on Shadow. He petted the dog and moved his feet to a different spot.

"Mild concussion. But the blood work came back positive for opioids."

Silence hung between them. Joe ran his hand over his face. "His back injury was months ago. He shouldn't still be taking them."

"He doesn't have a prescription for them. I'm heading over to his place later this afternoon to discuss this with him, get to the bottom of it. There are some serious ramifications here, for his health, his career. His actions put other men at risk, including you, and I won't have that in my fire station." O'Grady paused. "You want to come with me to talk to him?"

"I'll be there." Joe hung up and put the phone on the coffee table. Opioids. He scrolled through the last few weeks. A lot of Hardin's behavior made sense now. The irritability, the sluggishness. How had he missed it? And why hadn't Andrew come to him if he was struggling? Yeah, he knew all about male pride, but he hoped his leadership skills made their shift different.

Pushing himself off the couch, he headed to the kitchen to make a sandwich. But he couldn't shake the feeling that he'd failed Andrew somehow.

Chapter Fifteen

"Hi, Kyle. What's up?" Sarah kept her voice light as she answered her cell, but she couldn't control the pounding of her heart. Kyle wouldn't call unless he had news. She swiveled her desk chair so she could look out the office window, focusing on the green she could see.

"I have more information on Greg Connor. He may not be as 'disappeared' as we thought. The fire that burned down that building you designed? He might have been involved in that. Arson found a gas can from his construction company partially burned in the rubble. And gasoline was used as the accelerant. Plus, there were boot prints around the site that matched the ones in his truck."

Sarah was silent a moment, processing the information. "What does that mean?"

"Well, it makes us think he might have faked his disappearance so he wouldn't be a suspect. Though if he went to the trouble of disappearing so well, how come he left so many clues that obviously pointed to him? Which leads to the bigger question: Why would he want to burn that building down?

Or why would someone want to make it look like Greg did it? Have any ideas?"

"Did you talk to the owner to see if he'd worked with Greg on the project? Or maybe another project they had butted heads on?"

"He's next on my list. I just thought I'd talk to you first in case you knew something unofficial."

"Mark, my boss, might. He's been around the business longer than me and knows everybody. Today's his last full day in the office, but he's still going to be around occasionally, and I'm sure he'll be happy to talk with you."

"Sure. What's his number?"

Sarah gave it to him. "Thanks for keeping me in the loop. If I think of anything, I'll let you know." She set her phone on her desk and buried her face in her hands.

So was Greg alive? Was he behind the trashing of her condo and the fire at the building? There were pieces missing to this puzzle. Nothing made sense. Was she more in danger or less? Racking her brain for something to anchor her sanity to, Joe's face popped in her mind. She knew he'd do what he could to help.

She couldn't say the same about Ryan. She leaned back and sighed. She hated conflict, but she had to deal with him. It wasn't going to get better. But there was one thing she needed to do first.

Picking up her phone, she pulled up her Bible app. Thumbing to the Psalms, she started reading highlighted passages. "In peace I will lie down and sleep, for you alone LORD, make me dwell in safety." The one bit of stability she could cling to in a world that felt increasingly like it was spinning out of her control.

Joe watched the clock. Sarah should be home by now. Should he text her or just head over like he was walking Shadow? He wanted to check on her. And yeah, he wanted to know if she had plans to go out with Ryan tonight. And if not … Well, after he and Dan O'Grady had visited Andrew Rankin, he needed some positive distraction.

Andrew could choose to go into a rehab program for first responders. Or he could give up his career. He hadn't been too happy to see them, and when they left, he hadn't made a clear commitment to rehab either. Joe rubbed his hand over his face. Such a waste. And if he'd seen the signs earlier, maybe …

First things first. He clipped on Shadow's leash. "Come on, boy. Let's go visit Sarah." At her name, the dog's ears perked up. Did he know who Joe was talking about, or was he just excited about the walk?

Minutes later, they climbed the steps to Sarah's condo, and he knocked.

Smiling, Sarah pulled open the door. "Hey, guys! Come on in. I just got home."

Shadow pressed his way through the door and bumped Sarah's leg. She gave him the petting he wanted.

"Looks like he's making himself at home." Joe unclipped the leash and set it on the entryway table next to her oversized leather tote.

"He's good company after a day like today." She went into the kitchen and pulled out a jar of dog treats, Shadow right on her heels.

Joe laughed. "Ah, now I see why he likes coming here so much. You do bribe my dog."

Shadow waited patiently but intently while she set the treat on the floor. "Okay." At her signal, Shadow inhaled the treat. "Good boy." She moved into the living room and collapsed on her one chair. Then glanced up at him. "I'm sorry. I'm being rude, taking the only comfy chair."

She moved to stand, but he put his hand on her shoulder. "Stay. It's fine. I'll grab a kitchen chair." He gave her shoulder a squeeze then grabbed a chair from the kitchen and swung it around.

"The couch should be in next week. And hopefully my car will be ready by then too." She shook her head. "At least my life will look normal. I'm not sure it will be until we figure out what's going on." She leaned her head back and closed her eyes.

"Long day? Long week?" All he wanted to do was pull her into his arms and tell her everything was going to be fine. But he couldn't.

She nodded then opened her eyes, telling him about Kyle's update on Greg Connor. "An arson investigator called me at work today asking about the owner and the project, were there financial troubles or anything like that. Seemed pretty standard."

"That's where they usually look first. Most arson is done by the owner for financial reasons."

"I don't think that's what happened here. Unless I'm completely off base. It's always possible for people to have hidden lives, but this developer is well respected, and the project is well financed. He's going to rebuild and is anxious to do it. I don't see the motive there." She paused. "I really hope this isn't about me." Her voice was quieter.

He wished he could give her a hug, make things better for her and ease her mind. Instead, he reached for her hand. "That's what the arson guys are going to figure out."

She let out a long sigh but didn't move her hand away. "And today was Mark's last official day in the office. We gave him a going away party. Not only am I going to miss him, I have no idea how I'm going to fill his shoes at that company."

She was exhausted to her core; it settled on her like a heavy blanket.

"Did you sleep okay last night?"

"Surprisingly, not too bad. I think it's exhaustion after Heather's couch. And Shadow's presence. He really does live up to his name." Shadow pricked his ears in her direction, and she laughed.

He tapped the back of her hand. "Want to get something to eat?" He studied her face for her reaction.

She smiled and met his gaze. "Sure. That sounds good."

Yes. Another hour or so with her. And no date with Ryan tonight. Interesting. "How does Outback sound?"

She laughed. "Like a lot of food. But good. I'm hungry since I didn't get much of a lunch today. And the cake gave me a carb coma. Some protein sounds like a good idea." She stood and grabbed her bag. "You be a good boy, Shadow."

She really seemed to love his dog. And Shadow loved her. At least this was one thing Joe could do for her to make her life a little better.

They left her place, and Sarah locked up, then tugged on the door and tested it twice before walking down the steps toward Joe's condo.

He should have driven over, but then his dinner invitation would have seemed less spontaneous and more planned. And if she'd turned him down, it would have been dumb to drive back. Within minutes, Joe was helping Sarah into the truck, and fifteen minutes later they were walking into Outback. People lined the front porch area, waiting, and the inside wasn't any better. A couple of people glanced at them and smiled. He hadn't thought about that. Sarah's face was recognizable. He wasn't thrilled she was dating Ryan, but he didn't want to go out of his way to make trouble for her either.

"Ugh." Sarah walked through the door, oblivious to the looks she was getting. "Friday night. We're going to wait an hour for a table."

Joe shrugged. He wasn't sure how Sarah was going to take this. He walked up to the hostess podium. "Hi. Joe Romero."

She glanced at her sheet and grabbed two menus. "Right this way."

Sarah gave him an enigmatic smile before following the

hostess. Once in their seats she raised her eyebrows at him. "Call-ahead seating? That was advance planning."

He grinned and picked up a menu. "Be prepared, I always say."

"Were you a Boy Scout?"

"Nope. I just like their motto."

She laughed and looked at her menu.

He let out a sigh. She was amused, not upset by his planning. Good. Very good.

After the waitress brought their drinks and took their orders, Joe studied Sarah a moment, waiting until she finished stirring a stevia packet from her bag into her iced tea and looked up at him. Might as well jump into the deep end. "So. How is it you're not out with Ryan tonight?"

"He's at the Ethan Tate concert with the rest of the staff."

"I see." He picked up his own drink. "And since a few people saw you walk in here with me, are you going to be in trouble if word gets back to him?" He took a sip, watching her reaction over the rim.

Her eyes darted up and to the side, and she chewed her lip for a second before giving her head a quick shake and taking a drink.

"What?"

She looked up. "We just went on a couple of dates, and then Ryan made a big production out of it. I've been trying to call it off with him, but the timing hasn't been very good." She played with the corner of the menu.

The waitress came over and took their orders.

He studied her while she ordered, his heart pounding a little harder than it should be ordering dinner. Just because she wasn't interested in Ryan didn't necessarily mean she'd be interested in him. Unlike worship-leader Ryan, Joe had a past he wasn't proud of. And Sarah might not want to have anything to do with him once she found out. He gave the waitress his order and handed her the menu. But for now, he was going to enjoy the moment.

Sarah met his gaze. "Enough about me. What's been going on at work?"

He sighed and moved his glass around. "I've had some personnel challenges. One of my guys got addicted to opioids after hurting his back in a fall several months ago. When we responded to the fire that burned down your building, he was out of it. Then he fell and hit his head, and I had to pull him out. So now he has the option to choose a rehab program for first responders with addictions. But his future is uncertain." He shook his head. "I just wish I'd seen it earlier, or that he'd come to me. Something had been off with him for a while. He'd been irritable and not getting along with the rest of the team. As the captain, I should have seen it."

She touched his hand. "You can't know everything that's going on in everyone's life, especially if they don't tell you. Even if you'd confronted him about his behavior, he wouldn't have told you where it was coming from, and I'm sure you wouldn't have guessed opioids."

His hand was as warm and tingly as if he'd grabbed a hot doorknob. He didn't dare move lest she pull her hand away. "You're right. I did talk to him about his attitude. I assumed he was having some relationship troubles. Guys don't like to talk about that, and I figured it'd blow over in time. I still wish he'd come to me, though."

"If he was the type of person to share his problems with someone else, then he probably wouldn't have gotten addicted in the first place. He would have asked for help before it spiraled out of control."

He gave her a half smile. "Yeah. I don't think any of us firefighters are used to asking for help. We'd rather give it."

She smiled back. "And I, for one, am grateful. Though, I will admit it is hard to be the person receiving the help. Nobody wants to need help."

Joe wrapped his hand around Sarah's and rubbed his thumb over the back of it before she pulled away to make room for their dinners as the server returned with their plates. Joe asked the blessing, and they cut into their steaks, eating in silence for a moment.

"Since we've established firefighters like giving help, I'll do the emotional stretching and ask for help from you yet again." She grinned.

He grinned back. He liked this side of Sarah. Maybe she needed a little food in her to perk her up. And if he could help her in any way, he'd walk through a burning building to do it.

"Anything you need. I mean it." And he did.

She poked around her baked potato. "I've been thinking about this whole thing with Greg and the property, trying to figure out what we're missing here. The one thing that bothers me a bit is those artifacts."

She'd lost him. "What artifacts?"

"The ones you and Kyle found when you were kids. That's a pretty big deal in development. I can't figure out how that connects to burning down one of my buildings. But Greg seems to be involved in that and in the land where there might be artifacts. Somehow there's a link there we're missing."

She was like a dog with a bone, and he loved it. "We? I thought this was Kyle's case." He hoped she got the teasing tone in his voice.

"It is." She tilted her head to the side. "However, I can't resist a good puzzle. I think I'm going to do a little research on Orange County Native American artifacts. I might run across something that could help Kyle."

"Just be careful, okay?"

"I will."

"And let me know if you need any help."

She smiled.

This turned out to be a good day after all.

Tony's cell phone rang. A glance at the display told him it was Nick. Out of habit he scanned the area. His office door was open, but everyone had gone for the night. He answered the phone. "Did you follow them?"

"Yeah, they just went to dinner. They must be an item. I don't think there's anything to worry about. The evidence points heavily to Greg. The only one who even questions it at all is that cop."

"He won't find anything. This will all blow over soon, and we can get back to our plan. Keep an eye on her, and let me know if she needs any more persuading to mind her own business."

"Will do. The bugs are working fine, and she hasn't discovered the tracking program on her computer yet."

Tony pawed through his Jelly Belly bowl. No, he'd better not. He was going to eat dinner soon. "Good. I don't want to have to go to the next step. She's much too pretty."

Chapter Sixteen

J UST AS SARAH WAS GETTING ready to leave for church, she
heard the rumble of Ryan's Mustang and looked out her
front window. He crookedly parked in the spot in front of
her condo, hopped out, and ran up the steps.

What was he doing here? Sarah pulled open the door.

He grinned. "Want a ride? I brought you something. I got
up a half an hour early to be here, and I would have been mad
if I'd missed you. But I wanted it to be a surprise."

She smiled hesitantly. It was sweet of him to try to do
something nice for her. Though she hated surprises. And
she'd dragged this whole thing out long enough. But today
was the big service with Ethan Tate. She didn't want to upset
Ryan before that. *Excuses, excuses.* She shook her head slightly.
"What's the surprise?"

"You'll see. Are you ready to go?"

"Sure. Just let me grab my purse."

"Good." He turned and headed for the car.

She peered in her purse to make sure her Bible was there
and grabbed her travel mug filled with Lemon Zinger tea. Her

throat had been achy this morning. She locked the door behind her, double-checking it. Maybe this would work. She'd get to talk to him about their relationship on the way home. They'd be alone in the car with no one around and no distractions.

A minute later she climbed into the seat next to Ryan. She went to put her travel mug in his cup holder, but both were occupied by Starbucks cups. He handed her one. "Oh, thanks. Just let me …" She slipped her purse off her shoulder onto the floor between her feet, then pulled the seatbelt around and latched it. Travel mug in one hand, she took the warm Starbucks cup.

"Thanks. That was sweet of you." She took a sip then set it back in the cup holder. She worked not to grimace. It was strong with no cream. Nodding at the cup, she asked, "What drink did you get me?"

He backed out and headed for church. "I didn't know what to get you, so I just got you an Americano, black."

"Mmm." She nodded and tried to take a few more polite sips. Maybe she could dump it in the green room when he wasn't looking.

They pulled into the parking lot at church and were headed for the worship center when Ethan Tate walked up.

"Morning, guys."

Ryan slipped his arm around Sarah and pulled her closer. "Morning. Ready to sing?"

"Yep." Ethan's eyes cut to Sarah. "Hi, Sarah. How's the voice?"

"Not too bad." She slipped out from under Ryan's arm.

Ryan frowned. "What's wrong with your voice? You didn't mention anything to me."

"Just a little scratchy. Nothing to worry about."

Ethan nodded at her cups. "Coffee and tea? Covering the bases?"

"Yeah. Lemon Zinger for my throat, and Ryan brought me coffee. So I should be awake and in fine singing form." She smiled.

Ryan shot her a glare. Ethan opened the door to the worship center. Ryan headed for the sound guys, and Ethan walked with Sarah over to the risers where a few people were already gathered. People had seen her walk in with Ryan, and she caught a few knowing smiles. Inwardly, she groaned. This thing with Ryan had to end.

Ethan chatted up the people that gathered around him, talking about his performance the last two nights with humility and grace. He cracked a few self-deprecating jokes. He must have women all over him at every tour stop.

A few people stared past Sarah, over her shoulder. She turned. Ryan stood there with raised eyebrows. "Are we ready to start?"

"Sure." She moved into position. Ethan handed her her mic with a wink. Ryan cued the band.

Looking out over the worship center, a few people were beginning to trickle in. Then a familiar form strode in a side door. Dark hair, broad shoulders. Her heart flipped. Joe. She smiled and waved. He'd worked yesterday, so he must have come here straight from the fire station.

Ryan turned to see what she was looking at. When he turned back, he met her gaze with narrowed eyes and a scowl. Did anyone else see that? This was getting out of control if she couldn't even wave at a friend without Ryan getting annoyed at her. Though, if she was honest, Joe wasn't like her other friends. He was … she wasn't sure what he was. She finished up the sound check, being careful not to strain her throat, and Ryan dismissed them all to the green room to wait for the service to start.

"Sarah, stay a minute, please."

She nodded. She reached for Heather's arm as she walked by. "See that Starbucks cup over there next to my purse and travel mug? Can you dump it for me?"

Heather laughed. "If you tell me what's going on, sure." She waved at Joe and Kyle—who had found seats—and left the stage.

Sarah picked up her purse and travel mug and walked over to Ryan at the edge of the stage. She hoped he wouldn't notice she no longer had the Starbucks cup. "What is it?"

"I need you to be paying better attention to me when we're on stage. If people see you talking and not paying attention, then they think they can do that too. If everyone does it, we might as well give up and go home."

"Ryan, I wasn't—"

"I'm not going to argue with you while the worship center is filling up. Head on back to the green room with everyone else, please."

She didn't move for a long second but met his gaze. Then her eyes drifted off to the side. Joe and Kyle were watching the whole exchange. Yep, this whole thing needed to be over. Today. She turned and left.

But not before Joe's voice caught up with her. "Hey, Ryan? I don't think Sarah was being disrespectful to you. She was helping some of the altos with their parts."

Her knees weakened. Joe was defending her. He'd just gotten off shift and had to be tired, but here he was at church explaining her side of things. No one had ever done that for her. Blinking back tears, she hurried to the green room. She could only imagine what Ryan thought about Joe defending her. As she entered the green room, she sipped her still-hot Lemon Zinger tea, hoping to calm her emotions and keep her throat from clogging up. Her haywire emotions had to be from the residual stress bleeding off from the past week. *Lord, please, just get me through this service.*

A couple of the altos were gathered in the corner rehearsing. Cait turned and waved Sarah over. It was good to see her back at choir. "Sarah, do you remember our part for that second song of Ethan's we're doing?"

Everyone looked at her. Okay, this she could do.

"I still think we need to be up a third," Sharon said.

That was probably the problem. "Sharon, can you sing the melody? I'll sing the alto part."

Sharon started, and Sarah joined her, the other altos started trickling in until they got to the chorus and a few of them started getting lost. "Stop. That's the problem. Let's go over it."

She sang the harmony and then the altos joined in, going over it several times until everyone had it.

"Time to line up!"

"Everyone okay with that?" Sarah looked at each one, sipping the last of her tea.

They all nodded. "Good." She moved to get in line to go on.

They made it through the opening set of songs, and she was pleased with how well the altos did. The small core group knowing their parts carried through the whole section. Her voice was still doing okay. *Thank You, Lord.*

She collapsed in a chair in the green room. A warm hand landed on her shoulder. Turning her head, she spotted Ryan. "Hi."

"Hey, you." Ryan lowered his head closer to her ear. "Want to go to a movie this afternoon?"

Ryan had that little-boy grin on his face that would make him nearly irresistible to most women. But not her; not anymore. "Um, I probably should take a nap this afternoon." She was ending it on the way home.

"Good. Let's leave as soon as this service is over." He touched her shoulder and moved off, someone else grabbing his attention.

They had about ten minutes before the next service began. She stood and moved to one of the water coolers, refilling her travel mug with water. More tea would have been better. Now all she had to do was make it through the service. And the ride home.

An hour and a half later, Sarah picked up her purse from the chair in the green room and looked around. Ryan had a crowd around him as usual. She turned to find Heather and nearly ran into Ethan Tate. He caught her elbow to keep her from crashing into him.

"Sorry about that. Too much Lemon Zinger tea I guess."

He laughed. "No problem. Hey, I wanted to thank you for doing such a great job today."

"Oh. No problem. It was fun. And my voice didn't leave me yet." She glanced past Ethan to see if Ryan was done yet.

Someone was still talking to him, but he was looking at Sarah and frowning.

She wasn't in the mood to deal with his attitude again. She waved at Cait and Grayson as they left. Ethan said something that she missed, so she just smiled. Thankfully, Heather walked up. Ethan thanked her too and then said goodbye.

Heather tilted her head toward Ryan and raised her eyebrows.

Sarah let out a breath. "Pray for me. I'm ending it with him on the ride home." There. She'd said it out loud, and Heather would hound her until she did it. She glanced at her watch. "But he's still talking."

"Well go stand next to him, and maybe he'll get the hint."

Sarah stifled a yawn. "Yeah. I'll do that. See you tomorrow at Kyle's."

Heather waved and walked out of the green room.

Sarah made her way over to where Ryan was talking to Lou, Chris, and another guy whose name she couldn't remember.

He glanced at her, winked, and kept talking.

After a minute she sank down in a nearby chair. She was getting hungry, but she was so tired she didn't care. She just wanted a nap. Did any woman have the potential to be the most important person in Ryan's life? Or was it just her? As far as she could tell, the guys weren't talking about anything more important than some baseball game. If he could ignore her in the infatuated stage of first dating, what did that portend for the future?

She headed to the women's room. A cold, wet paper towel

on her neck might wake her up. It was probably a good thing Ryan had driven and trapped her here or she would have left. She checked her hair and reapplied her tinted lip balm. As she was putting it away, she noticed the power bar in her purse. If he took much longer, she could just eat that.

Coming out of the bathroom, Sarah scanned the green room. Empty. Maybe Ryan was outside. She stepped out and looked around. Still no Ryan. She glanced over the parking lot. No Mustang. She looked again, certain she'd missed it. Where had they parked this morning? Yeah, that was the spot, but it was empty.

A weird feeling washed over her, and she stumbled over to the concrete planter and sank down, pushing back the wave of irrational emotion engulfing her. There had to be a logical explanation. He wasn't abandoning her. Worst came to worse, he'd remember he was her ride and come back. But the little girl inside her wouldn't be appeased. Too many concrete benches. Too many times waiting for the car that never came.

She wrapped her arms around her middle and looked around, desperately trying to find something to distract her, to get her mind off the memories. People were still around, though the church was emptying. Heather had left with Kyle. But she would come back and give her a ride. Sarah reached for her purse and began digging inside while still looking around. Surely Ryan would come back. Though it would serve him right if she got a hold of Heather and left before he did. Then he could search for her. Petty? Oh yeah. And she didn't care. It was almost like he knew she was going to break up with him and left her here on purpose.

She dialed Heather's number and immediately got voice mail. Her chest tightened, and Sarah fought against it. *Not here.* She blinked back tears.

A group of kids streamed by, some sort of youth summer camp headed for the buses. Someone bumped her arm. She looked up into the hair-obscured eyes of a preteen but instead was transported back into the fifth grade and Kelly, the biggest, meanest girl in school.

"Thanks a lot, Kelly." She flipped her pencil over and started erasing the stray line.

"Doing your homework like a good little schoolgirl?"

Sarah didn't even look up. "Duh." Maybe Kelly would just go away. For whatever reason, she hated Sarah and picked on her relentlessly. Probably because she was the smallest person in class. There were third graders taller than Sarah. She looked around, pretending to search for her mom. No teachers in sight, though she could probably run to the office if she needed to. Kelly would beat her there, though. She had longer legs and was a fast runner.

"You gonna cry because your mom's late again?" She laughed.

Risking a glance, Sarah found Kelly staring at her. She stared back. If Kelly started something, Sarah was going to make sure she got suspended for it.

Kelly flipped up the edge of Sarah's notebook, but it didn't go anywhere. "See you tomorrow, schoolgirl." She sauntered off then tossed back over her shoulder, "If you're not still sitting here in the morning." Laughing, she ran to join a group of her friends.

Now she could get to her book. She picked it up but didn't open it to her bookmark yet. She'd count cars first. What would it be today? Ten? That should be enough. Mom would be here before the ten cars went by. This wasn't a busy street.

She counted twelve cars, just in case she'd gotten confused and lost count. When minutes passed without another car in sight, she opened her book. The smell of thin paper and ink carried her away, and she began reading about the blizzard that trapped Laura's family and the town of DeSmet.

The sounds faded away as the bus closed its doors and pulled away. A different cement bench than she had sat on after school so many days, but she was still waiting for someone who forgot her.

A familiar stride caught her eye. Joe. Without thinking she stood, unreasonable happiness and relief nearly started the tears again. *Get a grip.* What to tell him? She waved, trying not to seem too anxious, and he noticed her, veering in her direction.

"Hey, Sarah. You're still here." Dark circles rimmed his eyes. Had he had a busy shift last night? Had he gotten much sleep?

"Yeah. Have you seen Heather or Kyle? I was hoping I could get a ride home."

"They left about five minutes ago. Do you need a ride?"

"Yeah." She tried for a casual tone. "Ryan brought me this morning, but he seems to have gone somewhere, and I don't feel like waiting around." She swallowed a lump and hoped he didn't notice.

His gaze didn't waiver. "Let's go. I'll get you home."

Her relief was all out of proportion, but she couldn't help but feel like Joe had rescued her. She smiled at him. "Thanks."

Joe would have offered to take Sarah to lunch, but she looked so worn out on the ride home, her eyes closed as her head rested against the seat, that he thought she needed a nap more than anything. Luckily, he'd left his Bible under his seat and had gone back to get it. He was just coming out of the worship center when he saw Sarah sitting there, like some vision his imagination had conjured up. But the way she had folded in on herself and the almost-haunted expression she wore, made him wonder what was really going on with her.

Had she ended things with Ryan? That would explain Ryan's snarkiness this morning during sound check. But would he be that petty to leave her at church when he'd been her ride? Who knew?

As he pulled into the slot in front of her house, he

remembered what had happened last Sunday. "Hand me your keys. I'm going to check the house first, okay?"

She looked at him and blinked, opening her mouth then shutting it. Wordlessly, she handed over her keys.

He got out of the truck and strode up the steps to her door. He unlocked her door and stepped inside, doing a sweep of the house and the garage. Nothing looked out of place. Just in case, he'd bring Shadow over to keep an eye on her while she slept.

Back outside, he opened the truck door on her side. "Everything looks fine, but I'll bring Shadow over to keep you company so you can get some rest. You look like you're coming down with something."

She nodded, taking his hand as she crawled out of the truck. "My throat has been hurting all morning. Might just be all the stress of the past week. A nap should be just the thing." She let go of his hand and walked into her condo, moving more slowly than he'd ever seen her.

Something was definitely not right.

Chapter Seventeen

Sarah glanced at her ringing phone on the kitchen counter where she was making potato salad to take to Kyle's Fourth of July barbecue. Ryan again. That made—what—five times? She hit Silence with her knuckle, the only part of her hand that was clean. She was sure the voice mail would be the same too. Hearing it again wouldn't change anything. While she was glad he was apologetic—she'd listened to the voice mail he'd left yesterday about an hour after she'd gotten home—she didn't think it was right to end things with him over the phone. And she didn't want to see him.

Today was the Fourth, and she was going to spend it with friends and enjoy herself. She'd tried to nap yesterday and managed to sleep about twenty minutes. Hoping that a bit of research would allow her to rest, she spent some time in front of her computer using different search terms in Google, trying to find what was out there on OC artifacts. After a while, her eyes had glazed over as she clicked on the links. Nothing seemed to stick in her brain, and she was having trouble concentrating. She ended up just copying the info from the sites into a file.

She'd print them all out later and highlight them. The regional library might know more too, but she wasn't sure what she was even looking for.

When her head had started hurting again, she pushed away from her desk. With a hot cup of Lemon Zinger tea and Liz Tolsma's *Snow on the Tulips* she stretched out on the couch. She sipped as she read. Eventually, she dragged herself to bed.

And today she wasn't going to deal with it. Today she was putting work, trashed condos, burned-down buildings, and Ryan all out of her mind. Her throat wasn't hurting, and her headache was gone. She was going to spend the day with friends and enjoy the food and fireworks.

She packed the potato salad in a cooler with an ice pack. Shadow got up from where he'd been at her feet and headed for the door. A knock sounded. Shadow whined at the door. Must be Joe.

She unlocked the door and opened it. Joe stood there, a dark-blue T-shirt hugging his muscles in all the right places, sunglasses perched on his head. She was glad she'd thrown on a maxi dress and heeled sandals and taken some time with her hair and makeup.

"You look great. Are you feeling better?" He stepped through the door and tousled Shadow's ears.

"Yeah, I must have just needed the rest."

"Sarah?" The male voice came from behind Joe. Ryan.

Her heart pounded. This is what her procrastination got her. Awkward situations.

Joe narrowed his gaze at Ryan, who looked between her and Joe with a frown.

"You didn't answer any of my calls, so I came over in person." Ryan hovered in the doorway. "I wanted to make sure you were okay."

"Um, hi. Come on in." Because being polite was important no matter how awkward the situation. What would Emily

Post recommend in this situation? Probably to never let this situation develop.

Joe grabbed Shadow's leash. "I'm going to take him for a walk around the complex. I'll be back in a few minutes, and we can head over to Kyle's." He raised his eyebrows at Sarah, and she nodded. He shot Ryan an unreadable look as he headed out the door.

Ryan glanced over his shoulder at a retreating Joe. "What's going on? You're not answering my calls, so I think you're sick. And then I find Joe here and you're headed out somewhere."

She gave him a tight smile. "Look—"

"Is this about Sunday? I'm sorry. I've said it about a million times now to your voice mail and in texts. I'm not used to taking anyone home, and I just completely forgot."

"I understand. It was no big deal." It was, but it wasn't why she was breaking up with him, and she didn't want to get off on that rabbit trail when it wouldn't even matter. "I just don't think this is working out. We're too different."

Ryan shoved his hands in his pockets, jangling his keys. "It's not like you to be so moody. That's why I don't like to date singers or musicians. But you seemed different, above all that. That's why I asked you out." He gave her his movie-star grin. "You intrigued me."

She twisted her fingers together and took a step back.

"Ryan—"

"Sarah, you're just mad because of Sunday. I apologized for that, okay? Frankly, I'm a little disappointed with you. I thought you were more mature than this. I didn't think you were the type of girl to pull this, if-I-don't-like-everything-you-do-I'm-breaking-up-with-you thing."

Okay. She expected him to be upset. She didn't expect him to be mean.

"You don't want to discuss anything, you dodge my calls. You just want to be right. That's sin, Sarah. You need to make the effort to make this right with me. We need to talk and if you don't want to do it now, then tell me when." He glanced out the front door. "Some time when you don't have other plans." He practically spit the last word.

This was exactly why she'd been putting off talking to him. She knew he'd try to talk her out of it. "It doesn't have to be any big deal, Ryan. It just didn't work out between us. You're the limelight guy, and I'd rather stay home and read a book. Not everyone is a good fit. That's what dating is supposed to help you figure out." If he didn't walk away from the conversation feeling like he was the winner, then the consequences weren't going to be pretty. Sadness enveloped her soul. Relationships were hard work. But they shouldn't be filled with dread and stress. Not when she had a choice. She could do this. *For the Spirit God gave us does not make us timid, but gives us power, love and self-discipline.*

"So you waited until after I announced it to the whole choir that we were together to decide that we weren't a good fit."

"I'm sorry. I didn't know you were going to do that. And I did enjoy being with you. I just don't see it working out long term." She swallowed and hoped he didn't continue to argue with her.

He met her gaze, and she didn't look away. Something tight and broken flickered in his eyes.

His vulnerability triggered her sympathy. He wasn't a bad guy; he just wasn't the right guy for her. Joe's face flashed through her mind, and she pushed it away. One problem at a time. An overwhelming sense of rightness came over her, something that was outside of herself. She almost felt lighthearted, and for once, confident she could stand her ground.

"Are you sure?" He reached for her.

She flinched back a step instinctively.

Confusion, hurt, and something else filled his eyes. He gave her a hard look and spun, slamming the screen door on his way out. A moment later the Mustang roared and squealed out of the parking lot.

She squeezed her shaking hands together. Well, for better or worse, that was over. Now she could wait and see what the fallout would be. She couldn't control that, but she could rest in the confidence that she had done the right thing. Finally.

The jingle of Shadow's collar pulled her gaze out the screen door. Joe and Shadow came up the steps. She mentally switched gears. Joe. The barbecue. Her friends. She wouldn't have to think about Ryan.

His soft brown gaze sought hers. "You okay?"

She nodded. "Yeah. Glad that's over with."

He reached for her and rubbed her arm.

She was acutely aware of the fact that she leaned into his touch instead of jumping away from it.

Joe glanced over at Sarah as they rode in his truck over to Kyle's. She hadn't volunteered any more info, but Joe and Shadow had lingered around the corner of her condo, just out of sight but able to hear most of the conversation. He wasn't proud of eavesdropping, but he was concerned about Sarah and not thrilled to leave her alone with Ryan. He wanted to be in earshot if she needed him.

His first instinct had been to tell Ryan to step off. But then he realized that Sarah needed to do this. For her own sake, she needed to end things with Ryan or make things up with him and continue that relationship. As much as he loved helping, some things she needed to do for herself. So she could realize how strong she really was.

Joe's heart was already too far involved, beyond what was wise. And if she'd chosen Ryan, then he would have had to walk away. If she couldn't make up her mind about what she wanted, she wasn't ready for a relationship, at least not one with him. He'd played enough of those games and had the scars on his heart to prove it.

But the farther they got from her house, the more the tension seemed to slide off her shoulders.

She let out a big sigh. "I guess you weren't planning on all of that today. Sorry I made us late."

"It's a barbecue. Nobody's late. I'm glad I could be there for you. Are you okay with how everything ended up?" He had to be sure.

"Yeah. It's my own fault, really. I hate conflict, and I kept putting off talking to Ryan. If I had been strong enough, I would have said no to begin with. I let him steamroll over me. Anyhow—" she shook her head "—maybe I'll get better at this conflict thing. I survived." She smiled. "And now that Mark has me in charge of the office, I have a feeling I'll have to learn to navigate conflict a lot better than just avoiding it."

But she'd done it. And he was proud of her, not only because it left him free to pursue her, but because he knew how it felt to do something hard, something you're scared of, and come out the other side.

"Nobody likes conflict. But I've taken enough leadership and management courses that I'd be happy to be your sounding board whenever you need it."

She turned her full smile on him, and his heart tumbled like it fell off a three-story ladder. She had no idea. This might be the best Fourth ever.

The little niggle in his mind that when she met Scott she might be enamored of him dissipated. If she could resist the charms of someone like Ryan who went out of his way to be charming, she'd not fall for Scott who didn't go out of his way to attract either Joe's or Kyle's girls. Not that it hadn't stopped previous girlfriends from throwing themselves at him. But that was a story best left in the past and not dwelled on today.

He pulled in Kyle's driveway and saw that Scott's classic Corvette was already in the driveway. Based on the other cars parked along the curb, they were probably the last to arrive.

He helped Sarah out of the truck, holding her hand longer than necessary, but she didn't pull away.

The door was open, and they walked on in. Voices came from the kitchen, but from the entryway he could see through to the back patio where Kyle was messing around with the barbecue.

He handed Sarah the cooler of potato salad. "I'm going to rescue the grill before Kyle blows us all up."

She laughed and moved through the tiled entry toward the kitchen. He slid open the patio door then turned to look at her. She seemed lighter. As she gave Heather a hug, she looked over at him and smiled.

He winked at her then headed out to the patio.

"What was that all about?" Scott appeared from behind Kyle and grabbed his hand, wrapping him in a bear hug.

"Good to see you, man." Joe slapped Scott's back. He looked good, tired but good.

Scott tilted his head toward the kitchen. "Who's that?"

Joe stilled, trying to see if there was anything behind Scott's question. But he saw no interest in Scott's eyes, just simple curiosity. "That's Sarah. She's a friend of Heather's."

Scott raised his eyebrows. "And?"

Joe shrugged.

Scott slapped him on the shoulder and grinned.

Sarah stood in the kitchen with Heather and Melissa Ellis. They were pretending to put the finishing touches on the food, but mostly they were sneaking peeks out to the patio where the guys were grilling. They couldn't hear what they were saying, but laughter and the relaxed body language gave proof to the fact that the three of them were long-time friends.

"So that's Scott? The navy pilot?" Melissa leaned over the counter. "He come up often?"

Heather nudged her. "Not often enough. But he's not too far away. He's in China Lake. They're like the three musketeers. They've been friends since the fourth grade."

"We have one of our field offices down there." She turned to Sarah. "I work for a defense contractor."

Heather huffed. "That's an understatement. She practically runs the place."

Melissa shook her head and went back to stirring the dip.

Heather turned to Sarah. "How's your throat? And did you ever hear from Ryan?"

Sarah looked around. "Anyone else coming to this shindig? I thought we were going to be the last ones, being so late."

Heather smiled. "I see what you're doing. And I'm not going to let you get away with it. Everyone else had other plans, but Cait and Grayson are supposed to stop by for a bit. And Kim decided she'd rather do something with her friends than hang out here with her brother. Imagine that."

Sarah laughed. "Kyle and Kim actually have a pretty good relationship considering they live in the same house."

"As long as Kyle doesn't find out how much his little sister spends on clothes, they get along just fine." Heather wiped her hands on a towel. "Now spill. You've stalled long enough."

"My throat's fine, thanks." Sarah scanned the kitchen, wanting to keep her hands busy. She weighed how much more she should say. She didn't know Melissa that well. "Ryan came by after I hadn't returned any of his calls or texts."

Heather raised her eyebrows.

"While Joe was there."

"That must have been interesting." Melissa looked up from stirring the dip. "And I don't even know what's really going on."

Sarah gave her a quick recap. "So I ended it with Ryan. Finally. Choir practice should be interesting after this."

Heather gave her a quick hug around the shoulders. "You did the right thing. I'm proud of you. And however Ryan chooses to respond is up to him." She glanced out toward the patio where the three guys were deep in conversation. "How did Joe take it?"

"I thought he was going to punch Ryan, but instead he left us to talk. He's been such a good friend through all this craziness."

"Friend?" Melissa raised her eyebrows. "Honey, he's got a lot more than 'friend' on his mind, even I can see that."

Sarah's cheeks heated. "He is always finding a way to rescue me out of various predicaments. But he's got such a dangerous job. How do you do it, Heather?"

"I keep busy, don't think about it. And when I do, I remember how many people he's helping. People who need him. He's got lots of training, and he's good at what he does. And ultimately, God knows the number of Kyle's days. Or any of ours, for that matter. My fretting won't change that."

God's in control. She had to keep reminding herself of that.

"So, you didn't bring Shadow?" Heather set out paper plates while Melissa grabbed plastic utensils and napkins.

"No, Joe took him on a quick walk before we left. He's probably snoozing on my bed. Where he's not supposed to be." She'd seen the dog hair on her comforter, but he always looked so innocent.

"What did I do?"

Sarah spun around at Joe's voice behind her. Her cheeks heated again. What on earth did she have to be blushing about? At this rate, she was going to look sunburned. "I didn't hear you come in." She turned back and concentrated on sticking a chip in the dip. What had he heard?

"That's because I'm stealthy."

"They teach you that at the fire academy?" Kyle walked in and wrapped his arms around Heather's waist, giving her a kiss on the cheek before heading for the refrigerator. "Because it seems like there's a great need for stealthy firefighters."

"Hey, you never know." Joe reached around Sarah for a chip, his arm brushing hers.

She hoped he didn't see the tingles run up her arm. What was with her?

Scott leaned in through the patio door. "The grill's ready."

"Joe, should we do the manly thing and go play with fire and try to cook some meat?" Kyle handed him a platter of burgers.

"Of course. Toss me one of those Dr. Peppers while you're in there. Grab one for Scott too."

Kyle grabbed the sodas. "Medium okay for everyone?"

"Can you make one well done for me?" Melissa asked.

"Sure. One blacked hamburger coming up. I'll let Joe make yours. He's good with burning things."

The guys moved outside while Heather shook her head. "The three of them together are a sight to behold."

Sarah wrapped the camaraderie around her like a blanket. Just watching these life-long friends interact was almost as good as being part of it. Could she ever be part of something like that? Someone she could trust to stick with her no matter what?

Joe must have caught her staring at them, because he grinned at her through the patio door. Yeah, maybe she could.

"So what's going on there? By the way you're drooling, I'd say she was more than just Heather's friend."

Joe turned from staring through the patio door at Scott's question.

"Sarah?" He wasn't sure how to answer that. "She's had some trouble lately, and I'm trying to help."

"Yeah, we know how you help. I think I still have a scar from the last time you 'helped' me out of that tree." Scott pushed up his sleeve and pointed to a faint scar. He turned to Kyle. "Have you warned her?"

Kyle laid the burgers on the grill. "Actually, Joe's the least of her problems right now." He gave Scott a quick rundown.

"Did arson send you over a copy of their report on that building of hers that burned down?" Joe popped the tab on his Dr. Pepper.

"So far it looks like it's not my jurisdiction, and I'm not getting anywhere with the city planning department. Yeah, it could be a motive for Greg Connor's disappearance. Or is his disappearance a way to throw the trail off his arson?"

It wasn't the reassurance he was hoping for. "She likes working out puzzles. And that's what she thinks this is. I'm worried about her going off on her own. I don't think she has any kind of clue what danger she's in. The thing at her condo shook her for a bit, but if it's still bothering her, I can't tell." He took another sip. "Any way you can use your police persuasion to keep her out of the investigation?"

Scott smirked. "Just friends, huh?"

It didn't take Scott long to get up to speed without Joe having to give him all the details. That's what happened when you'd been friends for most of your lives.

Kyle poked at the meat then closed the lid. "I'll admit, she's been helpful. She knows the industry better than I do." He started to say something else, then shook his head slightly. "I'll make sure Sarah knows she's not to be going off on her own."

"Thanks." He was grateful Kyle would talk to Sarah, but also that he didn't harass Joe. He didn't realize his feelings for her were so transparent. Then again, these were the guys he let his guard down around. With them, he didn't have to be the best or achieve anything. He could simply be himself. "I'm calling the arson investigator tomorrow and see if I can't get some better answers."

Scott raised his eyebrows. "Gonna poke a hornet's nest at your own place of work?"

"If I have to. I hope it doesn't come to that." He sighed. "I wish I could just get her out of here until this whole thing blows over. I've got a lot of time off coming." He thought briefly of

DiMarco's offer of his cabin. Not that, but maybe just a place to get away and lay low. "What?"

Scott and Kyle both stared at him.

"Well, she'd never go for it. Her boss, Mark, has left her in charge of the company now, and she'd never leave him in the lurch."

Kyle lifted the grill lid. "You're doing a lot of advance planning for a woman who—last I knew—was dating the worship leader. You might have more than one hornet's nest on your hands."

"What? Dude." Scott crossed his arms. "I need the whole story. Not just the highlight reel."

"Ryan's done. He left her at church Sunday when he was supposed to be her ride home. Then he showed up at her place today before we left. She ended things with him."

"Sounds like a quality guy." Scott downed the rest of his soda.

Kyle slid the burgers on to a tray. "I know what it's like to risk it all to protect a woman you love." He met Joe's gaze. "Just make sure you know what the stakes are before you go all in." He opened the patio door and stepped through, Scott following him.

Joe stared out over the valley visible from Kyle's patio. Was he doing all of this just to be the rescuer he always was? Or was his heart already fully engulfed? He turned and looked inside, watching Sarah through the glass.

Yeah, he was a goner.

The doorbell rang, and Sarah slid off the barstool she'd been perched on.

"Sarah, can you get that?" Heather asked, almost like it was her house. It probably would be in just a matter of time, whenever Kyle decided to pop the question. Plus, Heather had painted every room of this house when she was under Kyle's protection.

Sarah opened the door to Cait and Grayson. She gave Cait a hug. "You feeling okay?"

"Almost back to normal. Just a few headaches, but nothing too major." Cait held up a bag of food. "Where do you want this?"

Sarah pointed to the kitchen. "Heather's got everything laid out in there. Burgers are being cooked even as we speak."

Grayson put a hand on Sarah's arm. "Any word on the missing contractor? And I heard about your building burning. A lot is happening in that corner of Orange County."

"No word yet. But have you ever heard of Native American artifacts showing up on any of your projects? Or any odd environmental impacts?"

He shook his head. "No, but if DiMarco is involved, you can bet something shady is going on. Nobody can ever pin anything on him, but I pulled out of working with him on a project earlier this year that skirted too close to the line. But if there are artifacts involved in that area, well with the future of that corridor, I could see why an unscrupulous developer would just plow them under. Too much money is at stake to have a project halted."

"That's what I was thinking too. But I still don't see what that has to do with Greg, my trashed house, or burning down one of my buildings."

Grayson frowned. "Maybe consider taking a vacation until this all blows over. You don't know what could happen next."

Footsteps sounded behind her that she instinctively knew were Joe's. "Talking shop. I should have known." He shook Grayson's hand. "Joe Romero. I don't think we've formally met."

"I've been wanting to meet you to thank you for rescuing Cait. You made a positive impact on a lousy situation. I really appreciate it."

"Happy I could help. Any of the guys would have done it. I'm just glad she's okay." He shifted his weight, seemingly uncomfortable with the praise, and slipped his arm over Sarah's shoulders. "Burgers are ready. Hungry?"

She nodded and followed him to the kitchen. While she made her burger and filled her plate, Heather's words played through her mind regarding Kyle helping people. Joe did too. If he hadn't been there for Cait, what would have happened? Could Sarah let go of her grip just enough to trust that God had a good plan even if she couldn't see it? Joe was an amazing guy. He'd already proven over and over that he could protect her and be there for her. Could she trust him with her heart? Even with his dangerous job? Dealing every day with the thing she feared most? Or was it like the mirage that shimmered off the pavement on a hot day, always just out of reach?

Everyone grabbed whatever seat they could find. She slid into the far seat of the dining room table, Joe next to her. Cait and Grayson at the opposite end. After a few moments, all was silent as everyone was busy eating. The food was delicious. There was just something about barbecued hamburgers. And her potato salad had turned out really well.

But it wasn't quiet for long as Kyle, Joe, and Scott joked and told stories.

"I'm just happy we've lived long enough to tell some of these tales." Scott tipped back in his chair, bracing his knees against the table top to hold himself in place. "Remember that time we put out that fire in the orange grove? I think that's when you decided to become a firefighter." He pointed at Joe.

"Okay, I've got to hear this." Heather leaned forward. "I can't ever get these two to tell me anything."

Joe nudged Sarah, his voice brushing her ear and sending shivers cascading across her body. "I wanted to be a firefighter long before this. Don't believe everything this guy says."

Kyle draped his arm around Heather's shoulders. "If I remember correctly, Scott, you started that rotten orange fight when we were walking home from school. The smell of hot, fermented oranges is imprinted in my brain forever. I don't even like orange juice anymore."

Scott tossed his napkin at him. "But Joe spotted the smoke and said we should go check it out. We ran to the edge of the grove, and the field next to it—full of brush—was burning. So we all ran to Joe's house, which was the closest. He yelled at his mom to call 911 and then darted to the garage, handing us shovels.

"We were like, what are we doing? You want us to put this thing out? His mom was yelling in Spanish for us to stay put. But Joe insisted that we had to do this because the fire department might not make it in time and there were houses right next to that field."

Sarah looked up at Joe. His cheeks were a little redder than usual. "Hey, I watched a lot of *Emergency* after school. Johnny and Roy would have done the same thing." He eased back, sliding his arm along the back of her chair. She leaned into it.

Scott let his chair thump back to the floor. "They were paramedics. Anyhow, Joe had us dig a perimeter, throwing dirt on the fire. We were covered in dirt and soot and sweat when the real firefighters showed up. They put the thing out pretty quick. They had a few words of warning for us, thinking we started the fire at first. But once one of the neighbors came out and said they saw someone toss a cigarette out a car window just before everything went up, we were off the hook. We got a tour of the engine and all. It was a lot of excitement for three eleven-year-old boys."

Kyle started in on another story, this one about them seeing a guy stealing a car and calling the cops. But Sarah studied Joe. He was relaxed, joking around. How would it feel to have such long-term friends? Comfortable? Safe? She didn't make friends easily; Heather was her closest one. She had acquaintances, and being an only child with distant parents didn't give her anyone to get close to. But something like this? She could get used to it. If they would let her in.

Melissa piped up. "So, stories about Kyle and Joe, but what about you, Scott? Just an innocent bystander in all of these adventures?"

He winked at her. "Classified."

She gave him a saucy smirk. "I bet my security clearance is higher than yours."

"Touché!" Kyle stood and took his plate to the kitchen.

Heather followed him and began putting the food away. Sarah joined her. The guys pulled out beach chairs and set them on the back patio. There was an easy comfort in everyone working together. It was similar to what she felt when it had just been Heather, Kyle, Joe, and her, but magnified. Was she attracted to Joe for who he was or for the sense of belonging he brought her?

Finished with the food, she stepped out on the patio. The ocean breeze had come up and the sun was going down. A beautiful summer twilight, palm trees silhouetted against the flaming sky. She would need to get her jacket soon; she was feeling a chill.

"Deep thoughts?"

She nearly jumped. Joe had come up behind her again without her knowing. "You've got to be serious about those stealthy firefighter classes. That's the second time today you've done that."

He grinned. "I think you're just not paying attention."

"I'll give you that."

"Cait put out the dessert she brought. I hate to break it to you, but you'll have to make a crucial decision."

She raised her eyebrows at him. "Really?"

"Yes. Whether or not to have ice cream with your brownies."

She laughed. "Ah, I can see how that would be crucial. But a brownie with vanilla ice cream is approaching perfection."

"Ah, perfection. Okay, well I will strive to deliver perfection if you'll grab us a couple of seats. But I have one more important question for you." His face turned serious.

What was he going to ask her? With Ryan out of the picture—?

"Coffee?"

It took a moment. "Oh. Yes, coffee sounds great." There she went, letting her imagination run off with her.

"Go sit down then and save me a good seat."

"It's the least I can do." Sarah moved over to a couple of chairs, sliding them a bit closer together with her foot.

A minute later, Joe came out balancing a plate and two coffee cups, her jacket draped over his arm. "You take cream in yours, right?"

"How did you know?"

"Comes with the stealthy thing." He handed her a cup.

She gave him a look.

"Okay, I confess. I'd noticed your coffee was light, but I didn't know if you put sugar in it. So I asked Heather."

"Smart."

"Occasionally." He held out her jacket. "It's getting cool. I thought you'd want this."

And a mind reader too. She slipped on her jacket then took the cup and plate he handed her.

Sarah sipped her coffee, mixed exactly right, to hide her smile. Joe was sweet. And way too handsome for her own good. She suppressed a sigh. Was Joe interested in her or just being nice?

The patio filled as everyone filtered out and found their seats. The fireworks started. Four different shows could be seen—in varying degrees—from Kyle's patio. Metallic flowers blooming and fading in succession, varying shapes, sizes, and colors.

Joe rested his arm on the chair arm. And since she had pushed them together, their arms touched, making more fireworks than just up in the sky.

The slight breeze kept the smoke cleared. It made for a great evening, but Sarah could barely keep her teeth from chattering, her coffee long gone.

"You cold?" Joe asked.

She nodded.

"It's not that cold out here. I hope you're not coming down with something." He rubbed her arm.

"Me too." The sky filled with a final barrage of fireworks before falling silent, the smoky air tinged pale orange from the light pollution of street lights.

As much as she was enjoying herself, if she was coming down with something beyond a sore throat, a good night's sleep would go a long way to curing it.

Cait and Grayson said their goodbyes and left, fatigue etched in Cait's face.

"We should head home too. You're not feeling well, and Shadow's going to want to be let out." Joe gathered up their cups and plates then stood.

"I should help Heather clean up."

"I got it." Melissa shooed her through the patio door. "You get home."

They said their goodbyes. Scott gave Joe a bro hug then reached for Sarah. "He'll take good care of you," he said softly in her ear.

She smiled. What had they been talking about on the patio?

Once they pulled up to her condo, Joe took her keys. "How about I take Shadow for a quick walk around while you get settled?"

Relief washed through her. "That would be amazing. Thanks."

He opened her door and scanned the area for a minute before stepping aside to let her in. Shadow bounded up to both of them, barely stilling enough for Joe to get the leash on him. "We'll be right back."

The door closed behind them, and she moved to the

kitchen, rinsing out the potato salad bowl and loading it in the dishwasher. She thought of making some tea but decided to pop a few ibuprofen instead.

Though her sore throat was back and she felt chilled, she couldn't remember the last time she'd had such a great night. The easy friendship, the laughter, the history they all had. And they included her, as well as Cait and Grayson. It almost seemed too good to be true.

She peeked out the front window. And Joe. So kind and thoughtful, even when Ryan was in the picture. Was it a risk worth taking? If things went sideways, there was a lot to lose. And yet, going back to an isolated life of only work and church didn't seem that appealing.

Joe and Shadow came up the walk, and she opened the door. Shadow trotted in. Joe unclipped the leash and set it on the entryway table. He held her gaze for a long moment then reached his hand up and stroked her cheek.

She leaned into his touch and closed her eyes for a moment, opening them to see his liquid gaze still on hers before flicking to her lips and back up again. She shifted her weight forward.

Shadow whined and bumped her leg hard. The spell broke. He bumped her again. Oh. "He wants a treat."

Joe laughed, dropping his hand but skimming it along her arm, leaving a trail of fire in his wake. "I'll let you spoil my dog." He squeezed her hand. "I'm on shift tomorrow, but I'll check on you when I have a chance. Sleep tight." He winked at her, turned, and left.

She locked the door behind him. She wished she knew what he was thinking. Heck, she wished she knew what *she* was thinking.

Chapter Eighteen

SARAH SHOOK ANOTHER COUPLE OF ibuprofen out of the bottle she had stashed in her desk. Popping them in her mouth, she washed them down with her lukewarm tea. Yuck. She'd been trying to do busy work, as much mindless stuff as she could considering she couldn't think straight. Between her headache and the way her thoughts were swirling, she probably wouldn't be too productive today. Plus, the smart people in her office had taken the day after the holiday off, so it was unusually quiet.

She headed to the break room. She needed coffee, not lukewarm tea. As she waited for the cup to fill, an image popped into her mind. Joe bringing her coffee, doctored just right. The intent way he studied her when he handed her the cup. The tingles she felt when his fingers brushed hers. Last night felt an awful lot like a date.

Something had definitely shifted between them last night. But he had texted her minutes after her alarm had gone off, wanting to know how she was feeling and if she'd mind putting Shadow in his condo. She had taken Shadow over there and left

Joe a key to her place as well. It was only right, she rationalized, since she had a key to his place.

Focus. She needed to get something done. At the very least, she could send Kyle what little information she'd found on Native American artifacts in Orange County. Though that really looked like a bust. But you never knew. She looked at the results on Google that had turned up and started clicking through them. Maybe she'd make some headway on this artifact thing.

After about an hour, Sarah read over the email one more time before hitting Send. She'd sent Kyle all the information she'd come up with on the artifacts, summarizing her findings and her thoughts in the body of the email. Was she over reacting? Everything she had come up with could all be nothing. She almost felt silly. She hadn't received any more threats or anything that made her think she was still a target. But it was the off chance that something might be important that pushed her to send it. And Kyle wouldn't make her feel like an idiot. Which was a plus.

Satisfied that she had done the right thing, Sarah opened AutoCad. She had the site plan and specs for a new project they had just landed. She was excited about it because the owner wanted something different, and she could use her creativity. And this was the first project she'd run completely on her own without Mark there to back her up. She already had a few ideas of what she wanted to do. Now she just needed to flesh them out enough to show the owner so they could further refine what they wanted. She was definitely feeling better; she was more excited about a project than she had been in a long time.

Since she'd started designing the one that burned down.

"Joe? A word." O'Grady motioned Joe to his office as Joe walked across the apparatus floor, returning from a medical call.

Joe snagged a bottle of water from the fridge before

entering the battalion chief's office and grabbing a seat. "What's up?" He unscrewed the lid and took a long drink.

O'Grady leaned his folded hands on his desk. "I got a call from arson. Seems you've been poking your nose into one of their investigations regarding a commercial building under construction that burned down. Sound familiar?"

Joe nodded. "Yeah, it's connected to a case LVPD is working on regarding that missing contractor. I was facilitating cross-department relations." He gave a small smile.

O'Grady didn't return it. "They don't need your help. This was a firm request for you to stay out of it. The next time it won't be a request. Understood?"

"Understood." Still, arson didn't seem to be taking the big picture into consideration. He didn't want to risk his job or create bad blood in a job where promotions could be as affected by politics as performance. And he wanted his next promotion. Badly. The brush fire had already put him out of the last round, and he didn't want to miss the next one. But whoever was threatening Sarah wasn't going to get away with it. Job or no job.

"There's something else. HQ has requested our cooperation with a fund-raising effort for our victims' fund. They are sending a representative over from a company that runs these kinds of things for all sorts of nonprofits and government agencies. She's supposed to be here this afternoon, and we are to give her our utmost consideration. I'm putting you in charge of the project."

Great. Babysitting some professional fundraiser sounds like as much fun as a full-gear tower climb. No, the tower climb would be better.

Tony's right hip vibrated. Giving a quick glance to his lunch companions, he unholstered his phone and looked at the display.

Nick. He tucked it into his pocket. He needed to take this but not here in the middle of an important business meeting in one of the nicer ocean-front restaurants in Newport Beach.

"Gentlemen, excuse me for a moment, would you?" He blotted his mouth with the cloth napkin and set it next to his plate as he rose. Flashing a quick smile around the table, he headed toward the men's room. The hallway that provided access to the restrooms was empty. He pulled out the phone and called Nick back. "What's up?"

"I got some info off her computer. She's hit on the artifacts. And she's getting info on the toll road. I don't know if she's putting the pieces together or not, but she's getting close. And she's friends with that cop. She emailed him everything she'd come up with."

Tony rubbed his eyes. Why couldn't she leave well enough alone? Why didn't people just mind their own business? Life would be easier for all of them. "Time to send her a message. Literally."

Sarah was just thinking about lunch when her phone vibrated. Her heart jumped, hoping it was Joe. Kyle's name appeared on the screen. A bit deflated, she answered.

"I got your email. Thanks for all of that work. I haven't had time to go over it yet, but it was thorough."

"I don't know if it'll be helpful or not, but I figured you should have it in case anything in there might be useful." She moved her mouse to wake up her computer screen.

"I appreciate it, but just leave the rest of it up to me and my team. If we need anything else from you, I'll let you know. We don't know what's going on with all of this, and I don't want you in any more danger."

"I—" An email notification slid across her screen. From Greg Connor. Her throat clogged. She swallowed, trying to speak. "Uh, Kyle. I just got an email from Greg Connor." Heat filled her face. "But maybe it's nothing. It's a common name." Maybe she was completely overreacting. She clicked on the notification to bring up her email. Oh. The words made her stomach twist. "The subject line reads: About the job site." The blood drained to her feet followed by a sick feeling. She took a shaky breath willing the blood back to her head. Was this some kind of sick joke?

"Don't touch anything," Kyle said in her ear. "I'm coming over." The line went dead.

She pushed back from her desk, breaking her stare from the taunting email. Grabbing her phone and her coffee cup, she escaped to the break room. She paced the length a few times, but the room was small. This was ridiculous and not helping anything, but she had to burn off this nervous energy. After scrubbing her cup clean, wiping down the countertops, and tossing old food out of the fridge, she was at a loss of what to do next.

Mark's office was empty. Back in her office, her computer had gone to sleep mode, so the nasty email was invisible. But she had read it, and she could still see the words imprinted on her mind. After unlocking the door to Mark's office, she slipped inside and closed the door behind her. The smell of leather, ink, and Mark's aftershave lingered still, wrapping her in comfort. It was like he had just stepped out for lunch instead of leaving her in charge.

She eased into his chair, the soft leather enveloping her. Picking up the phone, she told Malia to expect Detective Taylor. Then, swallowing, she dialed Mark's number. It was a mistake for him to trust her with his company. All she wanted to do was to keep it going so he wouldn't have to worry about anything other than taking care of Martha. And she failed. Maybe she should go away, leave all of this for Kyle to sort out and let Eric run the office.

Mark answered the phone, pleasure lacing his voice. "How are you doing, Sarah?"

She let out a sigh. "How are things with Martha?"

If he noticed her redirection, he didn't comment. "We're developing a new normal. But I'm glad I can be with her more now. Thank you for making that possible."

Tears burned her eyes. "You may not thank me after this. Did we lose any jobs recently, anything fall through that I don't know about?"

He was silent a moment. "Nothing unusual about that in this business. We bid on things, sometimes we lose. People change their mind, financing falls through. Why do you ask?"

She hated that he had to worry him with this when he had so many other things on his plate. "No. I just got an email from Greg Connor ordering me to stop investigating Indian artifacts, any project in the Foothill Corridor that wasn't ours, and his disappearance. Or we'd lose more jobs. Which implies that we've already lost some."

"Have you called Detective Taylor?"

"He's on his way over. What do you think?" Sarah played with the edge of his desk.

"I think it's a sick joke."

In some small way, this was Sarah's fault. She was hurting his business. And the worst of it was, she didn't even know what she'd done to cause it other than get directions from Greg Connor. "But we have lost business recently."

"Two bids last week and two cancelled contracts. I didn't tell you about them because nothing came of it."

She closed her eyes. He was worried. And if Mark was worried …

"Sarah, the office has more work than the team can handle. It's not a big deal. We've been through much worse times before."

"Not when we had this much staff." Her chest tightened, and she swallowed. Somehow, she had to fix this, to figure a way out. How had anyone known? Other than Kyle and Joe, she hadn't talked to anyone. Was there a leak in the police department? She'd begun research after her condo had been broken into, so they couldn't have gotten the information off there, except—

Stop. This is exactly what she'd promised Kyle she wouldn't do. She'd wait until he came.

Mark didn't say anything for a long moment. "Don't jump to conclusions. Talk to Detective Taylor. See what he says."

They ended the call with her reassurance that she would keep him up-to-date on what was happening. And his reassurance that he still trusted her to run the company. Which made her doubt Mark's wisdom for the first time since she'd known him.

She shook her head. It didn't matter. She was done. She'd give them what they wanted. She couldn't risk anyone else's safety or livelihood. Picking up a pad of paper from Mark's desk, she doodled around. Maybe thinking about designs for that new project she had been so excited about would take her mind off things. But nothing would come.

Where was Kyle? Shouldn't he be here by now? She glanced at her phone. No call or text from him.

Should she text Joe? He'd be upset if she didn't let him know what was going on. But he was also at work. She didn't want to distract him from his job. And he couldn't do anything about it anyway. She'd tell him tomorrow morning when they went for their walk.

In the meantime, she pulled up the Bible app on her phone. This was a better use of her time than sitting here fretting. She clicked through to the Psalms, the place she turned to over and over again for solace. It wasn't a cure all, didn't make everything all better. But as she forced the words from her head and pushed them down into her heart, willing herself to acknowledge their truth regardless of what she felt, that ache eased just a bit.

She read how David cried out to God for relief from his

enemies. For once she could relate. She'd never before felt like she had enemies when she read the Psalms. But this time … yeah. She just wished she knew who they were.

"Detective Taylor is here." Malia's voice came over the phone.

"Thanks, Malia. I'll meet him in my office." Sarah grabbed her phone and pad of doodles and left Mark's office and headed to her own.

Malia stood in the doorway to Sarah's office, Kyle behind her.

"Hi, Kyle. Come on in. Thanks, Malia." Sarah showed Kyle to her extra chair then closed her office door. "Here's the email." She pulled it up on her computer, hit Print, and handed him the paper.

After a moment Kyle said, "Can you copy what you need to keep working to another computer? I'm going to need to take this one in and have our tech guys look at it."

"Sure." She opened a drawer and pulled out a jump drive. She had figured this would happen and had mentally made a list of what she'd need but didn't want to touch anything until Kyle had come over. Plugging the little stick into the USB drive, she began dragging files over to it. Everything was on the server, and her latest projects were now on the jump drive. She wouldn't lose any work. And since they had brought on extra staff recently, there wasn't a spare computer for her. She'd have to go buy one. Well, it wasn't like she was getting any work done today anyway. Which was getting to be a problem. By the time her life settled down, she'd be buried under the things she needed to get to.

Files copied, she undocked her computer and shut it down then handed it to Kyle. "Thanks for hosting us last night. It was a lot of fun."

"You and Heather did all the work. I just offered the house.

But it was a great time. We'll do it again." He tapped her computer. "I'll let you know as soon as we find out about anything. In the meantime, don't go poking around anymore. You've done plenty. If we need any more info or have any questions, I'll call you. But these guys are serious, Sarah. I don't want anything to happen to you."

She nodded, her throat clogging. She cleared it. "I promise."

"Good." Kyle grinned. "I'll call you." Then he was out the door.

She blew out a breath. Time to get a new computer and something to eat. Maybe not in that order. Waving to Malia, she pushed out the front door of the office and pulled the keys to the rental out. She missed her car. Hopefully, she'd get it back soon.

Hopefully, normal would come back soon. But she wasn't holding her breath.

Tony slipped his sunglasses on as the marine layer burned off and the sun came poking through. He was standing just where he had last time he was here. Except now it was the afternoon and Greg wasn't here. He almost laughed at the irony, but the other guys wouldn't appreciate it. He studied the area from behind his glasses, wanting to see if there were any tell-tale clues. He couldn't see any. Didn't expect to, really. Nick was good with that stuff.

"Hey, Tony!" George, his new GC, came over, rolled-up plans in his hand.

"What you got for me?" Tony stepped to the front of his Lexus, noticing the dust from the job site was already settling on the black finish. He'd have his secretary call the car detailers to wash it. It was one of his favorite perks of his office building. A car detailing service right there. They'd come get your keys and wash and detail your car in a section of the parking garage.

George spread out the plans on the hood of the car. "Okay, we're behind schedule on the grading because we needed the new cut and fill amounts. But now that we have those, we should make good time."

Tony's phone rang. He glanced at the screen. Nick. "Yeah, what's up?"

"She got the email and decided to call that cop friend of hers. He took her computer. They'll find the tracking program easy."

He glanced at George then moved away, turning his back. "Did you cover your tracks?"

"What do you think? Of course."

"Then what are you worried about?"

"Nothing. Just thought you should know."

"Now I know. Hang tight until I decide what to do next." He hit the off button and slid the phone back to its place. Sarah was pretty smart for a girl. It didn't matter if they found the tracking program. In fact, that would just reinforce to her how serious they were. How easily they could get to her. They'd have no more problems from her, he was sure. But if they did ... well, that's what Nick was for.

He turned back to George. "These are guys you can trust to keep their mouths shut, right?"

"Oh yeah. I hand-picked them. And the nice bonus you're paying didn't hurt none either."

"Good. Because I want every trace of that stuff gone by next week. Got me?"

"I got it."

McCoy rapped on Joe's door before pushing it open. "Captain, you've got a visitor on the apparatus floor. A woman."

Joe pushed to his feet. Sarah? Would she have come by without letting him know? He glanced at his phone. No missed calls or texts. He followed McCoy. As he rounded the corner, his steps faltered. It wasn't Sarah. In fact, it might be the last person he wanted to see.

Macy Villanueva. The one person who almost destroyed his relationship with Scott and Kyle. For a moment he thought about ducking back around the corner, but she spotted him.

"Joe Romero. What a sight for sore eyes." She wore a dark-red, form-fitting dress with heels, her dark hair cascading around her shoulders. She tapped her way over to him, hand outstretched. "I was hoping I'd get to work with you on this project."

He shook her hand then quickly slipped it from her grasp, taking a step back. "What brings you here?"

"Didn't they tell you? I was told you'd be expecting me. I'm heading up the fund-raising campaign for the victims' fund."

No. This couldn't be. The person he'd been ordered to help out. *Lord* ... He didn't even know what to pray.

"I have some great ideas. Is there a place where we can go over what I have planned?" She looked up at him, her eyes as big and brown as ever.

"Uh, sure." He led her inside to one of the tables.

She pulled things out of her large tote and began spreading them over the table. "Now, this here has been our bestseller at other departments, and HQ loves the idea. We just need to set up a schedule for the shoots. I don't want to get in your way, but a mix of pose and action shots works the best."

It was like she was speaking a foreign language. She had pointed at a calendar of cops. At least he thought that's what they were, considering most of them had their shirts off. What did that have to do with them? Wait. No.

"You're not suggesting we do, uh, this?" He couldn't even bring himself to say it.

She beamed up at him. Even in those ridiculous heels, she didn't come to his shoulder. "Yes! It'll be fabulous. Just think of all the money we'll raise for the victims' fund. These hero calendars, as we call them, sell like crazy. The cops calendar broke all previous sales records. But I think you guys can do even better."

He wasn't going to fall for her attempt to goad him into a competition. This whole idea was ridiculous. He couldn't believe HQ had approved it. A few of the guys had gathered around the table, picking up the calendars and making comments.

Macy answered all of their questions with a bright smile and a little bit of flirting. If anyone could get a group of guys to do her bidding, it was Macy. A fact he knew all too well.

CHAPTER NINETEEN

YES GRITTY FROM LACK OF sleep—and given that he was
still at the station, he wasn't going to remedy that soon—
Joe picked up his phone. He had to tell Sarah he couldn't
meet her for their walk this morning since he was held over.
He could text her, but he needed to hear her voice instead of
just a text.

"Hello?" Her voice was scratchy.

He frowned. "Are you sick?"

"No, not really. Just this sore throat that's been hanging
around since last weekend." She gave a small laugh. "Given
what time it is, I'm guessing you won't make our walk."

"No, I've been held over. But you probably could use the
rest anyway. I was thinking either I could come get Shadow
from your place when I get home and then you could pick him
up after choir practice." How would she fare with Ryan after
their break up? Given how public Ryan had made their dating,
tonight had the potential to be awkward to say the least. "Are
you still planning on going?"

"Yeah, so far. We'll see how my throat is tonight." She
paused. "Have you talked to Kyle?"

"Not since the party at his house. Why?"

"Oh, he had to come get my computer yesterday. I got an email from Greg warning me to stay away."

He gripped the phone so tight he had to consciously stop squeezing it before he broke it. "What? *The* Greg?"

"Likely someone posing as him. I got a new computer yesterday." Her tone was matter of fact, but he could hear the exhaustion threading through it. "Anyhow, I'd better let you get back to work. If I don't go to choir practice, I'll let you know. Actually, an early night sounds like a good option right about now."

Frustrated by the distance between them, he simply said, "Be careful. I'll talk to you tonight." As soon as they hung up, he called Kyle.

Sarah dusted off the empty spot on her desk where her computer used to sit. She didn't want to put her new one down until she'd cleaned. She continued to wipe on the edge of the desk, procrastinating. Picking up her wire mesh pencil holder, she dumped it. Pens, drafting pencils, paper clips, confetti-like pieces of paper and dust scattered across her clean desk. Meticulously she began wiping every surface down. Really, she needed Q-Tips or something for this kind of detail work.

A drop splashed in the middle of the dust, turning it to mud. She started to examine the cleaning bottle in her hand, looking for the leak before she realized it was her. Annoyed, she sniffed and brushed at her eyes with the back of her hand.

Scooping up the pens and pencils, she slid them back into the gleaming cup. She scrubbed off the dusty mud and scanned the rest of the desk. The drafting light. Turning the cloth to a clean spot, she ran it over the brushed nickel. When had her life become such a soap opera?

"Sarah?"

She startled a little then turned.

Mark stood in her doorway. "We have a cleaning crew for that."

"What?"

He gestured to the rag and cleaning bottle she still held in her hand.

"Oh." Her cheeks felt a little warm. "It was just kind of dusty where the computer was, and so I thought before I brought the new one in I'd just clean everything up. Anyway, why are you here? Is everything okay?"

Setting the cloth and bottle on the desk behind her, she leaned against it. Her hands were dusty and sticky. She needed to wash them.

He stepped into her office and closed the door behind him, then handed her a steaming mug of Lemon Zinger. "A little bird told me you had a sore throat."

She wrapped her hands around the cup. "Would that little bird's name be Malia?" She smiled, breathing in the deep lemon scent.

"Everything's fine. Martha's with a caregiver right now. I thought I'd come by and check on you."

So . . . this was going to be one of those talks. She pushed her extra office chair toward him and sank into hers.

He sat, elbows on knees, studying her but not saying anything.

She started to play with the hem of her shirt but then remembered that her hands were icky. Maybe Mark would wait while she went to wash her hands. She started to say something.

"Sarah. How are you doing? Really?"

Tears warmed her eyes. Drat. She hated it when he was nice to her. Why couldn't he be stern, tell her to get to work and not let her personal problems affect her job? She knew how to deal with that.

She bit her lip and blinked. "I'm okay." She hoped he didn't hear that catch in her voice. Allergies. Clearing it, she said, "I'm not looking forward to all the work I need to do to fix my computer so I can use it, but I might as well do it now as later." Talking about work was good. Having a plan, that always helped.

Mark studied her more, concern in his eyes. Was she really that pathetic? She was going to have to reassure him.

But he spoke before she could get her thoughts together. "Hey, I don't want you to worry about the business. Okay? I've been through many ups and downs. I have some contingency plans." He leaned forward. "This isn't your problem, and it's not your fault. You just keep telling Kyle everything you know and let him do his job. He'll get this guy."

Sarah nodded, knowing she couldn't get words past that lump in her throat. She was incredibly grateful for this boss and this job.

"All right." Mark stood and so did Sarah. She started to say something, but too many words collided in her brain at once.

Mark smiled at her. "And. No worrying." He opened the door to her office and left.

Stunned, Sarah didn't move.

Malia walked past the open door, glanced in, then stopped and came back. "Everything okay?"

Sarah had been staring at the open doorway and hadn't moved. "Um, yeah. Just trying to think."

Malia nodded and went on.

Get it together, girl. Lunch would be just the break she needed. She hated emotional stuff. Life was easier when everything was logical. Grabbing her purse, she stood and took one final look around the office. No, she wasn't forgetting anything. She headed out to her car.

"Sarah!"

Her head snapped up. It wasn't— Oh. Ryan. What was he doing here? She kept walking toward her car. There wasn't anything left to say.

He stepped in front of her, blocking her from the car door. "We need to talk. Without anyone else around." He leaned against her car and crossed his arms.

Her legs got mushy, and she fought to hold herself still. She didn't want him to see her shake. What had she ever seen in him? And why couldn't she handle conflict with confidence? "We talked already, Ryan. There's really nothing else to say."

"I said I was sorry for leaving you at church, okay. Sorry. I'm human. I forget things. I have a lot of responsibilities and a lot on my mind. You of all people should understand that. But now you have an obligation to forgive me. And I'm not letting you sing again until you do."

Too many things tumbled through her at once. She hated confrontation. She hated emotional, spur-of-the-moment conversations when she was caught off guard and couldn't think of a thing to say. Why wouldn't her brain work? *Lord, please. Help me say something.*

"Ryan. I forgive you. I told you that. That's not what this is about. It's just not working, okay?" He wasn't going to let her sing. His words finally sunk in. Why had she even dated him to begin with? He was hurting her on purpose, taking away something that always brought her joy. Why was he being like this? What had she done to deserve this?

"Sarah, I'm saying this to you as your pastor not just as your boyfriend. You've got something in your life, some area of sin you haven't turned over to God yet. I don't know what it is, but you need to get down on your knees and confess it to Him. Until you do, you can't be on the worship team."

Anger, humiliation, shame, rage all fought for attention. Should she just play along, like she always had? Or should she stand up to him? If she did, she'd lose everything for sure. She couldn't imagine seeing Ryan again at rehearsal. Yet to leave a church she loved over a falling out with one person. But to not sing … She was torn. *Don't cry. Don't cry. Don't cry.*

"I can't believe you think that. If you really thought that, why did you ask me out to begin with? What is it? What is this great revelation about my character that you've gotten from

God? Because I would sure like to be enlightened by your wisdom." Her voice turned a little shrill at the end, but she was beyond caring.

Ryan crossed his arms over his chest and leaned against her car. "I don't know. It's just obvious you have an attitude problem. You think you're better than everyone else. You probably think you could do my job. You were disrespectful to me when Ethan Tate was here. I can't have that kind of attitude or dissension on my team."

"What did I do that was disrespectful to you?"

"Several people came up to me and said the same thing."

"Who? What'd they say?"

"I'm not going to reveal that."

She shook her head. This was unbelievable. She was back in Mr. Odell's office in junior high being accused of calling Tracey names, when Tracey was the one who had called her names. Sarah had just put her head down and ignored her, which had made Tracey even madder. She had no idea why Tracey hated her so much, but Tracey was mean to her in PE and on the bus and every chance she got. But the worst thing was pulling Sarah into the vice principal's office. That had been the ultimate humiliation. No, wait, that was when Mr. Odell didn't believe her. He said she was lying. And nothing she said could convince him otherwise. She had sobbed uncontrollably when she realized that.

Funny thing was, she'd seen Tracey years later at a party in college. Sarah had forgotten all about it until Tracey brought it up. "Yeah, I was pretty mean to you back then. I still feel bad about it."

Twenty years later, here she was again. "I can't believe you listen to gossip, Ryan."

"I don't consider it gossip when people bring their concerns to me."

"Why didn't you tell them to come talk to me? That's the biblical way."

"You intimidate them."

She wanted to stomp her foot, but she wouldn't give Ryan the satisfaction. This was going nowhere. "Okay, we have to agree to disagree. Please let me get in my car. I need to leave. I have things to do. This is still my work day."

He didn't move. "We're not done."

"Yes. We are."

"Is there a problem here?"

Sarah saw Ryan's eyes shift over her shoulder before she turned.

Mark stood, hands on hips, looking between Sarah and Ryan. The tears flowed in earnest now. Grateful and humiliated, she had to get out of here. Turning away, head down, playing with her keys, she said, "No, I'm just trying to leave."

Ryan moved slightly away from the door, but enough so she could open it and slide in. "For a smart girl, you're pretty dumb. Call me when you have something to say." He shut the door on her and walked off.

She didn't dare meet Mark's eyes, so she concentrated on getting her shaking hands to put the key in the ignition and starting the car. She pulled out and left. Now there were two more places she was mortified to show her face. What had she done that was so wrong?

And how could she run a company when her personal life was such a mess it was spilling into the office?

Joe rolled over, trying to locate what had awoken him. Sunlight leaked around the edges of the blackout blinds in his bedroom. His phone was ringing. He snatched it up. Kyle. Finally. Joe hadn't been able to reach him earlier.

"Sarah said she got an email from Greg. What's that about?"

Kyle filled him in on the details, of which there weren't too many more than what Sarah had said.

Sliding out of bed, Joe headed to the kitchen and grabbed a Dr. Pepper from the fridge. He took a couple of swigs. "This tracking program on her computer hasn't led anywhere?"

"Not so far. These guys know what they're doing. Joe, I probably don't have to tell you this, but keep an eye on her."

"I plan to." He paused. "On another note, guess who showed up at the station yesterday?"

"Who?"

"Macy Villanueva."

Kyle was silent for a long moment. "What was she doing there?"

"She runs a fund-raising company, and HQ has approved her latest efforts for our victims' fund." He let out a long breath. "She wants to do a calendar. And O'Grady has ordered me to cooperate with her."

"Don't mention it to Scott. He's forgiven you, and you guys were able to pull your relationship out of a bad tailspin, but there's no point in poking old wounds."

"Yeah, that was my thought too. But I could use some extra prayer around this situation. If it was up to me, I'd never see her again. Unfortunately, that's not an option if I want to keep my job."

"You got it, bro. Hey, up for some basketball tomorrow night?"

"Sure." Joe hung up and leaned on the kitchen counter, the past washing over him in painful waves. Macy had been the start of a series of bad choices, ones that almost derailed his life at the end of high school and the beginning of college.

Scott, Kyle, and he had done everything together since fourth grade. Including being the key players on the football team. Scott was their star quarterback, Joe and Kyle were linemen. And Macy was a cheerleader who had set her sights on Scott. She and Scott started dating and all of the sudden Joe, Kyle, and football were a distant second in Scott's life behind Macy. Joe and Kyle cornered Scott after practice, before Macy could show up.

"Dude, you've got to get your head on straight or we're not going to make it to the championship." Kyle straddled the bench Scott was sitting on in the locker room, tying his shoes.

Joe landed on the other side of Scott. "You've got to break up with Macy. She's messing with your head, and you're not focusing. Doesn't have to be forever, just until the season is over. You missed that easy pass from Marcus because you were too busy checking her out on the sidelines."

Scott was silent, tugging on his laces that were already tied. He straightened. "You're just jealous. You had your eye on her long before I did, and you're just mad that she chose me."

Joe swallowed. There was a little bit of truth in that. He had had a crush on Macy ever since freshman year. "We're seniors, and this is our last season. I don't want to see it go down in flames because of some girl."

Scott pushed to his feet, nudging Joe out of the way. "You just do your job and make sure I don't get tackled. And stay out of my private life." He stalked out of the locker room.

Joe started after him, but Kyle held him back. "You said what you wanted to say. It's up to him now what he does with it."

Joe gave Kyle a steady look. "Let's just hope we win tomorrow's game, or it won't matter anyway."

And they had won. It had been one of their best games with each of them playing at the top of their games, the way they wanted to finish the season. They were going to the finals. Joe thought his tough-love talk had changed Scott's mind, but after the game, Scott ignored him.

There was an after party at a cheerleader's house. Joe and Kyle had gone, partly to celebrate, partly to keep an eye on Scott. It wasn't long before Scott was drunk. Kyle hauled him home. Joe was getting ready to leave when Macy came up to him, sobbing. Mascara streaked down her face and her eyes were puffy. She was also really drunk. Joe steadied her as she flung herself into his arms.

"What's the matter? Are you okay?" He was trying not to

notice her curves pressed against him.

Between her sobbing into his shirt and the loud music, he couldn't hear anything she was saying. "Come on. Let's go somewhere quieter." He led her out to his car parked down the street. She swayed unsteadily, so he slipped his arm around her waist and held her tight against him, trying not to think about how good it felt to have her pressed against him. Or how Scott would take his head off if he saw them like this.

He settled her in the passenger seat of his truck and got around on the other side, handing her a napkin to wipe her nose and face with.

"Thank you, Joe. You've always been so sweet." Her breath caught on a soft hiccup. "I should have picked you instead."

His heart warmed at her words and then shame flared at his disloyalty to his friend. "Scott's a good guy. He's just got a lot on his mind right now since we're going to the finals."

"He broke up with me!" She burst into more sobs.

Whoa. He hadn't expected that. Pleasure that Scott had actually listened to him mingled with the regret of how much pain his advice had caused Macy. And apparently Scott, who had decided to drink his troubles away. Not something he usually did.

"It's going to be okay, Macy." He slid his arm around her shoulder, patting it.

She slid across the bench seat up next to him, curling her arm around his waist, her head on his chest.

He continued patting her shoulder, not sure what to do with her. He should take her home. He eased back. "Um, let me—"

She sat up and closed the space between them, capturing his lips with her own.

Stunned, Joe didn't respond for a minute. Then three years of pent-up attraction poured out as he kissed her back. As Macy's arm wrapped around the back of his neck and he pulled her closer, he had the vague thought that he hoped no one saw them.

Joe shook his head and pushed away from the counter. Bad memories, all of it. He'd taken Macy home and finally gotten her inside. Somehow, he'd resisted her invitation to come in, saying her parents were gone. But for a moment ...

The next day, Joe answered the door to find Scott standing there. Before he could say anything, Scott's fist landed against his jaw. "You slept with her!"

"No, Scott! I just took her home—"

They wrestled on the front lawn until Joe pinned him and was able to tell Scott what happened. But considering Macy had given quite a different story, he saw the disbelief in Scott's eyes as he pushed Joe off and stalked away.

Joe was stung by Macy's betrayal. She'd used him—and exaggerated what happened—to get back at Scott. But the loss of Scott's friendship hurt more than anything since his dad's death. It wasn't until Kyle organized a camping trip the following summer that they'd been able to repair their friendship. But the pain of doing the right thing and having it backfire on him had sent Joe into a spiral of poor choices. Ones he deeply regretted.

He wasn't going to give Macy Villanueva the chance to ruin his life again.

Chapter Twenty

Sarah dropped her bag on the entryway table, her keys next to it. No need to hurry through dinner tonight since she wasn't going to choir practice. She'd better text Joe and see if she could pick up Shadow earlier. Make it an early night. She tapped out the message and then moved to the kitchen. She opened three cupboards before it registered that she didn't have anything. She hadn't gone grocery shopping to replace everything that had been destroyed in the break-in. She plopped down on her new couch that finally had been delivered, trying to figure out dinner, when her phone rang. Joe. Warmth flooded her.

"Hey, is your throat worse? Is that why you're not going to choir practice?"

She let out a long sigh. "Not really. It's a long story, but Ryan kicked me off the team."

He was silent for a beat. Maybe she shouldn't have said anything. He was going to think she had nothing but drama in her life. Then, "Do you like hot and sour soup? It might feel good on your throat."

"Yeah, I was just thinking about that for dinner, actually."

"Great. I'll go to that little Chinese place around the corner and bring over dinner and the dog. Then you can tell me the long story. "

"Oh, wow, that does sound good. I had forgotten to pick something up on the way home from work. And of course, I've got very little in the cupboards here since … well, you know. Anyhow, I'd love to take you up on your offer."

"Okay, I'll grab you some soup and be over in a bit. Anything else you want or need? Anything from the store?"

"I think I'm okay. Thanks, Joe. I really appreciate it."

"No problem. I'll see you in a few minutes."

She hung up then pushed herself off the couch and studied her reflection in the entryway mirror. She looked tired. Maybe more makeup would do the trick? But then would she look like she was trying too hard? This wasn't a date, and Joe had seen her under less than ideal circumstances.

She moved to the kitchen. She'd make some passion-fruit iced tea. That was at least a useful contribution. And if she couldn't go to choir practice, spending time with Joe was a great alternative. She didn't even remember what she'd done after her confrontation with Ryan in the parking lot. Somehow, she'd ended up at the office supply store, where she'd wandered the aisles filling a cart with pens and paper and sticky notes. None of which she actually needed. But it beat sitting in her car crying.

Then she'd called Heather and given her the rundown. Heather had wanted to go give Ryan a piece of her mind tonight, but they decided that it would be better for Heather to wait and see what Ryan did.

She wasn't sure what she felt, actually. In a way, she was relieved she didn't have to face Ryan again. And though she loved singing, her sore throat would mean her voice wouldn't be at its best. Even if he hadn't kicked her out of the choir, he certainly wouldn't have let her solo. But what would people say about her when she didn't show up? What would Ryan say?

She couldn't control any of that. And Heather would be sure to give her a full report. And wouldn't she be interested to know that Sarah spent the evening with Joe instead?

Half an hour later, Joe rang Sarah's doorbell, carrying several plastic bags and trying not to tip the container of soup while Shadow tugged on the leash.

She opened the door and gave him a grateful, if tired, smile. "Thanks so much. Come on in."

He stepped through the doorway and continued on to the kitchen, setting the bags on the counter. He dropped Shadow's leash.

She shut the door and unsnapped the leash. "Hey, boy." Then she followed Joe into the kitchen. "Smells really good. And I didn't even think I was hungry."

He started unloading bags. "Now go park yourself in a chair while I get the food. I cleaned up the kitchen, remember? I know where everything is. Completely different than where I put things, but whatever." He tried to hide his smile as he glanced up to see her reaction.

She rolled her eyes but pulled out a dining room chair. "That's because I put things where they should go logically."

"Well, it's not like it really matters in a kitchen this small anyhow. One cupboard is just as close as another." He grabbed a bowl and plates out of the cupboard behind him.

"True. It's more of the principle of the thing."

"Which principle?"

"Form follows function."

He poured soup into a bowl for her. "Spoken like a true architect." He wanted to ask about Ryan but was afraid to lose the light atmosphere they had going between them. He picked up her bowl and a plate for him and carried them to the table.

He thanked God for their food, and then they began eating. Joe decided he would just have to bring up the subject of Ryan. Sarah hadn't come remotely close to touching it. "So what's this about the choir?"

Sarah set her spoon in her bowl. "Ryan showed up at work today." She gave him a summary of what happened.

The more she talked, the more Joe couldn't believe what was happening. He shook his head; he couldn't help it. Ryan was an idiot. "Have you thought about going to Pastor Tom about it? I can't think he'd want Ryan to get away with it."

"I thought about it. But it could become this whole he-said-she-said thing. And Pastor Tom would encourage me to talk to Ryan first before he would get involved. And I really don't have anything else to say to Ryan." She spooned up her soup.

"I know how much you love to sing. You have a gift. I hate to see you suffering for something you didn't do." He reached over and squeezed her hand.

She returned the squeeze and didn't pull her hand away. "Thank you. You're my cheering section."

He froze a bit at the word *cheering*, memories of Macy fresh in his mind. Memories that would stay buried in the past where they belonged.

"I think I'm going to let things play out for a bit and see what happens. Hopefully, Ryan will move his attention elsewhere and forget about me."

Joe didn't think any guy in his right mind could forget about her, but he didn't say so.

"Could be." Joe finished the last bit of beef and broccoli. Sarah's soup bowl was empty. "Do you want some more?"

"No, that was just right. Thanks."

He picked up their dishes and took them to the sink. He'd been thinking about this next part of the evening. His palms were sweaty, and he wiped them on a dish towel. He didn't want the evening to end. And he hoped she didn't either. "You know that movie you, Heather, and Melissa were talking about at

Kyle's? It's out on Netflix. The evening's still early so we could watch it without it getting too late." He looked over at her. She didn't seem horrified, so he kept going. "And I brought a surprise. You know what the best thing is for a sore throat?"

She laughed. "I can only imagine. What?"

"Ice cream."

"Of course it is. What kind?"

He reached into her freezer drawer where he'd stashed it. "Rocky road."

"How did you get that in there without me knowing?" She stood from the table and moved over next to him, her shoulder brushing his.

"That stealthy firefighter thing."

She grabbed clean bowls. "That's coming in real handy lately."

"Or maybe you just weren't paying attention. Too busy playing with the dog."

"Yeah, he's a real attention hog." She looked over at Shadow who was snoring in front of the couch. "You want some decaf to go with that?"

"Sounds perfect." He dished up the ice cream while she started the coffee. The companionable silence and the way they moved easily around each other made him feel like they'd been doing this forever. A fist gripped his chest. Forever. Yeah. He kinda liked the sound of that.

He stuck spoons in the bowls and carried them to the coffee table. He hoped she would choose the couch with him.

She followed with the coffee cups, hers doctored with cream, his black. She set them down next to the bowls and eased onto the couch next to him. "Shadow's making himself at home down there, leaving us about two feet of space."

He slid his arm along the back of the couch. "I don't mind."

She grinned as she picked up the remote, flipping through the options until the Netflix menu came up. She started the movie, propped her feet on the coffee table, and started in on her ice cream. Once the bowls were empty and back on the coffee table, she snuggled into the couch, next to his shoulder. He let his arm drop around her shoulder, lightly brushing it with his fingers. She didn't pull away.

She seemed to be enjoying the movie, but it couldn't hold his attention. Instead, every fiber of his being was focused on this amazing woman next to him. Her soft skin and silky hair.

The movie ended, though he couldn't have said what it was about. Sarah leaned her head back on the couch and looked at him. That was all it took.

He moved toward her, sliding his hand on the back of her neck, pulling her to him. Hesitating, seeking permission in her eyes before lowering his lips to hers. She tasted of sweetness and richness, and a hundred dreams exploded in his mind as she wrapped her arms around him and kissed him back with a passion he hadn't expected. The heat built in him, and he reluctantly eased her away. He traced the back of his hand down her cheek. "Have dinner with me Saturday. A real date, not take out."

She gave him a soft smile, her eyes still hazy. "I'd like that."

For once, something was going his way.

CHAPTER TWENTY-ONE

S UN BEATING DOWN ON HER head, Sarah scanned the food
court looking for Heather. Well, she was looking for Ryan
too, hoping to avoid him. She didn't want to give up
meeting Heather for lunch at their favorite place just because
Ryan might happen by. She spotted Heather over at a table in
a corner, partially hidden by a potted palm. Good.

She slid into the seat, setting her tray down. "Hey, perfect seat."

"I thought you'd appreciate it." Heather took a sip of her
Diet Coke and picked up her burrito. "You didn't miss much
last night."

Sarah blew out a breath. "Good. So he didn't say anything?"

"No. Other than continually looking at me like I was to
blame for your rebellion, Ryan led choir practice as usual. A
few people asked me about you, but I said you had a sore throat.
True enough."

Sarah poked around her chicken and avocado salad. "I love
choir, but it's nice to have a break from the Ryan drama. I don't

know how all of this is ever going to work out. I don't see Ryan announcing we broke up."

"I wonder what he'd do if you just showed up? If you're gone for more than a few weeks, people are going to start asking questions."

"True. On one hand, I can see him just ignoring me and pretending the whole thing didn't happen. That would be for the best. On the other hand, if the Ryan who came by my office and chewed me out showed up, it could be public humiliation disguised as church discipline." She took a bite of her salad, the creamy cilantro dressing easing away the unpleasant memories of Ryan.

"You might have to talk to Pastor Tom."

Sarah wrinkled her nose. "Yeah, Joe mentioned that too."

Heather raised her eyebrows.

"He came over last night. Brought me soup and ice cream." Her cheeks grew warm.

"Uh huh. And?"

"And what?"

Heather just stared at her.

"He might have kissed me."

"I knew it!" Heather set down her nearly finished burrito. "Are you guys together now?"

Sarah shrugged. "We're going out Saturday night. On a real date."

"You guys are good together. It's about time."

Sarah played with the straw in her Diet Coke. Last night had been great, relaxed and comfortable. She could have stayed in Joe's arms … well, it was good they stopped when they did. Still, when Joe was on shift, he was never far from her thoughts. And as he became more important to her, could she ever stop worrying about him?

Heather put her hand on Sarah's. "Hey. Don't borrow trouble, okay? Joe's very good at what he does. He doesn't take unnecessary risks."

Her head knew that, but her heart wasn't convinced.

"Up for some basketball?" Kyle was finally returning Joe's call.

"Sure. Thought you had small group tonight." Joe headed to his closet to pull out his basketball shoes.

"Tonight's our social night. The girls wanted to go see some chick flick, so the guys are going to play basketball. Meet us there in about ten minutes."

Joe hopped in his truck. Maybe there was a chance they'd meet up with the girls after the game/movie. He was hoping to see Sarah at some point today. She dropped off Shadow early, begging off their walk because she needed to get into the office to get caught up before anyone else got in and made her time theirs. He understood. And at least he'd gotten another quick kiss out of her before the day had started.

He pulled into the parking lot of a local park just behind Kyle.

Joe and Kyle met on the sidewalk and waited for Bernie and Gary to join them. It was twilight, but the lights already flickered on the tennis and basketball courts. One court had a full game on, the other just a few guys. Joe hoped they could get a game.

Bernie and Gary walked up, and Joe tilted his head in the direction of the courts. "Want to see if they'll share?"

"Sure."

As they headed over, Joe watched the four guys on the court. Two looked familiar. One was one of the guys who sang at church a lot, but he couldn't think of his name. One he didn't know—the guy had two full sleeves of ink—but the last one was all too familiar. Ryan. He forced his feet to keep moving ahead, but his mind raced. Ryan was pretty much the last person he wanted to see right now. He glanced at Kyle to gauge his reaction. Kyle shot Joe a look with raised eyebrows. Joe shrugged. Kyle nodded.

Joe stepped onto the edge of the court and waited for a

break in play. He knew the moment Ryan spotted him.

Ryan stiffened slightly and tucked the ball under his arm, eyes narrowed for just a second, then he recovered, his old amiable self back in place. "Hey Joe, Kyle." He nodded at them.

"Looks like the courts are all taken. You guys want to play a little four-on-four?"

Ryan looked behind Joe, clearly sizing up the competition. Joe knew what he was thinking: Bernie and Gary didn't look like much of a threat, especially compared to two of the guys on Ryan's team. Of course, Ryan didn't know Kyle and Joe had been playing basketball together for over twenty years.

"Sure." He turned to the guys with him. "This is Chris, Lou, and Nick."

"I recognize some of you from the choir." The guys exchanged handshakes.

Chris pointed at Lou. "He and I do."

Nick, the guy with the ink, grabbed the ball from Ryan. "I'm not into that church thing. I'm just here for the basketball. Ryan twists my arm."

Ryan stole the ball back. "Just trying to prove all church people aren't weirdos."

Nick raised his eyebrows.

Joe dropped his stuff next to the bench. This should be interesting.

The game started out friendly enough, each side taking their time, sizing up the competition. Ryan had the ball and made a break for the hoop with a layup.

Joe moved to block. And caught an elbow in the cheekbone for his trouble. The ball bounced uselessly off the rim.

Joe gave Ryan a hard look. Ryan returned it for a moment then jogged back down the court. Joe stared after him a moment before rubbing his cheek across his shoulder. Man, that stung.

They were up by three points, and the game hadn't gotten any less physical. They were supposed to be calling their own fouls, but that wasn't happening too much. Ryan had the ball, and Joe set up to screen him. Ryan lowered his shoulder, which was fairly obvious given he was taller than Joe. Ryan's shoulder slammed into Joe's chest and knocked him on his butt. What game was he playing? This was basketball not football.

Joe scrambled to his feet. "What's wrong with you?"

Ryan smirked and sent the ball to Joe with a hard pass. "Sorry. Just used to playing street rules."

Joe caught the ball and resisted the urge to roll his eyes. In south Orange County? *Give me a break.*

"If you can't take it ..." Ryan shrugged. Nick stepped up behind him.

"Is this how you run the worship team? By bullying everyone into doing what you want?"

Ryan's eyes narrowed. "What's that supposed to mean?"

"Just that you don't seem to appreciate all the people around you who support you, who work as a team to make you look good." Righteous anger surged through Joe. He should shut his mouth before he regretted it.

"Who *support* me?" Ryan gave a harsh laugh. "If you're talking about Sarah, she was actually undermining my authority. She's got some issues of her own she needs to work on."

Chris put his hand on Ryan's shoulder, but he shook it off.

Joe glanced around. Kyle watched him, arms folded across his chest, watching. He wasn't going to intervene. Bernie furrowed his brow, and Gary shifted his weight from foot to foot. Joe was done with this. He shoved the ball at Ryan. "You don't even know what you had in her. She met with the altos to teach them the parts because you were too busy schmoozing with Ethan Tate. And then you have the nerve to be mad at her because Ethan complimented her singing more than he did yours. Grow up, Ryan." He stalked off the court.

Just as he bent over to pick up his keys and wallet from the bench, Kyle came up next to him. "Wondered when you were going to do that."

Joe dismissed the men. They had training coming up in a few weeks on some new equipment that he was really excited about. Today's training was preliminary work that needed to be accomplished before then.

He came out on the apparatus floor to see what looked like a photography studio set up in front of one of the trucks. Lights, reflectors, a photographer. And Macy.

She turned and smiled at him. "Hey, Joe! Want to go first?"

"What is this?"

She touched his arm. "Didn't you get the message? We're shooting the calendar today. You should go first. Set a good example for your men." She eyed him up and down. "Maybe one in what you're wearing, then maybe your turnout pants with no shirt?"

He ran his hand over his face. After her last visit, he'd had a conversation with O'Grady that went nowhere. In fact, he was supposed to be the example of cooperation.

But he wasn't taking his shirt off.

Most of the men had gathered around. Joe pointed to them. "Why don't you start with these guys? Put them where you want them. But know that if we get a call, we're out of here."

She gave him a hundred-watt smile. "Of course."

It was going to be a long day.

It was a long morning of watching Macy and her photographer pose his men. Her flirty style got the guys to do whatever she wanted, especially the younger ones. She'd even gotten a bunch of them to take their shirts off, making it a competition to see which shift could have the most months on the calendar.

Tone sounded, and they ran for their gear. "Get your equipment out of the way!" Joe yelled at the photographer, who quickly dragged his lights out from in front of the engine and truck.

Joe was relieved. A car wreck. This was at least something he knew how to handle.

A short trip found them at a three-car pileup on Portola. A minivan and two sedans.

They were well into pulling out victims when voices drifted over to him as soon as they stopped using their equipment. Someone was arguing with one of the cops directing traffic.

Macy and her photographer had arrived. While Macy was talking to the cop and gesturing, her photographer was sneaking around, shooting Joe and his team in action. How long had they been there? He shook his head. As long as they weren't a distraction, the cop could deal with them.

Joe went back to work on the minivan. They'd gotten the mom out, now he stuck his head in back where two kids— one in a car seat and one in a booster seat—were strapped in. Shaken, but not hurt. Good for Mom for strapping her kids in well.

"All right, guys. We're going to get you out of here. Have you ever seen a fire truck up close?"

Two pairs of wide eyes looked at him. The blond boy in the booster seat shook his head, tears and snot streaming down his face. The baby in the car seat just chewed on a toy.

"Well, today is your lucky day. I can even get you your own fire helmet and some stickers. We've got a stuffed dog for your little sister here. And we'll take you to see Mom. Just let me and my buddies here get you guys out." He tugged a blanket over. "This is just to protect you from flying glass. It's going to get loud, but I'll be right here, okay?"

The boy nodded.

Once the door had been pried off, Joe unstrapped the baby and handed her off to Akino. He unstrapped the boy. "Okay, buddy. Let's go get you that helmet." He pulled the boy into his arms and backed out of the minivan, right into Macy's photographer.

"What are you doing? You can't be here." He scanned the area. Where was the cop controlling the scene? Talking to Macy while he was directing traffic. "Get out of the way!"

The photographer kept taking shots but backed toward his car.

Macy and the photographer had no business at the scene. In fact, this whole calendar thing was a bad idea. Somebody was going to get hurt. And Joe was going to make sure it wasn't his men or those kids.

Chapter Twenty-Two

J OE HAD JUST WALKED IN his house after shift when his phone rang in his pocket. He hoped it was Sarah. They'd texted briefly last night, and he was looking forward to their date tonight. He had a few thoughts of where he could take her, he just needed to see where he could get reservations.

He pulled it out and looked at the screen. His sister, Catrina. The youngest of his four sisters. "Hey, sis. What's up?"

"Just reminding you of Marcus's birthday party tonight. You never responded to the Facebook invite."

"That's because I never saw it. I never go on Facebook. Why didn't you call or text me?"

"That's what I'm doing now."

He sighed. Marcus was turning three this weekend, he knew that. He just hadn't known about the party. And not attending was not an option. But the idea of cancelling his date with Sarah had him rubbing his forehead.

"What? You had other plans?" His sister's voice came teasing through the line. "I know you're not working. I already checked."

"Yeah, actually, I did have other plans." He moved into the kitchen and pulled a bottle of water out of the fridge.

"Who is she?"

"What makes you say that?" He uncapped it and took a long swallow, buying time.

"Seriously? If you were just hanging out with Kyle, it'd wouldn't take you a second to cancel. Bring her."

"To meet all of you so you can scare her off? No, thanks."

"So she's just a fling? That's not like you."

"No," he said a bit more vehemently than he felt. "No, she's definitely not a fling. She's a friend of Kyle's girlfriend, Heather. I got to know her when I was helping Kyle with that situation earlier this summer."

"Then she'll have to meet us eventually." All the teasing dropped out of Catrina's voice. "We're not that scary, Joe. Believe it or not, we just want you to be happy. I promise we won't give her the third degree."

"Ha. It's not you I'm worried about. It's Gabi and Sophia." At ten and twelve years older than him, respectively, his oldest sisters acted more like his mothers; they considered him spoiled. Which he probably was. He'd been a happy surprise for his parents who'd thought their family was complete with four girls.

"Mom will keep them in line."

"True. All right. I'll talk to Sarah. She's very sweet, so even if she doesn't want to go, she'll agree to it. So you all be nice to her."

"We will be. Don't worry. I'm actually looking forward to meeting the woman that has finally caught my brother's attention."

He grunted. "What's Marcus want for his birthday?"

She rattled off a list of things. Looked like a trip to Target was now on his schedule for the day.

"By the way, I see you're famous."

"What do you mean?"

"You really don't check social media, do you? There's a

picture of you rescuing a little boy out of a car wreck yesterday. Go look it up."

Macy's photographer.

After he hung up with his sister, he grabbed his running shoes. He needed to bleed off some stress. He'd look up the photo later.

Sarah sat in Joe's truck on the way to his nephew's birthday party fingering the bow on the present in her lap, a set of oversized building blocks. The package was huge. She hoped it wasn't overkill. Her outfit was casual but nice. White jeans, sandals, a flowy print top. Hopefully, they would like her. It felt a bit like going on an interview.

Joe reached over and took her hand. Had her nervousness been that obvious? "Sorry again about springing this on you. But the food will be good, my sisters have promised to be nice, and I'll make it up to you."

"It's fine. I'm actually looking forward to meeting your family." She could get to know another side of him. Find out what she was getting herself into.

His truck pulled into the driveway of an older ranch house, music and laughter spilling over from inside. He leaned over and gave her a quick kiss. "You look great. Everyone will love you." He hopped out of the truck and came around to her side, taking both of their presents and helping her to keep her white jeans from getting dirty on his truck.

Once inside the house, he dropped off the presents on a table already overflowing with gifts. The living room was full of people. Joe waved but tugged her by the hand into the kitchen.

As long as he didn't abandon her, she'd be fine. At least she'd keep telling herself that.

A small woman with Joe's smile and dark hair shot through with gray worked in the kitchen.

"Hey, Ma." Joe let go of Sarah's hand to wrap his mom in a hug.

She patted his cheeks. "My big hero! You've got your picture everywhere now. You're famous."

He shook his head, an embarrassed grin creasing his face. He slid his arm around Sarah's shoulders. "Ma, this is Sarah Brockman."

"Hello, Mrs. Romero." Sarah held out her hand but was immediately enveloped in a hug that smelled like salsa and fresh tortillas. "Welcome! Call me Flavia. It's so good to meet you." She elbowed Joe. "This one tells me nothing. I have to find out from the internet that he's a hero. And he never mentioned how lovely you are." She fingered one of Sarah's curls. "Such a pretty color." She motioned to the food covering the counters. "Come, get something to eat."

But before Sarah could move, two women entered the kitchen, squealing and throwing their arms around Joe.

"I can't believe our little brother is a hero!"

"We can take all the credit for that."

Joe disentangled himself. "Gabi, Catrina, this is Sarah. Sarah, Gabi is the second oldest, and Catrina is the baby sister, right before me."

Both women wrapped her in hugs. Catrina was taller, with dark, cascading hair. Gabi was shorter and curvier, with her glossy hair in a stylish long bob.

"Sophia and Alyssa are somewhere." Catrina scanned the area.

"I saw their husbands in the living room as we came in." Joe moved over to a cooler and handed Sarah a Diet Coke. "We'll catch up with them later." He grabbed a Dr. Pepper for himself. "Where's the birthday boy?"

"Running around out back with his cousins. He'll be so glad his hero uncle is here. In the meantime—" Catrina looped her arm through Sarah's, drawing her away—"you can give us the scoop on my brother. He's not very forthcoming with information."

Joe grinned and shook his head. "Go easy, Trina."

"Joe, come fix your girlfriend a plate," said Flavia.

Sarah's face grew hot, and she glanced at Joe, who was just grinning. "Sure, Ma."

Catrina slid out a chair for Sarah and then took one side of her while Gabi took the other. "Joe says you're an architect. That's really cool. You must be smart." Gabi pulled out her phone and turned it to Sarah. "You saw this, right?"

Oh, had she. The photo kept her from having to respond to the barrage of questions. The image of Joe pulling out a little boy about the age of his nephew from a completely smashed minivan had blown up all of her social media feeds. But more than the rescue, it was the expressions on their faces that had made the photo go viral. The boy's face was streaked with tears, but he looked up at Joe with so much trust. And Joe gazed at the boy with tenderness and compassion. Something she'd seen from him more than once.

Yeah, he was good at his job. The world needed more men like him. She glanced back to where Joe was speaking with his mom while filling a few plates. "Do you ever worry about him? Was everyone okay with his career choice?"

Gabi leaned back. "We worry. Especially Mom. But we're really proud of him too." She tapped her phone. "When we see things like this, we know he's doing what God designed him to do."

"I wish that photo showed the whole story." Joe had come up and leaned over the back of Sarah's chair, setting a plate in front of her. "There's a whole crew of guys working to rescue seven other victims. It's never just one of us. We can't do what we do unless we work together."

Catrina stood and patted his shoulder. "You're a good leader. Who knew that such a bratty brother could be such a great guy? I'm going to check on the rest of my guests. But, Sarah, you want any dirt on this guy, just ask me." She gave a saucy grin before leaving the kitchen.

Joe took Catrina's seat and set a plate in front of himself.

Sarah's was loaded with homemade tamales, spanish rice, refried beans, pico de gallo, and a few tortilla chips. Joe nudged her. "That's not even half of what's up there. So don't go away hungry."

"You might have to roll me out of here." She had just taken a bite when two other women joined them, the other two sisters given their family resemblance. Joe introduced her to Alyssa and Sophia. A few children and some husbands also filtered by, but the names all started running together. She managed to get a few bites in between answering questions, but she was relieved when Catrina announced that it was time for the piñata.

Everyone moved to the backyard where a piñata hung from the patio roof. The little kids lined up to get blindfolded and take a whack at the toy-and-candy-filled papier-mâché monkey. Catrina's husband, Raoul, made sure none of the little sluggers hit something they weren't supposed to. Like the next kid in line.

Joe stood behind Sarah, his arms wrapped lightly around her waist. She leaned back against him, comforted by his presence and by the fact he hadn't left her to deal with all of these people by herself.

After all the kids had taken two turns and the piñata still hadn't broken, Raoul took the bat and gave it a good whack. The piñata flew off the string and landed in the yard, candy and toys spilling everywhere. The kids ran to fill their bags while Raoul got a round of applause and a few comments that the Dodgers could use his skills.

Sarah was fading, but there was still cake to be eaten and presents to be opened. A few of the kids were starting to fuss. Overstimulation. She could relate. Joe ushered her to a seat and brought her a piece of cake and a cup of coffee while Marcus tore into his presents. Hers was one of the first ones he opened. She held her breath, hoping she'd gotten the right thing, more for his family's approval than for Marcus himself. Silly, but she hadn't been around too many little kids. She didn't have nieces and nephews like Joe did. She swallowed and pushed the dark, painful bubble back down where it belonged.

"Wow! Look, I can build a fort!" Marcus began opening the storage bag that held the blocks. Catrina redirected him to thank Sarah. He flung himself into Sarah's lap. "Thank you, Tia Sarah."

She patted his sweaty little back. "You're welcome, sweetie. I hope you have fun with them." Aunt Sarah. She blinked. She'd never thought she'd be an aunt to anyone.

Marcus tore into the next gift. Joe's. It was a toy electric guitar. Marcus pressed the buttons, and it lit up and played a raucous noise.

Catrina gave Joe a mock glare. "Really? Just you wait, little brother. I'll get my revenge when you have kids."

Marcus gave Joe an equally exuberant hug. "Thank you, Tio. Did you bring your fire engine? Can I ride in it?"

"I didn't bring it today, but have your mom bring you to the station, and I'll let you climb all over it. You can even sit in the driver's seat."

"Can we go tomorrow, Mom?"

Joe ruffled Marcus's hair. "Maybe Monday. If it's okay with your mom."

"We'll see." Catrina ushered Marcus back to opening presents.

As soon as Marcus was done, Joe leaned over and whispered, "We can go." He gathered up their plates, and she trailed him into the kitchen.

Flavia followed them and wrapped Sarah in a hug. "It was good to meet you. Joe, you take good care of this one."

"That's the plan, Ma." He gave her a hug and a kiss on the cheek. "The food was amazing as always."

"I fixed you both plates to take home." She dug in the fridge and pulled out covered foil pans.

He peeked. "Oh good, I got tamales. I was hoping there were some left."

"Those tamales were amazing," Sarah said.

"Come at Christmas. We make tamales for days. You can learn." Flavia patted Sarah's hand.

"I would love to."

After saying thanks and goodbye to Catrina and giving hugs all around, they made their way out to Joe's truck. Once they were settled and headed back home, he reached for her hand. "Thanks for being a good sport. Everyone loved you. I hope it wasn't too overwhelming."

"It was." She smiled at him. "But in a good way. I've never been to a big family party. The closest I came was when I'd go camping with my friend's family from church. But they only had four kids."

"You are an only child, right?"

"My brother died as a baby, when I was four." She thought about not saying the rest, but she was too tired to analyze the pros and cons. And if she was going to have a future with Joe, he needed to know. She'd met his family. If this was a deal breaker, it was better to know now.

"A fire broke out in our house one night. I remember Dad rushing me outside in my nightgown. He'd grabbed a blanket off my bed and wrapped it around me. The grass was wet and prickly on my bare feet. It was so hot and bright out from the fire leaping up the back of the house. Mom rushed out of the house a minute later, my baby brother wrapped in a blanket. But she was crying and yelling at my dad. They laid my brother on the grass and did CPR. He wasn't breathing."

The images rolled across her mind as if it were yesterday. She could hear the flames, feel the heat of losing everything she owned. "The fire department showed up and some of them worked on my brother before taking him and my mom to the hospital. Dad and I followed in the car. I remember being afraid to walk across the parking lot and into the hospital barefoot. The asphalt was still warm from the day, but the tile floor was cold on my feet. One of the nurses sat me at her desk and let me draw. I remember thinking I had to draw the house as it was before it burned down, so they would know how to rebuild it. And I was frustrated that I couldn't get it right. I kept asking for more paper to start over.

"Then one of the firefighters showed up. He brought me Cindy, my favorite doll. She was a little dirty and smelled like smoke, but she was okay. Until that moment I had forgotten all about her. How could I do that? She was my favorite baby doll."

She shrugged and wiped the tears from her face. "After that, all I remember was staying in a hotel for days before we moved into a rental house. And my mom crying. All the time. I don't think she was ever happy again."

They were parked in front of her condo. She had no idea how long they'd been there. She unclipped her keys from her tote, but Joe took them from her.

He helped her out of the truck and into the house. Once inside, he wrapped his arms around her. But her tears had dried up. A cold hollow spot filled her chest.

"That explains all the smoke detectors," Joe whispered against her hair. "You're afraid of fire."

"Terrified."

CHAPTER TWENTY-THREE

SARAH FINISHED HER WEEKLY REPORT to Mark. He didn't expect it, but she liked to keep him in the loop. Plus, it helped her see concretely what their team had accomplished and what they needed to work on this week. And she needed some normalcy in her life after such an emotional weekend.

Joe had picked her up for church yesterday, and she'd been glad for his presence. She wasn't sure how she'd react to seeing the whole choir on stage without her. Kyle met them on the patio at church, and they found seats in the middle, the most crowded spot. She wanted to go unnoticed, lost in the crowd.

She ran her thumb over the pages of her Bible, the gilded edges fanning under her finger. When she was little, she used to imagine someone with a tiny paintbrush dabbing the gold on each thin page and marveled at their control and detail. It wasn't until she was much older that she realized the pages were probably gilded all at once when the book was bound. She glanced through the bulletin and kept her eyes off the stage, even though Heather was up there. Out of the corner of her eye, she saw Kyle wave to Heather.

See? She was fine. Until the music started.

Ryan came out and welcomed everyone. The worship team followed. She kept her eyes on the lyrics on the screen, but she couldn't keep Ryan's voice out of her head. How could he just stand there being his normal engaging self after what he'd said to her? Was he that good of an actor? Or maybe he really believed what he said. She didn't know.

As they closed in prayer, tears squeezed out of her shut eyes. With her head bowed, her nose started dripping. She tried to discreetly sniff and wiped at her eyes with the back of her hand. Then she opened them, staring, hoping the air would dry them out.

The prayer ended, and she glanced up. Big mistake. Ryan spotted her, held her gaze for a moment, before moving off stage.

She had no idea what he was thinking.

After the message, during the closing song, she made sure not to catch Ryan's eye. If he was looking for her, she didn't know. At the last note, Joe was already moving them out the row and up the aisle. She didn't want to give Ryan the chance to talk to her, and she was grateful Joe understood.

Outside she slipped on her sunglasses. She did it; she got through the service, but she was drained. They walked toward the parking lot. She waved and smiled at people but really didn't want to talk to anyone. She just wanted to go home and take a nap.

"Sure you don't want to come to lunch with us?" Kyle offered. Joe looked at Sarah.

"No, thanks. But I appreciate it." She gave a small smile. And then Joe took her home. They ate leftovers from the party for lunch and watched Netflix. He'd been able to keep her mind off it all.

Today on their walk, she'd deliberately kept the conversation light. And he hadn't brought up her revelation of her big fear of fire. She wasn't quite sure what to make of that. She sort of regretted bringing it up. But then again, she didn't. Her first instinct to be honest was the correct one. And it didn't seem to have scared Joe off. And since nearly a week had gone by with no more messages from "Greg," she could just about take a deep breath, relax, and enjoy Joe's company.

Even though she was acutely aware that he was working today. A verse floated through her mind. *Do not be anxious about anything, but in every situation, by prayer and petition, with thanksgiving, present your requests to God.* Philippians 4:6, if she remembered correctly from Bible camp. Every time she worried about Joe, she'd turn it into a prayer. Hopefully, it'd help her worrying. It would certainly benefit her prayer life.

Back from a medical call, Joe sat at his desk working on paperwork. The part of his job he liked least. Certainly Sarah had no cause to worry about this part of his day. He hadn't known what to say when she told him about losing her brother in a fire. His heart broke for her. And it was unfortunately something he'd seen in his line of work. Worse, there was nothing he could do to make it better. With her terror of fire, how could she even date him? At what point would her fear for him be too much? Did they even have a chance? He couldn't guarantee that he wouldn't be injured or killed.

No, only God could do that. In fact, Joe took great comfort in the fact that God already knew the number of his days. But he couldn't think of a way to say that to Sarah that didn't sound glib. And then Sunday she'd had to deal with Ryan trying to stare her down at church. The guy was such a jerk. He had half a mind to talk to Pastor Tom himself. Probably would have if he knew Sarah wouldn't throw a fit if she found out. And she would find out because Pastor Tom would call her in for her side of the story.

Joe knew her well enough now to know she hoped it would all just fade away. For her sake, he hoped so too.

A knock sounded, and his door opened, McCoy standing there. "Hey, big hero. You have company."

Not Macy. The dread must have shown on his face because McCoy laughed. "Just your sister and nephew."

Relief sluiced through him. He stood and hurried to the apparatus floor. The hero thing needed to stop. That's all he'd heard all day. An enlarged version of the photo had been printed out and tacked to the bulletin board, and the guys didn't let an opportunity pass to tease him about it.

The guys already had Marcus up in the truck. He gave Catrina a hug.

"This is all he's talked about since Saturday. Thanks for letting him come."

"Happy to. It's such a simple thing to make him so happy." They watched as Marcus pretended to drive and be on the radio. One of the guys had put a way-too-big helmet on his head.

Catrina eyed him. "Speaking of happy, you seem pretty content. Have anything to do with Sarah? Who we all like, by the way."

He glanced around. None of the guys were listening. They were helping Marcus, pointing out different parts of the truck, explaining how different tools worked. "Yeah. She's pretty great. She's had it rough lately with being the last one to see a missing contractor alive, and there's been some fallout from that. But being in the same complex, I can keep an eye on her. And I loan her my dog at night." He grinned.

"No ulterior motive there. So we didn't scare her off?"

He shook his head. "She's an only child. Her brother died as a baby." He left off how, not sure how much Sarah would want him to share. "But she had a family that took her under their wing when she was younger, so I think she's always longed to be part of something bigger, even if she watches from the sidelines."

Catrina nudged his shoulder. "Don't screw it up. Marcus already has you two married off. He said he's going to be your 'ring bear.'"

He laughed at that and moved to catch Marcus as he jumped off the truck. "Let's see the rest of this place." But Catrina's words rang in his head. No, he wasn't going to screw this up. In fact, there was one way maybe he could help her.

Shadow whined at the screen door. Sarah was running late this morning, for no real good reason. She just seemed to be moving through molasses. Joe would be here any minute for their walk. Probably why Shadow was whining.

Yep. Joe hustled up the steps to Sarah's condo.

"Come on in." She raised her voice. The screen opened. "Sorry, I'm running late. Just let me get my shoes."

"No problem." He petted Shadow while she dashed back to her bedroom for her shoes then came back to the living room, plopping on the couch to put them on.

Joe got Shadow's leash and clipped it on. "Hey, do you have any plans after work? I know I still owe you a nice date on Friday, but I was thinking about something."

"Sure. I'm not doing anything." And the idea of spending time with him was much more attractive than being alone with her thoughts. She tugged on her shoes and started on the laces.

"Good. There's still something about that project of yours that burned down. I don't like the answers I'm getting from Arson. I thought we might take a look around. We can't get too close; I'm sure they've fenced it off by now. I don't know that it'll accomplish anything, but I thought you might be curious. Since it stays light pretty late, I thought we could go after you get off work."

She stilled, hand on her laces. Shock, fear, and anticipation all raced through her in a confusing swirl. But he would be with her, and maybe seeing it in person would help with the nightmares. "Yeah. I think I would." She let out a breath. "Actually, we're working on another project not too far from there. I keep thinking I'd like to go check it out. But I know Kyle wouldn't want me to go alone. Maybe we could swing by it while we're out there." She finished tying her shoes and stood. But Kyle would be fine with Joe being with her. An image flashed through her mind of Joe's arm tight around her waist pulling her out of her trashed condo. She didn't doubt for a moment that he could keep her safe.

They headed out of her condo, Joe checking the door behind them, making sure it was locked.

Yep. He would keep her safe. But it was his safety she worried about.

Joe glanced over at Sarah sitting next to him in his truck. She'd been quiet ever since he picked her up. Answering questions about work but staring through the windshield a lot. Her hands twisted in her lap. A different Sarah than the one this morning or even the one he'd seen at lunch when she'd called and said the police had released her car and asked him to help her pick it up and return the rental.

They turned onto Via Flores. As the street snaked around, a chain link fence threaded with yellow warning tape slowly came into view; then the charred skeleton of the building.

He nosed the truck to the fence. They sat in silence a few minutes. Sarah's face was nearly expressionless as she stared out the window. He dealt with burned down buildings all the time. He knew the consequences were devastating when someone lost their home or property. He was glad she'd told him about the fire when she was little. Because he imagined she might be seeing images of that all over again.

"It's like a book burning."

Her voice startled Joe out of his thoughts, almost as if she were reading them.

"It's the same kind of senseless destruction of someone else's creative work. Yes, a book is just paper and ink. Just like this building was wood and nails. But what it represents is so much more. It was one of my favorite projects. It wasn't just a typical concrete tilt-up; I got to do some interesting and creative design on it. I put a lot of myself into that building." Finally, she turned her eyes to him. They were glowing, almost like they were lit from behind by a burning ember. "It's silly, I know. Really overstating things, I'm sure to most people. But it's the closest thing I've found to describe why this bothers me so much."

Joe couldn't think of anything to say. He didn't try.

"Can we go look around?"

"Sure." They got out of the truck. He was glad she was wearing leather work boots. Through the fence he pointed out the burn paths and where they found the gas can. "Didn't seem like someone wanted to hide the fact that this was set intentionally."

"I've heard about owners burning projects for the insurance money when they had financial difficulties or their financial backers pulled out. But that wouldn't make sense here. The owner could have easily doubled his profit selling it partially completed. Somehow it's related to Greg's disappearance." She wrapped her arms around herself. "Mostly it just gives me the creeps."

He put his hand on her shoulder. "Anything else you want to see here?" His pulse picked up.

She sighed and shook her head. "Thanks for bringing me, though. In a strange way, it helps."

"I'm glad." He glanced over the charcoaled building before meeting her eyes again.

Tony scrolled down the list on his phone. Just about once a day he wanted to chuck it out his window into the ocean below. Most of the time it was more trouble than just writing things down. But how would it look if he pulled out his old DayTimer? So he struggled with it until he was too frustrated. Then he got Nick to show him what to do.

The list consisted of everyone in the industry he thought might have a connection, no matter how slight, with Rankin and Associates. It was a game he played well. Just make a few calls, shoot the breeze, ask a few questions like "Hey, have you heard anything about Rankin and Associates? I'm thinking of doing some business with them, but I've heard a few things that made me question. Nothing specific, which is why I'm calling. Just checking it out." He knew how this industry ran on personal contacts.

And those he had a more intimate business relationship with … well, they got more pointed direction. Continuing down the list, he'd called everyone he could think of, spent most of the day on it. He stared at it a few more minutes. No one else came to mind.

He set the phone down and grabbed a handful of Jelly Bellys. He had dinner reservations in half an hour.

Nick pushed through the door a little too forcefully.

Tony studied him. "Did you get it done?"

"Yeah. But I don't even know if they'll go in. What if one of the workers discovers it tomorrow?" Nick's gaze darted around the room, barely landing on Tony.

Tony wondered if he was high, if Greg had gotten him into that crap. "They'll either move it to get down there, or they'll step through it. Which would be an unfortunate job site accident." No, Nick wasn't high, just agitated about something. "What's eating you?"

"Nothing." He shoved his hands into his jeans pockets, his tattooed sleeves disappearing. "I don't know. I just don't like the idea of her getting hurt. It could be bad if they fall down there.

Chapter Twenty-Four

THEY DROVE TOWARD THE JOB site in silence for a while, Sarah trying to visualize the route in her mind. She hadn't been out here since the day she got directions from Greg. And look how that had turned out. She shuddered.

"You okay?" Joe cut his eyes toward her.

"Oh, yeah. I was just thinking I whaven't been out here since Greg disappeared. Just a little weird is all."

They were getting close to the job site now. This was the part she always had difficulty with.

"Which street am I looking for?" Joe asked.

"Um, it used to be the first left after the eucalyptus, but now those are gone. And they even graded it, so I can't tell where they used to be."

Joe laughed. "I like how you find your way around."

Her heart warmed a little at that. She'd expected a little more teasing. "I think that's it up there. I'm not totally sure."

Joe turned on the street, but after going about a half mile it clearly wasn't the right street. He pulled over to the side of the deserted road.

Sarah resisted the urge to squirm. She felt like an idiot. What architect couldn't find the job site, multiple times even? She pulled her laptop out of her tote and opened it. Luckily, she'd been working on the file, so it was saved to her local drive instead of in the cloud. She pulled up the site plan, zooming and scrolling until only the site map showed. She turned the computer so Joe could see the screen. "This is where we need to be."

Joe studied it and got his bearings. "Ah, okay. I think I get it."

"Sorry I'm, um, a little directionally challenged, in case you didn't notice."

He shot her a smile before taking a drink out of his water bottle. Setting it back in the cup holder he said, "Well, I was getting a little worried you were perfect." He put the truck in gear and turned around.

The warmth in her heart spread throughout her chest. She wanted to dwell on it, on what he meant, but if she did he could probably see it on her face. She tucked it away to think about later.

In two minutes, they were pulling up to the job site. "Is this it?" Joe turned in his seat to face her.

"Yep." She looked at the plans for this site. Her eyes flicked back and forth between the building in front of her and her computer screen. She didn't even know what she was looking for, but she let herself get immersed in the drawing, feeling it come to life, as if she were actually walking through it.

Joe was watching her.

Her cheeks tingled as blood flowed to them. "Sorry. I tend to get a little lost in my work."

"No problem." He nodded at the computer. "Show me the plans." His gaze on her was intense, warming her clear to her toes.

She walked him through the plans and her ideas. What did Joe think of the place? He saw her vision, but he also looked at it through firefighter's eyes. Where were the exits, how would you get equipment in here, was this a fire-retardant building? Some of those she had to contend with when designing the building, but she treated them more like challenges, parameters that she had to design within, like disability access and parking requirements.

The fact that he was interested in what she did and asked intelligent questions filled her in a way she hadn't felt in a long time. Someone outside of work actually cared about what she did. She wasn't quite sure what to do with that.

She closed her laptop and slid it back into its sleeve and then her tote. "I think I'm ready to go look at the site." She shoved her tote in the extended cab area, out of sight.

Lengthening shadows of the fading day made her careful where she put her feet. She wore a pair of work boots that she kept in her car for when she needed to go to job sites. Nails and screws and pieces of metal could easily slice through a pair of regular shoes. Tetanus she didn't need. She alternated between looking at the building and watching where she was stepping.

It was quiet up here, only the crunch of Joe's and her footsteps, the toll road a distant hum. The building was in its awkward, gangly teen stage. All angles and bare studs and concrete subflooring. Yet she could envision how it would look when the ugly duckling turned into a swan. She always started with the swan stage and worked backward.

She tilted her head back and stared at the façade, the gaping holes in the sheathing, the bare metal beams, the dangling wires nothing like the final version she pictured in her mind. Squinting, she overlapped the two. Yep, so far so good.

Another step and she was in the shadow of the building. She pushed her sunglasses up on her head and waited for her eyes to adjust.

"See anything out of place yet?" Joe kicked his toe at a piece of rebar lying in the dirt.

She'd almost forgotten why they'd come. She scanned the

area, peering into the darker shadows. Slowly she shook her head. "No. Not that I can tell. Let's go inside."

She took a step forward, and Joe put his hand on her arm. She looked at him, eyebrows raised.

"Just … be careful. Okay?"

She nodded. He was always protective of her. It was sweet. And she'd come to rely on it.

She stepped onto the concrete and looked around. This was the main lobby. She loved this part of the building best. Open, airy, with a small intimate alcove off to the side. When it was done, the tumbled travertine floors, the polished wood, and the glass upper-level windows would make this space breathtaking.

She started down one of the side halls. The stairwell was around this way. The floor changed from concrete to plywood sheathing as they began crossing over the basement. All of the facility equipment would be down there. She didn't need to see that. Unless—

"Hey, Joe?" She turned. Her foot fell into nothingness.

Something clamped around her arm.

Joe's back was on fire. No, not fire. Cold concrete seeped in through his shirt and pants. He opened his eyes. It was dim down here, but as his eyes adjusted there was enough light filtering in to see the debris that filled the basement. At least that's where he figured they were.

They.

Sarah. He didn't see her.

"Sarah?" Did his voice really sound that panicky? "Sarah!" His voice echoed around him.

"Here." Pause. "I'm here."

"Where?" He pushed himself to a sitting position. Pain sliced through his back, sending a flood of warmth through his shirt and into the waistband of his pants. He was bleeding, pretty heavily by the feel of it. Okay. Triage. He had to figure out Sarah's status first.

By sitting up he could see her. She'd landed on a pile of lumber, just beyond his reach, her ankle twisted at an unnatural angle. That explained her shortness of breath. Pain. "Does anything else hurt besides your ankle?"

"My wrist—" she took a breath. "But it's—" breath—"just a sprain."

Joe's mind kicked in, working on autopilot, overriding the pain. He needed to know what was going on with his back, and he needed pressure applied. But Sarah couldn't move over to him. Maybe he could move over to her? Okay, but then she couldn't apply pressure. She'd be lucky not to pass out from the pain. And he needed to look at her ankle.

Okay, how to get over that pile of debris she'd landed on? He gritted his teeth and blew out his breath. He drew his legs close to his body. Concentrating on *not* using his back, just his legs, he squatted and pushed up to standing. A quick shove, followed by another warm gush, and he was standing. Okay, that hurt. He saw stars and grunted to push the blood back up to his head. He did not need to pass out and get a head injury.

Moving slowly toward Sarah, careful to keep his back as neutral as possible, he worked around the debris. But now he couldn't bend over without splitting his back open. Slowly squatting, and using his hands for balance, he hovered over Sarah.

He couldn't get a good read on her pallor in this light, but she looked pale. Her eyes were closed. "Sarah?"

They fluttered open. "My ankle's broken."

"Probably." He grinned at her.

She grimaced.

"Does your head hurt anywhere?"

"No, I don't think it hit at all. My foot took the brunt of it. Then my wrist. What happened?"

Joe studied the hole they'd fallen through. Plywood sheathing splintered all around the opening. "Looks like we fell through some plywood. I tried to grab you, but we both came tumbling down."

He stared at her eyes. Pupils equally dilated. Couldn't tell about their reactivity here in this dim light. But she said she hadn't hit her head. He didn't see any blood anywhere.

"Give me your non-sprained wrist."

She moved her hand away from where it cradled her other wrist and extended it toward him. Making sure he was balanced, he lifted his own hand to take hers, closing his fingers around her wrist until he found her pulse. Then, still balancing, he rotated their hands until he could see the second hand on his watch. And started counting. Okay, a little high but that was to be expected from the pain. Reluctantly he released her hand.

They both needed to get help soon. And he needed to get pressure on his back before he passed out. He started to reach for his phone but before his hand could get there, he could see it clearly plugged into the recharger in his truck.

"Do you have your cell phone with you?"

Her hand went to her pocket. Then the other side. "Yes. But it's under my sprained wrist. Let me maneuver a bit." She grimaced as she lifted her sprained hand out of the way and awkwardly reached for her phone with the opposite hand. She blew out a breath. "Got it." She thumbed it on. "No signal. Figures. Reception is terrible out here anyway. Probably more so in a basement." Her voice wavered at the end.

"Okay. So. No way to call for help. Right now, I need to figure out how to get us both comfortable."

"You're bleeding." Sarah's gaze glued to his side.

He looked down. The blood had seeped through his shirt and was oozing around the front. "Yeah, something ripped through my back. I need to get pressure on it to stop the bleeding."

Sarah eased into a sitting position. "If you can turn around, I can do it."

"Not sitting like that. You'd get tired too soon. I need …" He scanned the basement. "Okay, I can press my back against the wall and use my shirt as a pressure bandage." He stood again, just using his legs. The room faded. *Please, Lord. Don't let me pass out. Please.* The darkness faded slowly. He moved toward the closest wall and slowly lowered himself again. Taking a deep breath and biting down, he grabbed the hem of his shirt and started to lift. Six inches into it the pain was intense, blood was gushing, and he couldn't force the muscles on one side to work. The shirt was sticking to the wound, pulling. He dropped his arms and took breaths. Maybe in a minute he'd have the energy to try again.

Sarah was watching him. "Let me do that for you."

"No, you can't get over here. Give me a minute, and I'll come to you."

"I want to lean up against something anyway. Let me just try, okay?"

He nodded, not having the breath to argue. She'd figure it out soon enough.

He watched as she studied the area around her, formulating a plan. Her broken foot was resting on a piece of two-by-four. She eyed the distance to him, bent her good knee and grabbed the wood. Pushing with her good leg, she started toward him. A small, not-quite-stifled scream escaped her lips. But she did two more pushes in his direction before stopping, shoulders heaving.

"Sarah, don't." His breath was back, but he didn't think he could get up just yet.

She shook her head. "Just a couple more."

Sure enough, two more pushes, a couple groans and heaving shoulders and she was on his right side. She was pale and breathing hard.

"Put your head on my shoulder and rest a minute."

And she did without comment, which told him more about her pain level than anything.

He started thinking. Under normal circumstances they could spend the night down here without harm. Yeah, they'd be cold and uncomfortable, but they'd survive until the workers returned in the morning. But with her ankle needing attention and his bleeding, things were looking more dicey.

She took a deep breath and leaned away from him. "Tell me if I need to stop, okay?"

"Just do it."

She reached around him with her good hand and pulled at the hem of his shirt, lifting it up. He worked one arm out until the fabric bunched around his shoulder. Then she started in on the other side. As soon as she started tugging, he felt the material pull against the wound.

She stopped and looked at it. "It's stuck back here. The shirt's ripped, and it looks like some of it's embedded in the wound." The tension wove through her voice.

It was going to be fun getting that out. "Just do what you can. They'll clean it out better at the hospital."

"Okay. Here goes." She yanked hard on that last word, barely giving him time to suck in a breath.

It felt like half his back came away with the shirt. He was too weak with pain to help her get it off over his head, but somehow she managed and was folding it into a pad while warmth cascaded down his back. The room dimmed.

"Lie back."

He barely noticed she'd pressed his shirt against the wound. He eased back, muscles protesting all the while, until cool, hard concrete supported his back. He pressed as hard as he could to staunch the flow.

He swallowed, trying to keep the pressure on. "How'd it look?" His voice missed the light tone he was going for by a mile.

"About nine inches long, pretty jagged, into the muscle in places." If it weren't for the slight tremor in her voice, she could have been telling him what she had for lunch. And a gash like that couldn't have been a pleasant sight. If he wasn't so afraid of passing out, he'd be impressed.

"Thanks. I know that wasn't easy."

"I think it was harder for you." A wry tone permeated her words. "If I'd brought my purse with me, we'd at least have some Band-Aids and power bars. Though I think we're past Band-Aids."

He just sat there concentrating on breathing in and out. And staying conscious. After a moment, he studied her ankle. Distorted, swollen, turning purple. But no bone sticking through the skin, so that was good.

"We need to get you to a hospital. But there's no cell service, and neither of us is in any condition to try and find a way out of here." The glow from her phone lit up her face. She studied her phone. "Maybe we can get a text message out. If there's a little bit of a signal, it might send when a phone call can't. I think we should text as many people as we can who could come get us." She started tapping her screen with her good hand. "Kyle, Heather … do you know anyone else's numbers off the top of your head?"

He gave her Dan and Jeff's numbers, amazed that he even knew them. "I didn't know you were left handed."

She frowned. "I'm not. It's just the only hand that works."

"It's working pretty good. As good as your right hand."

She grinned. "I'm ambidextrous."

"Really?"

"Yeah."

"Cool."

"Most of the time. I think it jumbles my brain a bit. The left and right sides sometimes get confused as to who is in control. Causes paralysis."

He laughed a little. Too much hurt his back.

"Anyone else?"

"The only other numbers I know belong to my mom and

sisters. And that would just freak them out." He grinned at her. "And I know yours. But you're already here with me."

She gave him a soft smile and tilted her head. "You memorized my number?"

"It seemed important."

He reached over and took her good hand. "Weird as this situation is, I like problem-solving with you. Maybe we can do a puzzle or something when we get out of here."

She smiled. "A much safer way to solve problems." She paused. "Okay, here goes nothing. Let's pray this works." Tucking her phone in her pocket, she curled her good leg under her, and pushed up against the wall until she was standing on her good leg. She groaned but slid her phone out of her pocket and tapped it, then lifted it high above her head and waved it in a slow arc.

His heart squeezed in his chest as she levered herself up. He prayed. Hard. And hoped the Lord heard him even though this whole situation was his fault. And he couldn't even get them out of it.

Chapter Twenty-Five

SARAH'S FOOT THROBBED WITH PAIN as gravity pulled the blood into it. When she could stand it no longer, she looked at her phone. There was no red exclamation point saying her text didn't go through. So maybe it did. She slid back down, her good leg wobbly, landing with a thump.

Joe reached over, sliding his hand on top of hers, curling his fingers under her palm.

The warmth was comforting, soothing, traveling from her arm to her heart.

They sat in comfortable silence for a moment.

"So, think any of those messages will get to anybody?"

He was silent for a moment. "Nope. But don't worry. Someone will come get us. We might get a little cold and thirsty. But we should be okay."

Though if she had to bet, based on the confidence in his voice on that sentence, he was trying to reassure her more than anything. Given that he was a paramedic, he had to know that his bleeding back would not do well waiting until the morning for someone to find them.

Joe squeezed her hand. "Let's pray. Better than worrying."

She laced her fingers through his. "Good idea." She closed her eyes.

"Lord, you know this is a difficult situation we're in. But you see us, and you're right here with us. You know what we need. We'd love it if you'd send us some help tonight and if you could keep our pain levels manageable. But more than anything, we thank you for the gift of your Son. No matter what happens, that will always be enough. Amen."

Sarah blinked back tears. "Amen." Wow. His words, his comfortable relationship with God, bringing their focus back to the most important thing, curled around her heart and wedged peace firmly there.

She met his gaze. "Thank you."

He nodded. "We're going to be okay. No matter what." He shifted his legs and grimaced.

She clicked the flashlight app on her phone and checked his shirt bandage. The blood was still soaking through, though it seemed to have slowed some. How long could he go like that without needing some help?

"What's wrong?"

Had she spoken out loud? "What do you mean?"

"You're biting your lip, just the lower left side. Something's bothering you."

Only Heather had ever mentioned that Sarah did that when she was thinking. The fact that Joe had noticed pleased her more than she would have thought. Because it meant he noticed her. And it had been a long time since anyone had noticed her. Deciding not to ask why he'd noticed, she simply said, "The bleeding's slowed, but it's still there. How long before you need to get help?"

"Oh, about an hour ago." The light tone was strained, and he pressed his back further into the wall, bringing his shoulder firmly into contact with her. She didn't move away; it was comforting. He nudged her with his knee. "Why? Afraid I'm going to die on you?"

"You're not. I won't let you." The vehemence in her voice and the tingling in her eyes surprised her.

"I know. Sorry. That was a bad joke." He nudged her again with his knee, this time leaving his leg up against hers.

It was getting cold in here, the coolness of the concrete seeped into her back and legs. The faint light filtering in was growing dimmer. She craved the warmth his leg provided up against hers.

"In the meantime, let's make good use of our time. Now that I have your undivided attention—" she heard more than saw his grin—"I've got a few questions for you. Starting with, what made you want to be an architect?"

She leaned her head back against the wall. "I used to draw houses when I was little. Places I wanted to live with turrets and huge libraries and fireplaces and secret passageways. I think my parents hoped I'd be a doctor or an engineer, but I needed something with more ... I don't know. Something. Art, maybe? Beauty? It's hard to say since it really wasn't valued in my home. When I got to college, I had the opportunity to do the things that I had always ached to do, like draw and sing. And I wasn't too bad. Architecture seemed to be the perfect balance of brains and beauty."

"Like you."

It was completely dark now, so she couldn't read his face. She nudged his shoulder instead.

His voice got quiet. "You must have had a lot of time alone when you were young to draw and imagine."

"Yeah." Her voice matched his. "After my brother died, my mom was never the same. She pretty much didn't come out of her room. Anytime I went in there it was dark, the lights off, curtains pulled tight. Now I know she was clinically depressed.

"My dad tried to help, but he was gone all day working. He

bought me a dog when I was eight to help with the loneliness after school. Gaucho. He was a mutt." She laughed a little at the memory. "But he was an escape artist, and my dad was always after me to keep the backyard gate latched. I'd come home from school and go through the gate and Gaucho would be so happy to see me. It was nice, like I was important to someone."

"Dogs are good at that."

"Yeah. They are. But one day he ran past me. There was a cat in the yard across the street, and Gaucho headed straight for him. Right in front of a car. He got hit." Tears clogged her throat. Still. After all these years.

Joe tightened his hand around hers. "It wasn't your fault, you know."

She nodded and swiped at her eyes. "I know. In my head. But my mom ..." She couldn't even say what her mom had said to her. About not being able to take care of anything. About it being her fault.

"Your mom had an illness. It made her say things that weren't true. She probably said a lot of things that weren't true to you."

Somehow Joe had become a mind reader down in this basement. And a part of her heart that she could barely remember existing, began to glow and beat.

Joe didn't have to see Sarah's face to know tears were streaming down it. His heart was doing funny things in his chest. All he wanted to do was pull her in his arms and promise her that nothing bad would happen again. But look where they were. He should have been going first, testing the floor. Right now, his job was to keep her as safe as he could. And that meant being her emotional support, if that's all he could be.

Sarah cleared her throat. "So how about you? How did you decide to be a firefighter? Was it that fire that Kyle and Scott were talking about at the Fourth of July party?"

He gave a small laugh that he didn't feel. "No, it started before that. I know something about having a parent who has problems. My dad was an alcoholic. I think he was okay when my sisters were little. But by the time I came along ... well, he was drunk most of the time. And sometimes he was really mean." He let out a breath. Even Scott and Kyle didn't know all of it, though they probably suspected.

"One day I was running around shooting things with my Nerf gun. Trina grabbed my arm and told me Dad was sleeping and to stop making so much noise. I knew enough that I didn't want to be the reason Dad woke up. He had been yelling at Mom earlier for the kitchen being dirty and then had disappeared into the bedroom. Which I had been happy about.

"I ran into the living room. My mom was there. Her head was in her hands, her shoulders shaking. I hated seeing her like that. So I tried to do something that would make her happy and make Dad not be mad. As I was unloading the dishwasher, I managed to cut myself on a knife. I grabbed a paper towel and had just started to put pressure on it as I heard sirens. They got louder and louder and pretty soon firefighters came through the front door with their equipment. And I wondered how they knew I'd cut my finger. It wasn't that bad. It had mostly stopped bleeding.

"Then I heard my mom's voice. She led the firefighters to their bedroom. I followed them down the hall and peeked in the doorway." He swallowed and let out a breath. "My dad was on the bed. I thought he was asleep, but the firefighters couldn't wake him up. They put oxygen on him and loaded him on a gurney. I slipped into the hall bathroom so I could keep watching but be out of their way.

"My mom raced around gathering up her shoes and purse. She saw me watching and put her arm around me. She said that Dad was sick. She had to go to the hospital, and I was supposed to be a good boy. I told her that I had unloaded the dishwasher and showed her my paper-towel-wrapped finger. She told me I was a good boy, that I was the man of the house now and I had to look after my sisters. I told her I would, even though the oldest two were in college. Turned out my dad had just about died from alcohol poisoning. The firefighters saved his life. And the whole thing scared my dad enough that he stayed sober for a while. He would even toss the ball around with me in the yard after school. In my mind, the firefighters did something magical in our house that day. I started watching *Emergency* reruns on the TV when I got home from school."

He took a shallow breath. It'd be easy to stop the story there, on a happy note. But he wanted something more with Sarah than just the shiny image that everyone else saw. He wanted her to know *him*, behind the mask. All of him. "My dad was in and out of rehab. He finally passed away my senior year of high school. I didn't handle it well. I partied too much and just drifted out of high school and into community college. Made a lot of choices I regret. If it weren't for Kyle and Scott pointing out I wasn't much different than my old man, I don't know where I'd be. I committed my life to Christ and straightened out.

"But I hadn't thought about being a firefighter in years. Until I came across a car wreck on the backside of El Toro, just after it was decommissioned. No cell phones then. The mom was trapped, and she had a little baby in the back. I got the baby out, put him in my car, and tried to put out the fire. The other guy in the wreck had a fire extinguisher, but it only worked for a bit. We tried throwing dirt, anything we could think of to keep the flames at bay until someone with some equipment could get the woman out of there.

"Someone finally did call 911, and the fire department showed up. I was pretty glad to see them. But I was talking to one of the guys afterward, and he told me about these info meetings they had. Seemed like as good of a choice as any. Plus, the flexibility and lack of routine appealed to me. Turned out I was pretty good at it. I decided to start climbing the leadership ladder. And somehow, that led to me trying to keep you from falling through the floor and both of us ending up hurt in the bottom of a basement. Quite a ride, huh?"

Her head brushed his bare shoulder. "It suits you."

"Yeah, it does." What little energy he had drained out of him. Leaning next to Sarah it seemed like she might be holding him up even. "I've never told anyone that whole story before."

She rubbed her thumb over the back of his hand. "Me neither. It's too bad it took a dark basement and some massive injuries for us to bare our souls." He heard the smile in her voice, but he recognized the truth of her words. This was a bond that they shared with each other alone. No matter what came next.

Sarah let out a sigh and wiggled until her head rested completely on his shoulder. Her soft hair brushed over his bare skin. What he wouldn't give to be able to put his arm around her.

How late was it anyway? He couldn't press the button on his watch to make it glow, and he didn't want to break the moment by asking her to check the time on her phone. It didn't matter anyway.

He turned and buried his nose in her hair. He could smell vanilla and some sort of exotic fruit like mangoes or papaya or something.

A wave of sleepiness washed over him, and he sighed. Sleep and Sarah. A nice combination he could only enjoy while they were down here. Because bottom line, he'd failed her. And he didn't want to be one more person in her life who had let her down.

A distant shout filtered through to Joe's consciousness, and then Sarah moved away, taking her warmth and delicious smell with her. Joe couldn't see a thing.

Another distant shout, maybe a little closer. "Joe! Sarah!"

Kyle? How did he know where to find them? The memories of sending messages slowly faded into view. "Hey!" Which came out like a croak. He cleared his throat. "Hey, Kyle! Down here, in the basement! But watch your step. The wood's bad up there."

Shuffling steps above them.

He could feel Sarah's shoulder move against his as she took a deep breath and heard her whispered prayer of thanks.

Lights flickered overhead. Then a beam found their hole and filtered down.

Joe looked away and blinked. "Yeah, that's us. Man, that's bright."

The light moved to the wall behind him, out of his eyes, illuminating their cell.

He looked up.

The light reflected off Kyle's face peering down at them. More footsteps and shouts followed. Kyle grinned. "Want some company?"

Joe stole a look at Sarah, whose attention was focused on Kyle.

"Yes, thank you!" He could hear the relief in her voice.

But he kind of liked the company he had. And he was going to miss it.

Chapter Twenty-Six

J OE STUDIED HIS FACE IN the mirror. Dark circles rimmed his eyes, his dark beard was a scruff across his face, his hair matted where he'd slept on it. The pain in his back kept him up most of the night. He'd ended up on the couch on his side. But he couldn't escape the nightmares of Sarah falling over and over into a black hole, just out of his reach.

He splashed water on his face and washed up as best he could without being able to shower. He couldn't get the staples wet. He gingerly lifted his arm to run a wet comb through his hair. It would have to do. He was shaking just from getting ready, and he still had to make it over to Sarah's house to let Shadow out.

He texted Sarah that he was coming over and that he'd let himself in with her key. He didn't want her having to get up and maneuver with her crutches. He locked the door behind him, staring at his truck parked out front. One of the guys had driven it back to his place, and Kyle had brought him and Sarah home from the hospital. No, it was ridiculous to drive the short distance to her house. He could walk and should since it'd be the only exercise he'd be getting for a while. He headed across the parking lot toward Sarah's condo. Keeping himself from going stir crazy would be a real challenge.

Or maybe a puzzle he and Sarah could work on together. A much safer one than their last one. He kept his pace slow and deliberate. The light was on in her living room. He knocked quickly before inserting the key. "It's me," he said as he pushed her door open.

Shadow nosed his leg. "Hey boy." He ruffled Shadow's fur.

Sarah was on the couch, foot propped up and iced, the TV on softly. She had turned her head when he came in. "Morning. Hope you had a better night than I did."

He laughed. "Maybe I should have just stayed here, and we could have been up all night watching movies and getting each other ice packs." He grabbed Shadow's leash from the entry table and snapped it on.

"Would have been about as restful. Help yourself to some coffee." She pointed to the mug on the coffee table in front of her. "I managed to get myself a cup without spilling it."

"Aw, I would have gotten it for you."

"At five in the morning?" She gave him a wry smile.

"See? Should have stayed over."

She shook her head and grinned.

Shadow whined.

"Okay, I get the message. I'll grab the coffee when I get back. I think this guy needs a quick walk around the building. Or maybe a slow one, considering how I'm moving." He stepped outside and let Shadow explore all the bushes around the condo. Luckily, he seemed to know Joe was hurt and didn't tug on the leash or want to wander far. In no time at all, Shadow bounded back up the steps to Sarah's condo, almost like he was worried about her. "That makes two of us, boy."

They headed inside, and Joe made himself a cup of coffee. He knew Sarah's kitchen as well as his own by this time. He liked the feeling. Taking his coffee, he eased himself into the chair next to Sarah's couch. "So, you didn't sleep well either?"

She shook her head. "It's hard to sleep on my back, and I can't exactly sleep any other way with this cast. Plus, it throbbed all night. In fact, it's time for more ibuprofen but I need to eat something." She let out a sigh. "It's so difficult to do anything."

He gave her a wry grin. "I know the feeling. But I'm a little more mobile than you. Want some eggs?"

There was a knock at the door. He raised his eyebrows. "Expecting anybody?"

"No." She craned her neck to see out the blinds but was at the wrong angle.

He levered himself out of the chair and moved to the door, peeking through the peephole before opening the door. "Hey, Heather."

"Hey, Joe. I figured you'd be here." She grinned at both of them.

Sarah rolled her eyes. "He came to walk Shadow."

"Of course." Heather moved into the kitchen and set down the bag she was carrying. "I figured you both could use some food in your stomachs and wouldn't quite be up to cooking. So I brought muffins and a quiche."

"You're a lifesaver. I was just going to make us some eggs." Joe got out plates and silverware, and Heather dished up the food.

"Need anything while I'm here?" She pulled open the fridge. "It's pretty empty in here. I'll bring you some groceries this afternoon."

Joe started a mental list. They needed to think about what they would need and what would be difficult to do. He could have a larger grocery order delivered later, but there were probably other things they'd need help with. And the fact that he was thinking in terms of Sarah and him together made his heart do flips. They were in this together. And maybe this was God making something good out of one of Joe's stupid mistakes. Allowing him to spend time with Sarah. He carried their plates to the living room and handed one to Sarah.

"Diet Coke," Sarah said to Heather as she took the plate from him. "I think I only have one left."

Heather laughed. "Can't have that." She came over to Sarah with a fresh ice pack for her ankle then sat on the coffee table, her face full of concern. "I'm so glad you were able to get a text to me and Kyle. I can't imagine what would have happened to the two of you if you'd had to spend the night down there."

"Sarah gets all the credit for that idea. But it never should have happened. I should have gone first, testing the floor. I just didn't grab her in time." He set his plate down, not hungry.

Heather raised her eyebrows at him. "How well do you know Sarah, Joe?"

He tilted his head, not sure what she was getting at. "Pretty well, I think. Why?"

"You know she would have gone to that site without you, right? She's used to going to sites alone all the time. Maybe not always after work hours, but if you hadn't gone with her, she would have gone anyway. And she would have been at the bottom of that basement all by herself." Tears welled in her eyes. "You know Kyle wouldn't let me go with him to get you guys? He was afraid of what condition he'd find you both in, and he didn't want me to see it. The fact that you are both here and okay …" She swiped at her eyes. "I'm just glad you were with her, Joe. You helped her."

Oh. He didn't know what to say to that. But she had defended him with vehemence and corrected his thinking.

Sarah's hand landed on his knee. "She's right, Joe. Even though I was in pain, I was never afraid because you were with me."

He covered her hand with his and met her gaze. "I always want to do that for you." He blinked back the moisture in his eyes. He didn't deserve this kind of support. But he'd take it.

Sarah balanced her computer on her lap. Joe had brought it to her, despite his objections that she should be resting, not working. But she just needed to check a few things. She'd already talked to Mark on the phone and then Eric. Eric would be in charge of the office while she was out, but he had promised to come to her with any issues instead of going to Mark.

Unfortunately, she'd already gotten a couple of texts about things Eric had done that weren't going over well. She did her best to smooth things over and hoped that everything would hang together until she could get back into the office.

She set the computer on the coffee table.

"What do you want to watch next?" Joe had the Netflix menu open on the TV. "Or do you want something to eat?"

He'd been hopping up to get her anything she wanted or he thought she needed, even though she could see how it hurt him to move. She reached for her crutches wedged under Shadow. That couldn't be comfortable, but he hadn't left her side.

"What do you need? I can get it." Joe rose from the chair

"I have to go to the bathroom. You can't help with that." She tugged one crutch free. Shadow looked from her to Joe.

"Come here, boy." Joe patted his leg, and Shadow came over, freeing Sarah to get the other crutch.

She swung her leg off the pillow and sat for a moment as the blood readjusted itself across her body. Then using her good leg and her crutches, she pushed off the couch.

Joe had his hands out like a parent expecting a toddler to fall.

She laughed. "I'll be fine. It's not like this is a big place. I've got maybe four steps to go." She nodded to the kitchen. "I think Heather brought over some popcorn with the groceries. You could make that for us to go with our next series binge."

"Okay, but call if you need me."

"Not likely." Because she'd text Heather to come help her first. In fact, she'd need some help getting in and out of the bathtub at some point. She still smelled like a hospital. She looked in the bathroom mirror. Ugh. It was a wonder Joe hadn't run screaming from her. Though it was kind of nice to have gotten to this comfortable stage with him. After what they'd shared in the basement, there was a bond there. Something permanent, she hoped. Yep, she loved him, no doubt about that. And he was the sweetest guy in the world, but did he love her? And could she handle his job? All questions she didn't have the energy to deal with right now.

Crutching her way back into the living room, she settled on the couch. Joe brought her a new ice pack and handed her a bowl of popcorn. He slid his chair so it was touching the couch and a groan escaped.

"What are you doing? Don't hurt yourself."

"I'm fine. And it's worth it." He lowered into the chair.

"Why?"

He reached for her hand. "So I can do this." He interlaced their fingers. "I'm sorry this happened. But I'm not sorry I get to spend time with you."

Warmth flooded her as he held her gaze. Did she see in his eyes something more than the tenderness and compassion that she always saw? "Me too."

And what could he see in her eyes? She looked away. "And it's a good excuse to get caught up on our shows. So. What are we watching?"

His phone buzzed on the coffee table. *Macy* appeared on his screen with a text. Huh. That wasn't one of his sisters. Someone from work?

He scooped up the phone with a frown. Then let go of her hand and ran his hand over his face.

"What's wrong?"

He shook his head. "Macy is at my house with some sort of get-well gift. Apparently, she went by the station thinking I was working today, and they told her the whole story."

A hard ball settled in her stomach. "Who's Macy?"

He blew out a breath. "She's with the PR firm the department hired to run the fundraiser for our victims' fund. She's been at the station shooting pictures for the calendar they're doing. She also went to high school with me, Scott, and Joe. But she's expecting me to be home since I'm not at work and my truck is there."

So she was an old friend, and it was work related. But there seemed to be a bit more angst there than the situation warranted. Interesting. "Have her come here. That way you don't have to walk over there. She can drop off whatever she needs to and see that you're still alive." Sarah smiled at the end. And she could meet this Macy and gauge what was really going on.

He patted her knee. "Good idea. Thanks." He texted something and put his phone down.

She studied him, but nothing seemed amiss.

A few minutes later, her doorbell rang. Joe eased up to answer it. A curvy, dark-haired woman entered with a huge bouquet of balloons. Shadow barked and jumped at the balloons.

"Guess he's never seen balloons before. Come here, boy." Sarah patted her leg and Shadow reluctantly came over, still keeping a wary eye on the balloons. She rubbed his fur, glad to have something to do with her hands.

"Come on in. Macy, this is Sarah. My girlfriend." Joe stepped back in the entryway and met her gaze, a smile playing around his lips.

Her face heated. Okay, then. "Hi, Macy. Thanks for making the trip over here."

"Anything for Joe." Macy beamed up at him, pushing the gift basket anchoring the balloons into his arms. "These are for you. Though I guess you can share with your girlfriend." She flashed a bright smile at the both of them. "I did have a legitimate reason to run around town looking for you." She pulled something out of her bag. "The calendar proofs are in and each of the models has to approve their page. I already got all the guys at the station, so I just need you to sign off."

Joe stiffened and shoved the basket on the entry table and then mechanically reached for the calendar, but Macy pulled it away and brought it over to Sarah, perching on the arm of the couch. "Actually, you might like to see your boyfriend in action here." The cover of the calendar was the picture of Joe pulling the boy out of the wrecked car that had made the rounds. Blown up to eleven-by-eighteen, it was even more powerful.

"He's something, isn't he? You're a lucky woman."

Sarah met Joe's gaze, lightness filling her chest. "Absolutely." More than she could put into words.

He gave her a tender smile and moved to peer over Macy's shoulder.

Macy flipped through the other months with firefighters in different stages in and out of their uniforms. Joe appeared again in the December shoot with his entire squad. "He's the only one in here twice." She handed him a pen and the calendar. "Sign on the sticker on your photos." She turned back to Sarah. "Did Joe tell you he and I dated in high school?"

"He said—"

"I wouldn't say we really dated, Macy. You were into Scott." He handed her the calendar and pen. His face had shuttered.

She stood and tucked the calendar and pen in her bag. "We had something. I would have liked more." She patted his chest and then walked to the door. "You two enjoy." She slipped out the door, closing it behind her.

Joe took the basket from the entry table and carried it to the kitchen. Shadow jumped up and barked, following Joe.

"Cheese, crackers, fruit, chocolate. Anything sound good?" He didn't meet her gaze. Instead, he was busy putting things in the fridge.

"No, I'm not hungry." She wasn't sure what she was. Joe had called her his girlfriend, which set all sorts of swirling emotions through her. But what was the deal with Macy? There was something more there. Maybe it was none of her business. And it was in the past. But something about it was still bugging Joe.

"Joe?"

He looked up. "I think I'm going to fix myself something. Sure you don't want anything?"

"I'm sure. But—" here went nothing— "what's the story with Macy?"

He shrugged and went back to putting food on a plate. "Not much of a story, really. She was into Scott, and they were dating. But she was a big distraction to our football team. Scott was quarterback, and we were headed to the championships, but he wasn't focusing on the game. Macy was a cheerleader, and he was far more interested in what was going on over there than on the field."

Picking up his plate, he came over to the living room and sat in the chair next to the couch. "I convinced him to break up with her, and he did. But then Macy came up to me at a party, drunk and sobbing about Scott breaking up with her. I took her home and that was it. But she told Scott we'd slept together." He jerked his head up and met her gaze. "Which we didn't. But it did a lot of damage to my relationship with Scott." He reached for her hand and wove his fingers through hers. "It was a long time ago. But I don't trust her. And the sooner this whole calendar thing is done, the better."

Which explained why he was so uncomfortable around Macy. Sarah let the tension drop from her shoulders. She'd waded into a sticky area, and it had been okay. More than okay. She rubbed her thumb over the back of his hand. "Thanks for telling me the whole story."

He winked at her. "You're my girlfriend. I want to tell you everything." He slid over to the couch, nudging her with his hip, bracing his arm on the back of the couch. "You okay with that?" His voice dropped low and stirred embers inside her.

"Yeah." She smiled up at him, staring into those deep chocolatey eyes. "I am."

"Good." He leaned in and kissed her with a gentleness and sweetness at first, then he slid his hand behind her neck.

Her hands came up his chest and over his shoulders, the emotions of the past days built up and spilled over into a passion that had them clinging to each other. A bit of common sense broke through her fog, and she pushed him away but left her hands on his chest, feeling his heart pound under her fingers.

"We're in close quarters, buddy. We'd better be careful."

He picked up her hand and kissed her palm. "You're right." He eased back into his chair. "We'd better watch an action movie then. Nothing romantic."

She grinned at him. This she could get used to.

CHAPTER TWENTY-SEVEN

JOE LEANED AGAINST THE ICE pack and pressed. It was the only way to reduce the itching of the stupid staples. Luckily, they were coming out today. His doctor's appointment couldn't come soon enough. And then, a long, hot shower.

But he had laundry to do. Maybe it'd take his mind off the itching. He finished sorting and carried a load to the washer. Sarah had gone back to work today, leaving him with an oddly empty space. For the past week and a half, they'd spent nearly every day together, binge watching shows and eating far more junk food than they should.

He tossed the clothes in the washer and started it. Then he looked in the fridge. He might as well do some grocery shopping while he was out. He'd been at Sarah's so much, he hadn't bothered to stock his own fridge. He was looking forward to hearing how her day went.

There was a comfortable rhythm they'd fallen into, and he didn't want to lose it. The first time he'd called her his girlfriend, it hadn't been planned. Which wasn't like him. But Macy showing up had been unexpected, and he wanted

Sarah to have no question where his heart belonged. Yep, it belonged to her, one hundred percent. And a weight he hadn't even known he was carrying lifted when he told Sarah about Macy. He was letting her into his heart, letting her see behind his carefully constructed mask that only Kyle and Scott had seen. There had been no judgment in her eyes, only compassion and understanding. He wasn't sure what he'd expected, but it hadn't been that.

He closed the fridge and jotted down a few things. She was bound to be tired after her first day back. He should do something nice for her tonight. Tomorrow, he'd be back at work on light duty. And she was talking about going back to choir practice on Wednesday. Heather had come over, and they'd had a long discussion about it. He'd agreed with Heather that Sarah needed to go and not let Ryan push her out of doing something she loved. Even though she'd probably be content to slink away and not risk the chance of conflict.

So that left Thursday. They hadn't had their big date, and they needed one. It might be a little tricky with her ankle, but he'd figure something out. He grinned. Thursday was going to be a night to remember.

Her leather tote slung diagonally across her chest, Sarah guided her knee wheeler into work. This glorified scooter was ridiculous, but it took the weight off her ankle and didn't make her sprained wrist—still in a brace—hurt the way the crutches did. Only a sprain, but it still hurt and made maneuvering difficult.

Heather had picked it up for her when she heard of Sarah's plans to return to work. As much as she loved spending time with Joe, she was sick of TV and junk food. She needed to do something and get out of the house. Eric hadn't been very forthcoming about the status of things at work, simply telling her to rest and heal. And that was driving her nuts too. She wanted to know what was going on at the office, how things were going, if they were busy enough or not. That wasn't something Eric could hide from her if she were there.

"Sarah!" Malia came from around her desk and started to give Sarah a hug. Then obviously figuring out she just might topple her, she stood back. "I can't believe you're here."

"I don't know for how long. I just needed to get out of the house." She wasn't even dressed professionally. Hard to do with a cast, so dark yoga pants and a knit shirt had to do.

She pushed herself toward her office, Malia behind her. Parking the scooter close to her desk, she pulled her bag over her head and set it on the desk.

"Anything I can do to help?" Malia hovered.

"Can you see if I left any Diet Coke in the fridge?"

"Sure."

"Thanks."

Sarah tugged the extra chair in her office over, then lowered herself into her desk chair and propped her foot up on the guest chair.

Eric appeared in the doorway, filling most of it with his ex-football player build. "Hey, what are you doing back?"

She smiled. "I was bored."

"Well, take it easy. Don't overdo it or anything."

"I won't. I'll probably just stay a few hours and go back home."

Malia came back with the soda and handed it to her. "Thanks."

"Sure, let me know if you need anything." Malia glanced up at Eric and smiled before leaving Sarah's office.

Giving her a few seconds to get out of earshot, Sarah lowered her voice. "How are things?"

Eric shrugged. "Don't worry. We'll be fine. Nobody's been laid off." He rapped his knuckles on her doorframe and turned away. "Holler if you need anything." Then he was gone.

Sarah stared at the empty doorframe for a minute. That

wasn't reassuring at all. How much was truth and how much was Eric being Eric? Now that she was here, she wasn't sure what to do. She slid her computer into the dock. She checked her email—nothing new there since she'd checked it at home this morning.

She opened her files, trying to decide where to start. Oh, that proposal she was working on. She should check with Eric to see where they were on that. He probably had finished it up while she was out. Not wanting to duplicate his efforts, she reached for her phone. Wait. She'd go talk to him in person. That'd be the pretense anyway, and maybe he'd tell her more on the status of the company. If not, then she'd get on his calendar for a status-update meeting.

All of this trouble had started with her. If there was anything she could do, she wanted to do it. It wasn't really rational. Still, knowing everything about a situation created a sense of control. Yeah, it was an illusion; she knew that. She didn't care. It was better than nothing.

Reaching for her scooter, she shifted her weight and pushed up. She was getting good at this now. And her arms were definitely getting a workout. She glided down the hall to Eric's office. A few people waved as she went by. The mood was subdued but not depressed. The frenetic activity of this year was definitely missing, but people were still working at their desks, talking quietly.

The door to Eric's office was closed. Odd. She and Eric almost always kept their doors open. Everyone did. Raised voices floated out from behind the door. Who was he talking to? And what sort of trouble was he making that she'd have to fix? Taking a minute on the pretense of catching her breath, she adjusted her grip on the handlebars and tried to figure out who was in there. Didn't seem like an employee. Which meant it was either personal—in which case she needed to leave before she overheard something she wished she hadn't—or a client. She studied the ceiling as if inspiration would fall on her from above.

"Ron." Eric's voice trailed off, but the tone was placating. Ron Richards was one of their best and biggest clients.

Sarah stayed where she was.

"Sorry, Eric. I've got my own interests to think of." Yep, Ron Richards was in Eric's office. His firm supplied a huge chunk of their work. He was one of their best clients. And this conversation didn't sound good. Why hadn't Eric told her Ron was coming over? And why didn't he include her? Frustration filled her, tightening her grip. This whole thing had been a nightmare. No way could they keep everybody on if they lost him as a client. Sarah's heart pounded, and she willed it to slow so she could hear better.

"You know I like Sarah's designs," Ron continued. "She's a great girl to work with, and she always does an excellent job." Sarah was used to the condescension and chauvinism in this field. His comments barely fazed her. What was he getting at? "But the lawsuit, that's a whole other ball of wax. True or not, rumors of that kind of thing can ruin a man's business. And I'm getting ready to retire in another five years. I've got to have a business that's worth something."

What lawsuit? What did that have to do with her? Without deliberating and coming up with a plan—there wasn't time—Sarah pushed open Eric's door.

"Hi. Sorry to interrupt. I came down to ask Eric something and then heard Ron mention my name and a lawsuit. What's that about?"

Surprise registered on both men's faces. Eric was leaning against his desk, beefy arms folded. Ron got halfway to his feet. "Oh, hi, Sarah. Nice to see you. What on earth happened to your foot?"

She shook his extended hand before grabbing the other chair. But she kept a steady gaze on Ron, not letting him off the hook in answering her question. One thing she'd learned in this business was you couldn't back down with men.

"I broke it falling through subflooring and into a basement.

So, what about this lawsuit?"

He fiddled with his hands, hands of a working man. Ron didn't wear a suit; he still looked like he worked in the field. Probably did. She liked him; until now he had reminded her of her grandfather. "Well, I guess you'd know about that."

"No. I don't."

He raised an eyebrow at her like she was lying. "You're being sued over one of your projects."

"Which project? Why? And by whom?"

Ron raised his hands and gave her a don't-look-at-me look. "I didn't hear. Look, Sarah, you're a nice girl. You made a mistake. That's what E&O insurance is for. Just fess up and put it behind you. You don't want to drag Mark's company down with you."

A sharp pain in her hand caught her attention. Her fingers clenched so tightly, her nails cut into her palms. This was ridiculous. "I'm not being sued, Ron. I don't know what you've heard or from whom. But it's not happening. Who told you it was?"

He looked toward Eric, then out the window and shifted as if he was going to get up. Sarah blocked the doorway still. "Everyone's talking about it. You know how it is."

Yeah, she did. Construction and development was still a relatively small circle of people, an old boys network. But she still didn't get it. Why would someone start a rumor that she was being sued when it wasn't true?

Because it was one more way to make her pay. She just wished she knew who and why. "So, let me get this straight. Based on some rumor—you don't know who told you or where it came from—you're pulling your work from us, who you've worked with, quite well I might add, for years. You're just going to toss all of that history, all of that fact, away, because of a rumor?" Anger laced her voice as it rose. Everyone up and down the hall could hear her, she was sure. And she didn't care.

"So, you don't really care about the relationship we've built over the years. Or all the extras we've done for you without charge. Or all the times we've made last-minute changes to your plans without complaining. The times we've worked you in ahead of other clients because of your history with us. You're going to throw all of that away because of some junior-high-level rumor? I'm sitting here telling you it's not true. I don't know anything about it. But you don't believe me. I bet Eric told you the same thing." She saw in Don's face it was true.

She glanced at Eric. His eyes were wide, and he leaned forward, almost looming over Ron. She didn't know what Mark would say if he were here. She'd call him after this. And if there was any fallout, she could quit and then Mark could disavow all of her actions and let Eric take over. Though right now, Eric looked like his solution was to pound Ron into a pulp.

"Look, blame me if you want." Ron stood and stepped back from Eric. "But I'm not the only one who knows about it. Nobody wants to do business with you guys. And anyone who does won't get any other subs to work for him. It's a sue-happy world. Nobody needs an excuse to sue someone. Just the rumor of something gone wrong can get a lawyer's blood up faster than anything. None of us can afford that kind of expense or exposure." He turned to Eric. "Sorry. Wish it were different. I'll call Mark myself and tell him, if you want."

"Don't bother." The last thing she needed was Ron disturbing Mark with problems she was supposed to be handling.

He started toward the door, forcing Sarah to turn in the chair. All of her fire burned down, and she was spent. He was leaving; she hadn't changed his mind. "You still didn't say where you heard it from."

He gave her a smirk and walked out.

Sarah tossed the remains of her lunch into the trash. Malia had brought her Baja Fresh, but her favorite burrito left a bad taste in her mouth. After Ron had left, Eric had suggested suing him for breach of contract. But that wouldn't solve the problem and would simply ensure they never got work from Ron again.

Though if they didn't need the work so badly, she wouldn't care if she ever saw the man again. What was it with people? She couldn't imagine Mark doing that if the situation were reversed. Maybe she was just out of touch, but were people only motivated by money? Wasn't there any sense of loyalty, of history, of building relationships?

Joe's face flashed through her mind. Yes, she'd definitely built a relationship with him the last week. That was the one solace in this whole stupid mess. But she couldn't think about him now. She had to figure out what to do to salvage the company Mark had entrusted to her.

She dropped her head in her hands. She'd failed. She'd let down Mark and everyone else in the company. It was her fault they were all going to lose their jobs. Why couldn't she have left well enough alone? Why did she have to get lost that fateful day? Like her parents always said, for a smart person, she was pretty dumb. Ryan had said the same thing.

Her phone rang. A brief flicker of hope flared that it was Joe. She could use his calm reassurance about now. A glance at the screen showed her it was Kyle. With leaden arms, she picked up the phone.

"I thought you'd want to hear this. The plywood sub floor-ing that you fell through had been cut nearly through in the back so it would break away. Someone sabotaged that site."

"Not again. It seems like everything I touch turns into a disaster. Maybe I just need to go away until this whole thing is over. But why would hurting some worker at the job site profit someone else?" Her head hurt, and she couldn't parse any of this out. The lawsuit, the sabotage. Why did someone hate her so much?

"Did anyone know you were going to the site?"

"No. Just Joe. We talked about it that morning before we left for our walk and then we went after work."

"I'll call him next and see if he told anyone. Even if he did, how would it get back to whoever did this?" Kyle's let-out breath came through the phone. "I'd like to send a tech over to your house. They planted a tracker on your computer when they broke in. Maybe they left something else behind too. It would explain a few things."

A chill froze her entire body. She nearly dropped the phone. Someone had been spying on her?

"Okay, sure." Her voice sounded small even to her own ears. She updated Kyle on the lawsuit; maybe he could unearth something. If it was even relevant.

She hung up with Kyle. All she wanted was a pint of rocky road and a good book and to forget about all of this. But she couldn't do that. She had to call Mark.

This was his company. He'd built it up. And she was tearing it down. It wasn't fair to him. His association with her was costing him. She thought back over what Ron had said.

She stared at her phone. She knew what she had to do. It was best for everyone. He'd try to talk her out of it. His kindness toward her could cost everyone at Rankin and Associates big time. If she put it in writing, she could email it to him. That would be for the best, wouldn't it? Or was she just being a coward, once again avoiding conflict? After all Mark had done for her, she owed it to him to do this right.

Bracing herself mentally, she selected his number before she could talk herself out of it. She studied her office. It had a lot of memories, almost palpable today. The chill from earlier settled into a hard ache in her chest. Why was doing the right thing always so stinking hard? *God, please. Help me get through this.*

"Hey, Sarah. How's the ankle doing?"

"It's fine. I'm back in the office today. But I wanted to talk to you about something."

"Ron Richards. He called me."

"I told him not to. I didn't want him to bother you."

"I've known Ron over twenty years. If he's dumping my firm, I deserve to hear it from him. While I'm not happy about the news, Ron has to protect his people. I can't say I wouldn't do the same thing in his position."

She shook her head. "No, you wouldn't. You'd figure out a way to do the right thing." She took a sip of soda, buying time, screwing up her courage. "That's what I've been trying to do. I've been trying to figure out what the right thing to do in this situation is. I don't want to dump the firm's problems on your lap when you have so much going on. And I don't take lightly your trust in me. But I can't help but feel that I've let you down, and I've put everyone at the firm in jeopardy." She took a breath. "I want to resign. I think it's best for everyone."

It was a minute before he spoke. "I appreciate that offer. I know you didn't make it lightly. But, Sarah, I'm not going to let you do it. You can take some time off, you can work from home, you can do whatever you need to. But unless you start working for another company, you're still running my firm."

The ache moved to her throat. She couldn't push it down. It made her jaw cramp and tears well in her eyes. Making herself perfectly still, she willed it to go away, to go numb, to stop feeling.

It was working until Mark said, "Sarah, I don't regret one minute putting my trust in you."

The ache splintered, and tears began to fall. Mortified, Sarah stared at her computer, unable to gain enough control to talk. She tried to stop them, tried to suck them back down, to blink away the wetness. They came too fast, dropping on the desktop. Oh, what must Mark think of her? This should be proof that his faith in her was misplaced. Good grief. She swiped at her eyes and nose with the back of her hand. She reached for a tissue and began wiping. This was so embarrassing.

"I've been through a lot of ups and downs in my time. Things somehow turn around. And since Martha's diagnosis, I've had more time to reflect on God's faithfulness. It doesn't always look the way we expect it to. But, he never leaves us."

Sarah nodded, then realized he couldn't see her nod and whispered. "Yes, I know." She sniffed. "But I needed the reminder."

"You going to be okay?"

She couldn't help but laugh. "I can't believe you're worried about me after everything I just told you."

"You are more important than the company."

She nodded. She hated it when people were nice to her when she was crying. Made it harder to get those tears under control.

She hung up with Mark. Nothing about this day had gone like she planned.

CHAPTER TWENTY-EIGHT

JOE WASN'T THRILLED WITH SARAH going into work today. Driving with a cast on wasn't recommended. But he also understood how stir crazy she was getting. He wished she'd let him take her and pick her up. She could be stubborn when she wanted to.

He'd taken a walk after getting back from getting his stitches out. He'd tried running a few steps, but the jolting hurt his back. But the shower after had been one of the best ever, rivaling those after coming off the fire line.

After Kyle had called him and updated him on the sub-floor sabotage and the potential bug in Sarah's house, he'd gone over to let the LVPD techs in. They had found a bug in Sarah's house. One in the living room outlet and one in her office desk lamp. Sarah didn't seem overly disturbed by the news when he'd called her at work. More like resigned to a continual string of bad news.

Now it was about time for Sarah to get home, unless she'd returned early. He texted her to ask. Yep, she was home. After spending so much time with her lately, today had felt ... off.

Even Shadow wasn't the same.

"Let's go, boy. Let's go see Sarah." He clipped on the dog's leash and headed out the door. At Sarah's front door, Joe bounced on his toes. She wasn't answering, though he'd knocked and rung the doorbell. She knew he was coming over, so she wouldn't have laid down for a nap. The back patio slider was open. His pulse picked up its pace. She had to be back there. Maybe she just couldn't hear him. He had her key, but he didn't want to startle her either. But what if she had fallen?

He slid the key into the lock and turned. "Sarah? Are you here?" He pushed the door open the rest of the way. And came inside. "Sarah?" Shadow bounded out the slider. Joe shut the front door and followed the dog. "Sarah?"

A teak chair was knocked over. A Diet Coke lay on its side by the patio door, brown fizzy liquid seeping into everything else.

And in the middle of it all sat Sarah, desperately trying to replant some fuzzy purple plant. She had her casted leg out to the side and was up on her good knee, trying to get some leverage to push the roots back into the dirt.

"Sarah? Are you okay? What happened?"

She looked up and blinked, almost as if seeing him for the first time. She swiped a torn, dirty sleeve across her nose and shoved her hair back from her face. Tendrils stuck up all over, more frizzy than her generally soft, well-tamed curls. Her eyes were red rimmed from crying. As if noticing him notice, she rubbed at a wet spot on her cheek and left a mud smudge.

Joe was next to her in two strides. "Are you hurt?"

She shook her head.

He looked around, grabbed and righted a chair.

"I need to get it back in the ground, before it dies." Tears overflowed her eyes. "I can't do anything right."

Joe knelt in front of her, taking her dirty hands in his. He noticed cuts and scratches, broken nails. "We'll get a new one." He waited until she met his eyes. "Okay?"

She nodded.

"That's my girl. Now let's get you inside and cleaned up."
He reached for her. "Here. Let me help you up."

"Oh, no. You'll rip open your back. Just get the other crutch and hold this one."

"Not if we do this right." He put his hands around her waist. "On three. One, two, three." He straightened and lifted her, keeping his back straight while she pushed with her good leg. He handed her the crutches.

She grabbed them but winced.

"Where's your knee wheeler?"

"In the car. I couldn't get it inside."

All he wanted to do was to pick her up. But he couldn't even do that.

Her foot pounded on the wood deck with a hollow echo. It had to be throbbing. She hobbled through the door, and he pointed to the kitchen sink. He dragged over a chair, and she plopped in it.

He turned on the water and let it run until it was warm. "Wash cloth?"

"In the bathroom."

He nodded and headed down the hall. "Don't go anywhere."

A moment later he ran the cloth under the now-warm water and added soap to it. He picked up her hand, and she tried to pull it back. "I can do that."

"I know." He pulled it toward himself again. "But I want to." Gently, he washed the dirt off the cuts, cleaning them with soap. She winced a few times but didn't try to pull away again. He rinsed the soap off. They weren't bleeding anymore so he'd just let them dry. He'd bandage them before she needed to use her crutches, though.

He headed to the garage and retrieved her knee wheeler from her car. He set it in front of her. "I wish I could just carry you to the couch."

She eased on to the knee wheeler and looked up at him.

She reached up and touched his face. "Thank you for coming over." Tears welled again.

"Let's get you to the couch." He helped her wheel to the couch and got her settled with an ice pack and some ibuprofen. "Need another Diet Coke?"

"Yes, please."

He brought it to her and sat on the edge of the couch. "What happened?"

She let out a long breath and told him about her perfectly awful day. "I thought spending some time in the garden would help. It always does. And it needed some work. But I lost my balance trying to deadhead the roses and I fell, grabbing the butterfly bush on the way down and pulling it out. And then suddenly, the one thing that had always brought me joy and peace was something I was ruining and had become a source of frustration. I just don't even know what to do any more. Maybe I do need to take a vacation somewhere away from here." She thumped her cast. "Though I can't go very far with this stupid thing."

Joe wrapped her in his arms and kissed the top of her head. He'd never felt so helpless.

Actually, he had.

Joe slid into his truck and leaned against the seat, already warm from the August heat, even though it was still early in the day. His first day back at work, even if it was light duty. His back was still a little tender. As he pulled out of the parking lot, he missed his morning walk with Sarah. It would be awhile before those could resume. He hoped she stayed safe today even though she was determined to go into the office again. She did promise him she wouldn't work in the garden again without him.

Last night he'd cleaned up her patio then brought her a pint of rocky road and a spoon. Her red-rimmed eyes told him he'd made the right move with ice cream. He hadn't followed through on his plan to ask her out for their first real date. It hadn't seemed the right time with her so upset. At least by the time he'd left her and Shadow, she wasn't as upset.

He'd called Kyle later and pressed him on how they could wrap this thing up. It was eating Sarah alive, proven by her offer to resign to save Mark's firm. Maybe he should take her away somewhere away from all of this, despite her cast.

He was still thinking about it when he pulled into the fire station parking lot twenty minutes later. The rest of the guys filtered in, greeting him and teasing him about the time off.

"Oh, and I see you made the calendar twice," McCoy razzed him. "And you didn't even take your shirt off."

"How's the back?" Chief O'Grady headed toward Joe.

"Just got the staples out. I'm here to help you reduce that fire hazard on your desk you call paperwork."

"Good. I could use the help. Hey, you gotta minute?"

"Sure."

"Let's head to my office."

When they got in O'Grady's office, he motioned for Joe to sit, as he moved behind his desk and took a seat. Folding his hands on his desk he studied Joe. O'Grady wanted to say something, Joe just didn't know what. But he didn't think he'd like it.

"So, how are you feeling?" O'Grady was stalling for time, but he was also looking for something specific.

Not entirely sure what O'Grady wanted to hear, Joe shrugged, the movement still restricted by the unhealed muscles in his back. "The muscle was torn pretty good back there. The doctor doesn't want me doing any lifting for four to six weeks. Then I'm sure it'll take some time to regain that strength." Joe leaned back in his chair and flashed a grin. "Can't happen too soon for me, though. I'm going a little stir crazy."

O'Grady's return grin wasn't as enthusiastic. "That equipment training we have coming up in two weeks. You won't be one hundred percent by then, so I've asked Micah Flores from alpha shift to take your squad."

Joe nodded. Disappointment slapped him like a spray of water, because he'd been looking forward to that for months, but he understood. Still, it was a bitter realization.

"What were you doing over at that building anyway?"

Caution lights flashed in Joe's head at the change of subject. He switched mental gears, shoving the disappointment away. He didn't want to say something that would end up putting Sarah in any further danger. Considering they only had a vague idea where the danger was coming from, that made it pretty difficult. "Sarah wanted to show it to me. She'd designed it."

"Any particular reason you went at that time, after work hours?"

Joe frowned. "I didn't ask. I assumed it was easier to check it out without the crews around. I don't know. I didn't think about it too much." He reached for a typical male line of reasoning, pulling out his phone. Trina had taken a picture of Sarah and him at Marcus's party. It was now his phone's wallpaper. He flashed it at O'Grady. "This is Sarah. I'd pretty much do anything she wanted to without question."

O'Grady nodded but looked distracted. "You've got a review coming up, Joe. You've done really well. Got potential to go far. You don't want to do anything to jeopardize that."

Joe tilted his head. Where was this going? "What does that mean?"

O'Grady met his gaze. "Look. This is a political organization. We both know that. Tick off the wrong people and your career is over in this city. Sarah is a person of interest in the arson case. And if your fall turns out to be caused by sabotage … All I'm saying is you might want to keep a low profile, maybe not get too close to her until all of this is resolved."

Anger and suspicion flared in Joe. "Where's this coming from?"

O'Grady shook his head. "I don't know. I just got a vague

phone call from the chief asking about you and your relationship with Sarah."

"That's not his business."

"I know. But it doesn't matter. It can still affect your career."

Joe stood. "Anything else?"

"I'm sorry. I'm just trying to warn you." O'Grady got to his feet. "You're one of the best at what you do. I'd hate to see you become a victim of politics. Maybe just play it cool for a while until it all blows over."

Joe walked out of the office and out to the back apron. He didn't want to talk to anyone else right now. Why would the chief or anyone care about his relationship with Sarah? And how on earth would that affect his career? He didn't know, but politics were unpredictable. He pondered it some more, still coming up with nothing.

Ah, what did it matter? It wasn't like it was anything he could control. God knew what was going on. At least he could tell himself that. Whether or not he could actually let the problem go was another thing.

Fortunately, he had a pile of paperwork to get his mind off things. Yeah, he was looking forward to that.

Sarah heard a plate clinking on her black wood coffee table. Slowly she cracked open her eyes. She'd plopped on the couch as soon as she'd gotten home from work. Joe and Shadow had shown up with something that smelled wonderful. Savory. Charo Chicken. Yum. Chicken marinated in citrus juice and spices then slow roasted, eaten with salsa and tortillas. Messy but delicious. She heard a pop and hiss, then a Diet Coke can was plunked down next to her plate.

Pushing herself to more of a sitting position, she smiled at Joe. He leaned over and kissed her. It was quick but definitely left her wanting more. Even hurt, he took good care of her. And they hadn't even been on a real date yet. But that was changing tomorrow night. Joe had called her at lunch today and asked her out. Which was funny considering he'd been arranging all of her meals for the past two weeks.

"Thank you. Didn't realize I was so hungry." She picked up the plate.

"You're welcome. I thought it might sound good. Still planning on going to choir practice?"

Sigh. "Yes." She glanced at her phone. "Heather should be here in a bit."

"You don't have to go." Joe had his own plate balanced on his lap.

"I know. I just want to get it over with. My injury is a good excuse to arrive late and leave early."

Joe didn't respond. He didn't have to; she knew what he was thinking. Ryan would be there. Yeah. Still, she needed to get this over with.

They finished eating just as Heather knocked on the door. Joe got up and answered it.

Heather grinned at Joe. "Ooh, smells good." She stepped through the door. "Charo Chicken, huh?"

"Yep. There's some left if you'd like it."

"No, thanks. I already ate. Unfortunately, it was a TV dinner from the microwave. Yuck. Why do I buy those things anyway? They're a step above plastic. I should have come over earlier."

Sarah grabbed her crutches and pulled her leather tote over her head like a cross body bag. Once outside, she scowled at Heather's Miata. "Nope, we're taking my car. You can drive if you want." She unclipped her keys from inside her bag and handed them to Heather. She'd parked out front today. No more trying to maneuver in her tiny one-car garage. She slid into her car. It was weird sitting on the passenger side.

Joe tucked the crutches in the back seat. "Sure you don't want your knee wheeler?"

"No, the ramps would be more effort. Heather can drop me close."

He leaned over and kissed her. "I'll clean up."

She snaked her hand around the back of his neck. "I wouldn't mind it if you were still here when I got home."

He kissed her again, this one with more promise. "Your wish is my command."

"Heather, watch her and bring her home if she's getting too tired or in too much pain. She'll be too stubborn to admit it." He said that last with a wink and a smile at Sarah.

"You and Kyle compare notes? Gee. I think we managed to survive this long without you two." Heather started the car.

"Yeah, but it's more fun with us." Joe closed Sarah's door and waved.

Heather had driven out of the parking lot before she sighed. "I'm so glad you guys are finally together. Are you worried about seeing Ryan tonight?"

"Trying not to think about it. I'm hoping everything will just fade from people's minds."

"Other than asking me where you were, no one has said anything to me about you and Ryan being a couple." Heather reached over and squeezed Sarah's hand. "I think it's good for you to do this. It'll be closure so you can move on with Joe, and no one will think anything weird about seeing the two of you together. The way he looks at you, no one has any doubt about how he feels about you."

"I hope tonight is the end of it. Joe and I are finally going on a real date tomorrow night."

"Ooh, where?"

"I don't know yet. It's going to be a surprise."

They pulled up to the church. Heather got as close as she could and helped Sarah out.

Sarah focused on adjusting her crutches. She could hear people coming over to her. She hated being on display. They had arrived later than usual, hoping to slide in as practice began. So why were all these people still outside? A chorus of "Are you okay? What happened? What did you do?" surrounded her. Maybe she could get through the explanation just once or twice if she waited until everyone was gathered around.

She moved with her audience toward the rehearsal room. "I was looking at one of my buildings, and I fell through to the basement and broke my ankle."

The great chorus erupted in "Oh, no! I can't believe it! Thank the Lord you weren't hurt worse." Two more hops. "We'll be praying for your speedy healing." This from Sharon.

She just wanted to get to her seat. Her pulse had ticked up. From the exertion and from knowing she was going to see Ryan any minute. People were talking to her, and she hoped the combination of maneuvering the crutches and her "uh huhs" made it seem like she was paying attention more than she was. Someone got the door, and she swung through it. Her foot was throbbing; sweat beaded on her forehead. She just wanted to sit down and put her foot up. Luckily, the alto section was closest. She plopped into the first chair she reached. Someone dragged another chair over, and she propped her foot up and caught her breath.

A whole new chorus of voices asked again about her injuries, but Sharon stood by, giving everyone else the play-by-play. For once, Sharon's desire to have the inside info on everything was proving useful.

Maybe Sarah shouldn't have come. Didn't matter, she was here now. Taking a final deep breath, she looked around. For Ryan. She might as well admit it.

He stood in the back talking near the soundboard, but he was facing her direction. He had to have seen her come in. Chris was standing off to the side, so if Ryan hadn't seen her, Chris would be sure to give him all the details.

As if he felt her stare, Ryan looked her way, caught her gaze. She managed a weak smile and then looked off. Crud. She should have planned that better. She probably looked guilty.

Which she wasn't. She was terrible with these kinds of situations.

Wasn't this rehearsal ever going to begin? It was five after now.

She heard Heather's voice and a slap of paper on her arm. "Here's your music."

"Thanks." Sarah looked up at Heather, hoping she conveyed lots of gratitude with her eyes.

Then Ryan appeared over Heather's shoulder. Sarah's stomach tightened, and the music stuck to her hands. What would he say? Wait. He couldn't say anything about her ankle without revealing that he didn't know. Which would either make him look like a jerk of a boyfriend or let everyone know they weren't together.

This should be interesting. What should she say? She willed her brain to work. The perfect quip would come to her in the middle of the night, waking her out of a deep sleep. When it'd do her a fat lot of good. Sigh.

Ryan patted her on the shoulder and winked at her. "Glad you made it."

She stared at him. Not blinking. That she could manage.

He looked away. "Okay, we're running late. Let's get started."

Chapter Twenty-Nine

THIS SHOULDN'T BE THAT HARD. She put together designs all day long. So why couldn't she figure out what to wear? It was the cast, that was it. It messed everything up. Nothing looked right with it. Half a dozen outfits were draped over her duvet, she was sweaty, and her hair stuck up all over the place. Great way to get ready for a date.

She flopped on the bed. Joe had certainly seen her worse. But still. This was their first real date. She wanted him to want a second.

On the other hand, why shouldn't today be a complete disaster? Ever since she'd gotten lost going to the job site all those weeks ago, her world had been one disaster after another.

She studied the ceiling. "Sorry, Lord." She really did have a lot to be grateful for even in the midst of everything. It could all be so much worse. She sat up. Besides, those kind of thoughts were only going to make her miserable and make their date a wreck. There was nothing she could do about it now anyway. Tonight after their date, she could lay in bed all night worrying if she wanted.

She finally decided on a floral print dress with a draw-string neckline and cap sleeves with ballet flats. Nice but still maneuverable on crutches. Now if she didn't trip and make a fool of herself, everything should be fine.

She had no idea what they were doing. Joe said it was a surprise. Normally, she wasn't too fond of surprises, but she trusted him. He'd certainly been around her enough to know what she liked. And he seemed so excited about it, she didn't want to ruin it for him.

Hobbling into the bathroom, she washed her sweaty face and reapplied her makeup and curled her hair, something she hadn't done before on crutches. Her foot throbbed from being down, but it was getting better. Still, by the time she was done, she was shaking.

She reached for her tote bag, but it was truly too large to take, and it didn't go with her outfit. Carefully balancing, she reached for a small cross-body bag on her closet shelf. Unpacking the essentials from her tote, she moved them into the bag. She crutched out to the living room and performed a final check in the entryway mirror before plopping into the chair. She was already wiped out, and their date hadn't even begun. *Please, Lord, let this be an enjoyable evening and don't let anything go wrong. Just for one night.*

Please don't let anything go wrong tonight. Joe rapped on the door three quick times and then turned the knob. He didn't want her to have to get up and get the door. But the knob didn't turn. His hand was slick, and he wiped it on his khakis. Instead there was the thump and creak of her crutches. The door swung open, Shadow raced past him inside, and he was speechless.

Sarah appeared in a pretty dress, hair curling softly past her shoulders. She'd been wearing it pulled back lately, but he liked it down. Lines began forming across her forehead, and her smile started to fade.

He was standing there staring like an idiot. "Hi. Wow. You look terrific."

The smile came back. "Thanks. I'm ready to go if you are." She leaned over and reached for a sweater on the back of the chair.

"Let me get that." He took a quick stride inside and picked up her sweater, bumping into her as she was reaching for it.

She wobbled, and he grabbed her arm. Shadow jumped against her leg.

"I'm so sorry. Are you okay?" He reached to push Shadow away just as she did and they almost bumped heads. They were so out of sync, unusual for them. He hoped this wasn't how the whole date was going to go.

She laughed, but it was edged with nervousness.

He held her gaze for a moment, then stepped close to her, winding his arm around her waist. He lowered his head, touching her lips with his, softly, then as she balanced herself with her hands against his chest, he deepened the kiss. Now they were in sync, and the world faded away a moment before he pulled back. They needed to leave if they were going to make their reservations.

He touched her cheek. "Better now?"

She smiled, a genuine one that lit up her whole face. "Much."

He pulled open the front door and stepped to the side so she could maneuver past him.

"Mind locking up?"

"Sure." He pulled the door shut and locked it.

Sarah stood next to the passenger door. He wanted to just scoop her up and place her on the seat, might not have even given it a second thought if it weren't for his still-tender back.

"Would it be easier on you if we took your car? Then you wouldn't have to try to climb into the truck?" Plus where they were going, parking her car would be easier.

"Good idea." She handed him her keys then moved around to the passenger side. Carefully, he opened the door and gently held her arm while she lowered herself into the seat. He put her crutches in the back seat and closed the door.

As they headed for the ocean, all he wanted was for this to be a nice, relaxing date for them, a contrast to all the stress they'd been under. They weren't off to a great start. Well, the night was still young. Hopefully, his surprise would be a good one and not a terrible mistake.

Sarah studied Joe as they neared the harbor. She'd never seen him so dressed up in his pressed khakis and a black button-down shirt that made his eyes into dark pools. Her stomach swirled, especially thinking about that kiss before they'd left.

They must be getting close to their destination since a grin played around his mouth. It made him happy to surprise her. She couldn't remember the last time someone had taken so much care to do something special for her. He was a keeper all right. He was so entwined into her life that she couldn't imagine life without him. Which she hoped she'd never have to find out. Now that he was back at work, she'd been doing a lot of praying.

They pulled into a parking lot next to a marina. There were several restaurants along the water. This should be fun. A valet opened her door and then was confused when she couldn't get out. Joe hurried around and got her crutches out of the back. Once she was on her feet, so to speak, Joe led her down to the marina instead of the restaurant. This was interesting. He indicated a ramp, and she eased her way down it to a smaller tour boat tied up at the end. There were four people on board already and it looked like it could hold about fifteen. She turned to Joe, but he just grinned.

"I hope this works." He handed tickets to the captain standing next to the boat, and the two of them practically lifted her on board. Seats ran around the edge of the boat, so she didn't have to do anything but collapse into it. Joe tucked her crutches away and sat next to her. "I thought a sunset harbor cruise might be a nice first date."

She leaned back into the cushions and tilted her head up. "I've never done one before. This is amazing." The gentle sway of the boat and the briny air drained every bit of tension from her.

Joe slid his arm behind her shoulders, and she snuggled into him.

One other couple joined the boat, and then they pushed off and were on their way. As the captain took them around the harbor, another crew member passed out glasses of wine and small artichoke tart hors d'oeuvres. They cruised around Lido and Balboa Islands, the captain pointing out all the multi-million-dollar mansions and the famous people who lived in them. The sky deepened into indigo and crimson, and the water turned inky. She sighed and laid her head on Joe's shoulder. Nothing could be more perfect than this moment right here with him.

He kissed the top of her head and trailed his fingers along the skin of her shoulder below her cap sleeve.

The one-hour cruise was over in a blink, and they were pulling back to the dock. She squeezed Joe's hand. "Thank you. This was wonderful. I love that you put so much thought into this."

He kissed her cheek then winked at her. "It's not over yet."

The captain and Joe helped her off the boat, and she crutched up the dock. Joe led her up a ramp to a restaurant and inside. He gave the hostess his name, and she guided them to a window seat with a bay view.

Joe helped Sarah into her chair, watching her carefully, then leaned her crutches against the window next to her before taking his seat.

She leaned forward. "I know I keep saying it, but I'm completely blown away. This is so sweet."

"I'm glad you like it. I wanted it to be special, but not difficult for you to get around with your crutches. So that left off a picnic on a mountain top, which was my first choice." He grinned.

The waitress brought them both a cup of clam chowder. When she left, Sarah had a good view of the front door.

A young blonde woman walked in, vaguely familiar. Sarah was still trying to place her when she saw who followed her in, his hand on her lower back.

Ryan.

"Huh."

Joe frowned. "What?"

She tilted her head and cut her eyes toward the host-ess station. He raised his eyebrows. "They're coming this way." There was an empty two-top behind Joe. She prayed Ryan and his date wouldn't be seated there. She didn't want to spend the whole evening seeing Ryan's face over Joe's shoulder. She sipped her chowder, the creamy, salty broth filling the empty spots in her stomach that the little tarts on the boat didn't satisfy.

"Hey, Ryan." Joe lifted his hand and waved as Ryan and his date neared.

Ryan nodded. "Joe. Sarah. Enjoying yourselves?"

"We are, thanks. You do the same."

Sarah just smiled as the hostess led Ryan and his date to a table deeper in the restaurant. "Well, Ryan must be over whatever grudge he had against me. The last two times I've seen him he's been civil. I'm glad that is over."

Joe shrugged. "He wasn't too civil on the basketball court, but I'd rather he take his frustration out on me. Besides, by the time I'm playing basketball again, he'll have moved on."

"We'll see if he ever lets me sing a solo again." She took a sip. "Actually, as much as I enjoy singing, I've had so much going on that even if I weren't on crutches, I don't think I could give it the attention it deserves. Maybe it's a season of life that has passed."

"You don't have to make any decisions now."

"True."

Their waitress brought their entrees. Grilled salmon with wild rice and haricot verts for Sarah and blackened swordfish with tropical fruit salsa and coconut rice for him. They fell into their comfortable routine over the meal, but every time she looked up at him, he met her gaze with something deep in his eyes. She hoped he loved her as much as she loved him.

She didn't think she could fit in another bite, but the server brought chocolate lava cake ala mode for them to share with coffee. It was the perfect ending to the perfect evening.

When they had finished dinner, Joe directed her around the corner to a deck where several benches overlooked the bay. Lights twinkled on the water from the other restaurants on the bay and the building across it. Soft bistro lights lined the deck. "We can enjoy a few more minutes of tonight before we have to head home." She sat on the bench, and he moved her crutches to the side. He sat next to her and pulled her close with his arm around her waist. His other hand grazed her cheek. Her body hummed from his presence.

"You are simply stunning, Sarah. You take my breath away, whether you're dressed up like tonight or in your yoga pants and a pony tail." He paused, and his eyes were inky pools. He touched his forehead to hers. "I love you. Fallen head over heels."

The question hung in his eyes. She crept her hand around his neck. "I love you too."

CHAPTER THIRTY

SARAH FLOATED THROUGH THE WORK day. At least that's what it felt like after last night's date. Even her heavy cast didn't weigh her down. Joe loved her. That thought still managed to stop her in her tracks. She still couldn't believe it. Yes, the words just formalized what his actions had been saying all along. But there was this new security, a sense that someone was in her corner. She couldn't remember the last time she'd felt that way.

And work had been okay too. They hadn't lost any more clients, and Eric hadn't irritated anyone else, so this week was ending on a high note. And since their fall at the job site, no more word from "Greg" or his henchmen. Maybe they did finally believe that there was nothing she could give them. Maybe she could finally take a deep breath and relax. Life was looking up.

She had gotten a quick text from Joe this morning. He worked today, so she didn't expect to hear from him. But it was sweet hearing how much he enjoyed last night and that he loved her.

She clicked through a few more emails and double

checked her projects list. Yep, she could go home early. She'd text Heather and see what she was up to. If she didn't have plans with Kyle, maybe they could hang out.

She picked up her phone, but it buzzed in her hand. Heather. Reading her mind.

Did you hear about the fire? Have you heard from Joe?

There was a link to a news video. Sarah clicked on it. A news reporter stood in front of a nursing home complex with smoke and flames billowing behind him. Fire engines and trucks were off to the side with fire personnel in the background. She couldn't see the numbers on the equipment to know if Joe's station had been called out. But given the amount of equipment and the number of people that needed to be evacuated, it was likely his men were there. And if she knew Joe, he'd be there too, light duty or not.

Her hands shook. The reporter didn't have much information other than the name of the facility and that staff and first responders were doing everything they could to manage the situation. She set the phone on the desk.

"I've just received word that two firefighters were injured. No details on the extent of their injuries, but they are being transported to local hospitals, along with several of the nursing home residents. I'll have another live update as soon as we have more information."

The room spun and faded out. Images of her childhood home in flames, cold prickly grass on her bare feet, invaded her office. She gripped the arms of the chair and practiced breathing.

Lord, I can't go through this again.

Somehow, she made it home. She didn't remember the drive at all. But now she was on her couch, scrolling through videos and tweets, trying to find out anything she could on the fire. Or the two injured firefighters. Shadow laid next to her and whined.

She tried Joe's phone again. She'd called three times and texted him twice. If he was busy, she didn't want to be a distraction. But she needed info. This not knowing was driving her crazy.

Shadow jumped up a second before a knock at the door sounded.

"It's me." Heather pushed the door open. Sarah hadn't locked the door behind her? She shook her head. It just proved what a wreck she was.

"Hey, do you mind letting Shadow out for a minute?"

"Sure." Heather clipped Shadow's leash on and led him out around the front of the condo. But they were back in under a minute, Shadow taking up his position next to her on the couch. "Need an ice pack? Or a Diet Coke?"

Sarah shook her head.

Heather closed the door. "How are you? Actually, I don't even need to ask. You look terrible."

"Thanks." She picked up the remote and flipped on the TV. It was time for the local news to come on.

"Have you heard from Joe?" She went into the kitchen and opened the fridge.

"No. Does Kyle know anything?"

"He couldn't find anything out, but he promised to let you know if he did." She popped open a Diet Coke and plopped on the chair next to the couch. "He's on light duty. Likely he's there coordinating information and teams and is too busy to respond to you."

"That's what I keep hoping." But the cold lump in her stomach told her differently. She rubbed her hand over her face, the images of her little brother being worked on by firefighters appearing on the back of her eyelids. Every time she closed her eyes, the images came back. "I can't live like this. It's bringing everything back, all my worst nightmares. I love Joe, but I can't be with him."

Heather rubbed Sarah's shoulder. "I feel that way every

time I hear about a police shooting. Earlier this year, one of Kyle's trainees was shot, senselessly. Bad things happen in this world. There are no guarantees in this life. Look at Mark and Martha. I'm sure her dementia was not in their plans."

Sarah knew Heather was right. In her head. But her heart wasn't listening.

The same reporter from the video appeared on the TV. Sarah turned up the volume. But she couldn't hear anything the reporter said because in the video they were rolling, a firefighter was backing down a ladder, carrying an elderly lady. And on the back of his turnout coat she could clearly read ROMERO.

"See? There he is. He's fine," Heather pointed out.

They cut back to the reporter. "Now that video was shot earlier today. Since then two firefighters have been injured in this fire and at least a dozen elderly residents have been transported to the hospital. No word on anyone's condition. Back to you in the studio."

"Sarah." Heather waited until Sarah turned to look at her. "God has Joe's days numbered. Just like yours, mine, Kyle's, and Martha's. You don't control that. Your worrying doesn't change it. You can choose to trust God, or you can cut Joe out of your life now. And it will be as if he's already dead, since you'll be depriving yourself of his love for you and what the two of you could have together for as long as God has planned for the two of you. How is that protecting your heart?"

Sarah brushed the tears from her cheeks. "I can trust Joe with my heart. But can I trust God with Joe?" All she could picture was her little brother's empty crib.

A ringing woke Sarah from her fuzzy state. She didn't remember falling asleep. She reached for her phone on the coffee table, the pale sky outside her living room window told her she'd spent the night on the couch.

Was it Joe? Her heart rate picked up as she scrambled to

get her fingers around the phone and tilt the screen toward her. Kyle?

"Hey, Sarah, sorry to bother you so early."

His voice seemed steady. Surely he wasn't calling with bad news about Joe. Then again, he'd had practice, so maybe. "Is it Joe?" She couldn't wait.

"Huh? No, I haven't heard from him. I thought maybe you had."

"I—so that's not why you're calling?"

"No, it's about Greg Connor. Some hikers found his body off a trail near Ortega Highway, not too far from where we found his truck. He still had his wallet and ID on him. The coroner hasn't examined him yet obviously, but from the on-site examination, he had a significant blunt trauma to the back of his head. So this looks like it's a potential murder investigation at this point. I want to bring over some mug shots to see if you can ID anyone. It's a long shot, I know. But it's the best we've got right now. And since it's not easy for you to get around, I figured I'd come to you."

The sketch she and Heather had done trying to capture the man's face surfaced in her mind. It hadn't helped, but maybe this time would.

"That's fine. I'm home all day."

He paused. "We're going to release this information to the public, see if it stirs up anything. But it may blow back on you. I need you to be extra vigilant. Joe—well, I'll see what I can find out on him. I'll be over in a bit."

She hung up and tossed the phone on the coffee table. If Kyle was coming over, she needed to look a little better. Some coffee would help. She pushed off the couch and hobbled into the kitchen, Shadow trailing her. While she waited for the coffee, she crutched into her office, searching for that sketch. But by the time her coffee was done, she still hadn't found it.

Joe sat in his truck in front of Sarah's condo. One of the guys had given him a ride back to the station from the hospital, where he picked up his phone from the desk where he'd left it. He saw the calls and texts from Sarah. All the way home he prayed about how to handle this. He was nearly certain she wouldn't want to see him. It was her worst nightmare come true, and he couldn't guarantee it wouldn't happen again.

There just hadn't been enough time for them to be together, for her to have him come home unscathed from many shifts. Yes, he'd lived. But he could only imagine the panic she felt when she couldn't get ahold of him.

He opened his truck door and slid out. *Lord, give me the right words. If we're supposed to be together, give us both wisdom on how to handle my job.* In front of her door, he took a deep breath and then winced as it pulled across his re-injured back. Shadow snuffled at the door. Who had walked him last night? Had Sarah managed on her crutches?

He knocked before Shadow started barking. The blinds in the front window jiggled then a moment later the front door opened. Shadow dashed out, but Sarah stood there on crutches, her face unreadable for a moment before it crumpled, and she burst into sobs, covering her mouth.

Two steps and he pulled her into his arms, but she didn't return the embrace.

"How could you? I was so worried. I'm glad you're okay." Her words tumbled out between sobs and her head found his chest, her arms curled against herself.

He rubbed her back. "I'm okay." He let her cry it out, relishing the feel of her in his arms, knowing it might be the last time.

She pulled back, wiping at her face then wiping her hands on her yoga pants.

He reached under the coffee table and handed her a handful of tissues from the box there. The front door stood open still. He stepped out and whistled for Shadow who reappeared and bounded into the house. Closing the door behind the dog, Joe studied Sarah as she crutched over to the couch and collapsed.

She hadn't kicked him out, so he took the chair. "I'm so sorry I left my phone on the desk and you couldn't reach me. I was originally on the call to help coordinate the teams and relay information. But the fire started moving fast, and they needed help getting all of the residents out of the nursing home. I had to jump in."

She nodded, sniffed. "That's what Heather said. I saw a video of you pulling an elderly lady out."

"Really? I didn't know I'd made the news. Anyhow, guess I reopened the wound in my back. The bleeding wasn't too bad, but there were so many folks from the nursing home being treated that I didn't get seen until the wee hours this morning. I'm all butterflied back together and have to take a course of antibiotics. I've probably increased my light duty time too."

She just stared at him, her dark green eyes stormy as a winter ocean. "The news said two firefighters were transported."

"Yeah, one of the guys was venting the roof, and it collapsed. He broke his ankle." He reached for her hand, and she didn't pull away. "I'm so sorry you had to worry about me. I know given that a fire burned down your childhood home and took your brother's life, I might be the last man you'd want to love."

Her eyes filled with tears again.

"But Sarah, you might be the only person, even more than Scott and Kyle, who knows who I am when I'm not a firefighter. You know the me behind the mask. And I hope you can love that man even if the firefighter part of me scares you to death."

She pulled her hand from his.

Yeah, he expected that. Still hurt. A hot poker speared his chest. He should go. There was no reason to prolong it.

But she shoved her phone toward him. A video was playing. A video of the nursing home fire and him pulling people out. It was surreal watching himself on screen. He hadn't even noticed the camera crew, he was so focused on getting people out.

Sarah grabbed his knee. "You saved those people. At a cost to yourself. Because you aren't the kind of man who can just stand by when others are in trouble. You jump in with both feet." She gave him a watery smile. "I'm case-in-point of that. God made you that way for a reason. And, yes, it terrifies me. But it's also part of the man I fell in love with."

She let out a wobbly breath. "Heather reminded me last night that God already has numbered our days. No amount of my worrying will change that. And look what happened to Mark and Martha? I know this isn't the last time I won't hear from you and worry. And I guess God and I will be spending a lot of time together when that happens. But I'd rather have as many days with you as I can get than not have you at all."

His heart picked up tempo the more she talked. He flew off the chair and onto the couch next to her, sliding his arm around her waist, the other pushing back the hair from her face. "You are an amazing woman. I know how hard this is for you. And I'm honored that you are trusting me with your fears and your heart." He touched his forehead to hers, closing his eyes and breathing a prayer of thankfulness for an outcome he had never expected and didn't deserve.

Then he kissed his girlfriend with every bit of promise and hope he had.

Chapter Thirty-One

S ARAH STOOD OUTSIDE HER OFFICE on her knee wheeler waiting for Kyle. He'd texted her that something had come up, and he would swing by and get her. Probably to make an ID of someone they'd picked up, but she didn't know for sure. When he'd brought over the mug shots last weekend, they hadn't gotten anywhere. Maybe today they would. She wiped her sweaty hands on her pants. It would be great if this thing was finally over, though.

Kyle's truck swung into the parking lot. Huh. Where was his unmarked cruiser?

He hopped out of the truck. "Ready?"

"Yep." He helped her into the truck, practically lifting her in. Then he took her knee wheeler and put it in the back. "Will I need my crutches?" They were still in her car.

"Nope, there aren't any stairs." He made small talk during the drive, telling her about the movie he and Heather saw the other night.

While Sarah wanted to know what she was walking into, she trusted Kyle to do his job and tell her whatever she needed to know when she needed to know it. Still, she couldn't help but wonder.

They pulled up in front of the fire station. Joe's fire station to be exact. And he was working today. She frowned and turned to Kyle.

He gave her an enigmatic look and hopped out of the truck. He came around and opened her door, setting her knee wheeler in front of her.

"What's going on?" She slung her tote across her body then grasped the handles of the knee wheeler.

"I have some information for you that I think you'll find helpful."

What in the world? She followed Kyle into the station. Maybe it was a surprise for Joe? But then, why wasn't she in on it? She'd never visited him at the station, not wanting to be a distraction. But it would be nice to see where he worked.

She glanced around. No Joe. But another firefighter approached them, shaking Kyle's hand.

"Thanks for bringing her." He turned to Sarah. "I'm Jeff McCoy, and I'll be your tour guide today. If you'll follow me."

Confused didn't begin to describe what she was feeling, so she followed him over to a series of metal racks that held helmets, boots, and turnout gear. Jeff began putting his gear on, explaining each piece and what it did. She looked around. She expected to see a group of school kids behind her, since this seemed like something he would explain to them. Kyle stood off to the side, but no one else was around. She raised her eyebrows at him, but he just grinned.

"So you see how well protected we are from fire in our personal protection equipment." He had a mask on so his words were muffled.

She nodded. The gear was heavy and looked claustrophobic. She didn't know how they managed to do anything with it on. Kind of like a space suit.

He handed her a piece of paper. "This is for you." He began

taking his gear off as she opened the paper and read it.

It was from Joe. She recognized his strong, sure print. He'd leave her little notes with something to make her smile when she'd picked up Shadow from his place.

Sarah my love,

Jeff has shown you how our gear works. I want you to know as much as possible about all the equipment that goes into keeping me safe so I can come home to you after every shift. I know you'll still worry, but this will give you some ammunition to fight those worries with.

Love, Joe

Tears pricked her eyes, and she blinked. Scanning the area, she still didn't see Joe. Odd. Shouldn't he come out?

Jeff had finished putting his gear away and another firefighter approached. "I'm Jesse Lin. Come this way."

Tucking the note in her tote, she pushed off on her knee wheeler, gliding across the smooth concrete floor.

Jesse stopped in front of the vehicles in the open bay. "These are the different vehicles we have for responding to emergencies." He walked over to the first one and began pointing out the features and equipment. She got to peek inside the cab and see where the firefighters rode. It was interesting, but … where was Joe? And Kyle had disappeared.

Jesse opened a compartment and reached inside, pulling out a bouquet of wildflowers. He handed them to her with a card.

She couldn't help but smile. She had no idea what was going on, but she opened the small card. *These are the first of many I hope to bring to you. Love, Joe.* She slipped the card into her tote and the flowers into the small pouch on the front of her knee wheeler. She rather liked the look. It was something Heather would do.

Then Jesse introduced her to rookie Zach Akino, who gave her a tour of the station. She got to see where the firefighters ate, slept, hung out, worked out, and even Joe's office. But no

Joe. At the end of the tour, Zach presented her with a small gold box.

It smelled like—yep, she popped open the lid. Godiva truffles. She was amazed that he'd remembered. It was one of the conversations they'd had while they were recuperating. Favorite treats. His was peanut brittle. Another note lay across the chocolates. *Not nearly as sweet as you, but a reminder of how much I want to bring you the things that bring you joy. Love, Joe.*

She grinned and shook her head. Okay, she'd play along. She tucked the box in her tote just as another man strode up.

He stuck out his hand. "Battalion Chief Dan O'Grady." She shook it. This was Joe's boss. Interesting.

"If you'll follow me, I'll take you out back where we do much of our training."

Once out back of the fire station, the chief ordered Zach Akino and Jesse Lin through demonstrations with a ladder and a hose. The sun beat down, and sweat popped along her forehead.

When they were done, he turned to her.

Was he going to give her a gift too?

"Let's go back inside."

Okay. Her eyes adjusted to being inside as he led her though the bay.

"Of all the safety equipment we have and all the training we do, this is the most important thing of all." He gestured to one of the engines.

What? She'd already seen inside. Oh.

Joe came striding around in his dark blue uniform, looking dangerously handsome. A grin split his face as he neared her and pulled her into a hug, lifting her off her wheeler for a moment. "The most important piece of safety equipment we have is this." He gestured behind him.

She looked over his shoulder where a whole line of firefighters stood. And Kyle.

"We're a team, and we have each other's backs. I always

have someone looking out for me and willing to help, even in matters of the heart." Then he kissed her to the whoops and hollers of his coworkers.

Chapter Thirty-Two

SARAH STRUGGLED TO PULL OPEN the glass door etched with the name Martin Development without knocking her crutch out from under her. Through the reflection on the glass she could see the receptionist inside watching her from behind a dark wood desk. She was wearing a headset, so Sarah couldn't tell if the woman was talking on the phone or to someone Sarah couldn't see. Probably making fun of the crippled girl. Sigh. Maybe she'd get sympathy points. She needed everything she could get in her favor for this task.

Flinging the door open, she hobbled through before it could reverse its course and come back to whap her in the butt. Whew! One goal accomplished. One more to go.

"Hi, I'm Sarah Brockman. Is Eddie in?"

"Do you have an appointment?" She tapped a French-manicured nail on the polished wood.

"No, I was hoping he'd see me anyway. We've worked together for years."

The French-manicured nail punched a button on the phone and then began flipping through a magazine while she spoke into her headset. A moment later she said, "Go on back" without looking up. Sarah wasn't sure if she was speaking to her or someone in the headset, but it didn't matter. Sarah was heading to Eddie's office.

Swinging herself down the hallway, she almost chickened out. She'd never done anything like this. Begging for work. She hated the very thought of it. But when she imagined the people she worked with every day losing their jobs, because of her … There was nothing else she could do.

She paused in Eddie's doorway, slightly out of breath, either from nerves or the exertion of propelling herself down the hall. She allowed herself three deep breaths before rapping on the doorframe.

His gaze shifted from his computer to over the tops of his reading glasses. "Oh hey, Sarah, come on in." He stood and came around the desk. "What happened to you? Did you finally kick Mark in the shins?"

She smiled and hoped he couldn't tell it was fake. "I fell through a subfloor." She seated herself.

"On a job site?"

This wasn't how she wanted the conversation to go. "Yeah, but I'm fine. I was actually hoping to talk to you a bit and bounce some ideas off you."

"Sure, sure. Can I get you anything?"

Her first inclination was to say no, but then she said, "Sure. Water's great."

Eddie moved behind her and out the door. That was a surprise. She thought he would have had Miss French Manicure bring it. Or maybe she didn't do that.

Glancing around Eddie's office, she tried to find some common ground to talk about before she launched into her plea. She was terrible at small talk. A trade magazine sat on the side table next to her chair. "OC Builder Makes Waves" was the top headline on the front cover. Hmm. Who could that be? She flipped open to the article. Tony DiMarco apparently. So that's what he looked like. Sarah hadn't worked with him before. She skimmed the article, but the photos captured her attention. She knew this man. But how? She didn't know, but she knew that face. It would bug her all day until she could figure it out. Maybe they'd met at an industry event? She would have remembered his name though.

"Here you go." A frosted bottle of water hovered in front of her face.

"Thanks." She took the bottle and twisted off the cap. "Have you ever worked with Tony DiMarco before?" She held the magazine up for Eddie to see.

He was around his desk and starting to look down. He paused. "Not directly." He sat and folded his hands on his desk. "Interesting article on him, though. Take it if you want. So, what brings you here?"

She pushed Mr. DiMarco from her mind and took a sip of her water. "We've worked together for many years. I guess I was a little confused when you cancelled your contract. I was hoping maybe there was something we could talk about."

Eddie touched a paper on his desk, moving it slightly, then a pen. "Um, yeah, that wasn't personal. I like your work, you know that. It was just a business decision."

Sarah tilted her head. "Based on what?"

"Just additional information. Cost-effectiveness, that kind of thing."

"Are you saying someone underbid us?"

He met her eyes for the first time. "Oh no. Not at all."

"Then what kind of cost effectiveness are we talking about?" She'd come this far; she wasn't going to let him give her the run around with a bunch of buzz words.

He was silent for a while. "Sarah, I like you. I liked Mark. You guys have always done good work for us. But it's just time for us to move on. Now, I really need to get back to work.

Sorry to hear about your leg. Hope it heals quickly. Tell Mark I said hi." He stood and came around the desk, handing her the crutches.

Failure settled over her, nearly heavy enough to keep her in her seat. With extra effort she pushed out of the chair and took her crutches. Her mind was spinning. What could she say to change his mind? What should she say? Why couldn't she think on her feet? Thoughts were spinning too fast for her to grab onto any one of them.

She stuck her hand out, crutch tucked under her arm. She could be classy; that, she could do. "Thank you for your time, Eddie."

He wasn't looking at her until she spoke and then seemed a bit taken aback. "Oh yeah, no problem." He grasped her hand and quickly let go.

She propelled herself down the hall and past Miss French Manicure who never even looked up. Struggling with the door once again her eyes started to fill. Dang it. Not doing that. Not now. She wedged herself between the two sections of glass and side stepped out the door.

With a sigh of relief, Sarah slid under the cool sheets. After propping her foot up on the decorative pillows from her bed, then stretching to get the sheets properly over the mound—good thing she could still do her yoga—she laid back and let her muscles begin to relax. She reached for the book on her nightstand and instead her fingers touched glossy paper. The trade magazine she'd tossed there earlier after realizing she'd had it in her hand when she left Eddie's office. It was crumpled from where she'd crushed it against her crutch handle.

She flipped back to the Tony DiMarco article again, trying to figure out where she knew him from. It was floating around on the edges of her mind like a dream she couldn't quite remember. Like trying to grab fog.

She read the article twice more and stared at his pictures for at least five minutes before closing the magazine, setting it on the table, and turning out the lamp. It was probably something totally ridiculous, like they'd been at some fundraiser together. The things she worried about. Good grief.

Sleep had just started to cuddle her when it popped into her head. She knew why Tony DiMarco looked familiar. Drenched in a cold sweat, she pushed herself up and reached for her phone.

Chapter Thirty-Three

JOE REACHED ACROSS THE TRUCK cab and squeezed Sarah's hand. They could finally relax. Kyle had picked up DiMarco last night for the murder of Greg Connor and everything seemed to be wrapping up.

Even better, Sarah had loved Joe's grand gesture, had seen underneath it to his heart, a heart that desperately wanted to be a part of her life.

Just one thing niggled at him, and Sarah had agreed to take a long lunch with him. He glanced at the Google Earth printouts she had on her lap. "I think this is it." He turned onto a dirt road and rounded the corner. There it was. The property that started this whole mess. It looked a lot different than when he had been up here as a kid. A stop-work order was stapled to a stake pounded at the edge of the lot.

He slid out of the truck and came around to help Sarah out, handing her the crutches. They moved onto the property. The wind had picked up, carrying on it a distant rumble.

"What's that noise? Sounds like some machinery." Joe took another step, squinting into the sun.

"Sounds like grading equipment." Sarah hobbled up next to him. "But the site is supposed to be shut down."

A dozer moved into view at a rate of speed that seemed excessive. The driver pushed large amounts of dirt over the edge of the hill.

"That doesn't look like any kind of grading. It looks more like he's filling a hole." Sarah shaded her eyes.

"Hiding evidence?"

The driver caught sight of them and increased his speed, moving off into the brush. Flames crackled up in front of the dozer.

"He sparked a fire and is trying to put it out with the dozer. But he doesn't know what he's doing. Everything's tinder dry out here. He's just going to make it worse. I gotta stop this guy." Joe sprinted across the lot just as a gust of wind caught the flames and pushed them hard and fast across the brush. He ran back to the truck, shouting, "Call 911. We've got a fire with a rapid rate of spread."

He pulled out the fire extinguishers and shovel he always carried and hurried over to Sarah.

She was waving her phone in the air. "I can't get a signal."

"Keep trying. I need your help. Move over there and keep a path clear for me to get back here. I have to go get the dozer driver."

He knew what he was asking of her. Fear flashed up in her eyes, and her body shrunk and recoiled. Yes, not only was he abandoning her to her greatest fear, he was asking her to help him fight it. But there was no other choice.

"Sarah, listen. I've got to go rescue that guy. He's not going to make it if I don't. But I need you to make sure I can get back here by keeping the fire back. Those rocks up there will make a good fire break. I'm going to put the fire extinguisher and the shovel down over there. You make your way there while I get the guy." He held her gaze. "I know you can do this." He gave her a hard kiss. "I love you." And ran off, dropping the tools where he said then looking back.

She hadn't moved. He hoped he hadn't just killed them both.

Sarah couldn't stop shaking. She couldn't make her arms move the crutches even if she wanted to. *God has not given us a spirit of fear, but of power and a sound mind. Okay, God. I can't do this. I need you to.*

She glanced at her phone. Still no signal. The flames now ran up the side of the hills, licking around to where she was. If she didn't move soon, the fire would cut Joe off from coming back to the truck. She tapped Kyle's name then voice text. "Joe and I are at the DiMarco grading site and there's a fire. We need help. Please send help." She hit send, shoved the phone in her pocket and hoped that somehow it would go.

Crutching over to where Joe had dropped the fire extinguisher, her arms shook. *Please don't let me fall, God.* Once at the rocks, she dropped one crutch and picked up the fire extinguisher. She had practiced using one many times. But never on a real fire.

Squeezing the other crutch under her arm, she pulled the pin and balanced the canister on her good leg. Pointing the nozzle, she laid down a stream of white powder against the encroaching flames. The sight of them pulled her stomach into a solid mass. But she forced herself to focus on the job.

She scanned the area where Joe had run, but only hungry flames were visible. *Please, Lord. Keep him safe.*

She glanced back at the truck. Unless she put the extinguisher down, she couldn't check her phone to see if her message had gone through. And the extinguisher itself wouldn't last long. At some point, she'd have to get back to the safety of the truck. Given how the flames were eating up all the brush around her, that would be sooner rather than later.

But how much longer did she give Joe? What if he was hurt? Fear hummed in her chest. A lick of flame had crept closer. She sprayed it. The canister was growing lighter. Fiery pieces of chaparral landed around her and behind her, fire brands starting new fires all around, the wind pushing them forward.

Where was Joe?

Joe reached the dozer operator standing on the bucket, surrounded by flames. Joe sprayed down a path. "Jump!"

The guy jumped and crumpled on landing, letting out a groan. The heat and smoke were thick. They didn't have much time.

"I twisted my knee. I can't walk."

Joe grabbed him under the arms. "Put your arm around my shoulder." He sprayed the last of the extinguisher in front of them, giving them a few more seconds, then dropped the canister.

He finally saw the guy's face and his sleeves of tattoos. "Nick?"

The guy nodded, and they hustled forward, Joe practically carrying him back the way they had come. Back to Sarah.

The embers were falling hot now. They landed on him, stinging, but he couldn't slap them out and hang on to Nick. The smoke thickened, making it hard to breathe. They were heading the right way, but he couldn't see anything but flames and smoke.

As fast as this thing had blown up, Sarah wouldn't be able to keep a clear path for them. He tried to peer between the smoke and flames, but his eyes were watering too much, and there was too much smoke. He wouldn't say going after Nick had been a mistake, but it might be the last thing he did.

Sweat poured down Sarah's face as she tossed the empty extinguisher aside. The flames were higher now, so much higher. She couldn't stop the trembling that shook her. Where was Joe? Shouldn't he have been back by now?

She grabbed her phone out of her pocket. A red exclamation point followed her last text. Not delivered. No help was coming.

Snatching up the shovel, she began digging, tossing dirt toward the flames, making a pathetic break the towering flames could easily leap over. This wasn't going to last long. The heat burned her face, and embers landed all over her, spot fires springing up all around. Could she even get back to the truck?

She hated that Joe had left her so he could go rescue that dozer operator. Yes, it was the right thing to do, and there was no way Joe wouldn't help that man. But now she was left to face her fears alone.

What if Joe couldn't make it? How long could she try before it was too dangerous? The thoughts felt traitorous. Shouldn't she do anything to save the man she loved? But what if it wasn't enough? Because right now, it didn't seem like enough.

With watering eyes, she tried to see through the smoke, to spot any sign of movement. Any moment now, she was going to be overrun and have to dash for the truck hampered by crutches. And possibly make a decision she never wanted to make.

Please, God.

Sarah's form came into view like a mirage. She had tossed both of her crutches away and was holding the shovel, trying to throw dirt on flames which grew far too close for comfort. His knees nearly buckled with relief. They might actually make it.

"Sarah!" He waved her back. "Head to the truck!"

She looked up, and relief lifted her sooty, tear-streaked face. She dropped the shovel and reached for her crutches. She hadn't gone very far when they caught up to her. But he had Nick, so he couldn't grab her too.

The heat pressed in from behind them. Ash coated his truck and embers fell around them like hot rain. Spot fires gobbled up the chaparral and underbrush all around, leaving them the narrowest of escape routes. Getting to the truck might not be enough. They might not get off this hillside.

Joe yanked open the truck door and shoved Nick in the extended cab. He ran a few steps back and lifted Sarah off the ground, carrying her to the truck. "You did it, babe. You did it. I'm so proud of you." He kissed her sweat-and-dirt streaked forehead.

"I was so scared. I didn't want to lose you." Her green eyes were luminous and wide. She reached up and touched his face.

"You saved me. I couldn't have done it without you." He tossed her crutches in the back and slid her in the truck.

Keys still in the ignition, Joe started the engine, ash and embers blanketing the windshield. The smoke made it hard to see, and the wind pushed the flames hard in their direction, eating up the ground they had just been on.

As loud as it was with the fire and wind, one sound was missing: sirens. Somebody should see all this smoke and call 911. But help might not get there soon enough for them.

He gunned it, hoping he was heading out of danger.

"The text didn't go through." Sarah said. "I'll keep trying." She pulled out her phone with shaking hands.

"This is all my fault." Nick bounced against the front seats as they hit a rough patch. "Thanks for coming after me, Joe. But you probably should have left me there and saved yourselves."

"We're gonna be fine. Don't worry."

"I shoulda told Tony no. But he's a powerful guy. He doesn't take no for an answer. He knew Greg and I were using his sites as drug drops, and he held that over us. I still should have taken my chances with the cops." He touched Sarah's shoulder. "You didn't deserve any of this. I'm sorry for trashing your house and bugging it, for burning down your building, and cutting the plywood so you guys fell through the floor. I tried to tell Tony ..."

Joe glanced in the rearview mirror. The flames filled it, the inside of the truck was like an oven. He struggled to keep his bearings and the truck from hitting something that would disable it. But he couldn't slow down. The fire was gaining on them, being pushed by stiff winds in their direction.

Sarah patted Nick's inked hand. "Thanks for saying that, Nick. It means a lot." She glanced at Joe. "Still no signal." She turned to Nick. "But why me? I don't understand what Tony had against me."

"It's the Indian artifacts. They're on the site, and Tony didn't want anyone to know. So he devised an elaborate grading scheme to bury them. And Greg gave that to you. As insurance against Tony. I think he would have gotten it back from you. And you pretty much figured out what he was doing. That land was worth millions if it got picked for the toll road. Once everyone knows about the artifacts, it'll be shut down and studied for years. He'll lose all the money he put into it."

Sarah nodded. It was just as she had figured, almost exactly what she had told him and Kyle. Joe risked a quick squeeze of her hand. "Good job. You were right."

He racked his brain for an escape plan. Then it hit him. "Hang on, it's going to get rough." He pointed the truck downhill. "We're heading for the nearest development. It'll have some defensible space and a greenbelt, if we're lucky. Get ready to jump and run."

The smoke parted a bit, and there it was. Not too far from

the brush fire he fought a few months ago. "Okay, get ready." He braked hard, the nose of the truck resting against a wrought-iron fence.

Throwing open his door, he hopped out, grabbing the extended cab door on his way out, opening it. Running around the back of the truck was like jumping into a blast furnace. Sarah had pushed her door open. Nick was already limping toward the fence.

Joe lifted Sarah into his arms. He carried her to the fence. Nick was already over, favoring his knee but standing on green grass. "I'm going to lift her over to you." He hoisted Sarah over the six-foot fence, straining against the angle and the warm metal. Nick grabbed her as she slid down the other side.

He planted his foot and threw himself over the fence. He'd bought them some time. But with two injured, he wasn't going to get them too far too fast. He scanned the perfectly landscaped yard. The pergola-covered patio with the outdoor kitchen, the negative-edge pool. It was like everyone in this neighborhood had the same landscape designer. And nothing that could help him.

Sarah had her phone out, leaning against Nick. Her face lit up. "I got it! I've got 911 on the line. Where are we?"

"Nick! Move toward the house. Let's get to the street." He scooped up Sarah. "I'll take her and run ahead and get an address." He had a pretty good idea where they were and relayed it to Sarah to give the 911 operator. She wasn't the first one to report in, but the more info the better. They opened the side gate and came out into the street. A few neighbors had gathered in their yards, watching the smoke, some carrying belongings to their cars. But it was the middle of a work day. Most people weren't even home.

"Evacuate now! The fire's too close!" He carried Sarah to the first person he saw, a woman taking video on her cell phone. "I've got to get one more guy. Give me two minutes to get back and then get out of here. Whether I'm here or not."

He didn't wait for a response, just ran back, met Nick at

the side yard gate, pale, sweat trailing through smoke-blackened skin. He hoisted Nick on his shoulder and quick timed it back to see the woman backing out of her driveway, Sarah in the passenger seat.

And a fire engine coming up the street.

Sarah was grateful Kyle had let them go home and wash up and change clothes before reporting to the Laguna Vista police station. Though the station was cold, she could still feel the scorching heat burning her skin. Her hair still reeked of smoke.

Joe's arm slipped around her shoulders as they waited in the viewing room. She leaned gratefully into him. Things could have been so much worse. She still couldn't quite believe they'd made it out of the fire alive.

The door to the room on the other side of the glass opened, and a uniformed officer led in several men, including Tony DiMarco. He was rumpled from a night in jail, with none of the polished air about him that was present in the magazine article.

Kyle moved next to her. "Which one of these men, if any, was the one you saw with Greg Connor on June 20?"

"That's him. Number four."

Kyle spoke to another officer then took a chair across from her. "He'll be out on bail soon. He has a whole slew of lawyers working for him. He covered his tracks well. But Nick told us everything. He'll get some leniency because of his cooperation. Apparently, DiMarco had some financial problems and couldn't afford to lose the property to the lengthy investigation that would happen because of the Native American artifacts. One thing led to another and somehow he ended up killing Greg. We don't know for sure if it was intentional or not, and DiMarco isn't saying. Needless to say, his house of cards is tumbling now. Likely that fancy house of his that you saved from the fire, Joe, is going to be sold to pay his legal fees."

Joe shook his head. "Ironic."

"Yeah." Kyle nodded. "Sarah, you just happened to be at the wrong place at the wrong time. DiMarco knew you saw him with Greg the day he disappeared. He also knew Greg had given you the site map with the cut and fill amounts that he had rigged up. He knew if anyone could figure it out, you could. He hoped to intimidate you into silence." He paused. "Maybe worse."

A shiver passed through her. "I know a lot of developers hope and pray that artifacts aren't found on their projects because it will bring them to a halt while the site is investigated. And if it's found to have significance to the local tribes, developers can be extremely limited in how they can use the land. A toll road would be out of the question. DiMarco's land became useless to him with that discovery. A lot of money wasted. Sounds like money he couldn't afford to lose."

"Like you said, that land has been in his family for a long time with rumors of Native American presence. Even Joe and I knew about them when we were kids. He got greedy, and for once, it didn't pay off."

She sighed. "What's going to happen to Nick?"

"That will take awhile to determine. The prosecutor's office will likely cut him a deal for his cooperation. Apparently, hanging out with Ryan had done him some good because he felt guilty and wanted to get out of working with DiMarco. After burying the evidence, he had planned to get out of town." Kyle put his hand on her shoulder. "Thanks for your help. I'm so sorry for everything you went through, but I honestly don't think we could have figured out all of these pieces, including Greg Connor's likely murder, without your help."

She nodded, and tears welled up. It was over. All of this nightmare was finally over. "Can I go now? No offense, Kyle, but I hate it here."

He grinned. "Yeah, you can go." He turned to Joe. "I think you guys need an evening off from your adventures. Take it easy."

Joe kissed her head. "I plan to."

Epilogue

SARAH ROTATED HER ANKLE IN the cab of Joe's truck, relishing how light it felt without the cast.

Joe saw what she was doing and smiled. He reached over and intertwined their fingers, lifting her hand to kiss the back of it. "Feels good to get that cast off, doesn't it?"

"I can't believe how light my foot feels. It's going to take some work to get it strong again."

"You can do that."

Yes, she could.

They pulled into the parking lot of Capistrano Beach. Tonight, they were having a bonfire on the beach with their friends celebrating her cast removal, Joe's return to full duty, and one more surprise only she and Heather knew about.

And while only one of Rankin and Associates' clients that had left returned, several more had signed on when the full story about DiMarco hit the news networks.

She tucked her tote underneath the back seat and slid out of the truck.

Joe grabbed a grocery bag out of the back of the truck and

handed her a beach chair. "Don't you want your purse?"

"No, I don't need it. I have everything I need."

He grinned at her.

They settled around the fire ring where Melissa, Heather, Bernie, and Gary had already arrived. Joe settled her chair where the smoke wouldn't blow on her and a good distance from the fire. She was still a bit wary, but the flames in the concrete ring were low, the sunlight heading for the horizon washing everything with a golden glow.

Joe roasted her hot dog for her, but she watched. Maybe she'd try roasting a marshmallow later. After all, Joe was with her.

Cait and Grayson arrived while they were roasting hot dogs, and Kyle came in a bit after them. His hands were jammed in his pockets and his shoulders hunched. A bad day at work? He headed toward her and Joe.

Joe stood and grasped Kyle's shoulder. "What's up?"

"Did you hear from Scott's mom?"

"No. What?"

"Scott was hurt in a training accident. He's been taken to the hospital, but there aren't any more details. She's supposed to let me know more."

Joe nodded. "We can pray."

Kyle gave him a quick nod then headed to Heather and pulled her into a long hug.

Sarah let out a breath. She barely knew Scott, but the ache etched in Kyle and Joe's faces tugged on her heart. Deep friendship had the potential for deep loss. Sarah wrapped her fingers around Joe's and laid her head on his shoulder.

The smell of smoke and the crackle of fire wasn't so bad when she was with Joe. Maybe these new memories would replace the old ones.

"Who's ready for s'mores?" Heather tossed a bag of marshmallows to Kyle. An assembly line of graham crackers, chocolate squares, peanut butter cups—Joe's favorite version—and marshmallows made its way around the circle.

Grayson took a skewer from Cait. "I'll make yours."

Joe looked at Sarah and raised his eyebrows. "I'll go first, but you can try if you want."

She nodded and watched while he stuck the marshmallow not over the flames, but over the glowing coals. She could do this.

He handed her a skewered marshmallow. She scooted to the edge of her chair and eased the skewer over the concrete lip. She let out a breath. These flames were small and contained, and while the heat from them warmed her hand, it was nothing like the scorching of the brush fire. She smiled at Joe, who rubbed her back.

"I knew you could do it," he whispered in her ear, sending tingles all through her. Her marshmallow was barely golden brown, but she pulled it out of the fire. Good enough for her first try.

"Wait. What?" Cait's confused voice floated over the fire pit. "Grayson?"

A diamond ring balanced on top of the s'more Cait held.

Grayson knelt. "Caitlyn Bellamy, will you do me the honor of becoming my wife?"

Cait put her hands over her mouth, nodding, her eyes bright. She nodded, then pulled her hands down. "Yes!"

Grayson took the ring from the graham cracker top and put it on her finger, pulling her into a hug to the applause of their friends.

Sarah shifted her gaze to Heather, who was smiling up at Kyle who wore an enigmatic grin. They would be next, Sarah was sure. She turned to Joe, who surprised her with a kiss.

"Bonfires on the beach are awfully romantic, don't you think?" he whispered to her.

She couldn't agree more.

Are you curious about what happened to Scott?

And how did Cait and Grayson end up together?

And what other adventures await Kyle, Heather, Joe, and Sarah?

Find out by signing up for my latest news and updates at www.jlcrosswhite.com and you'll get the prequel novella, *Promise Me*— Grayson and Cait's story.

My bimonthly updates include upcoming books written by me (Scott and Melissa's story, *Special Assignment*, will release in summer 2019 and you'll be the first to know) and other authors you will enjoy, information on all my latest releases, sneak peeks of yet-to-be-released chapters, and exclusive giveaways. Your email address will never be shared, and you can unsubscribe at any time.

If you enjoyed this book, please consider leaving a review. Reviews can be as simple as "I couldn't put it down. I can't wait for the next one" and help raise the author's visibility and lets other readers find her.

Acknowledgments

The expertise on fire fighting procedures came from a lot of research. I'm greatly indebted to all of the first responders who post photos and training online. A special shout out to Yermo/Calico firefighters Matthews and Wynne who took the time to answer all of my questions, show me all the equipment, and run through scenarios with me. They added a richness and details that I would not have discovered. Any liberties taken are my own.

This book would not be possible without the patience and willingness to read many, many drafts by Diana Brandmeyer, Liz Tolsma, Jenny Cary, and Danielle Reid. Special thanks to Sara Benner for her expert proofreading and Danielle Reid for her eagle eyes! Many thanks to my beta readers and reviewers!

Much thanks and love to my children, Caitlyn Elizabeth and Joshua Alexander, for supporting my dream for many years and giving me time to write. And most of all to my Lord Jesus, who makes all things possible and directs my paths.

Author's Note

Laguna Vista isn't a real town, but it's based on the area of Orange County that I lived in for twelve years. It's a beautiful location with the ocean to the west and foothills and mountains to the east and the austere-but-beautiful desert within driving distance.

Life in Southern California is routinely overshadowed by wildland fires. As I was writing this book, we had a devasting fire season up and down the state, experiencing some of the deadliest fires in our history.

I wanted to explore how fire and fear impacts people's lives. And how we navigate our fears with the assurance we get from God's Word. Joe and Sarah wrestle with understanding and accepting God's unfathomable journey for their lives and trusting Him with the outcome.

I hope you will take away from reading *Flash Point* that you can trust God with your future, no matter how incomprehensible it may appear to you and be encouraged with how uniquely God has crafted your life.

ABOUT ME

My favorite thing is discovering how much there is to love about America the Beautiful and the great outdoors. I'm an Amazon bestselling author, a mom to two navigating the young adult years while battling my daughter's juvenile arthritis, exploring the delights of my son's autism, and keeping gluten free. A California native who's spent significant time in the Midwest, I'm thrilled to be back in the Golden State. Follow me on social media to see all my adventures and how I get inspired for my books!

www.JLCrosswhite.com
Twitter: @jenlcross
Facebook: Author Jennifer Crosswhite
Instagram: jencrosswhite
Pinterest: Author Jennifer Crosswhite

Sneak Peek of
Special Assignment

Prologue

Orange County, California, 1995

THE ANNOUNCER'S VOICE CAME OVER the loudspeakers at the El Toro Marine Air Station saying that the Blue Angels, the finale for the airshow, would be taking to the skies shortly. The sun was hot, but the breeze coming off the ocean cooled Scott Blake as he hustled across the concrete airfield with his friends Joe Romero and Kyle Taylor. They had seen all the static displays of the planes, many of which he had hanging as models in his room. He'd taken pictures of his favorite ones with the camera he got for his birthday. But he had only enough film for thirty-six photos, so he had to be careful.

Dad had brought them and then staked out a good spot at the center of the runway to watch the airshow, and there he'd sat all day. At eleven, Scott and his friends were old enough to run around and see everything by themselves. They even had their own money for snacks. Scott hadn't been sure Dad would even bring them to the airshow. After Scott's older brother, Christopher, had died, Dad hadn't been in the mood to do much of anything. But he knew how much seeing the Blue Angels meant to Scott. He'd hadn't even had to beg too much.

It had been a full day so far, one of the best ever. Kyle was even checking out the weapons the marines carried. He wanted to be a cop when he grew up. A parachutist had kicked off the show by descending from the sky with an American flag flying from his heels while the National Anthem played. Everyone had clapped as he landed on the infield.

Scott couldn't believe they were going to close this base in a couple of years. His whole life had been lived out to the sound of the planes landing and taking off on maneuvers. There was even a sign on the Carl's Jr. drive-thru that warned people not to place an order when the jets were overhead. They were loud, but it was cool.

He glanced at Dad who was staring off into space. Was he thinking about Christopher? He'd have been finishing his final year in college now, playing football on a scholarship somewhere. Scott's chest hollowed out like it did whenever he thought about his brother. He'd make his parents proud, just like Christopher would have done.

The roar of an F/A-18 shrieked above them. Those were the coolest planes. He nudged Joe and Kyle. "That's what I'm going to fly. You just watch."

The announcer switched over to the Blue Angels' emcee, and the show began. Scott wiped his hands on his shorts. This was it!

The planes split the sky with their tight formations and acrobatic moves in a mesmerizing routine. Unbelievable! He couldn't tear his eyes away. The planes came so close to the ground that he could see the pilots' helmets. What would it be like to be one of them? Feeling the positive and negative G's as they made those tight turns and sweeping loops?

When the last Blue Angel came in for a landing, Scott let out a breath. His sno-cone had dripped all over his hand. He hadn't even noticed.

Dad stood and folded his chair. He nodded in the direction of the parked planes with their canopies popped open. "Want to go meet them?"

"Yes!" He had two pictures left on his camera roll. He dropped the sno-cone paper in a trash can and snagged a couple of napkins from a hot dog stand that was closing up.

By the time they got to the pilots standing on the other side of a waist-high plastic fence, a small crowd had already formed. The pilots were chatting with the kids, signing programs, and taking pictures. The pilot closest to them was smiling as he talked with a couple of older girls.

Scott nudged his way forward, comparing the pilot with the picture in his program. He folded it back so the pilot's picture was up and got his pen ready. "Excuse me, sir?"

But the man didn't seem to see him. He was too busy paying attention to the girls. They didn't even have a program for him to sign. Scott's stomach sank.

He turned, but a voice snagged his attention. "You interested in planes?" Another pilot stood there, grinning at Scott.

"Yes, sir. I'd like to fly an F/A-18 one day. And I've got models of just about every other plane hanging from the ceiling in my room." Scott thrust the pen and program at the pilot. "Would you sign my program?"

"I'd be honored to. What's your name, pilot?"

"Scott, sir. Scott Blake."

"Well, Scott Blake—" the pilot scribbled on Scott's program but didn't give it back to him. "Do you know how to fly this kind of airplane?" He began folding the program into a complicated paper airplane before handing it back to Scott.

"Wow, that's cool! Thanks!"

The pilot winked at him. "You can fly that kind of plane most anywhere." He gestured to the camera in Scott's hand, the one he'd nearly forgotten. "Can we get a picture together? That way when you're famous, I can say I knew you when."

"Sure!" Scott handed the camera to Kyle. "Get a picture of us." He moved to the fence and turned around.

The pilot set his hand on Scott's shoulder, and Scott held up the paper airplane and smiled.

"Say cheese!" Kyle said as he snapped the shutter.

Scott smiled then turned to the pilot. "Thanks a lot!"

The pilot stuck out his hand. "Anytime. See you in the air!"

Scott shook it and grinned.

They moved off to let someone else get closer to the fence. He glanced over at the other pilot who was still talking to the girls, ignoring the kids trying to get his attention.

When he was a pilot, he'd be like the cool one that had talked to him and not the one that just wanted all the girls' attention. Who needed girls anyway when you could fly those awesome planes?

"Dad, did you see that? We got a picture together, and he made this cool paper airplane for me."

Dad squeezed his shoulder and smiled. "I did. Looks like you had a good time."

"I did. Thanks for taking us, Dad." For a moment, all was right in their small world. Him, his friends, and even Dad seemed like he'd had a good time. He'd do whatever he could to keep that feeling.

Chapter One

Orange County, California, Present day

MELISSA ELLIS SCROLLED THROUGH THE profit-and-loss statements on her computer screen. The numbers blurred. She blinked and tried to focus. The financial meeting was in thirty minutes, and she had to make sense of these numbers. The problem was, they weren't making any sense. Unease swirled in her stomach, making her regret the third cup of coffee. According to these numbers, Broadstone Technologies was hemorrhaging money. She just couldn't figure out why.

She stepped away from her standing desk and paced her office. Moving around usually helped. She'd suspected something was wrong for a while now, yet all of her digging uncovered nothing. But numbers didn't lie. Something didn't add up.

As vice president of operations, she should have her finger on the pulse of how the company was running. Her ability to sniff out problems and deliver solutions had rocketed her to her position, the youngest VP ever in the company's history. Which was saying something in an industry staffed by an old-boys network.

But this had her stymied. Maybe it was beyond her abilities. The old imposter syndrome raised its ugly head, and she forced it back down. There was no time for an emotional crisis. She was still in charge, still had a problem to solve.

She stopped pacing in front of her credenza and picked up a framed photo of her and her two best friends, Halley and Gracelyn. They were in middle school at Camp Eureka, a science camp. In the photo, slimy Oobleck had splashed on their tie-dyed shirts. They were grinning, arms slung around each other. It had been the best summer of her life, working with the girls to solve science riddles and having fun. Not having to worry about being in charge. Sharing the load and accomplishing something as a team.

She set the photo back on the cherrywood and let out a breath. Maybe she should call Halley and Gracelyn, see if they had any ideas. She nixed the idea the second it popped in her brain. As much as she'd like to, as a defense contractor, security clearances prohibited that.

Pulling open her door, she stuck her head out. "Danielle? Do you have a minute?"

Her perky assistant peered over the top of her monitor, Bluetooth headset firmly in her ear. "Sure. What do you need?"

"I'm going to send you the P&L I'm working on, see if your fresh eyes can make sense of it. The meeting's in—" she glanced at her Apple Watch— "twenty minutes. Sorry, just do what you can. Maybe it's obvious, and I'm just missing it."

Danielle gave her a soft smile. "I'm happy to look at it. Why don't you close your eyes for a few minutes, and I'll let you know when it's time to head over?"

"Good plan." The best she'd heard all day. She stepped back in her office and closed the door. Heading over to the couch, she kicked off her heels and laid down. Maybe just a few minutes.

Who knew? Maybe the solution would appear in a dream.

The caffeine coursing through her bloodstream kept her brain spinning. Maybe she needed to head to the pottery studio tonight and throw a pot. That always helped. She visualized what she might create and concentrated on breathing steadily in and out.

But all she could see were all the people who depended on her, whose jobs were in danger if she couldn't solve the company's financial crisis.

Melissa set her tablet and phone on her desk, blowing out a breath. The financial meeting had not gone well. In fact, Gavin Broadstone—the namesake of Broadstone Technologies and her boss and mentor—seemed to be blaming her. He was kind about it, but he made it clear that he thought the problem was in operations and she needed to solve it. She'd never seen him blame anyone without evidence. One of the things she admired about him was his fairness, waiting until the facts were in before making a judgment.

Her phone vibrated. She swiped the screen. Anything to get her mind off what just happened. A text from Heather inviting her to dinner tomorrow. Her finger hovered over the screen. She really didn't want to drive anywhere but home on a Friday night. Though dinner with friends seemed a better option than what she'd likely be doing, going over those financials again. And didn't that just show what a well-rounded life she lived. She started to reply when she got another text from Heather.

Scott's coming too.

Oh. She hadn't seen him since the Fourth of July barbecue at Kyle's. He'd been injured in a training accident—which was what they always called it—and was back home on medical leave.

What she had thought would be a relaxing time with friends morphed into something else. She didn't feel like the vibrant, confident woman she had projected at the Fourth of July party. She didn't even think she could fake it. Her friends wouldn't mind, but Scott? She just didn't know him that well.

She really should go throw pots instead. That always eased the tension from her shoulders. The wet clay slipping through her fingers, creating something new from a formless lump. She hesitated. Then again, being alone with her thoughts hadn't been helping. Maybe being around company would. And it's not as if this was a date. There would be plenty of people to carry the conversation. In fact, Joe, Kyle, and Scott would likely tell stories the whole time.

Plus, it could possibly be the last break she'd have in a while, since their avionics system being tested by the Navy was coming back for review, and it would require all of her attention. That Navy contract would provide a needed cash infusion, saving the company, .

And Scott was a Navy pilot. He might have an idea or a new perspective. At least she could talk to him about it.

She texted Heather that she'd be there. Checking the time, she saw she had a few more hours of productive work. She popped out the door. "Danielle, did you come up with anything in your scan of those numbers?"

"No, but I didn't get to do much more than a cursory look. Want me to keep looking?"

"Yeah. The answer has to be there. I'll start looking at all of our recent projects."

"Sounds like a plan." Danielle spun back to her computer.

Melissa closed the door and went back to her desk, plopping in her chair. She started pulling up the recent projects. But her mind kept drifting to the handsome naval aviator.

An automated voice came over the speaker in her office,

and the light in her ceiling strobed. "There is a fire. Please evacuate your office via the stairs on the northside of the building and gather in your assigned area on the west parking lot." The strobe in her office added to her headache. She powered down her computer, grabbed her coat, her purse—shoving her phone and tablet inside—and made sure her badge showed around her neck. She pulled her office door shut behind her, double checking that it locked.

"Danielle?"

"On it."

Danielle held the emergency evacuation sheet, and she and Melissa moved through the cubical farm, making sure everyone was headed out the door and all computers were powering down for security purposes. "Was everyone here today?"

"Dana called out, but that's it."

They'd do a head count once they got to their assigned area in the parking lot. Likely it was just a drill, but security would come around and check to make sure everyone complied. Not a great day for a drill. Then again, when was it ever?

They headed toward the stairwell, their footsteps echoing off the walls along with everyone else's. She heard sirens. Outside, a cold gust of wind made Melissa pull her coat on and wrap it around her.

The fire department's equipment and personnel added to the controlled chaos. Was Joe Romero on this call? She scanned the area briefly, but first she and Danielle had to make sure everyone on their team was accounted for. Then they had to wait for the all clear.

While their computer whiz, Jeremy Chao, kept them entertained with stories of his adventures and near-death experiences, Melissa studied the firefighters. The one who seemed to be in charge turned so she could see that his coat said ROMERO on the back. That was Joe. She didn't want to interrupt his work, but it was somehow reassuring that someone she knew was taking care of things.

Gavin Broadstone strode over. "Everyone out okay?"

"Yep." She gestured behind her. "What's going on?"

By the look on Gavin's face, this wasn't a drill. "Did you see anything in your area? Smell any smoke?"

"No. Why?"

"The alarm was manually triggered from your zone."

She frowned. "Why would someone do that? I can't imagine—" She scanned her team huddled against the wind, talking in small groups. "If someone from my team had done it, they'd have told me what they saw. It wasn't someone from my team."

"The CCTV will show us who it was." He nodded toward Joe. "Let's talk to the fire captain and see what they've discovered."

Melissa followed Gavin, and they headed toward Joe. Her mind shuffled through the information, trying to make sense of it. Joe was talking to Broadstone's head of security, Adam Martinez. Joe spotted her, and she waved.

"Hey, Melissa."

Gavin's head swiveled. "You know each other?"

"Yes. Gavin, this is Fire Captain Joe Romero. Joe, this is my boss and the president of Broadstone Technologies, Gavin Broadstone."

Joe nodded. "As I was telling your head of security here, we've been through the building. Your fire system detection control panels aren't showing any heat, and neither are our thermal imaging cameras. None of the clean fire suppression agents were triggered. We can't detect any fire."

Melissa blew out a breath. "That's a relief."

Adam turned to her. "From a fire perspective, yes. But it creates another problem for us. We don't know how the alarm got activated."

"Can't you just look at the CCTV?" Gavin asked.

Adam winced. "We took a quick look, but it seems like the cameras were out in that particular area. Additionally, the alarm can be triggered via the control system by anyone that has access to the computer. But as of right now, that doesn't seem to be what happened. We'll do a thorough examination of the whole system and figure it out."

Joe motioned with his head for Melissa to step to the side while Gavin tore into Adam. She was happy to be out of the line of fire and glad that Gavin was targeting someone besides her. Though she felt bad for Adam.

Joe lowered his voice. "We're going to wrap up here, but I think you might want to call in Kyle to take a look at things. Something's not right. And be careful."

Melissa nodded as Joe moved back to his engine, his words still echoing in her head. The missing money and now this strange situation. Could they be connected? And what could she do to find out? She pulled out her phone and scrolled for Kyle's number. At least she could bounce ideas off him, and maybe he'd tell her she was worrying for nothing.

But she doubted it.

Books by JL Crosswhite

Romantic Suspense
The Hometown Heroes Series

Promise Me

Cait can't catch a break. What she witnessed could cost her job and her beloved farmhouse. Will Greyson help her or only make things worse?

Protective Custody

She's a key witness in a crime shaking the roots of the town's power brokers. He's protecting a woman he'll risk everything for. Doing the right thing may cost her everything. Including her life.

Flash Point

She's a directionally-challenged architect who stumbled on a crime that could destroy her life's work. He's a firefighter protecting his hometown... and the woman he loves.

Special Assignment

A brain-injured Navy pilot must work with the woman in charge of the program he blames for his injury. As they both grasp to save their careers, will their growing attraction hinder them as they attempt solve the mystery of who's really at fault before someone else dies?

Books by Jennifer Crosswhite

Contemporary Romance

The Inn at Cherry Blossom Lane

Can the summer magic of Lake Michigan bring first loves back together? Or will the secret they discover threaten everything they love?

Historical Romance
The Route Home Series

Be Mine

A woman searching for independence. A man searching for education. Can a simple thank you note turn into something more?

Coming Home

He was why she left. Now she's falling for him. Can a woman who turned her back on her home-town come home to find justice for her brother without falling in love with his best friend?

The Road Home

 He is a stagecoach driver just trying to do his job. She is returning to her suitor only to find he has died. When a stack of stolen money shows up in her bag, she thinks the past she has desperately tried to hide has come back to haunt her.

Made in the USA
Columbia, SC
08 November 2020